SUFFER THE WITCH

ALSO AVAILABLE
FROM TITAN BOOKS

Conan: Blood of the Serpent

Conan the Barbarian: The Official Motion Picture Adaptation

Conan: City of the Dead

Conan: Cult of the Obsidian Moon

Conan: Songs of the Slain

Conan: Spawn of the Serpent God

SUFFER THE WITCH

SHAUN HAMILL

TITAN BOOKS

Solomon Kane: Suffer the Witch
Print edition ISBN: 9781835411865
E-book edition ISBN: 9781835411872

Published by Titan Books
A division of Titan Publishing Group Ltd
144 Southwark Street, London SE1 0UP
www.titanbooks.com

First edition: January 2026
10 9 8 7 6 5 4 3 2 1

This is a work of fiction. All of the characters, organizations, and events portrayed in this novel are either products of the author's imagination or are used fictitiously. Any resemblance to actual persons, living or dead (except for satirical purposes), is entirely coincidental.

A CIP catalogue record for this title is available from the British Library.

EU RP (for authorities only)
eucomply OÜ, Pärnu mnt. 139b-14, 11317 Tallinn, Estonia
hello@eucompliancepartner.com, +3375690241

Printed and bound by CPI Group (UK) Ltd, Croydon CR0 4YY.

Dedicated to Robert E. Howard (1906–1936):
that starry-eyed dreamer from Texas,
whose dreams we're all still dreaming.

PROLOGUE

"Thou shalt not suffer a witch to live."

–EXODUS 22:18

"And if a man or woman have a spirit of divination, or soothsaying in them, they shall die the death: they shall stone them to death, their blood shall be upon them."

–LEVITICUS 20:27

"What is divine is full of Providence. Even chance is not divorced from nature, from the interweaving and enfolding of things governed by Providence. Everything proceeds from it."

–MARCUS AURELIUS,
THE MEDITATIONS

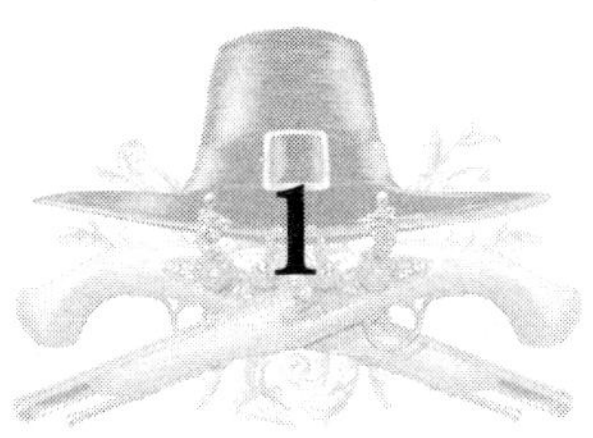

Lightning Over the Black Forest

On a stormy night in late September, Solomon Kane soared high above the treetops of the Black Forest, sure he was going to die.

The sky above was pitch black, the stars and moon obscured by heavy storm clouds. The air around him was an endless sheet of brutal, relentless rain. It fell hard and stinging and cold against his exposed skin.

Kane did none of the flying himself, but instead clung to the neck of a great winged beast with his right arm. In his left, he gripped a staff almost as tall as himself. Its bottom was pointed and sharp, and it was topped with a strange carving of a cat's head.

Lightning slashed the night sky, momentarily filling the world with light, and Kane got his first good look at the beast. In the darkness of the forest below, it had seemed similar in shape to a great black horse, but the light made clear several differences. First were its eyes, which burned red like coals. Second, when its lips parted, it had not the large, flat teeth a man could expect in a horse's mouth, but several rows of razor-sharp teeth, perfect for rending flesh from bone. Third, of course, Kane had needed no extraordinary light to see: the great skeletal wings sprouting from the creature's back, which now carried it, whinnying and huffing, through the night sky.

The beast's hide was not soft and smooth, like a horse's, but cold and repulsive to the touch, almost like the skin of a lizard. Its flesh was slippery as well, and the only thing between Kane and a steep drop was his grip upon the demon-steed's oily black mane. Even now, he could feel the greasy black hair slipping between his fingers.

He looked down and experienced a moment of wooziness as he realized just how high he was, then looked back up at the demon-steed. He needed to act quickly, if he was to survive this. With his strength divided between the staff and the creature's mane, he could not swing himself up onto its back and ride it. Nor could he hang on for more than another moment or two.

Death was inevitable, then. But would he die falling, letting this beast get away? Or would he try to stop it once and for all, and make a noble end for himself?

Kane lifted the staff in his left arm. To the unlearned observer, it would appear to be a handsome wooden stave—but the wood was older and stranger than any still found upon this earth. It was hard and strong as iron, and possessed of powerful magic.

He shifted it so that his grip fell nearer the middle than the top, pointed its sharp bottom end at his opponent, and drove the weapon into the beast's side.

The beast screamed, and dropped a dozen feet through the air. The jolt and fall caused Kane to lose his grip upon the demon-steed's mane, leaving him hanging only by his staff, impaled into the beast.

He raised his right arm and gripped the staff in both hands. The extra weight caused its sharp end to grind upward through the beast's innards. It screamed again and lost more altitude. Below, the treetops grew alarmingly close.

Using his grip upon the staff as leverage, Kane swung back and then forward, up into the air. For a second, he felt as if he were flying himself. Then he landed upon the beast's back, and gasped as most of the air was knocked from his lungs. His body, operating almost on instinct now, leaned forward and wrapped arms about the demon-steed's neck. As his mount fell out of the sky, the treetops flew up at him. He closed his eyes and braced himself. This was going to hurt.

Hurt it did.

They crashed into the trees. Pine needles and sharp branches stabbed and scraped at Kane's exposed face and hands. Their descent slowed as the demon-steed's wings tangled in the branches—and then the beast, blind with pain and panic, trying to free itself lunged forward, and slammed face-first into the thick trunk of a huge fir. Kane was dully aware of a great cracking sound. Had that been the tree? The beast's skull? Perhaps both?

He had no time to ponder, because the beast's body flailed about once more, tossing him off, and then he was falling once more. The forest floor smashed into him, knocked the air from his lungs all once more, and the entire world went gray around him.

The call to action had been simple enough. Lately, Kane had been moving through Europe, tracking a coven of vampires, who seemed to be perpetually one step, one move ahead of him. While stopped for supplies in a small German town, he had overheard tavern talk about a great black horse and rider running other riders off the road.

The story reminded Kane of a similar incident from his own younger days. Many years before, he himself had encountered such a horse and rider in the Black Forest. They had almost run Kane and his horse off the road, but instead of a painful collision, the figures had passed right through Kane.

The event had set young Kane's mind spinning, but as the phantoms had done him no injury, and he had already been about on urgent business, he had moved on. But there in the tavern, years later, he had at last seen an opportunity to revisit an old mystery. The talk had changed—it seemed that the horse and rider no longer passed through travelers on the road, but instead were taking on physical weight and dimensions, and were maiming and killing other travelers.

Kane had paused his vampire hunt to come to the Black Forest, hunting the beast and its rider. His quarry made no effort to hide. Soon after the sun had set, Kane entered the forest, and found himself shortly set upon. There had followed a short battle with the rider. Kane had managed to unseat the hooded figure, and run him through with a sword, whereupon the rider screamed and burst into smoke. The demon-steed, however, had proved a far more difficult matter.

The world gradually filled itself back in around Kane now: the forest floor, covered in fir needles; the trees standing about him like a gawking crowd; the rain falling from above, pelting his exposed face; and the sound of his own wheezing breath, as his body tried to fill itself with air once more.

He sat up with a groan and looked about. In the darkness of the wood, he heard no whinnying or neighing, or sounds of struggle; nor did he see any remains of the demon-steed. His staff lay nearby. It seemed unsullied, despite having recently been used to stab a monster. The monster itself must have burst into smoke and vanished. So it was dead, then.

And you, somehow, are still alive, he thought.

He ran his hands over his body, looking for broken bones or other injuries. Miraculously, he seemed unhurt.

Once his breathing returned to normal, he tried to stand, but as he did so, his right knee barked with pain, and sent him right back to the ground. He grunted as the pained knee struck the earth and sent a fresh wave of agony through his leg.

He crawled over to his staff, a few feet away on the ground. He drove the pointed end into the earth, and leaned upon it for support as he tried to stand once more. This time he managed it, but only barely.

He grinned through gritted teeth. This pain in his right knee had started a year ago, occasional flares of discomfort in his right leg. Pain when walking or putting weight upon it. While it occurred seldom at first, it had slowly increased in frequency and intensity, like an unwanted guest who decides to move into your home. Still he ought not complain. He was relatively spry for a man in his fifties and retained most of his strength and skill.

He put his fingers to his lips, and whistled. The rain seemed to dampen the sound, and he briefly worried that it would go unheard, but his concern proved baseless, as, a moment later, a spotted gray destrier clopped out from between the trees and to Kane.

"Inglewood," Kane murmured, speaking the horse's name as he patted her neck.

The horse snorted gently and nudged Kane with her snout. Kane limped over to the saddlebag, removed an apple, and offered it to her. It disappeared from his hand in a single bite. He stroked her snout twice more, and then strapped the staff to the saddle and mounted the horse, groaning with the effort. He picked up the reins and, after a moment's indecision—God above, it was difficult to determine directions in all this darkness and rain—started back toward the road.

2

Dream Palaver

Kane was thoroughly lost, but Inglewood seemed to have an unerring sense of the direction they needed to go. She found the road, and brought them back to the village of Baumstadt, where Kane was staying.

It was a tiny place, nestled deep in the Black Forest, and on a rainy night like tonight, it was shut up tight against the elements. Windows glowed orange with hearth light, and Kane found himself eager to be back indoors.

Inglewood went straight to the barn. Kane found no hands to help him stable his horse, so he did it himself, unsaddling her, brushing her mane, and feeding her, before hobbling across the muddy yard and into the inn. He had to knock and give his name before the door was opened to him.

The common room was warm and cozy, full of the smells of fire and good food. The innkeeper, a gaunt little man, was bent over a table, setting out bowls of stew for two men. His daughters were likewise serving other tables with tankards of beer and plates of bread.

Kane limped to the nearest empty table, and sat down heavily upon one of the benches. He felt, rather than saw, the innkeeper approach. His name was Lauderman, and he was the one who had reported the black horse and rider to Kane earlier today.

"Good evening, Herr Kane," Lauderman said, in heavily accented English. "How do you fare?"

"I am tired and hungry, Herr Lauderman," Kane said. "But your demon-steed and its rider are dead."

"Oh?" Lauderman asked. He stood up straight, and Kane lifted his head to look the innkeeper in the eye. The old man was clearly surprised.

"Aye," Kane said. "I slew them. Or sent them back to Hell, since I am not sure such a thing can *be* killed. I would have brought you proof or a trophy, but both corpses vanished upon their defeat."

"I suppose it is just as well," Lauderman said. "I would not want such a cursed thing in my home. But I must tell you, Herr Kane—it will be difficult to prove to the rest of the village that you have done this thing. I know they have offered a reward, but without proof..."

"The proof will come in the days and months to come, as travelers will traverse the roads outside this village unharried by Hell's own minions," Kane said. "But worry not about your gold. I did it not for the reward."

"So noble," Lauderman said. "Perhaps it is true what people say about you. That you are God's vengeance made human. His angry right hand."

"People say many things," Kane said.

But even as he discounted the compliment, he felt it warm his breast. The innkeeper had spoken to Kane's secret feeling about himself. That he had been chosen by God to travel the world, right wrongs, and punish evildoers. That it was God's own Providence that guided Kane's steps, and His righteous fury that directed Kane's sword, gun, and staff.

"You will have the undying gratitude of this village, I am sure," Lauderman said. "I shall see to your supper at once."

He took a few steps away before he stopped and snapped his fingers.

"I almost forgot," Lauderman said, returning to the table. "A courier arrived while you were out. Said he'd been chasing you all across Europe, and was very relieved to find out you were staying with us."

He reached into his apron and removed a battered envelope, which he offered to Kane. Kane took it and nodded his thanks to the innkeeper. He waited until Lauderman had left to turn the envelope right-side-up and read it. It was addressed to an inn in France where Kane had been staying for several weeks. He thought he recognized the small, neat hand in which it was written.

Kane broke the wax seal, removed the letter inside, and unfolded it upon the table to read:

Dearest Solomon,

I know it has been quite some time since we last spoke. I hope you will forgive me dispensing with the usual courtesies of asking about your health and latest adventures. The situation is dire, and I must be quick.

I write to you from my home in the village of Windsend. We are a young settlement, less than five years old, and several miles from the hamlet where you and I grew up in Devonshire. My husband Enoch and I were among the group of Puritans who helped found the town, which sits in a valley outside of a dark wood. Here we hoped to make an Eden, a paradise on Earth that the Lord would look upon with favor.

Unfortunately, life in Windsend has been difficult. Our crops fail. Our livestock ails. Our children are often born sickly, and we lose too many babes and mothers in childbirth. We have struggled and fought for everything we have in this valley. Each victory is hard-won.

I do not tell you this to garner your sympathy. You know as well as any that life is hard, and ease is not guaranteed. The Lord has His plans and we but move within them. I tell you these things because I want you to understand the mindset of my neighbors. We have lived five years of unceasing hardship. We are all tired, and scared, and we now face a new problem.

Men in town have begun to die in horrible ways. All have been prominent leaders—town elders and businessmen and the like. The deaths only seem to occur at night. Sometimes we hear the screams of the victims. Sometimes we do not. There have not yet been witnesses to any of the deaths, but too many of us have discovered the aftermath. Ruined human bodies, mutilated in ways that no Christian should ever see.

The people of the town—including my own husband, Enoch—are convinced that something inhuman and unnatural is committing these murders. The focus of this suspicion seems to be coalescing about my friend Sybil Eastey, the local midwife. She lives just outside the village, and is one of the only members of our community who is not of the Puritan faith.

Rumblings of witchcraft have already begun. They suspect her of plotting against the town. A few now openly accuse her—of the killings, yes, but also the poor harvests, the dying livestock, and worst, the sickly children. They are convinced that she is the root of our problems here.

Enoch and the town leaders have not yet made an arrest, but the talk grows louder. I fear it is only a matter of time now.

Sybil has been a good and true friend to me—the only one I have in Windsend. She delivered my youngest son, Isaac, through a difficult birth—a birth many women and children might not have survived. I now fear for Sybil's safety. I do not believe her capable of this evil, but I know that my perspective is skewed by my love and gratitude.

If anyone can discover the truth at the root of our woes, and pronounce Sybil innocent or guilty, I know it will be you, Solomon. You are among my oldest and truest friends. I implore you to return to England, and help me if you can.

Please hurry.

Your sister in Christ,
Catherine Archer

Kane ran a thumb over the signature. *Your sister in Christ.* There was a time when he and Catherine Archer (née Hyland) might have been more. They had grown up together, and gotten along well. If not for Bess, Catherine would have been the obvious choice. But then life had unfolded as God had willed. Kane had left home young, and set upon a life of adventure—a path that had guided his footsteps up until this very moment.

He read over the letter thrice more while he ate his supper, and carried it up to his room after he'd finished eating. The stairs were a trial, his knee crying out with each step. Thankfully, Kane's room was close to the top of the stairs.

He suppressed a groan of relief as he latched his door behind himself and sat upon the room's narrow bed, where he glared at his traitorous knee.

This was only the latest betrayal of his aging body. On the rare occasions when he looked into a mirror or saw his reflection in a body of water, he scarcely recognized himself. Silver now threaded his dark hair, and his gaunt face was marred with heavy lines. The image in the reflection told the truth: he was growing old. And old men's bodies failed.

After a moment's rest, he rose, set Catherine's letter on his nightstand, then washed his face in the room's little basin. He stripped his cloak, hat, and weapon belts, hanging them on the wall, pulled off his boots and stockings, and lay down upon the bed, staff in one hand, pistol in the other. The pistol he slept with every night, as a precaution. The staff he only brought to bed on the nights when he needed to speak with N'Longa.

Sleep came quickly, as it usually did for Kane. One moment, he was setting his head upon his meager pillow, and the next he found himself in an empty white space, facing N'Longa.

Kane had known N'Longa many years. He had met the African priest as a young man, during one of his first trips to that distant continent. N'Longa had helped Kane defeat a rogue murderer named Le Loup, and thereafter the two considered themselves blood brothers. They had met several times during Kane's subsequent travels in Africa, and had worked together quite successfully. It had been N'Longa who had given Kane his staff, which was made of a wood no longer found upon this earth. The staff had helped Kane to defeat an ancient city full of vampires, but it had also allowed Kane to communicate with N'Longa across vast distances in dreams.

Kane had availed himself of this second power often of late. He and N'Longa had been working together to wipe out nests of vampires across the world. N'Longa, a powerful sorcerer, could see much, and had proved an able guide to Kane, setting upon the path in Africa, but lately sending him after a mobile coven traveling across Europe, leaving a trail of dead bodies and vampire fledglings in their wake. Kane had put down many confused fledglings in the last several months, although it gave him no pleasure to do so.

In the vast whiteness of the dreamscape, N'Longa sat upon a log, near a crackling fire. He looked up at Kane and smiled, his wrinkled face breaking into a thousand small lines.

Kane nodded a greeting as he sat down on a log opposite N'Longa's. Around them, a dark and dense jungle began to sketch itself in.

"You have been busy," N'Longa said. In the dreams, he spoke perfect English, a far cry from the more accented trade language he and Kane spoke to one another in person.

"Very," Kane agreed.

"But not with our business, I see," N'Longa said.

"I still hunt the coven," Kane said. "But the people in Baumstadt needed help. I could not abandon them in their hour of need."

"Mm," N'Longa said. "Perhaps Le Loup had the right of it, when he teased you. Monsieur Galahad, he called you. A famous knight of legend in your land, was he not?"

"He was," Kane said.

"And now I sense you plan to delay our work once more," N'Longa said.

Kane shifted upon the log. "An old friend in England has asked for my help. I cannot ignore her."

"No, indeed," N'Longa said. "You stop to investigate every stray cry, and right every wrong upon your path. And as you do, our prey gets further away."

"I am not asking your permission, N'Longa," Kane said.

"I know," N'Longa said, and sighed. "And I know that what I say next will not affect your decision, but I will say it anyway. You were closing in on the coven before you stopped for this ghost horse business. The coven have gained ground since then. England—where you plan to return—is over seven hundred miles from the place where you sleep tonight. You will give our quarry ample opportunity to do more harm while you travel, and tarry in England."

"Do what you can to mitigate it," Kane said. "Send dreams to the people. Put them on alert. We might not be able to stop these villains yet, but mayhap we can make them go hungry for a time and lose speed."

"I will do what I can," N'Longa said. "But you must understand—right now, the coven are unaware of our pursuit. If I do too good a job, they may catch wind of us, and our task will become much more difficult."

Kane nodded his understanding. N'Longa would try to save some, but would not be able to save all, of the coven's intended victims.

"It may be you can speed my own work," Kane said. "I am bound for the village of Windsend, where a great many murders are taking place. A local midwife is suspected of using witchcraft to commit the murders. Can you see the truth of it from here?"

N'Longa took a deep breath and closed his eyes. His face was placid for a moment as he reached out with his powers, trying to see what Kane asked for. His calm was broken by a frown a moment later, and he grunted with surprise.

"What is wrong?" Kane said.

"It is strange," N'Longa said, keeping his eyes closed. "I can... almost see the village. But it refuses to come into focus. It is almost as if..." he shook his head.

"Almost as if what?" Kane said.

"Almost as if something there is blocking my magic. Obscuring my sight." He opened his eyes. "I have never seen anything like this, Solomon Kane."

"All the more reason for me to set off at once, then."

3

Windsend

Kane woke early the next morning. He left the innkeeper more than enough gold to settle his bill, then went to the stable to retrieve Inglewood.

The hard rains of the night before had continued through the predawn hours and forced Kane to keep Inglewood to a canter as they left the town and entered the woods once more.

The rains remained heavy but Inglewood seemed to intuit her master's impatience, and picked up speed as they rode, stretching her neck forward and galloping down the road. Trees flew past on either side. Some clung to their last leaves, but most were bare, their branches like dark, gnarled arms reaching for Kane from either side. The road squelched and splashed beneath the horse, spattering her coat and Kane's pants with mud and puddled rainwater. Fallen leaves gathered in Inglewood's wake, creating a nimbus of brown and gold amid the gray and brown of the road and trees.

Each of Inglewood's strides jostled Kane's bad knee. He gritted his teeth and leaned forward until his own neck was extended almost parallel to the horse's. Rain pelted his slouch hat and ran down his face, while the wind tried to snatch the hat off his head. Kane ignored it and kept this eyes on the furthest point visible to him at any moment—be it a bend in the road, a signpost, or, when they emerged from the woods onto a wide, grassy plan, the horizon itself.

It went this way for several days. Kane knew the muddy road made the going more difficult for his mount, so he tried to enforce frequent breaks, and to travel no more than twenty-five to thirty miles a day.

Perhaps N'Longa was aiding Inglewood, or perhaps the horse was one of those rare beasts that outperforms all others of its kind through accidents of birth and chance. Whatever the reason, she seemed to move faster, and need less rest than expected, and they made it out of Germany and into France ahead of schedule.

In Calais, Kane reluctantly sold Inglewood to a stable, and bought passage on a merchant vessel across the channel to England. In his native country, he bought another horse, Holiday, and started the long overland journey from Dover.

This part of the journey lasted a fortnight, with the heavy rains seeming to follow Kane, and Holiday proving a slower mount than Inglewood.

As they approached Windsend, Kane found himself entering yet another dense wood, and here, Holiday slowed further. He could feel her weariness, and considering stopping for the night, making camp one last time before arrival. It would be a cold and miserable night, but if Holiday was at the end of her rope, it might be for the best.

Before he could make up his mind, however, horse and rider emerged from the woods and back into the open air. Kane found himself looking down into a steep valley. In the dark of night, it was hard to see what was below, but Kane thought he could make out another forest—and abutting that, a small group of buildings. A few lanterns were lit here and there, giving vague shape to a village.

This must be it. He'd arrived in Windsend.

Kane dismounted Holiday at the lip of the valley, held her reins and gently led her down the path. He kept his lantern high, and watched his step. He would have liked to use his staff to support his weight, but with the reins in his right hand and the lantern in his left, he had no way to hold it. So he trod slowly and carefully. The path was probably treacherous in fair weather; in this storm, it was all the more dangerous.

With a bit of extra care, however, Kane and Holiday made it into the valley unharmed, and crossed a wide field into the village of Windsend. As they approached the small clump of buildings against the woods, four lanterns wobbled toward them in the distance. These lights grew larger and brighter, eventually giving shape to their carriers: four men in the black garments of Puritans, carrying muskets over their shoulders.

"Halt!" one of the men called.

Kane came to a stop. He continued to hold his lantern aloft, to let the men get a good look at his face.

"You need no weapons," he said. "I am no threat."

"Name yourself, stranger." It was the same man who had spoken before. He was small, with narrow shoulders, a red beard, and a pinched, unhappy face.

"My name is Solomon Kane, and I come to Windsend as a friend."

The men exchanged glances. All three of the others seemed to defer to the little red-haired man, who turned back to Kane with a less suspicious expression. He handed his musket to one of his companions, and came forward to offer Kane his hand.

"Master Kane," he said, as they shook. "We were told you might be coming, but..." He trailed off, then seemed to remember his manners. "My name is Nehemiah Lockwood. I am the town carpenter."

"It is late," Kane said. "What business keeps a carpenter out of bed at this hour?"

Lockwood frowned. "If you have come, I assume you have received Goodwife Archer's letter, and know how things are in our village. I have fashioned too many coffins in the last few months. We have set a watch to patrol the village and protect her citizens."

"So the matter of the killings is not yet resolved," Kane said.

"That remains to be seen," Lockwood said. "The local midwife—an awful woman named Sybil Eastey—was arrested earlier this week, after the mayor was killed. There have been no more killings since her arrest, but we expect you, with your expertise, will be able to discover the truth at the heart of our woes."

"I shall do all in my power," Kane said. "But I am weary tonight. Is there an inn where I might rent a room?"

"Of course," Lockwood said. "Please, come with us. We will show you the way."

Kane stashed his lantern and took up his staff, allowing the men to lead him. On the way, he was introduced to Lockwood's companions—Thomas Blackwell, a merchant, as well as Edwin Wilton and John Howlett, both farmers. They passed several locations, which Kane marked but did not remark upon, including the village's cemetery, which seemed large for such a young village. Life must have been difficult here indeed.

The village had only one inn. A sign hung from the eave, featuring a crude painting of a comet streaking across the night sky, and beneath this image, the inn's name: The Falling Star.

Lockwood went inside while Kane waited in the street.

A moment later, Lockwood returned in the company of a young man with curly dark hair, bushy eyebrows, and a broad, round face. He had heavy-lidded eyes, as if he had just woken from a deep sleep, and he wore his nightclothes.

"Master Kane," Lockwood said, gesturing to the sleepy young man. "This is Roger Kidby. His father, George, owns the inn."

Roger seemed to come fully awake upon hearing Kane's name. "A pleasure to meet you, Master Kane," he said, shaking Kane's hand perhaps too vigorously, and for too long.

He was still shaking Kane's hand in both of his own when Kane said, "I need a room, and a stable for my horse, if you have them."

"Of course," Roger said, releasing Kane's hand. "I can see to your horse, if you would like to go inside."

Kane thanked the young man, and allowed Nehemiah to lead him into the inn.

The sight that greeted Kane was almost the perfect picture of an inn: a wide room lined with wooden benches and tables, all arranged before a stone hearth. To the right stood a bar with its stools, and to the left, a staircase led up to a second floor, presumably with rooms for guests. The only things missing were a roaring fire, a cheerful crowd, and the smell of fresh meat and bread.

An older man emerged from a doorway behind the bar. He wore night clothes as well, but had fastened an apron around his considerable middle. He had a ruddy face, and wispy white hair.

"Welcome, sir," he said. "My name is George Kidby, and this is my inn. I apologize we have not a warmer welcome for you, but we are unaccustomed to late visitors here."

"I apologize for waking you," Kane said.

Kidby waved the apology away. "My wife is not well, so I am up late most nights caring for her—but I admit you caught me unprepared. I might be able to find some cold meat, bread, and beer, if you would like to eat before you retire."

Kane's stomach rumbled at the thought of food, but his prevailing exhaustion was stronger.

"Thank you, no," he said. "I would find a bed as soon as possible, so I might rise early. I would take some water, if you have it."

"Of course," Kidby said. He disappeared for a moment, then returned with an earthenware pitcher in one hand. He came out from behind the bar and headed for the stairs on the opposite side of the room.

Kane thanked Lockwood and the watch for their assistance.

"We are happy you have come, Master Kane," Lockwood said. "Perhaps our long nightmare is finally at an end."

At the top of the stairs, Kidby lit two candles, one of which he gave to Kane.

"You have your choice of rooms at the moment," Kidby said. "Not many visitors these days. And those we do have tend to stay with family when they come. But we keep the rooms and bedding clean, just in case."

Kane took the room closest to the stairs. He had experienced his fair share of misadventures at inns (he shuddered to think of his night at the Cleft Skull tavern), and wanted the quickest means of egress, should evil befall in the night. He thanked Kidby and offered the man some coin from his purse.

Kidby looked at the coins and raised a hand, which froze between his body and the proffered money. He sighed as he accepted it, and it disappeared into his apron.

"Normally I would not ask for payment until you leave," he said. "But things are… difficult right now. My wife is sick. Our midwife—Sybil Eastey—used to brew a concoction for her, one that soothed her pain, and helped her rest, even if it could not cure her ailment. But now that Sybil is in jail, we are forced to buy medicine from the traveling physician. Cheesebrough is a godly man, but his medicine does not work as well as Sybil's, and seems to run out faster. He will be here in the next few days, if he keeps to his regular schedule. Having the money to pay for his wares will be a blessing."

He seemed to realize that he was sharing private concerns with a stranger and waved all of it away, handing Kane the pitcher of water.

"I talk too much," he said, with a small smile. "Goodnight, Master Kane. I hope your dreams are… tolerable."

Kane noted the odd turn of phrase, but did not question it. Instead, he nodded his thanks and let himself into his room. It was small but cozy, and surprisingly well-appointed: a wide bed sat against the far wall, with a table set beside it. On the nearest wall stood a wardrobe, and to Kane's right stood a small washbasin on a stand.

He limped over to the bed. He set the candle on the table, dropped his bag on the bed, and leaned his staff against the wall, between bed and table. He unstrapped his slouch hat and hung it on the hook by the door. He undressed, hanging his gun and sword belts in the wardrobe, but not before pulling one of the pistols from the belt and setting it upon the table by the bed. He washed himself with cold water in the room's little basin, then limped to the bed, pulled back the blankets, and lowered himself onto the mattress with a grateful sigh. He picked up the pistol off the bed and put it in his right hand as he closed his eyes.

Kane was asleep almost as soon as his head hit the pillow.

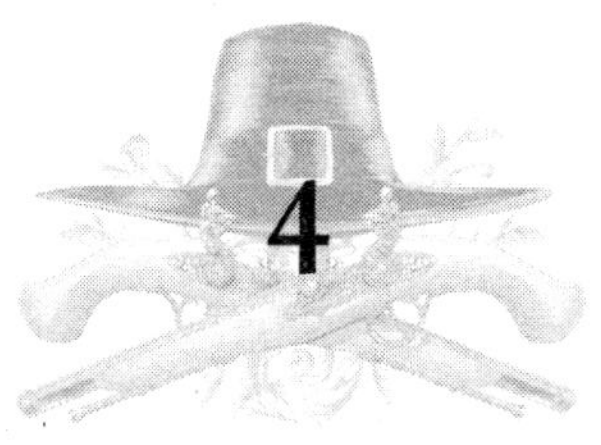

Screams in the Night

Kane wandered through a dark, narrow place, lit only by the wavering flame of the torch in his left hand. In his right, he carried one of his pistols. Although his rapier hung at his side, he did not carry his staff. Moreover, his knee did not hurt. His steps were as steady and easy as they had ever been.

The floor beneath him was stone, as were the walls and low ceiling above him. It *felt* like a cave, but was lined with flat, regular blocks, which had clearly been placed with intention. Kane stopped for a closer look at the stones, which appeared marked or marred. As he leaned forward, he realized he was looking at etchings, carved into the walls.

As Kane examined these carvings, a great wind swept in from the gaping dark. The blast and force were so great that Kane staggered, and his torch blew out like a candle.

Out of the dark came a chittering, skittering sound. It reminded Kane of the roar of jungle insects magnified a thousand-fold in both volume and size. He cocked his pistol and closed his eyes, trying to pinpoint the origin of the sound, which seemed to come from everywhere at once.

He dropped the torch, useless now as anything but a club, and reached for his rapier, only to find it missing. How could that be? He had seen it at his belt only a moment before. He cursed himself for the worst sort of fool, as the sound grew louder, and louder—

Kane opened his eyes with a sharp intake of breath. He found himself looking at his own extended right arm, pointing his pistol, not into a strange narrow corridor, but rather into a small, unfamiliar room. He was not standing, but lying down in a bed.

His memory finally caught up to his reflexes. He was in his room at the Falling Star Inn, in Windsend. He had come to see Catherine. But he saw no light leaking through the closed window shutters, and smelled no aromas of breakfast cooking below. It must be the middle of the night. Why was he awake now?

He heard the sounds of people in the street outside—unusual for this time of night, especially in a small Puritan village—and then a great scream rent the night. Kane launched himself out of bed and across the small room. He barreled through the door, not bothering with shoes, cloak, or hat, pausing only long enough to grab his weapon belt, which he tossed over one shoulder as he stormed down the stairs, across the common room, and out the front door of the inn and into the street.

He was only dimly aware of the earth beneath his naked feet, wet, cold, and soft from the rains. Mud squelched between his toes as he came to a stop at the bottom of the inn steps, and took in the scene before him.

A crowd had gathered in the street outside the inn. Kane saw the members of the night watch he had already met, now joined by several men and women in their night clothes. None of them seemed to mark Kane's arrival. Their faces were turned toward the sky, as if stargazing. Kane followed looked up to see what they were staring at.

It was George Kidby, the innkeeper who had so recently wished Kane a good night's rest. His body hung suspended a dozen feet in the air, facing the crowd, his back to Kane. His arms were stretched out to either side. His feet dangled, toes pointed down. The image put Kane in mind of the crucified Christ, missing only a cross. There were jagged tears in the back and sleeves of Kidby's white shirt, which was darkening with blood.

The gathered onlookers murmured among themselves. One woman pressed an alabaster hand to her mouth, eyes wide with terror, as Kidby whimpered and cried like a babe. Kane experienced a moment of disgust, which he forced out and replaced with pity. He was not in the company of fellow hard men and adventurers here, but among civilized men. Innocents who should never have to expect or fear a fate like this.

"George?" called one of the night watchmen. This was John Howlett, the farmer. "What is happening?"

"I—I do not know!" Kidby shouted back. "It hurts! Please, someone help me! Lord God, deliver me!"

The innkeeper had barely finished speaking before he began to scream again. His arms stretched further away from his body, and his back arched. He threw his head back to the sky and wailed, his agony loud and ugly.

As he watched, Kane became aware of a smell, almost hidden among the bouquet of an English village in October. Amid the smells of fire, wood, earth, rain, and animal scat, there was also a sulfurous stench on the night's chilly breeze—a stink that seemed to come from Kidby himself.

"Master Kane!" This came from Nehemiah Lockwood, standing at the front of the crowd. "Can you not help him?"

"I am not sure what is happening, Master Lockwood," Kane called back. "What would you have me do? Fire a gun into the air? Anything I do now would be as likely to harm as help."

"We cannot do nothing!" Lockwood shouted, over Kidby's screams.

Kane understood Lockwood's panic but was unsure what he *could* do.

The staff, he realized. *Perhaps my staff could reveal the source of this devilry. But he had left his staff up in his room.*

He was about to turn back, to run upstairs and retrieve it, when Kidby's screams grew louder. These cries were more than fear and pain—this was life-ending agony. Kane had heard it before, too many times. He forced himself to remain still, and witness the sight. It was all he could do for Kidby now.

As the innkeeper paused for breath between screams, there came a small popping sound, as if something had been freed from its socket deep in his body. This was followed by a tearing, not unlike what one might hear when pulling a leg off a roasted chicken.

Half a second later, the visual followed, as the innkeeper was ripped apart like a rack of lamb thrown to a pack of wild dogs. His arms, extended past their limits, came off his torso, unleashing freshets of blood into the air. Crimson droplets sprayed the faces of the crowd below. A couple of the women screamed. A few of the men did, too. Edwin Wilton dropped in a faint.

Kidby's remains hung in the air for another second, then dropped back to earth in a quick series of thumps, where they continued to gush blood into the mud. The crowd cried out, but Kane kept his eyes up to the place where the innkeeper had hovered a moment before. He could see nothing, but that hellish stench of sulfur remained, and... was there a sound? Something soft, like a chittering?

Lockwood gestured at the body on the ground, opening and closing his mouth. "You see," he said to Kane.

"I do," Kane said.

"Nothing in God's creation can commit such atrocities," Lockwood said, and although it was a statement, it had a hint of the question. Like a child looking for reassurance. "It must be witchcraft."

Kane did not answer right away, but looked from the corpse back into the air. He took a deep breath. The sulfurous smell was fading, and the chittering sound was gone—if indeed it had ever been there to begin with.

"I agree that something evil is afoot," Kane said. "But if it is witchcraft, it is like none I have seen before."

"Will you not come to see Sybil Eastey now, then?" Lockwood said. "Interview her. Ascertain her guilt or innocence."

Kane shook his head. "Nay. I will speak to her in the morning."

"We cannot let these evils continue," Lockwood insisted.

"And yet I shall speak to her in the morning, whether you like it or not," Kane said.

"Why?" Lockwood demanded. "Why not now?"

"Because I need my rest, Master Lockwood," Kane said. "I have had a long road, and will need all my wits for the interview. I *must* be sure of this woman. If you are truly interested in the truth, you must trust my methods and counsel."

"If you will not interview her tonight," Lockwood said, "I will lead the men of the town to the jailhouse and execute her right now. We cannot risk another death!"

"So, you will ensure one?"

"To save my people? Yes."

"And if Mistress Eastey is innocent?" Kane demanded. "What then? What happens if you execute her, and the killings continue? Will you sleep easily, knowing you have added another undeserving body to the pile?"

Lockwood's jaw worked, and his nostrils flared. He did not like what Kane said but heard the wisdom in it.

"What has happened here is a tragedy," Kane said. "But tonight, you and your watch should clean this mess out of the street, and see to the young man and widow that Master Kidby left behind."

Lockwood glanced at something behind Kane. Kane turned to see Roger Kidby, the innkeeper's son, standing on the porch, one hand to his mouth, eyes wide. Kane knew this look, too. This was not terror, but shock. Disbelief. The lad's mind could not understand what his eyes showed him.

As Kane mounted the steps back into the inn, he put a hand on Roger's shoulder.

"You will need to be strong now, for your mother's sake," he said.

Roger stared at his father's body in the darkened street for another moment, before looking back at Kane. He blinked slowly, like a small child waking from a dream. Kane tried to guess the lad's age. He could be no older than seventeen. Eighteen at most.

"Yes," Roger said. "Mother is sick."

"Let her rest, while she may," Kane said. "This ill news can wait until tomorrow."

"Yes," Roger agreed. "Tomorrow." His gaze went back to the scene in the street. Kane squeezed the boy's shoulder once more and went back inside.

Up in his room, he hung up his belt, cleaned the mud off his feet as well as he could, then returned to bed, and his uneasy night's rest.

5

Catherine Archer

Kane's dreams returned him to that dark corridor, full of strange sounds, and they stayed with him until he woke.

This time the waking happened without great ado. No cocked pistol, no screams in the street. Just the natural return to consciousness—awareness of light seeping through the window shutters; the sounds of bustle in the common room below; the smells of hot food.

He sat up and set his pistol on the nightstand. He used both hands to rub his face, and groaned softly into his palms. He felt all the miles of his long journey this morning, and the interruption of his rest the night before.

The memory came back: Kidby, the innkeeper, torn apart in the air in front of his home. Roger, the innkeeper's son, had seen at least some of it. He would be downstairs now, working. Kane ought to check on the boy, and then get about his own business.

He stood, testing his knee. It was sore, but less so today than yesterday. He paced the length of his room a few times, and found the process uncomfortable, but by no means intolerable. He could live with discomfort.

He washed in the room's basin, using the rest of the water George Kidby had given him the night before. Then he dressed, strapped on his weapons, grabbed his staff, and snatched his hat from the hook by the door.

Downstairs, he found Roger Kidby working a much livelier common room than the one Kane had observed the night before. There was a roaring fire in the hearth, and clumps of villagers were gathered at tables about the room, talking, smoking their pipes, and enjoying breakfast.

Their conversations came to an abrupt stop when Kane reached the bottom of the stairs. He was used to this. In other places in the world, his Puritan garb often caught the attention of strangers. They were often curious, and occasionally hostile. It was strange to receive such a welcome in a Puritan village, however. All the men here were dressed like Kane. Their clothes were less road-worn, but the types of garment—the black trousers and shirts—were the same.

Despite their similarities of dress, Kane treated these men as he would any other strangers. He gave them a curt nod and a "Good morrow," as he crossed the room to the bar, where Roger Kidby worked, looking harried.

Roger gave Kane a tired smile upon his approach. He was so damnably young. There was a light in his eyes, which Kane associated with youth. The only things marring the lad's broad, pleasant countenance were the dark bags beneath his eyes.

"Good morrow, Master Kane," Roger said. "How was your sleep?"

Kane noticed that the room behind them remained silent, aside from the crackling fire in the hearth. The other customers were listening to this conversation as well.

"It was fine," Kane lied. "How are you?"

Roger's tired smile became a grimace. "The watchmen took my… took the… the mess away, after you went back to bed," Roger said. "Master Lockwood is building a coffin for what's left of the body. We will bury him later today. My mother…" Here he looked down at the bar, rather than at Kane. "I fear she will not be well enough to attend the funeral."

"You have a trial before you," Kane said. "One I do not envy. But also know that the Lord has chosen it for you. It is all in His plan. It may be difficult to accept, or understand, but remember that all things serve Him. This is divine Providence at work."

Roger gave a short nod of his own. "Of course, Master Kane. You are right. I will pray for guidance." He stared down for another moment before shaking himself back to the present moment to look at Kane.

"Would you like some breakfast?" he asked.

Kane allowed that he would, and Roger fetched him a plate of bread and a tankard of milk. Kane quickly consumed both, then asked for directions to the Archer home, which Roger eagerly provided.

Kane strapped on his hat and set off. The rain had stopped, but the skies remained gray and foreboding. The air held an unpleasant chill. The earth squelched beneath his boots as he walked. He did his best to avoid the worst of the mire, but it was difficult, and he arrived at the Archer residence with new spatters on his already dirty boots, pants, and cloak.

The Archers lived in a small house that abutted a smithy. Catherine's husband, Enoch, was a blacksmith. As Kane paused before the front door to gather himself, he heard Enoch hammering away at the day's work.

Kane knocked on the door. A moment later, it flew open, and Kane found himself looking down at a pale boy, probably no older than nine or ten. His breathing was loud, and labored, and he had heavy bags under bright blue eyes. Those eyes looked identical to those of the boy's mother. Kane found himself transported, for a moment, back to his own boyhood in Devon. He might have been staring at Catherine's sickly twin.

"Who are you?" the boy said.

Kane tipped his hat to the lad. "I am Solomon Kane, young master. And I come seeking the lady of the house."

The boy turned his head. "Mother!" he shouted, in a high shrill voice. "You have a visitor!"

A few seconds later, Catherine appeared in the doorway, and Kane stood up a little straighter.

He had not seen her in many years. Much was the same—the alabaster skin that seemed to glow from within; those bright, merry blue eyes; the brown hair so dark it was almost black. But other things had changed. She had given birth to four children, and the shape of her body showed it. She was wider at the hips and bust. There were lines around her mouth and eyes. And although her hair was mostly tucked under a coif, what Kane could see now showed gray at the roots, like his own. Time had marked them both.

Catherine put a hand on the boy's shoulder. "Isaac," she said. "Is that how we greet a visitor?" She wore a hint of a smile as she said it, as though charmed by her son's spirit, even as she corrected his behavior.

"Sorry," the boy mumbled.

"What do we say?"

"Good morrow, master," the boy said, eyes downcast. "How may I help you, sir?"

"Good morrow, young master," Kane said. "You have helped me plenty, young Isaac, and I thank you."

Isaac, recovering a bit of his spirit, looked up at Kane. "Are you the adventurer mother told me about?"

Before Kane could answer, Catherine used her grip on the boy's shoulder to turn him about and direct him back into the house.

"Go help your sisters finish cleaning the table," she said.

"Yes, Mother," Isaac said. He disappeared into the house, leaving Kane and Catherine alone in the doorway. She smiled down at him from the porch, and he felt that strange movement back through the years.

"Hello, Catherine," Kane said. "It has been long."

Catherine surprised him by stepping out of the doorway and into the street, where she wrapped Kane in a tight embrace. Kane was shocked by the lack of decorum, but, after a moment, returned the hug.

"I am so grateful you came," she said.

She invited him into the house. He hesitated, wondering at the propriety of entering a woman's home when her husband was not present. It ought to be Enoch who invited him inside. He allowed himself to be carried forward by the force of Catherine's personality now. He entered the house, taking off his hat and cloak and allowing her to hang them near the door. He started toward the kitchen and its table, but Catherine stopped him, gesturing to his guns and sword.

"Would you mind hanging those up as well?" she said.

Kane was so used to keeping his tools close at hand, he sometimes forgot the niceties of civilized life. He unstrapped his weapons and hung them up as well. He felt naked without them, and it took willpower to leave his hands idle at his sides rather than feel for the missing weight against his thighs as he followed Catherine toward the kitchen, where four figures bustled about, cleaning and putting away the remains of breakfast. Three were girls, who Catherine introduced to him now: Mercy, aged eighteen; Faith, sixteen; and Grace, twelve.

The girls all favored their father, with light blonde hair,

brown eyes, and broad, pleasant faces. Only the boy, Isaac, had Catherine's dark hair and small features. Kane shook hands with all four, greeting each in turn.

Kane politely declined an offer of food, but did sit at the table while Catherine finished up in the kitchen. The girls disappeared into the house, off about their days. Only Isaac remained behind. He stood before Kane, openly staring.

The boy's breath was heavy, and came through an open mouth. He occasionally sniffled, snot rattling in his nose. He sounded as if he had a cold.

"Are you an adventurer?" Isaac asked.

"Of a sort," Kane said.

"Have you really been to Africa?"

"I have."

"What is it like?"

"Beautiful," Kane said. "But full of danger."

The boy's eyes widened. "Is it full of monsters?"

Kane opened his mouth, to tell the boy that the entire world was full of monsters. But then he glanced into the kitchen, where Catherine watched this exchange with her eyebrows raised.

"The world is full of strange and fascinating things," Kane said. "Things you cannot imagine."

"Yes, but I asked about *monsters*," the boy said. "Beasts from Hell."

"That is enough," Catherine said. "Leave us now, Isaac."

The boy's mouth twisted, as if clamping down on a retort or argument. Kane knew the look well. He had seen it on Catherine's face many a time when they were young. She had never been one to blindly trust authority, even that of her parents. She had had to learn to quiet her defiance. It seemed Isaac was learning similar lessons now.

"Mother," Isaac said, a whine in his voice. But before he could finish the sentence, his entire face bunched up. His hands flew up to cover his mouth as the coughing fit began. It racked his body, knocking him to and fro. Catherine crossed out of the kitchen and knelt beside him, gently rubbing his back.

Gradually, the coughing subsided, and Catherine said, "See what you have done. You have made yourself too excited. Go rest in your room. Read from your psalms."

The boy's shoulders slumped. "Yes, Mother."

Then he, too, disappeared, and Kane and Catherine were alone in the kitchen. She joined Kane at the table. A moment of silence passed between them. It was not a comfortable one.

"I saw the innkeeper die last night," Kane said.

Catherine folded her hands on the table, and lowered her head. "George Kidby. I heard. It is... the first of the deaths anyone has actually seen. With the others... we only heard screams. The mayor—Edmund Arrowsmith—was the worst. It was awful. The screams were unmanly. A few of the men in town heard and came to help. They found the front door locked fast. They broke down the door and raced upstairs, but by the time they arrived, it was too late. Enoch told me that it was like looking at the remains of a rag doll, one that has been shaken apart in the frothing mouth of a dog. But instead of stuffing scattered about the room it was..." She swallowed. "The man's innards. The deaths are always the same. All the victims are men. Until last night, each man was alone for his death, and there have been no witnesses. And then, four days ago, they arrested the local midwife, Sybil Eastey, on charges of witchcraft."

"This troubles you," Kane said. "Why?"

Catherine glanced back at the part of the house into which her children had vanished moments before. She turned back to Kane and leaned forward, conspiratorial.

"Sybil Eastey cared for me during a difficult pregnancy, and delivered Isaac through a traumatic birth. She may not be a Christian, but she is a good woman, and has been a good friend.

She only came to Windsend because I asked her to make the move with me. Friends have been difficult to come by since my marriage, and I wanted one nearby. I do not believe her capable of the crimes of which she has been accused. I know your history, Solomon. I trust you, and—"

Her speech was interrupted as the front door to the house opened. A silhouette stood framed in the gray morning light, that of a large man with shoulders so wide it seemed momentarily doubtful he could pass through the door.

He managed, however, and as he shut the door behind himself, Kane made out the details of Enoch Archer, Catherine's husband. He had blond hair, dark eyes, and a thick, rough-looking beard. His face was flush, and his skin coated in a sheen of perspiration, despite the chill.

Kane stood, as seemed polite upon the entrance of one's host. After a moment, Catherine stood as well.

"My love," she said. "You return early." Was it Kane's imagination, or did her voice quaver slightly?

"Grace told me we have a visitor," Enoch said. "I would not be a poor host." He crossed the room and shook Kane's hand. "Master Solomon Kane. It is good to meet you."

"And you, Master Archer," Kane said.

"Why did I have to hear from Grace that Master Kane arrived?" Enoch asked, turning to Catherine.

"I would not disturb you at your work," Catherine said, eyes upon the table. "I know how you hate to be interrupted."

Enoch stared at her, and Kane knew he had not imagined her anxiety before.

"I meant no disrespect," Kane said. "I hope I have not caused offense."

Enoch looked away from his wife. "Walk with me," Enoch said. "I will show you to Sybil's hut, where you may begin your investigation."

Kane glanced at Catherine, then away. He ought to know better than to defer to a woman when her husband was making a request.

"Of course," he said.

Kane and Enoch made the walk across the village together. Enoch walked quickly, his hands tucked into his coat pockets, his head down.

"I assume others have already given you all the grisly details," he said.

"Yes," Kane said. "And I saw for myself, last night."

"Awful things," Enoch said.

"And you suspect Sybil Eastey?" Kane asked.

"She is... strange," Enoch said. "She lives in a little hut outside the village proper. She has never shared our faith. She has never married, or issued a child. She seems to distrust all men, and prefers the company of women. No matter what ails a person, she seems to have the solution. Are these not signs of trouble, in and of themselves?"

Kane grunted. "Some people prefer solitude, and do not share our beliefs. This is not witchcraft in and of itself."

"There is more," Enoch said. "My friend, Nehemiah Lockwood, lost a child last year. He and his wife Joy believe that Eastey killed the babe."

Kane remembered Lockwood. The small red-haired man leading the patrol last night. He had seemed a decent enough sort.

"What proof does he offer?" Kane asked.

"No proof," Enoch said. "More of a... feeling in his gut." When Kane did not reply immediately, he went on. "I know Brother Lockwood is a stranger to you. But I trust his judgement. If he suspects Sybil Eastey, I think it is worth investigating."

"Why would she kill an infant?" Kane asked. "Or these men in your village? What would be her motive?"

"Do Lucifer's disciples need a reason?" Enoch said. "Is it not enough, to do harm to good Christians?"

"In my experience, killers have reasons," Kane said. "Even witches and demons have agendas."

"Oh," Enoch said. "And our dreams… our dreams are odd. That seems another sign."

"You believe Sybil Eastey haunts your dreams, as well?" Kane said. But he remembered his own dreams last night. They were not nightmares, not exactly, but they had been odd. Dark and foreboding.

"I do not know," Enoch said. "But we came to this place, and not long after, our village began to dream strangely."

They walked in silence for a moment. Enoch's jaw worked as though he were chewing some tough bit of meat. His face remained red, despite the cool air. Either the heat of his forge was slow to fade, or he was upset.

"I was against Catherine contacting you," he said at last. "But my wife is stubborn as a mule. She trusts you more than she trusts her own husband." He laughed a little, as if in jest, but Kane heard no humor in the sound.

"Nehemiah believes you can help our cause," Enoch went on. "He believes you will speed the process of discovery. So go on. Interview Sybil. Declare what we all already know. Denounce her as a witch. Put my wife's mind at ease, so she can focus on her duties, and our children. And then quickly be gone from here."

"I will discover the truth, as Catherine has asked," Kane said. "I will proceed with all my expertise, without prejudice, and it will take as long as it takes."

The look on Enoch's face suggested he didn't appreciate Kane's words. Kane cared not; he did not possess mildness when it came to men like Enoch Archer.

They arrived at a small hut on the edge of the village.

"Here is her hut," Enoch said. "I leave you to your work, Master Kane, and return to my own.

He did not shake Kane's hand, or offer any other pleasantry, but rather turned on his heel and marched back the way he had come.

6

Sybil Eastey

Kane entered the hut. It was a small, one-room dwelling, with a narrow bed in a corner. The bed had been made, as if its inhabitant had expected company, or just appreciated a tidy home. The rest of the space was taken up with shelves full of jars, a small fireplace, and a worktable along one wall. Strings of herbs hung from the ceiling. Kane recognized sage, dill, mint, parsley, and rosemary, among others.

He explored the hut, checking in each jar. Some contained herbs. Others liquids. Kane recognized no poisons, either in the jars, or in the herbs strung about the place. He searched each nook and cranny, but found nothing suspicious. No Books of Shadows. No poisons. No marks of the devil. He checked under the bed, and beneath the rug. There were no hidden doors, or traps. As nearly as he could tell, this was an ordinary midwife's hut.

He left, and headed for the town jail. Like the hut, it was a small, simple building, albeit in the center of the village, about a street away from the inn. The interior was one continuous space, the back third taken up by a barred cell. A small desk stood near the front door, and a portly, beardless man with thinning dark hair sat behind it. He smiled, taking Kane aback. This was not the smile of a jailer, a man who ought to be charged with the keeping of drunks and suspected criminals. This fellow would look more at home in a schoolhouse, teaching children.

The portly stranger smiled at Kane. "Good morrow, master."

Kane nodded to the man. "My name is Solomon Kane. I have come to question the woman Sybil Eastey, who has been accused of witchcraft."

The jailkeeper's eyes widened, and he hastened to his feet, knocking over his chair in the process. At his full height, he only came up to Kane's shoulder.

"Master Kane," he said. "Of course, of course. We were told you might be coming. Please, right this way."

Kane followed the little man from the desk to the cell in the back of the room. As they approached the bars, Kane saw a small figure lying on the cell's single cot. It began to stir at their approach, and sat up as the jailer produced a keyring from his belt and opened the cell door for Kane.

Sybil Eastey was a slight, slender woman, with sharp features and a wide mouth. Her hair was silvery blonde, and her eyes were green. She wore a blue dress with yellow sleeves. A coif for her hair lay nearby, but she did not reach for it now. Instead, she looked at Kane with a skeptical expression, like a woman dissatisfied with the wares on offer at a market stall.

After Sybil glanced at (and apparently dismissed) Kane, she turned to look at the jailer.

"What now, Ezekiel?" she said. It was a dry, throaty voice, not unlike a twig snapping underfoot on a forest floor.

"Good morning, mistress Eastey," Ezekiel said. There was warmth and kindness in his voice, and Kane felt a twinge of despair. You could not trust such a soft man in the company of criminals or witches. Kane would have to speak to the other men in town about this.

"This is Solomon Kane," Ezekiel said, gesturing over his shoulder at Kane. "The famous adventurer and righter of wrongs. He is going to interview you." With a placating smile, he stepped out of the doorway and gestured Kane inside.

Kane stepped into the cell, and looked back at Ezekiel. "I will need a small table, a chair, a quill, some ink, and parchment."

Ezekiel hurried away and returned a moment later with the requested items. Kane helped him set up the table and writing implements inside the cell. When they were finished, Kane said, "You can lock us in and leave now, Ezekiel."

Ezekiel's eyes widened. "I beg your pardon, master?"

"Lock the cell door. Then leave us. I would prefer privacy with Mistress Eastey for this interview. Return in half an hour."

"Are you sure, sir?" Ezekiel said. "That you want to be locked up, alone, with a woman accused of witchcraft?"

"Quite sure," Kane said. "Go on, then."

Ezekiel did as Kane ordered but did not look happy.

Perhaps he thinks to protect the witch from you, he thought. *Perhaps Sybil had bewitched this man.* He supposed that she would be considered beautiful. Kane could imagine the effect this had on lesser men.

Once Ezekiel had shut the jailhouse door behind himself, Kane turned back to Sybil Eastey. She sat with her knees pressed together, hands folded in her lap. Her posture was that of a demure Englishwoman, but there was something arrogant in her shoulders, and the set of her mouth. She might have been royalty in exile as she continued to regard Kane, unimpressed.

Kane's suspicion grew. An innocent woman would not look this proud in his presence. This defiant. An innocent woman would be frightened.

"You know who I am?" Kane asked.

"I am in possession of my hearing and my memory," Sybil said. "I heard you introduce yourself to Ezekiel, and heard Ezekiel introduce you to me, Solomon Kane," she said. "I was told you might be coming. That you would prove my innocence or guilt."

"Did they tell you that I am friend to Catherine Archer?" Kane said.

Her haughtiness broke for a moment, and genuine surprise showed through. Kane had at last told the woman something she did not already know.

"Catherine sent for you?" she asked, the first note of hope in her voice.

"She did," Kane said.

"Catherine Archer is a good woman," Sybil said. "If she is a friend of yours, then so am I."

Kane bristled. "Make no claim of friendship upon me, woman. You are accused of devilry, and grievous crimes against your neighbors. Ungodly acts."

Sybil rolled her eyes, all softness gone from her voice. "You men and your godliness. Go on then. Ask your questions."

Kane's temper flared, but he took a deep breath and calmed himself. He leaned his staff upon the bars and sat at the writing table, suppressing a grunt as he lowered himself onto the chair. He was forever grunting, groaning, and sighing whenever he sat or stood these days. Even on the days his knees behaved.

He picked up the quill off the table, dipped it in the inkwell, and held it over the top sheet of parchment.

"Sybil Eastey," Kane said, writing her name on the parchment. "You are aware of the crimes of which you are accused?"

"Yes," Sybil said. "I have been accused of using witchcraft to murder five men in the village. And one baby."

"Six men, actually," Kane said.

"Oh?" Sybil said.

"Heard you not the screams of George Kidby last night?" Kane said. "He was pulled into the sky and torn apart like a ragdoll in the street outside his inn."

Sybil frowned and looked at the floor. "I did hear the screams, but no one bothered to tell me what had happened. That is a shame. I liked George Kidby. I have been treating his wife. A very sick woman."

"I heard as much," Kane said, scratching out Sybil's answers and his own notes as quickly as he could. Perhaps he ought to have asked Ezekiel to stay behind and act as a scribe, freeing Kane to talk and observe. Kane found the process of transcribing laborious and boring. He only recorded it now for the sake of propriety. So that he could turn something in to the village leaders upon the completion of his investigation.

"Did you murder these six men? And the babe?" Kane asked, looking up from the parchment to ask the question.

Sybil met his eye, her gaze steady. "I did not *know* George Kidby was dead."

"Answer my question," Kane said.

She sighed. "No. I have never killed anyone."

Kane returned to the parchment. "And how long have you been a resident of Windsend?"

"Since the village's founding, five years ago," Sybil said.

"Are you a Puritan?"

She laughed, throwing her head back, her neck fully extended. She rocked back toward the wall, her hands to her chest.

"Is that a 'no'?" Kane asked.

"That is most assuredly a 'no,'" Sybil said.

"Windsend was founded as a haven for Puritans," Kane said. "Why live here, if you are not of the faith?"

"Catherine Archer asked if I would come, when she and Enoch came," she said. "She is a good woman, and a true friend. That is part of it. But there is more, a piece that is harder to define. I felt… compelled, when I heard about this place. Something drew me here."

"You moved to an untested place on a whim?" Kane asked, with a raised eyebrow. "Or did you perhaps hear—and heed—the call of some darker force?"

"If there was darkness in the call, I noticed it not," Sybil said. "But there was a financial aspect as well. I saw an opportunity—a community without a physician or midwife of its own. I hoped to make a good living, tending to the people and delivering their babies. But that is not a crime."

"No indeed," Kane said. "'*A slack hand causes poverty, but the hand of the diligent makes rich*,'" he said, quoting Proverbs 10:4. He dipped his quill back into the inkwell and began writing anew. "Tell me—how has life been for you in Windsend?"

"Life here has been difficult," Sybil said. "Since the village's founding, we have struggled. Our livestock have failed to multiply, or merely survive. Harvests have been meager. Citizens are prone to illness. Babes are oft stillborn, and those that live are plagued by sickness. And our dreams are strange. We dream of odd things that do not make sense. At least, not when we wake and discuss them. None of my remedies seem able to cure our affliction."

Kane noted the use of *our*. As if she were a member of the community and not a true outsider.

"And the people here are afraid," Sybil said. "They believe in a God who takes an active part in their lives. They do not understand why such a God would allow them to suffer so. After all, have they not dedicated their lives to worshipping him? And yet, here they are, working themselves to the bone and starving and dying still. Suffering, still. Surely, their God would not let them suffer like this. No, there must be an external cause for their misfortune. A third party. Someone in league with the devil. Once men jump to this conclusion?" She shrugged. "Once they start looking for someone to blame? It does not take long for their gazes to settle upon someone like me. A woman who lives in the community, but who does not share the faith. A woman without a husband. Without children. Who does not attend worship. It is an easy jump to make, for a certain mind. 'She does not live as we do. She must be a witch.'" She spoke this last sentence with a mixture of weariness and contempt, riling Kane's sympathies for the villagers. Did this woman not understand she mocked at his faith? Or did she simply not care?

He looked up as he finished transcribing her words, his face impassive, stony. "So you deny the accusations of witchcraft?" he said.

"Of course I do," she said, reaching up with her right hand to brush a lock of hair from her face. As she did so, the sleeve of her dress shifted, and Kane caught a glimpse of something: a dark mark on the woman's wrist.

He dropped his quill, stood, and crossed the cell. Sybil was so startled by his speed that she froze, hand raised. That made it easy for Kane to grab her arm and push her sleeve up to her elbow.

It had not been a shadow, or trick of the light. The pale flesh of her right arm was darkened by a large brown birthmark in the shape of a star, well-defined, its edges and points clear and sharp.

Kane looked from the birthmark back to Sybil's eyes. For the first time they betrayed an emotion aside from weariness and disdain. They were now full of fear.

"I am surprised you live," Kane said. "That the villagers bothered to contact me at all, when you bear such a clear mark upon your forearm."

Sybil yanked her hand away and stared up at him. He heard a dry click in her throat as she swallowed.

"It is a birthmark," she said. "Only a superstitious fool would use this as reason to end a woman's life."

Kane released her arm and crossed the cell to retrieve his staff. He returned to Sybil, grabbed her right arm, and used his left to touch the staff's cat head carving against the birthmark. The mark changed from dull brown to a bright white, like the light of a star in the night sky. It was so bright that Kane had to release her arm to stop from blinding himself.

He lowered the staff so that its pointed end touched the ground, then glowered at Sybil once more.

"Do you still protest your innocence, Sybil Eastey?" he asked.

She glared at Kane with something like pure hate. Kane had seen the look before, when he ferreted out a hidden criminal, or cornered a wild monster. With no power left to cause harm, hate was the only option left to the evildoer. Kane was used to it.

But then something new happened. Sybil's glance darted to Kane's staff, and her expression softened to one of curiosity.

"What is that you carry?" she asked.

"A powerful stave," Kane said. "It has proven useful in defeating evildoers like yourself."

"Where did you get it?"

"What does it matter?"

"I am curious."

"It was given to me by a friend," Kane said. "A man I call blood brother."

She frowned.

"Make your peace with your master, Sybil Eastey," Kane said. "You shall meet him soon enough."

He turned away from her, toward the cell door—and only then did he remember that he had sent Ezekiel away. He was stuck in this cell for at least a few moments more. He could try to call for the jailer, but that would be unbecoming and undignified.

Sybil laughed behind him. "Your dramatic exit is ruined, Master Kane."

Kane whirled and re-crossed the cell to loom over and glare down at her. "Laugh not at me, witch," he growled.

Sybil did not flinch. Instead, she stared back at Kane with those wide green eyes, a hint of mirth on her face. "Or what? What will you do to me? You already plan to assist my neighbors in scapegoating and murdering me."

"How *dare* you call it murder? What will happen to you will be nothing less than the Lord's justice," Kane said.

"I call it murder when the innocent are slain," Sybil said. She rose from her seat and stood, so fast that Kane took a step back. He was not used to a woman addressing him so forcefully. Though she was nearly a foot shorter than himself, she seemed to fill the room. "And I tell you, you foolish man: *I am innocent.*"

"My staff says otherwise."

She rolled her eyes. "Your staff says I am a witch. And in that, it is correct. All the women in my family have had the knack, for as far back as we can remember. But we are none of us murderers. Hear me when I say, I did not kill the men of Windsend."

Her green eyes were aflame, her voice strong and steady. Kane stopped himself from taking another step back, and felt a click in his own dry throat as he tried to swallow. He realized that he believed her.

He shook his head, trying to clear it. This must be a trick. Some witchcraft upon his head and heart. She was using her powers to exert control over him, surely. The same way she had ensnared Ezekiel. He meant to tell her this. To demand she get out of his head. But that was not what came out of his mouth. What emerged was entirely different.

"Why should I believe you?" he said.

"Because," she said. "You may dress as a Puritan, but you yourself are unusual. You have taken no wife. You have fathered no children. And you carry a magical staff, given to you by… someone powerful. Would your brothers and sisters in Christ approve of you carrying such a talisman, Solomon Kane? If they had seen what I just saw, I believe you would be in this cell with me, awaiting trial."

"You know nothing about me, witch."

"You know as well as I that magic is a tool," she said, trampling over his words with her own. "It has no inherent morality. It may be used for good or evil, the same as your sword, or pistols. Or, yes, your staff. You use these things to help people. I use my tools to help my neighbors. I have never used them to kill a human being."

"Then how do you explain the murders?" Kane said.

"Go east," Sybil said. "Two miles into the woods at the edge of the village, starting at the Lockwood house. You will smell it before you see it. Follow the stench of death, and you will find your answers. But be on your guard. What you find will not be to your liking."

"What will I find?"

"I am not entirely sure," she admitted. "I saw the place once, and was too frightened to return on my own. Something strange guards that place. Something for which I have no easy explanation. Bring your weapons with you. Be on your guard."

Kane frowned. "If this is so… if you have a possible alibi, in this cave… why have the men in town not already gone to investigate?"

"They do not listen to anything I have to say that is not a full confession," she said. "But if you are interested in truth, that is where you shall find it."

Ezekiel returned shortly thereafter, opening the cell door. Kane had already gathered up his papers, leaving only the ink and quill on the desk. He stormed out of the jail without a word, slamming the door behind him.

As he re-entered the fresh morning air, he found a small group of men gathered outside. Nehemiah Lockwood stood at their front, wearing an expression of fearful expectation.

Kane did not stop as he reached the bottom of the stairs.

"Master Lockwood," he said. "Would you walk with me?" He continued to move without waiting for the other man's answer, heading in the general direction of the woods.

Lockwood almost had to run to keep up with Kane. He used one hand to keep his hat atop his head. Behind them, Kane could hear the other men trotting along as well.

"Master Kane?" Lockwood said.

"Which way to your house, sir?" Kane said.

"Oh." Lockwood stopped in his tracks, as if unsure, then remembered himself and pointed to his left. "This way."

Kane let Lockwood lead the way for a moment, then resumed his steady pace. It felt good to move like this. To have his leg cooperating. To command his body in the way he had as a young man.

Within a few moments, they came to a house considerably larger than the Archer residence, and here Lockwood stopped.

"This is my home," Lockwood said. "Would you like to come inside? I am sure my wife Joy can—"

"No, thank you," Kane said. He walked past the house, heading for the trees. He looked to his left and saw that Lockwood was no longer beside him. Instead, the little man remained at his own front door, looking confused.

"I do not understand," Lockwood said. "Where are you going?"

Kane gestured toward the trees with his free hand. "The woods."

"Why?"

"Because my investigation is not yet complete, Master Lockwood."

"What about Sybil Eastey?" Lockwood said. "Her trial begins tomorrow!"

Kane did not answer as he allowed himself to be swallowed by the forest.

7

The Woods

Entering the woods outside of Windsend was like stepping from bright daylight into a small, dimly lit room. Kane had to slow his pace, and wait for his eyes to adjust as he carefully moved forward. When, after a few moments, he looked back in the direction he had come, he could no longer see the town. When he glanced up, the canopy of trees almost completely blocked the daylight.

Those same trees seemed to crowd in around him now, dense and close, like a bullying mob.

Kane, wary after Sybil Eastey's warning, and no stranger himself to the perils of a dark wood, kept on his guard. Although his eyes eventually adjusted to the darkness, visibility remained limited. The air around him felt stuffy and stale, like a room that has been shut up for too long. It was also as quiet as a night after a new-fallen snow. Far too quiet for this time of year. In October, there ought to be wind rattling the tree leaves and small creatures moving about. There ought to be birds that had not yet flown away for the winter. Kane's own footsteps ought to sound louder. Instead the sound seemed to be absorbed by the woods.

Something strange was at work here.

It was impossible to measure time in this preternaturally quiet darkness. Kane lost himself to it. He continued to move in a straight line, away from Windsend, guided only by his innate sense of direction, a compass that had never yet failed. The trees grew closer and closer, so narrow in places that Kane was forced to turn sideways to pass between them. Roots seemed to reach up to snag the toes of his boots. He struggled on, waltzing with this hostile place, choosing each step with care.

Eventually, he noticed a new smell. It began as a tickle in his nostrils, amid the earthy potpourri of the forest, but quickly grew to blot out the inviting smells of tree, earth, and decaying wood. This new scent put Kane in mind of standing upwind of an outhouse on a breezy day, the smell of waste wafting toward him. But that was not all. The outhouse stench was part of a bouquet of its own, accompanied by sulfur and something sickly sweet, like rotting meat. The breakfast in Kane's stomach rolled over as he breathed it in.

Sybil Eastey had spoken truly when she named it "the stench of death."

As the malodor grew stronger, the trees stopped crowding so close. There seemed to be fewer roots in which to snarl his feet. It was as if the woods were a living thing, and now gleefully invited Kane forward, to see the source of the smell.

He did not trust this new freedom of movement but continued to move forward slowly, pistol at the ready, listening hard to the eerie quiet about him and trying to look in all directions at once.

He was so busy looking at the trees that he almost stepped right into the source of the smell.

He stopped abruptly, planting his staff to keep his balance, and silently cursed himself for a fool as he crouched for a better look.

The fox lay on its side. It could only have been dead for a few days. Most of its reddish-brown fur remained intact, but its eye sockets had become writhing maggot pits. Its mouth, full of sharp little teeth, was wide open in what looked like a silent scream. Its throat had been torn open, but most of the meat remained. Whatever had killed this beast had not done so for food.

Kane looked up, and noticed another small form, several feet away. Hard to discern in this light, but drawing into sharp relief as Kane approached. But even close up, Kane remained unsure what the thing had been in life. It was less a corpse than a pile of muscle and bone. Like a living creature had been turned inside out. Kane did not kneel before this sight. Although no stranger to the gruesome, he felt no desire to be closer.

Instead he stepped around the fetid mess and continued forward. He came to the next body a few paces later. And the next. And the next. He had stumbled upon a trail of death and mutilation. All were animal corpses, but most appeared to have been killed in a manner similar to the deaths described by the townsfolk.

The trees grew sparser, and Kane shortly found himself in a large, circular clearing. The break in the tree cover allowed the weak gray daylight to shine down, and gave him a good view of the tableau before him: dozens of dead animals, scattered about like children's toys in a nursery, all seeming to radiate from a central point, which was a large hole in the forest floor.

Kane approached the hole now.

It was a silly notion—he knew this—but he could not help thinking (or feeling) that the silence he'd experienced since he had entered the forest was radiating from this hole, and spreading out through the woods like a blanket. As he drew close to the opening, he saw that it was rimmed with rough stone. Also, it was not a hole, but more a ramp, leading down into darkness.

Kane holstered his pistol, and quickly fashioned a torch from a fallen tree branch and scraps of cloth. He carried this light and warmth down into the darkness.

The ramp was surprisingly wide, and tall. Kane had no trouble standing upright as followed the stone.

The passage widened and heightened quickly, the further Kane walked, and he became aware of another smell to replace that awful stench of decay. What came now was like rotten eggs or flatulence.

He kept walking. As he did, the rough-hewn, natural stone corridor became large rectangular blocks, which had obviously been placed with deliberate intention. They were rough and slightly irregular, not the work of modern craftsmen—but surely this was man-made all the same.

The stone placement was the same upon the floor, walls, and ceiling of the corridor. At first glance, the stones seemed to be cracked, like a thin pane of winter ice. Kane approached one of the walls for a better look. When he placed his fingertips upon the stone, he grunted in surprise. These were not cracks, but rather etchings, carved into the rock. Elaborate, spiraling designs. And was it a trick of the light? — the stone also seemed to be giving off a slight, blueish glimmer. He leaned in for a closer look, and realized that there were chips embedded in the stone, which shone blue. It seemed familiar somehow, although he could not place it.

Kane stepped back from his examination of the wall, and tried to stand up. His retreat and ascent were interrupted as he bumped into something where there ought to have been nothing but empty air. His instincts told him what his mind struggled to frame. He had not hit a wall, but rather a body—something smaller than his own broad, solid frame, but real enough.

He turned around, swinging his torch in front of him. It passed through the air, and Kane found himself staring around an empty corridor.

He swung the torch a few more times, hunting for the body he'd bumped before, but found nothing but air.

"Who is there?" Kane demanded. "Show yourself."

There was a skittering sound on the stone floor, a clicking like a dog's claws on a hard surface. And a small chittering noise.

Kane swung his torch again, this time he hit something. A shape became briefly visible in the firelight—a head and shoulders, taller than a child but shorter than the average man. It was little more than a silhouette, and disappeared almost as quickly as Kane had seen it.

Camouflage. Somehow, this thing was camouflaging itself.

Something hit Kane's arm from behind and the torch was knocked out of his grip. It somersaulted through the air twice before hitting the floor and rolling away down the hall. It remained lit, but its illumination moved away, leaving Kane's immediate environs in darkness.

Kane swapped his staff to his newly free left hand so he could use his right to draw his sword. He closed his eyes, listening for his invisible attacker. But, like the forest above, he heard only silence.

When Kane opened his eyes, he was surprised to find that he was no longer in the dark. The walls of the corridor glowed a faint blue, the chips in the stone providing their own eerie illumination. In this dim blue light, Kane suddenly saw the creature.

The thing was short, and alarmingly thin, with small, paper-thin wings on its back. Its head only came up to the bottom of Kane's chest, and its arms were about as thick as fallen tree branches—the kind that could easily be picked up bundled for firewood. Kane had seen such scrawny limbs before, in villages where people were struck by illness or starvation. In the past, these sights had filled him with despair, a sense of helplessness, a dull rage at a thing he dared not name. Seeing something so similar on this bizarre creature engendered no sympathy now, however, only a mute disgust.

The creature's head was so large that he wondered how the thing's body and tiny neck supported it. The pate was wide and hairless, the ears large, upper tips as sharp as a predator's teeth. And the eyes. The eyes were most disturbing—large, yellow, with vertical pupils and blue where the other eyes were white.

The creature hunched forward, arms out in front, its long, clawed fingers curled. Its legs were bent, and he realized—almost too late—that the creature meant to spring at him. He barely had time to raise his rapier before the thing shrieked and leapt. It was fast, but Kane's instincts were equal. He sidestepped out of the creature's way, and slashed his blade across its chest.

The creature landed a few feet away, stumbling for balance, and Kane thrust forward, driving the tip of his rapier into the creature's back. The beast screamed as his sword emerged from its chest, the blade coated in the thing's black blood. Kane lifted the creature, using his sword as the point of leverage. The beast slid down the length of the blade, shrieking, flailing, and kicking all the way. Kane kept his arm fully extended, to stay out of reach until the creature's body slid flush against the guard of his rapier.

Then he planted his foot against the small of its back, and shoved it away with all his might, ripping his sword free as well. Blood arced through the air, black in the blue light, and Kane heard the meat of the monster's body tearing for a brief moment before the creature's screams began to echo. The sound was painfully loud in the small space, and he gritted his teeth and squinted his eyes, as if this might alleviate the pain.

He stepped back and gave the rapier a quick shake to get rid of any excess blood. The creature writhed on the stone floor, blood pouring from both sides of its body. Its limbs flailed and stamped against the stone like a toddler throwing a tantrum. Kane waited a few seconds, for the creature to bleed out and die. Instead, its agonies went on and on. It did not get back to its feet, or try to attack, but wailed and wailed.

Kane stepped forward, meaning to stab his rapier through the creature's throat and silence it, but paused as his keen ears picked up a new sound, almost buried beneath the dying creature's racket—a clattering, tapping sound, echoing down the corridor toward him out of the dark. It was difficult to tell because of the echo, but it sounded as though many creatures approached, a great horde drawn by the cries of their fellow.

He turned away from his wailing assailant and toward the corridor at his back. In the dim, eldritch blue light, he saw them coming: a wall of creatures, each identical to the one he'd already fought and injured. They approached, claws tip-tap-tapping on the stone floor, forelimbs raised, ready to tear him apart. Nor, Kane was disturbed to see, were they *only* traversing the floor. Some clung to the walls and ceiling, clambering forward on all fours.

Kane raised his rapier with his right hand, and his staff in his left. He bent his knees slightly, ready to spring into action, as he bared his teeth. And then a voice spoke up in the back of his mind:

Do not be a fool.

Kane knew the speaker well enough. This was caution. Self-preservation. This voice had saved his life many times. In his youth, Kane had learned to listen to this voice. It spoke to him more and more often lately, and these days it had taken on the tone of a hectoring parent or spouse, too concerned with safety to allow a person to live a life.

You cannot win against so many, the voice said now. *Flee, and return in strength.*

He knew it was wisdom, but something in him rebelled at the idea.

"Be damned," he said, both to the voice in his head and to the creatures before him.

As if answering his challenge, the first of the creatures leapt, springing toward him from its perch on the ceiling. Kane met it with a spinning slice of his sword, followed by a bash at the thing's head with the cathead of his staff. The creature crumpled to the ground, skull caved in, as Kane turned to face its fellows.

The creatures regarded Kane for what might have been the length of a single breath, but that breath seemed to stretch on into infinity.

"Be damned," he repeated. He was Solomon Kane. He would not run from this fight, or any other.

The creatures, now seeming to intuit that their strength lay in numbers, rushed Kane *en masse*. Kane let his body do what it did best. His mind sank into a red haze, calm and full of rage at the same time. His muscles moved of their own accord, directed by years of training and instinct, honed as fine as any blade.

Kane became a dervish in the cave, swinging and slashing and smashing, never staying still long enough to let any creature lay a single digit upon him. He felt their claws slice the air a fraction of an inch before his face. His ears were filled with the hisses and clicks of their rage, the screams of their agony as he cut them down in droves. Bodies began to pile up at his feet, and he had to slow his movements, to think more strategically about where to place every footfall.

Unfortunately, he could not see and understand everything at once.

He stabbed one of the monsters through the eye and, with it impaled upon his blade, swung it like a bludgeon to knock away a wave of its fellows. The side of his right boot brushed against a stack of bodies. He turned, shifting the weight on his right knee. Perhaps the turn was too abrupt? Kane could not be sure. All he was sure of was that the red haze, his battle calm, evaporated as agony flared up from his right knee, and the leg gave out beneath him.

He landed on the knee with a cry, and for the second time in the space of a few moments, he lost his grip upon something in his hand as his rapier hit the ground beside him and his right hand went instinctively to his knee, as though cradling it could alleviate the pain.

The creatures sensed the turn in the battle, and surged, coming at Kane from all sides now. Kane swung the staff in his left arm, tracing a wide arc about his body, knocking the creatures away. It bought him a second or two before a new wave of creatures clambered over the pile of their fallen fellows and rushed at Kane. There on one knee, he swept the staff back and forth, trying to knock away his assailants, to buy himself a chance to think, to regroup. The creatures gave him no such quarter. He was overrun. He tried to stand, but his knee cried out in protest. He would need the staff in order to stand, but the staff was all that stood between himself and certain death.

The staff. The staff, which was made of wood more ancient than any known to men. The staff, gifted to Kane by his blood brother, the priest N'Longa, in Africa. The staff, which granted Kane the ability to communicate with N'Longa across great distances, in dreams. Kane had never tried to communicate while awake. It was a long shot, but Kane had to try.

"N'Longa," Kane growled now, swinging the staff about in a wide circular motion. "Can you hear me?"

The staff vibrated in Kane's hand as it knocked back another wave of creatures. A strange buzzing sound filled Kane's head. It sounded like the roar of the ocean, and drowned out all other sound. Yet, somewhere in that din, Kane thought he discerned a voice speaking. He recognized it as N'Longa's voice, but could not make out the words.

"N'Longa, I cannot hear what you say," Kane said. "Can you understand me?"

The staff vibrated in Kane's hand, and there came a fresh wave of white noise. Kane took this as an answer in the affirmative.

One of the creatures got past Kane's defenses. It landed on his back and bit his neck. Kane cried out, more in surprise than pain as he grabbed the creature by its own neck, yanked it off him, and threw it forcefully into the crowd, knocking it back once more.

"I need your help, blood brother," Kane said. "If you can aid me now, I ask that you do so."

The staff vibrated once more. It started softly, a twin to the previous sensation, but this time it grew in power and frequency, until the stave shook so hard that Kane needed both hands to keep hold of it.

The horde seemed to understand that something unusual was happening, and stopped its onslaught. They looked to Kane, and to one another, confused. It took Kane a moment to realize that the ocean roar he'd heard before was no longer in his own head, but emanating from the staff.

As Kane made this realization, he made another: the head of the staff was glowing. The ancient wood had turned from a blackish brown to a lighter color. As Kane watched, it turned entirely white, like a tiny sun in the middle of this dark, evil place.

Just when Kane thought the staff would explode into a rain of splinters, the light at the top of the cat's head burst and sent a great white wave in all directions. The horde of creatures screamed as the light struck them. The closest were smashed to dust in an instant. The ones a little further back were knocked against walls, ceiling and floor, and the air was full of the sounds of screams and breaking bones.

The sights and sounds filled Kane with a grim satisfaction, but he could not linger to enjoy it. Instead, he planted the staff in the floor and used it to pull himself to his feet with a groan. His right knee screamed in protest, and he froze for a moment, waiting to see if the pain would lessen.

He looked at the fallen monsters about him. Many were still. A few moved and chittered softly. He tried to spot his rapier, but it was out of sight, buried somewhere among the bodies. Kane wanted it back badly, but also understood that this gift from N'Longa was fleeting. He could not count on the priest to provide another magic blast from across the world—at least, not anytime soon. Nor could Kane count on these creatures being the only ones down here. There might be hundreds or thousands more in these tunnels—and perhaps worse things, too. No, he had to make his escape now, if he meant to honor his friend.

Using his staff to stay upright, Kane limped back the way he had come. Each step sent a new blast of pain up from his knee, and he gritted his teeth against crying out. He moved as quickly as his body would allow, which was not quickly enough for his taste.

The journey back up the corridor, into the cave, and onto the forest floor seemed to take an eternity. When Kane emerged from the darkness, into the too-still clearing of the Windsend woods where he had entered, he knelt, breathing hard, his face hot with shame.

The pain did not bother him. Agony was not a new experience. No, what bothered him was his weakness, and the fact that he found himself gripped by fear. He had been genuinely afraid for his life in that corridor. That knowledge was hard to bear.

8

The Funeral

Kane limped back the way he had come, practically dragging himself forward with only the staff for support. His progress was embarrassingly slow, and painful. Each step sent a fresh jolt of discomfort up from his right knee. Kane gritted his teeth and put one foot in front of the other, following his sense of direction back toward Windsend.

The journey gave him plenty of time to listen to the forest, and think. The woods remained unnaturally quiet, except for the sounds Kane himself made. If he had been stealthy and quiet as a panther before, he now sounded like what he was: an old man in a great deal of discomfort. His footfalls were loud and clumsy in tandem with the thump of his staff as it dug into the forest floor. His breath came in labored, ragged gasps.

The voice of reason spoke up in his mind once more: *Your adventuring days are at an end, old man.*

"Be damned," Kane growled aloud. He felt slightly foolish but could not help himself. The voice felt so real. It demanded an answer.

He buried these dark thoughts, trying to focus instead on what he had discovered in the cave. The way it gave way to strange, man-made architecture. The designs etched into the stone, and the eldritch blue light those etchings had emitted, once his torch had been snuffed.

And then there were the creatures in that corridor, which had *only* become visible once the torchlight was gone, and the strange blue glow became the only illumination. Those small, wiry creatures with giant heads. Creatures that stank of brimstone.

It took no great deduction to surmise that these were George Kidby's killers. And although Kane had not witnessed the other deaths in Windsend, the manners of death were too similar. This had to be the source of the village's woes.

But Kane still had to determine the provenance of these infernal creatures. Was it possible Sybil Eastey had summoned them, and was commanding them? Such a thing was surely possible… but Kane's gut told him this was not the case. She had lied to him about being a witch, yes—but she had only done so to try to save her own life.

"'*The righteous should choose his friends carefully, for the way of the wicked leads them astray*'," the Voice said.

Kane sighed. Proverbs 12:26. When he could not trust his head, his heart or his company, he could trust in the Lord. It did not matter what he wanted to believe. His task was to follow the evidence, and see where it led. So far, that evidence seemed to lead away from Sybil, but he could not rule out the possibility that she had made a pact with some great evil. Witches did such things.

One bright side to all of this rumination was that it kept Kane's mind off his pain during the trip back to Windsend, and he was somewhat surprised when he emerged from the woods at the edge of the village, within sight of Nehemiah Lockwood's house.

Here he stopped and looked about. He cocked his head, listening. The town was as quiet as the forest had been. Kane's stomach sank. Had something happened while he was gone? Had Sybil Eastey led him away from the village, and then summoned an army of those creatures from another subterranean doorway and flooded the village?

But no. As Kane explored, he found no bodies in the street. No bloodstains on the sides of buildings or in the mud. The town was quiet, and the streets were empty, but that was all. It took his mind, full of the haze of combat, a few moments to calm enough to reason out what must be happening. George Kidby had died last night. They must be holding the funeral now.

He pointed himself toward the village cemetery, which he had passed upon his arrival. Along the way, he passed homesteads where animals roamed gated yards. Almost all had a thin, sickly look, and Kane was put in mind of villages where starvation had struck—and of the creatures he had so recently battled.

Worse than the beasts' appearance, however, was their carriage. They moved slowly, haltingly, as if unsure how to manage the trick of simple locomotion. And although their eyes were not human, their stares seemed distant and unfocused. Not unlike the stare of a man who has had too much wine. None of the beasts seemed to mark Kane's passage. They seemed focused on something in the middle distance.

A voice reached his ears as he drew near the cemetery. It was a man's—nasal and reedy, and not at all what one thought of when one imagined a good, Puritan preacher's voice, but it carried well and clear as it recited verses from the book of Matthew:

"'*Blessed are they that mourn: for they shall be comforted. Blessed are the meek: for they shall inherit the earth. Blessed are they which hunger and thirst for righteousness: for they shall be filled. Blessed are the merciful: for they shall obtain mercy. Blessed are the pure in heart: for they shall see God. Blessed are the peacemakers:*

for they shall be called the children of God. Blessed are they which suffer persecution for righteousness' sake: for theirs is the kingdom of Heaven. Blessed shall ye be when men revile you, and persecute you, and say all manner of evil against you for my sake, falsely. Rejoice and be glad, for great is your reward in Heaven: for so persecuted they the prophets which were before you.'"

Kane followed the sound of the voice until at last he emerged between two buildings and into view of the cemetery, a patch of flat land bounded by a low stone wall and an iron gate. It appeared that the entire village had gathered within—a mass of pale figures in black and white, their heads bowed toward the open grave as they listened to the preacher.

Among them, Kane spotted Catherine, Enoch, and the Archer children, including the young boy, Isaac. Catherine's eyes remained upon the ground and she dabbed at her cheeks with a handkerchief. Her free hand she left on the boy's shoulder. The lad wore the expression of someone who does not quite understand what is happening, or why it is so important, but does understand that it *is* important, and that he ought to pay attention and look serious.

At the front of the crowd, nearest the hole in the earth, stood Roger Kidby. Roger held his hat in both hands. He did not weep, but stared at the open grave with the same blank intensity Kane had seen upon the faces of the village beasts. Kane had not met the innkeeper's wife and Roger's mother, but Kane assumed that if the woman *were* present, she would be clinging to Roger's side and weeping. She must have been too sick to attend in person.

Kane stopped outside the iron gate, close enough to hear the sermon, but far enough away that (he hoped) he would not be disturbing the mourners.

"I knew George Kidby well," the preacher said. "He was a friend, and a good man—as good as any sinner can be, in this fallen world."

The preacher, who stood at the head of the grave, was a tall man with slouched posture and a graying beard. He did not cut a conventional figure, and his voice was not immediately pleasant to the ear. But despite all of this, he spoke eloquently, and well, as he sketched in a list of George Kidby's virtues: the dead man had been friendly, welcoming, and kind. He had been a good neighbor and a good friend to those who knew him, a good husband to his ailing wife, and a good father to his son, Roger.

The reverend reminded the assembly that salvation was a gift from God, and only God knew who would be saved. It was not given to any man to decide or deduce the fate of another's soul, but only to pray on their behalf. The reverend then led the assembly in prayer, and pled with the Lord for George Kidby's soul, and for the futures of Roger and Esther Kidby, who would need His guidance and love in this trying time.

After the prayer, the crowd dispersed, but paused near the gate when they saw Kane. Kane did not understand their fearful faces until he looked down at himself. He was filthy, covered in his own blood and that of his recent opponents. He looked a fright. He stepped some distance away, to show the mourners he meant no harm, and only approached again when the preacher exited the cemetery.

"It was a good sermon," Kane said.

The man seemed less frightened of Kane's appearance than his neighbors, and approached to shake Kane's hand, introducing himself as Reverend Pelham.

"It is kind of you to say, Master Kane," he said. "I only hope it helped."

"I am sure it did," Kane said. He meant to elaborate on this compliment, but his attention was drawn by the sound of hushed, angry voices. He glanced past Pelham and back into the cemetery. Most of the crowd had gone, but three figures remained by the open grave: Roger Kidby, staring into the earth, and, a little further away, Catherine and Enoch Archer. Their children were gone—perhaps ushered home by the older girls—leaving the parents to lean toward one another in postures of heated argument.

Enoch, who stood several inches taller than his wife, leaned down in her face and shook a finger at her. His face was flushed red. Catherine's mouth was drawn into a thin line, and she kept her hands together before her, as was meet for a woman, but her fingers worried at one another. They moved like the hands of a woman shredding lettuce. Her fingers were red from pinching themselves.

Pelham saw that he had lost Kane's attention, and turned to look at the Archers. When he turned back to Kane, he wore a sad expression.

"These are dark days, Master Kane," Pelham said. "We have struggled, here in Windsend. The Lord has seen fit to test us, and we have done our best to meet His challenges. But the trials of these last few weeks have been nothing short of extraordinary. I feel our beliefs—our sense of civilization—is slipping. Men no longer speak to their fellows with respect. They argue with their wives in public. Sybil Eastey has driven us mad with fear."

"You believe her guilty, then," Kane said.

Pelham considered. "I know some of the men in town are disgruntled by your arrival. They would prefer that we go ahead with her execution, and stave off further hardship. But I am glad you are here. I hear you interviewed Mistress Eastey this morning. Have you a verdict?"

Before Kane could answer, Enoch Archer stormed past, out the iron gate, his face redder than before, hat pressed low on his head, a scowl embedded on his face. His shoulders were hunched, and his boots squelched through the wet earth with purpose.

Catherine remained behind, close to the grave. She approached Roger and put a hand upon his shoulder, murmuring words Kane could not hear.

Kane refocused on Pelham. "Is there a council of leadership in this village?" he asked. "I would speak with them and discuss my findings."

Pelham nodded. "I sit on that council. I can have us gathered in a quarter-hour."

"I am hungry, and a bit weary," Kane said. "I would prefer to break my fast and gather my thoughts. Can we meet in two hours?"

Pelham said this could be done, and directed Kane to the village meeting house at five o'clock. Kane thanked the man, shook his hand, then moved to join Catherine at the graveside. His progress was arrested, however, by Pelham's hand on his shoulder.

"I know you and Goodwife Archer are friends," Pelham said. "But I would urge you to exercise caution in how you spend your time here. Her relationship with her husband is already… strained. And it does not look good, to be seen in the company of another man's wife, and not the man himself. People talk, and if the talk turns against you, it could hurt your credibility, and your ability to help us solve our problem."

"I thank you for your counsel, Reverend Pelham," Kane said, and then he approached Catherine anyway, nodding a greeting to the two young men who stood nearby, shovels in hand. They were ready to begin filling the grave but waited respectfully for Catherine and Roger to finish their goodbyes.

Catherine continued to look into the grave as Kane approached, and did not look up as he stopped beside her.

"Are you well?" he asked.

"No," she said. "I am not."

Kane waited with her, and Roger. He leaned on his staff, his knee throbbing. How he longed to sit! But he refused to betray his discomfort. He would stand here with Catherine for as long as she needed.

"Your father was a good man," Catherine said to Roger. "Pious, but more than that. He wanted the best for everyone. I never heard him say an unkind word. He did not deserve this."

Roger nodded, but did not speak. Catherine squeezed his shoulder and walked away. Kane followed her, but waited until they had exited the cemetery to speak.

"And the other men who died?" Kane asked. "Did they deserve to die?"

Catherine glanced at Kane. "Of course not, but they were more like… well, like men. Good. Pious. But hard, and not necessarily kind. George Kidby was made of softer stuff, and so the tragedy seems greater for it."

Kane said nothing to this, although he was not sure he agreed. In this world, so full of evil and mischance, a man had no business being soft. Softness got one killed. If George Kidby had not been felled by this current evil, he would surely have fallen some other way.

"You are weary," Catherine said. "And in pain. I see it in your face."

Kane's surprise must have showed, because Catherine laughed. "Do not worry, Solomon. I do not think anyone else can tell. But I know your face of old. You cannot fool me. Will you walk me home? You can sit with me, and I will feed you."

Pelham's warning sounded in Kane's memory. It might not look proper, if he accompanied Catherine home now. And yet, she was right. He *was* tired, *and* starving. His only other option was to return to the inn, but Roger Kidby remained at his father's grave. There would be no food for Kane there.

"That would be nice, thank you," Kane said.

9

Fencing Lessons

Kane escorted Catherine home, where they found Mercy at work on a pottage. While Catherine helped Mercy finish cooking, Kane sat on the back porch. He leaned his staff against the wall beside him, and sat, gratefully, in a wooden chair.

He rubbed at his knee, trying to massage out some of the discomfort. However, each touch only seemed to summon fresh sparks of pain, rather than relief. Was this permanent, he wondered? Would his knee always hurt now? He hoped not, but the Voice of Reason spoke up once more in his mind:

Your adventuring days are at an end, old man.

He leaned back and let his hands fall into his lap. He closed his eyes. The world seemed to recede. The sounds and smells of the day lost their sharpness, and a great softness spread from the middle of his mind, tendrils seeping down through his neck and shoulders. The softness seemed to offer relief from all that ailed him, if he would but give in.

"Where is your sword?"

Kane's eyes snapped open as his head jerked toward the voice on his left.

Isaac Archer, Catherine's youngest, stood at Kane's elbow, staring up at him with grave seriousness.

Although different in features, the boy's face reminded Kane of Roger Kidby. They shared an openness, as though they expected the world to be a kind, loving, and interesting place. Kane thought the look more forgivable in a child. After all, Isaac was yet a boy, close to his mother's loving gaze. Roger was a man now, and responsible for an ailing mother. The innkeeper's son ought to know better than to expect anything but trials, difficulties, and pain.

"Hello," Kane said.

"Your sword," the boy said, pointing to Kane's waist. "The one you had this morning. Where is it?"

Kane was not used to the company of children, and was somewhat taken aback by the lad's directness.

"I lost it," he said.

"Do you lose many swords?" Isaac said. "Is that a common peril for adventurers like you?"

"There are no adventurers like me," Kane said.

The boy nodded gravely. "The loss must be terribly embarrassing for you, then."

Kane's face contorted into a rare smile. The muscles used to form the expression felt creaky, rusted from disuse.

"You are right, Master Isaac," he said. "I am deeply ashamed." He said it lightly, with mock seriousness, but felt a pang as the words exited his lips and he realized they were true.

"Fear not, Master Kane," Isaac said. "I shall not tell another soul."

"You would keep my shame a secret for me?" Kane asked.

The boy considered his answer, and as he did so, he looked an exact duplicate of Catherine, whose vivid expressions of thoughtfulness had endeared her to him.

"It is not that I would hide a secret for you," Isaac said at last. "It is that I would not needlessly spread the tale of your misfortune for the sake of gossip."

"You are well spoken, for such a young man," Kane said. "And you have a noble heart."

"I mean to be an adventurer like you," Isaac said. "When I am old enough. Tell me—how did you come by your staff?"

Kane eyed the staff, leaning up against the house. "It was given to me," he said. "By a friend. N'Longa, my blood brother. He is a priest in Africa."

For the first time, Kane noticed that the boy held something in his right hand: a wooden sword, about half the length of his body. He held it to one side so that the tip neither brushed Kane nor touched the ground.

Isaac followed Kane's gaze, and offered him the sword. Kane took it, and made a show of inspecting it. The "blade" was smooth, finely sanded wood, which had been painted gray. The handle was wrapped with leather strips, and the guard had been painted black.

"It is not a real sword," Isaac said. "Only a toy."

Kane stood up, suppressing a grimace as his knee protested. He walked down off the porch and into the yard, to hold the sword up in the weak afternoon sun, and give it a few swings through the air. It had the shape of a longsword, but was light enough to handle as a rapier. It had a nice heft, and was surprisingly well-balanced. It might be a toy, but it was a toy whose making had clearly been undertaken with thought and care.

"Who gave you this?" Kane asked.

"My father," the boy said. "I told him I wanted a sword, and asked him to make me one, since he is a blacksmith. Instead, he had Master Lockwood, the carpenter, make me this. I have two, actually. So I can practice with friends, until I am ready for a real blade."

"Do you practice with friends often?" Kane asked.

The boy's expression drooped. "No, sir. I do not have many friends."

"Am I not a friend?" Kane asked.

Isaac's expression lit up. He ran back into the house, and returned a moment later with a second wooden sword, identical to the first, which he brought out onto the grass. Out of the shade of the porch, the boy's usually pale face was flushed red. Kane thought of Enoch, who had looked so angry at George Kidby's funeral. The boy was not angry, however, but excited. He raised his sword and brandished it at Kane.

"Have at thee, brigand!" the boy shouted.

"Stop," Kane said, with such gravity and command that Isaac immediately lowered the blade and looked at Kane wonderingly.

"You have had no training with this sword?" Kane said.

The boy's face fell. "They are only toys, sir," he said, voice barely above a whisper. "And none here know the art of swordplay."

This made sense. What need had farmers and carpenters for fencing? Kane's own training, with his father back in Devon, had been an unusual occurrence in their village—a rarity for which Kane had been thankful most of his life. Years of discipline and training during his boyhood had saved his own life on many occasions.

"You bring up a good point, Master Archer," Kane said. "But while I am here, and you duel with me, you will observe the proper forms. Would you learn?"

The boy nodded and Kane approached. He put one hand on the boy's back, and another on his chest.

"First, we must correct your posture," Kane said. "You cannot slouch, or you will end up dead."

The boy allowed Kane to stand him more erect. When Kane was satisfied with this, he began to work on the boy's stance.

"Put your right foot forward," he said. "Toward an imaginary adversary. And your left foot goes a shoulder's width behind you, toes perpendicular to your right. Bend your knees—not that much, only slightly. And stand up straight, lad."

The boy's brow furrowed as he worked to obey. "It feels unnatural, sir," he said.

"Practice it often enough and it will feel as natural as breathing," Kane promised. "Now, hold your left hand slightly before your chest. Edge toward the adversary. It is important to keep the hand close to your body, to protect from attacks or injury."

Next, he showed Isaac how to hold the sword, with thumb and forefinger over and around the guard, other fingers around the hilt. The boy's grip was awkward and unsure, and Kane wondered if his own had ever looked so clumsy. Had his own father bitten back criticism during those early lessons, knowing that mastery would come in time?

Once the boy's stance was more or less correct (or as correct as Kane could reasonably expect, for a first lesson), they moved into wards. They started with the broad ward, the sword held to the right of the body and parallel to the ground at shoulder height.

"The sword is heavy," Isaac said. "I cannot hold it this way for long."

"Aye," Kane said. "You will have to practice this ward every day, and build your muscles." Were he teaching an older boy, Kane would have insisted that Isaac practice this form until his arm shook with fatigue. It was the way of good teachers, to push a pupil past their perceived limits, past exhaustion, and to heights they could never have expected of themselves.

But this boy was small, and sickly too. So they moved on to the inside ward, where the swordsman held the blade at an angle, pointed toward the opponent's shoulder.

"This is much easier," Isaac said. "I think I will use this ward whenever I battle an enemy."

"You must learn them all, and know when to use them," Kane said. "Relying too heavily on any one trick or technique will give your opponents an advantage. They will see that you cannot change your strategy, and they will change their own to exploit your weaknesses."

The boy blinked, shocked, as if this thought had never occurred to him before.

"Now we practice moving with the sword," Kane said.

He showed Isaac the basics. The proper form of advance and retreat, as well as the cross-over. These the boy grasped quickly. He was eager to learn.

Kane stepped from his place behind Isaac, walked a couple of paces away, and lifted his own wooden sword toward Isaac.

"Are we going to duel now?" Isaac asked.

"You are going to practice defense," Kane said. "Show me your stance."

Isaac stood with his feet more or less as Kane had shown him, and lifted his sword parallel to the ground, at shoulder height, pointed toward Kane.

He is trying to impress me, Kane realized.

"Good," he said. "Now: advance."

The boy came at him, eyes bright, swinging the sword. Kane easily countered and deflected his attacks, but did his best not to make it look *too* easy as he stepped past a thrust and lightly touched the tip of his sword against the boy's chest.

"You are dead, young master," Kane said.

The boy looked down at the blade, pressed into the fabric of his shirt, then back at Kane, startled. He said nothing, but Kane read the truth: this was not how any of Isaac's imaginary duels had gone in the past. Those bouts of play were likely long, drawn-out affairs, full of fancy sword work and heroics. Only now did the boy begin to understand just how quickly an experienced fighter could take his life. That bravery and valor only carried one so far, in the face of technique. Here were Isaac's first taste of the realities of violence. Death came fast, without mercy.

To his credit, Isaac did not complain, or argue, or make up imaginary reasons why he could not be dead. Instead, he backed into the starting position, carefully resuming his stance, and raising his sword in the broad ward once more.

They went through this several times: the boy advancing, Kane parrying and dodging, then launching attacks of his own. He forced himself to slowness, exaggerating his movements so that each was clearly communicated ahead of time. So that Isaac had time to make decisions on how to counter.

At first the boy seemed not to notice at all. But after his third defeat, he also slowed down. His brow furrowed with concentration. He stopped doing what felt heroic, and began to strategize. His attacks remained clumsy and easy to avoid, but nonetheless grew more effective.

Kane was impressed. The boy showed potential. Kane was enjoying himself so thoroughly that he almost forgot to worry about his knee. Each step hurt a bit, but it mattered less now.

As they dueled, Isaac's fatigue grew apparent. His mind might be sharp and quick, but his body was not cooperative. His face flushed, and his breathing grew labored. He began to breathe through his mouth, and Kane detected a slight rattle in the breath. Isaac did not complain, but Kane knew a coughing fit could not be far off now.

Kane knew what it was like, to have a superior mind trapped in a failing vessel. It was one of the sorest trials the Lord could visit upon a soul.

He was debating whether or not to cry off the duel himself, citing his own very real exhaustion, when he and Isaac were interrupted by a shout from the back porch.

"And what is this?"

Kane and Isaac stopped to look at Catherine, who stood on the porch with a tray in her hands. It was laden with food and plates.

"Dueling practice," Kane said. "Isaac is keeping me sharp."

"And do you mean to steal my sweet son into a life of adventure, then?" Catherine asked. "Will you have him traveling the world and battling monsters? Leaving his poor mother alone at home?"

"Yes!" Isaac shouted, full of glee, but no sooner had the word passed his lips than he began to cough. The fit was deep and powerful, each cough wracking his small body. He dropped his sword and put both hands to his mouth. He bent forward, struggling to keep his balance.

Catherine set her tray on a table by the back door and hurried into the yard. She put one hand on Isaac's back and the other on his shoulder.

"Easy," she murmured. "Easy now, sweet boy. You grew too excited, that is all."

Kane stood to the side, helpless to do anything but watch until the fit had passed, and Isaac's breathing returned to normal.

"That is enough adventure for now," Catherine said. "Come and eat."

"Yes, Mother," Isaac said.

Kane bent to pick up the dropped sword, unable to suppress a quiet grunt as he did so. He stood and followed Catherine and Isaac back to the porch. They arranged the chairs around a small table, and sat.

"Are the girls not joining us?" he asked.

"They ate inside," Catherine said, "and are off to a friend's house for the afternoon."

She served Kane a hot bowl of cabbage stew, a portion of bread, and a cup of ale. Kane tried not to make a pig of himself as he dug in. Despite his efforts at restraint, he finished eating before either of his companions. The food was not fancy, or particularly flavorful, but it was filling, and settled the animal urge in Kane's stomach.

When his bowl and plate were clean, he said, "Too often must I eat what I can find in the wild. It is a rare treat to enjoy English home cooking."

"You are too kind," Catherine said.

"Nay," Kane said. "Only honest."

Isaac took over the conversation then, repeating all he could remember of Kane's lesson. Soon, he claimed, he would be a master swordsman just like Master Kane, and would travel the world, righting wrongs.

"Can I accompany you on your next adventure?" Isaac asked Kane. "You could teach me."

Kane kept his face grave and straight, despite his amusement.

"Adventuring is a lonely life. Would you leave your family so soon? Would you surrender a chance to have a wife and children of your own? Or your chance to learn your father's craft and take over his smithy someday?"

Isaac's brow furrowed. He had not considered these possibilities until now. He looked to Catherine, as if for permission or guidance.

"I know what I would prefer," she said. "But you will have to make your own choices, when the time comes."

Isaac mulled this over for a moment before looking back at Kane. "Can I think about it first?" he asked. As if Kane had already offered to take him on as an apprentice adventurer.

"Of course," Kane said. "It is nothing to undertake lightly."

After Catherine and Isaac finished eating, Isaac asked Kane for another lesson, but Kane refused.

"I have important matters to discuss with your mother," he said. "But go practice, if you like. I will watch your form."

The boy picked up his sword and ran into the yard. He stared down at his feet as he put them into position, then raised the blade parallel to the ground in a basic ward. He looked back at Kane, to make sure Kane was watching. Kane waved to show that he saw, and the boy returned to his practice.

"He has a noble spirit," Kane said.

"He reminds me of you," Catherine said. "Injustice sends him into a rage. He has your restlessness as well. So eager to leave this village and see the world."

Kane looked away from Isaac and over at his old friend. Her own gaze remained upon her son, squaring up against invisible opponents. At first his movements mimicked what Kane had taught him, but soon his excitement got the better of him, and he was swinging and spinning and shouting at invisible villains. This went on for a moment, the lad's face growing more and more flush, until he stopped, breathing hard, and bent over to cough. He brought a hand to his mouth as the coughing fit racked his little body.

Catherine stood as if to go to him, but Isaac waved her off. "I am all right!" he called.

Catherine sat, but did not look happy.

"The boy has been sickly all his life," Kane said, remembering what Catherine had told him before.

Catherine nodded. "Many children born here face frequent illness, but Isaac is sicklier than most. His was a difficult pregnancy and birth. Maybe it is my own fault, for having another child so late in life, but the birth nearly killed us both. We would both be dead now, if not for Sybil Eastey."

"Indeed?" Kane said. He kept his voice neutral. He had learned this during his years of travel. It was best to make space for a speaker's story, their point of view. To seem interested and open, so the speaker would tell you more. It felt strange to use this technique on Catherine, but necessary. He was, after all, conducting an investigation. He cared for Catherine, but he had to see her, for the moment, not as a friend, but as a witness, one who might be biased in Sybil Eastey's favor.

"Indeed," Catherine said. "Why would Sybil Eastey have saved me, and my son, if she were capable of the things the townsfolk believe?"

"People are complex," Kane said. "I once caught a killer in France. The man was a beloved husband and doting father. Well liked in his community. And yet he was luring young girls into the darkness, despoiling them, and then strangling them. A person can be good in many ways, and abhorrent in others."

"How awful," Catherine said.

"Indeed."

"How goes your investigation?"

"It proceeds apace," Kane said. "But I am more interested in what you think. Why do you think life in Windsend is so difficult, if it is not witchcraft?"

"If I knew the answer to that, perhaps I would not need your help," Catherine said. "But it is the test the Lord has set for us, and it is up to us to meet it the best we can, yes?"

"Do you ever wish that you had stayed in our village?" Kane asked. "Where we came of age?" He was surprised at himself. This question was not pertinent to his investigation.

"Do you?" she said, looking away from Isaac to meet Kane's gaze. Her blue eyes were electric, and for a moment, Kane found himself struck dumb, unable to reply.

Finally, he nodded. "I believe I followed the path that God laid out for me. I believe it was Providence that set me upon it, and that Providence brings me wherever I may roam. But yes. I sometimes wish it had been different. That this restlessness in my soul were absent, and I could be content with a simple domestic life of faith and love and hard work."

"Do you think Sybil is guilty?" Catherine asked. "You avoided my question before."

Kane considered his response for a moment, watching Isaac play in the afternoon gloom.

"I do not have all the facts," Kane said. "So I hesitate to speak too freely. But my instincts tell me she is not behind the recent deaths. As far as the larger issue of innocence or guilt? That is a far trickier question."

"Why is that?" Catherine said.

"She has commerce with dark forces. Forces with which no good Christian ought to interact."

"Indeed?" Catherine said. "And do you believe she is using these forces to hurt this village, or its people?"

"I have found no evidence of such," Kane said.

"So what does it matter, then, what she believes, and to whom she gives her spiritual allegiance?" Catherine said. "After all, are we Puritans not persecuted by the monarchy and the church of England?"

"We are," Kane conceded.

"And who have we hurt, by our beliefs? No one. Do we deserve mistreatment simply for believing something other than the majority?"

"No," Kane conceded again.

"So there you have it," she said. "I have known Sybil Eastey for years. She is a good person. She helps her neighbors and tries to earn a decent living doing so. Does she not deserve the chance to live her life in the way that makes sense to her, the same as you and I?"

"But the forces with which she is in touch," Kane protested.

"What does it matter, if she harms no one?" Catherine asked.

Kane sighed, but did not argue further.

"Help my friend, Solomon," she said. "If you can."

10

Elders

Kane lingered too long at the Archer house, and it was already a quarter hour after five, the sun setting, when he mounted the steps of the village meeting house, a plain and undecorated building with a steep pitched roof and several square windows.

The inside of the building was dark, lit only by a few lanterns and candles. Kane walked through a small lobby and into the building's main chamber. A group of men sat in chairs before a pulpit at the front of the room. At first, Kane could not make out faces, only silhouettes, and he had the eerie sensation of being on trial himself, before a panel of judges. But then he came closer, and the faces of those gathered became clear in the candlelight.

The men here were past the prime years of labor, toil, and battle. Their faces were lined, their beards gray. Kane recognized none of them, aside from Reverend Pelham.

Soon, this will be you, said the voice in Kane's mind. *A senseless, gray-haired prattler with nothing to offer this world but your mouth.*

Kane pushed the thought aside with effort and removed his hat to face the assembly.

"Good evening, masters," he said.

"You are late, Master Kane," said one of the men.

Kane ducked his head in deference. "I was reminiscing with an old friend. Catherine Archer. I lost track of the time, and I beg your pardon, sirs." He noticed now that the men had not set out a chair for him, but he refused to ask for one. Instead, he stood, stoic, and waited.

"It is not meet to be seen alone in the company of another man's wife," said a second man.

"Goodwife Archer is distressed at the situation with Sybil Eastey," Kane said. "I sought to comfort her."

"Comfort falls to her husband," the man snapped back. "Not a stranger."

"I am no stranger to Goodwife Archer," Kane said.

"But you are a stranger to us," the man said. "And ought to remember it when you act and speak."

A hot reply came to Kane's lips, but before he could unleash it, Pelham spoke:

"We are not here to pass judgement on Solomon Kane's conduct." He said it lightly, his tone friendly, and warm, but also full of authority. "We have welcomed him here as an expert on the supernatural, and gathered in this meeting house so that he can tell us about his investigation."

The tension bled out of the air. Kane's interlocuter—a bearded man with a face like a gnarled oak tree—continued to scowl, but ducked his own head, in deference to the preacher.

"Thank you, Reverend Pelham," said another of the men, who sat at the center of the gathering. He turned to Kane. "My name is Jeremiah Bartlett, and I am serving as interim mayor of Windsend until we can hold a proper election. I sit in temporary charge of the council of elders." These he introduced to Kane in turn—John Hurlbirt, Isiah Legge, Samuel Munt (the cranky man who had interrogated Kane upon his entrance), and Reverend Gideon Pelham.

Once formalities were complete, Kane related his investigation so far. He told of his interview with Sybil Eastey, and her protestations of innocence (although he left out the discovery that Sybil was, in fact, a witch). He related Sybil's suggestion that he investigate the cave in the forest. He told of his journey into the woods; his discovery of the cave; the creatures he found there—their wiry bodies; their ability to conceal themselves in most lights; and his battle with them.

"I scarcely escaped with my own life," Kane admitted. "But I believe these creatures are the culprits behind the recent deaths, and that Sybil Eastey is innocent."

The elders sat in quiet contemplation of his words for what felt like an eternity—certainly long enough for Kane to wish, once more, for a seat, and a chance to rest his knee, which was softly throbbing now. Still he refused to make the request. He would not show weakness before anyone.

Finally, Samuel Munt (the cranky fellow) spoke up. "You expect us to believe that there is a cave outside of this village, full of invisible monsters that only you can see?"

"I did not say they were visible only to me," Kane said. "I said that the illumination in the tunnel disrupted their camouflage."

"You will forgive us," Mayor Bartlett said, "if we are skeptical, Master Kane. The story you tell sounds more like a fairy tale for children than something that might happen to a man in the real world."

Kane sighed. Lord save him from the provincial mind.

"You brought me here for my expertise," he said, "which I am providing. Do you not trust me?"

"It is hard," Munt said, "to trust a stranger who comes to our home, makes wild claims, and tries to exonerate a witch."

"You believe in witchcraft," Kane said. "Why is belief in the creatures I describe such a stretch?"

"Witchcraft has been documented, Master Kane," Pelham said, in his patient manner. "It is in the scriptures. There are recorded trials throughout Europe. Men and women have been convicted by courts of law. There is no record of these creatures, at least none I know of. You ask us to take an additional leap of faith here."

Bartlett made a *there you have it* gesture with both hands and raised eyebrows.

"If you be Doubting Thomases," Kane said, "simply come to the woods with me now. I shall allay your doubts myself."

"It is late now," Bartlett said, "but early tomorrow we will send a party of men out to the woods to find this place and investigate."

"Good," Kane said. "Make sure the men are well-armed. These creatures have killed several of your neighbors already. You must be prepared to descend into that darkness without the benefit of light, and to fight."

"It is strange to me," Munt said, "that you insist upon Sybil Eastey's innocence."

"Is it?" Kane said, voice cold. "I insist because I believe it is the truth. I have seen the actual killers myself."

"Say, for a moment," Bartlett said, "that you are telling us the unvarnished truth. That you interviewed Sybil Eastey, and could find no evidence that she is a witch. That you then followed her advice and went into the woods, where you met monsters never before recorded in human history. Does it not worry you? How Eastey knew to send you there? How could she know?"

Kane paused there. How *had* Sybil known? Had she gone out there herself, and somehow escaped unscathed? Or was it related to her supernatural gifts? Either answer raised more questions than it answered, and if he admitted this to the council of elders, that would not help her case.

"She is a midwife, is she not?" Kane said. "It is part of her job to traverse the woods, hunting the plants and herbs needed for her remedies and potions. She could easily have stumbled upon the cave in the course of her daily labors."

There was a grudging murmur of agreement as the council considered what Kane had said, and found wisdom in it.

"And what of my wounds?" Kane said. He stepped forward, pointing to scratches on his face and rolling his shredded sleeves to show similar wounds upon his arms. "Did I inflict these upon myself?"

"This is dangerous country, Master Kane," Reverend Pelham said, not unsympathetically. "You could have acquired those wounds from any forest beast."

"Unfortunately, you have not given us enough evidence to acquit Sybil Eastey," Bartlett said. "But we thank you for the investigation, and as a token of our respect, we have taken up a collection for payment." He reached into his lap and lifted a bag Kane had not noticed before. It jangled with coin. "You may take it and be on your way."

Kane glared at the coin purse. "Keep your money, good masters. I came at the request of a friend, to see that justice prevails."

Bartlett kept the bag extended another moment before he shrugged and placed it in his lap once more. "Be that as it may," he said. "You are dismissed. Your services are no longer required here."

Kane heard the dismissal, but remained in place. This felt wrong.

"Tell me, Mayor Bartlett," he said. "If I had come in here and pronounced Sybil Eastey guilty, would I have been interrogated and disbelieved so soundly? Or are you trying to rid yourself of me because I tell you things you do not want to hear?"

Munt gave Kane a small, surly smile, but Bartlett answered first.

“I see no point in arguing hypotheticals, Master Kane. Please leave us to our own counsel.”

“When does Miss Eastey’s trial begin?” Kane asked.

“Tomorrow morning,” Bartlett said.

“Before or after you have confirmed my story?” Kane said.

“After, of course,” Bartlett said.

“Then I shall see you all on the morrow,” Kane said. “At the trial. I intend to speak on Sybil Eastey’s behalf.”

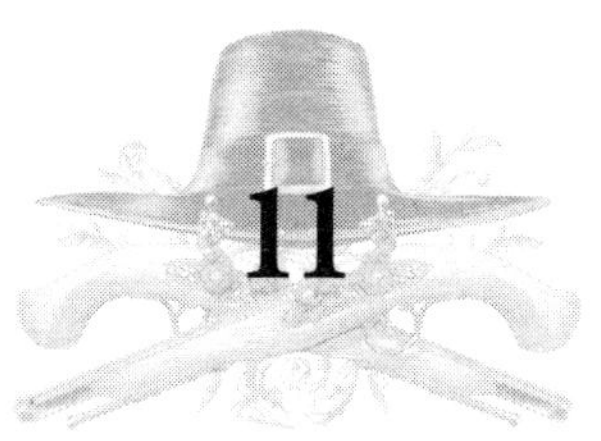

Esther Kidby

Kane left the meeting hall and made his way back to the Falling Star Inn. The common room was abuzz with customers, and Roger Kidby was working hard to keep everyone's tankards and plates full. His brow remained furrowed, his face flushed with effort. He looked a bit like Isaac Archer, right before a coughing fit.

The gathered villagers looked up when Kane entered, and the lively conversation died down. Kane nodded to his fellow customers, and made his way to the bar to sit down. He sighed as the pressure came off his knee, and he leaned forward, arms crossed on the bar. He waited to be approached by a curious or talkative villager, as he had been this morning, but gratefully, they left him alone tonight. He was allowed to bow his head over his arms, and, for a moment, free himself from the need to plan the next move, or the next conversation. He was allowed to just be, and let some of the tension out of his body. He hadn't realized how much he was carrying until this moment.

Did I always carry it thus? he wondered. *Is this situation so much more stressful than any I have encountered before? Or is the voice right? Am I just growing old?*

He was almost startled when Roger Kidby appeared behind the bar, looking harried.

"Can I bring you supper, Master Kane?"

"Please," Kane said.

Roger disappeared into the kitchen and returned a moment later with a bowl of stew, a hunk of bread, and a mug of beer. Kane was not especially hungry after his conversation with the council of elders, but he made himself eat and drink anyway, cleaning the bowl of its contents and wiping away the remains with the bread. In the adventuring life, one ate when one had the chance, for there were no guarantees about the timing of one's next meal.

When Kane had finished, he left some coin on the bar and stood, using his staff to pull himself to his feet. He turned to walk toward the stairs, meaning to go up to his room and retire for the evening, but stopped when he heard a long, low moan.

The sound was quiet—so quiet that Kane wondered how it had reached him, amid the din of the common room. He stood still, and waited for the sound to repeat. When it did, he followed it to a small hallway at the far side of the room. There were two doors here, one in each direction. One was slightly ajar, and the moan came through it. It sounded like a woman in pain.

Kane pushed the door open, and looked in on a small, modestly furnished bedroom, lit by a few candles. There was a familiar stink in here. Kane took a moment to identify it: stale beer. It smelled like old beer in here.

An old woman lay on the bed, propped up on thin pillows, her silver hair tied into a bun over her head. Her body, tucked under a blanket, was entirely too thin. Kane thought of the creatures he had encountered earlier today. Their limbs had looked similarly wasted.

This must be Roger's mother. George's widow. Esther Kidby.

"Is that you, Roger?" the woman said. Her eyes fluttered open and she frowned at Kane, confused.

"Roger is… busy, Goodwife Kidby," Kane said. "I am a friend. Solomon Kane."

"Oh yes," Esther said. "I heard about you."

"I overheard your cries," Kane said. "I came to see if I could help."

"I do not know what you could do for me, Master Kane," she said. "Unless you mean to prove Sybil Eastey innocent?"

Kane frowned at the woman. "And how would that help you?"

Esther picked up an empty bottle from the bedside table. "She …" and here her speech stopped, because she was racked with a coughing fit. The bottle slipped from her fingers and Kane dashed forward to snatch it from the air. He examined it in the dim candlelight. It was a simple earthenware vessel, with a curious mark upon it. Kane had seen the same mark upon several other bottles in Sybil's house.

"Mistress Eastey made you medicines," Kane said.

Esther nodded between coughs, her hands pressed to her mouth. Kane sniffed at the bottle, and caught a faint potpourri of herbs. As he had noticed at Sybil's house, he could not detect the smell of anything unnatural, any substance which did not grow in the earth. He set the bottle back on the table beside the bed.

When Esther's coughing fit subsided, she lay back against the bed. "I have had consumption for so long. Mistress Eastey's medicines were the only ones that helped."

"How many years have you ailed?" Kane asked.

"Oh…" She closed her eyes as she considered. "How long have we been in Windsend? Five years? It seemed to grow unbearable and constant not long after we opened the inn."

"Is that right?" Kane said.

Esther gave Kane a feeble smile. "I know what you are thinking, Master Kane."

"Do you?"

"You think to yourself, 'Is it not convenient that your illness began as soon as Sybil Eastey became your neighbor?'"

"Is it not?" Kane said.

"And you also ask yourself, 'Would it not behoove a witch to pose as a midwife, and keep her patients sick, so that they would need her care forever?'"

"Would it not?" Kane said.

"I tell you," Esther said. "I was already sickly. And I knew other midwives. I bought their services, drank their medicines. My husband George..." and here she paused, and grimaced, as the memory of his death seemed to strike her anew. "George also bought medicines from a traveling physician—Cheesebrough, by name. None of the other medicines worked the way Sybil's did. I do not think it is Sybil Eastey who keeps me sick. I think it is..." She gestured with one arm, indicating the room about them, "... this place. Windsend itself is sick. If we had any sense, we would have left years ago. All of us. Every man, woman, and child. But it is so hard to admit we have made a mistake, when it is of this magnitude. And there is no easy cause to point to. How do you say to your neighbors, 'We have come to a bad place'?"

"And you do not believe Sybil Eastey is in league with whatever makes Windsend so sick?" Kane asked.

"As far as I can tell," Esther said, "she was the only one here who seemed to be doing anything about the sickness. The men—the ones who run this village—seem intent on ignoring it. To talk about the Lord testing us."

"Do you not believe in Providence, Goodwife Eastey?" Kane asked. "The Lord's plan for us all?"

"I possess no great learning," Esther said. "But I see that

Sybil Eastey sees no point in needless suffering. She refuses to sit by and do nothing when she can help."

The last words came out of Esther on a strange up note, and gave way to another round of coughs. Esther leaned forward, a handkerchief pressed to her mouth to muffle the sound, her narrow shoulders hunched. At last, she leaned back against the headboard of her bed. She looked exhausted, as if the speaking and coughing had tired her out.

"I am sorry to have disturbed you," Kane said. "I meant only to ask if you needed my help, and to give my condolences about your husband."

"Thank you," she said. Tears ran down her cheeks, and she wiped at them with the back of one hand. "It was… hard, to miss his funeral today. I would have liked to say goodbye. Instead, I was trapped in this bed while my husband—as kind and dear a man as ever lived—was laid in the earth. And my poor Roger." She opened her eyes and looked to Kane. "He is not ready to be without his father. To have to look after his sick mother alone."

"Then you must get well soon," Kane said. "So you may look after him instead."

Her smile returned. "I do not think I will get well. If Sybil Eastey cannot cure me—if the best she can do is make me comfortable—I do not think there is more that can be done. I shall be with my husband soon enough. I only hope Roger is ready."

Kane knew the appropriate things to say now. How she must not speak so. How Roger would need her. But he saw how ill she was. He knew death would be a mercy. And that the Lord would decide her fate, one way or the other, regardless of his thoughts or prayers.

So instead of saying useless things, he set his staff against the wall and sat down on a chair next to the bed. There was a Bible on the nightstand, and he picked this up now.

He opened the book to the gospel of Matthew, chapter 18, and ran his calloused, dirt-caked finger down the pages until he found the verse he was looking for:

"*Come unto me, all ye that are weary and laden, and I will ease you. Take my yoke on you, and learn of me that I am meek and lowly in heart: and ye shall find rest unto your souls. For my yoke is easy, and my burden light.*"

He continued on from there, jumping from favorite passage to favorite passage, letting inspiration guide him, and the word of God do the speaking. It might not be as immediately effective as Sybil's medicines, but there was comfort here to be found and given.

Kane read to her until the soft sounds of her snores filled the room. He read for a few minutes after this as well, to make sure she was truly asleep and resting, and because the verses comforted him as well. He had felt shaken today—by Sybil Eastey's accusations, by the women who defended her, and not least by Windsend's council of elders, who had dismissed Kane's counsel out of hand.

By the time he stood and placed the Bible back on the table, he felt a little better. He took up his staff, and quietly let himself out of Esther's room into the little hallway outside the common room. The change in atmosphere was immediate. The stuffy air and stench of stale beer left his nostrils, replaced with the smells of a crackling hearth, and warm food and bread. The din of conversation from the common room was lower now, as time had passed and many had retired for the evening.

Kane found Roger Kidby just outside Esther's room, a dishrag in his hands, an expression of confusion upon his face.

"I was coming to check on Mother," Roger said. "I did not think to find you here."

"You seemed busy, and I took the liberty," Kane said. "I spoke to her, and read scripture. She is resting now."

"Thank you," Roger said, but the words sounded stiff and forced.

"I apologize if I overstepped," Kane said. "I did not mean to intrude on your family's privacy."

Roger nodded slowly, and stepped aside, to let Kane pass.

Kane was in the doorway to the common room when Roger spoke again.

"I never wanted to be an innkeeper," he said.

Kane stopped and turned back to the young man. Roger leaned against the wall, shoulders slumped, head hung. He looked exhausted. His long fingers worried at the rag in his hands.

"I wanted to be like you," he said. "I thought I would come of age and set off on a great voyage on some ship to a distant land. I thought I would see the world. Learn swordplay. But Mother has ailed, and my life has never been my own."

Kane bowed his own head. "None of our lives are our own, young Roger. The Lord sets a path before us. He decides what happens, and why, and it is not ours to question, but to strive for understanding. And my life is not one I would recommend. It is difficult, and lonely. I travel from one disaster to another. Everywhere I go, I see things like what is happening in this village. But it is my path, just as this inn, this family, this grief, is yours."

Roger nodded, his Adam's apple bobbing as he swallowed. "Of course. You are right."

But he remained slumped against the wall as Kane left.

When Kane was alone in his room with the door shut fast, he leaned back against it, breathing hard. Exhaustion swept over him, and pain as well. His hands shook as he pulled off his hat and unbuckled his weapon belt, hanging both in their appropriate spots.

There was a fresh jug of water near the door. Kane poured some into the basin, and scrubbed himself with a cold cloth. When he was as clean as he could be, he crossed the room and sat down upon his rented bed.

He was so tired. When was the last time he had felt so tired? He could not remember. He let gravity carry his body down toward the mattress, keeping his staff clasped to his chest as he did so. N'Longa. He needed to speak with N'Longa, and seek counsel.

He had no memory of his head touching the pillow. No sensation of soft cloth on his cheek. He was asleep that quickly.

12

Le Loup

Kane fought Le Loup. Their swords flashed and sparks flew as they dueled. Le Loup, the murderer, rapist, and brigand, was fast and flashy. He moved with incredible ferocity and grace. Kane's movements were tighter, more restrained. He wasted no energy on fancy flourishes, things that might impress a casual voyeur. Instead he kept after his opponent, staying wary, protecting himself, looking for any opening, any opportunity to strike and end the duel.

"You are strong, Monsieur Galahad!" Le Loup shouted. "But I shall have you, in the end."

Only… this was wrong.

"I…" Kane's thoughts came slowly, even as his body went through the motions of combat with their usual blunt effectiveness. "You and I have already had this duel. I killed you." His voice sounded odd, and seemed to echo around him.

"Do you say so?" Le Loup asked.

Kane tried to focus. How could Le Loup be here, when he had died upon Kane's sword, deep in the jungles of Africa?

Where were they now? This was not a jungle clearing, but rather a dark corridor of stone. And the light around them… it was not sunlight or starlight, but rather a strange blue glow that seemed to emanate from all around them, at once.

"How are you here?" Kane demanded.

"I cannot say, Monsieur Galahad," Le Loup said, with a sly smile. "But know that I am grateful for a second chance to end your life."

He pressed his attack anew, and Kane let himself be driven back, settling into an automatic defense, counting on his decades of training and combat to guide his body, freeing his mind to observe more fully. Le Loup looked exactly the same as he had on the day he had died. He had not aged a day, despite the many years. Kane checked in with his own body but found he had no such rejuvenation of his own body or spirit. He felt the weight of decades upon his shoulders and back. His body might still operate like a finely tuned machine, but he could feel the extra energy each movement cost him, while Le Loup moved as fast and smooth as ever, gestures as fluid as running water.

"Tell me, sir," Le Loup said. "Does it do your heart good, to tell yourself that you only fight for the cause of justice?"

"I do only fight for justice," Kane growled.

"So you say, both aloud, and to yourself. But have you ever looked closer at the darkness within? Have you ever admitted to yourself the truth we both know: that you *enjoy* hurting others?"

"Lies," Kane said, increasing the force of his own attacks.

Kane widened his frame of observation, so that he now took in not just Le Loup, but the dark corridor in which they fought. It felt achingly familiar, like the face of an old acquaintance, glanced briefly in a crowd. What was this place? What was happening? How had he come here?

His train of thought came to an abrupt halt, and he gasped

before he knew what had happened to him. He focused on Le Loup, a triumphant grin upon the Frenchman's face.

Then Kane looked away from Le Loup's face, and down, and understood. Le Loup's sword had buried itself in Kane's chest—no, not just in his chest. Le Loup had stabbed Kane through the heart. Kane wore black, and it was dark in this corridor, so he could not see the spread of his own blood across the fabric of his tunic, but he certainly felt it.

"Oh," he said.

He had felt hot during the duel. Now, the cold seeped in, as his life blood seeped out.

"Your adventuring days are at an end, Monsieur Galahad," Le Loup said, as he tore his rapier free of Kane's chest in one swift move.

Kane's legs gave out beneath him and he spilled to the floor. His head bounced against the hard stone, but he barely felt it. Everything—the corridor, Le Loup, his own body—seemed very far away. Impossibly distant.

Le Loup began to laugh as the world went dark.

13

Cheesebrough

Kane opened his eyes and his hands flew to his chest, searching for the wound. He pressed both hands over his heart, but found his shirt, and the flesh beneath, intact. His heart pounded beneath, alarmed but unharmed.

A dream. Only a dream.

He looked around. He was lying on a small, hard bed in a small, sparsely furnished room. It came back to him quickly, as it had yesterday: he was staying at the Falling Star Inn, in Windsend. He had come here to help Catherine Archer, and, as of yesterday, to save Sybil Eastey, if he could.

And today was Sybil Eastey's trial.

He glanced at the closed window shutters. Weak daylight seeped in at the edges. It was early yet, but he could hear sounds coming from downstairs. Hushed voices, and a low keening. A man who sounded like he was in pain.

Kane stood up, and as he did so, something fell off his bed and banged against the floor, startling him. It was his staff. Then he remembered another thing: he had meant to contact

N'Longa last night. He had fallen asleep with the staff in his arms, but for the first time ever, N'Longa had not come. Instead, Kane had faced the specter of Le Loup.

That was worrying, but Kane did not have time to think on it. Instead, he dressed as quickly as he could, grabbed his gun belt, and hurried downstairs.

He found a very different scene than the one he had encountered the night before. A crowd had gathered near the back of the common room, near the hallway which led to the Kidbys' bedrooms. There were men and women there, and few glanced back at Kane's entrance. Kane recognized John Howlett, one of the farmers from the night's watch.

"What has happened?" Kane asked. His question was partially drowned out by another wail, coming from somewhere beyond the crowd, in the depths of the inn.

"Esther Kidby has passed," Howlett said. "Roger found her dead this morning."

Alarmed, Kane pushed through the crowd. Most of them, startled by the force of his movement, parted without argument. They barely seemed to notice themselves being moved aside.

Kane came to the door of Esther's bedroom, and the stale beer stink caused his empty stomach to turn. He swallowed the bile in his throat.

Roger Kidby knelt at his mother's bedside, cradling her body in his arms, his face red and streaked with tears. Kane felt embarrassed for Roger, and this unmanly show of emotions. But mixed in that masculine shame, there was pity as well. The lad had lost both parents in the space of as many days.

Another man stood beside the bed, one Kane did not recognize. He was stout, bald, and bespectacled. He wore typical Puritan dress, but there was a stiffness to his carriage and posture unlike that of the farmers and craftsmen in Windsend. Kane could tell at once that this man was of a higher class than the villagers.

Kane entered the room fully, bracing himself against the stench as he approached the bed. He stopped beside Roger, trying to examine the body.

"I see no wounds," he said.

"No," the stranger said. "She does not appear to have died of violence."

Kane frowned at the man. "Who are you?"

The man offered a hand. "Doctor Calvin Cheesebrough."

Kane shook and introduced himself as well. "I have heard of you," he said.

"I travel between several towns and villages, offering my services," Cheesebrough said. "I only arrived this morning, to provide evidence for the trial, and happened to be here for this unhappy event."

"Indeed?" Kane said.

Cheesebrough nodded. "The council of elders requested my presence."

"Are you an expert on witchcraft, in addition to your work as a physician?" Kane said.

Cheesebrough gave Kane a withering smile. "I have taken part in several witchcraft investigations and trials here and on the continent. I know whereof I speak, Master Kane."

"What about Esther Kidby, Doctor Cheesebrough?" This came from Howlett, who had pushed his way to the front of the crowd but remained outside the room, as if afraid to be so close to death.

"Her death seems, at least at first glance, a natural one," Cheesebrough said, looking past Kane to his new interlocuter. "As Master Kane pointed out, there are no visible wounds. But..." and here he picked up the medicine bottle on Esther's bedside, and sniffed it. "As Roger has told me, Goodwife Kidby had truck with Sybil Eastey, and often bought 'medicine' from the midwife." He made a distasteful face and set it back down on the table. "Who is to say what is in this so-called 'medicine'?"

Roger looked up. "Mother said that Sybil's medicine helped."

"My dear boy," Cheesebrough said. "Poison may be cloaked in comforting clothing. Neither you, your father, nor your mother would have the knowledge to discern the truth."

"Can you prove it?" Kane said.

"My investigation is not yet complete," Cheesebrough said. "I will offer my findings later today at the trial, Master Kane."

Kane put a hand on Roger's shoulder. "I am sorry for your loss," he said.

Roger looked up at Kane. He seemed more a child than before. His eyes crinkled, his face contorted. He looked completely lost. Kane, not knowing what else to say, left the room, pushing back through the crowd. He was nearly back to the foot of the stairs before a voice called after him.

"I cannot help but notice," the voice said, "that you were present at the deaths of both George and Esther Kidby."

Kane turned back to see Nehemiah Lockwood standing with his arms crossed and glaring. Kane had not seen him before. The carpenter must have arrived during Kane's conversation with Cheesebrough.

"Aye," Kane said. "I was in town for both. I saw George Kidby die, just as you did, Master Lockwood. And I read to the widow Kidby last night before she slept. What of it?"

Lockwood shifted his stance, seeming uncomfortable, but determined. "You are the only person to have been in close proximity for both of these latest murders."

"Are you so sure that the widow was murdered?" Kane said. "She had been ill for many years, and had been denied Sybil Eastey's medicine for over a week. It seems likely that she died in her sleep."

"A likely excuse for a poisoner," Lockwood said.

Kane stalked back across the room until only an inch

remained between himself and the carpenter. Lockwood was short, and Kane glowered down from his full height.

"Do you have something you wish to accuse me of, sir?" he growled.

Lockwood swallowed hard, but, to his credit, stood his ground. "I accuse you of nothing yet. But I am not blind. None of us are."

"There were murders happening ere I ever arrived," Kane said. "What, exactly, do you think you see, with such keen eyes?"

Lockwood's jaw worked. He was clearly angry, and frustrated. But Kane saw something else in his demeanor. Fear and confusion. He could not seem to find the words, with Kane glaring down at him.

Kane tired of waiting for an answer. He turned away, and returned to his room, to finish preparing for the day.

14

The Testimony of Joy Lockwood

Fully dressed and shaved, Kane made his way to the village jail. He trudged quickly, marking each step with his staff. His knee hurt less this morning. The night's rest had done his body good, even if his mind remained a chaotic mess.

He meant to see and speak to Sybil Eastey ahead of the trial. To tell her what he had seen in the woods, and to let her know that he planned to speak on her behalf. But when he arrived at the jailhouse, he found Enoch Archer and Thomas Blackwell at the foot of the stairs, blocking his way. They stood with muskets across their chests, their faces masks of solemnity. They looked like children playing at being soldiers.

"Good morrow, Master Kane," said Archer.

"I would speak with the accused," Kane said.

"I cannot allow that," Archer said.

"Why not?" Kane asked.

"Mayor Bartlett's orders," said Thomas Blackwell. "No one is to see the accused before the trial."

"Is she some shy bride, to be protected from visitors before a wedding?" Kane asked, glowering. Sometimes his stare was enough to change a man's mind. And both men did look uncomfortable. Neither would meet his gaze for more than a moment or two, but they remained in place, blocking his way.

He considered pushing past them. He felt reasonably certain they would not shoot him. And if they tried to, well... muskets were slow and clumsy. Good for hunting, but not close combat. Even without his rapier, Kane could dispatch both men with ease.

You like to hurt people. This was not the voice of reason, but of Le Loup, from last night's dream. Taunting Kane from beyond the grave.

He felt himself tensing up, preparing, but stopped himself. These men were not his enemies. They *were not.* They were just villagers—and Puritans besides. Up against a force they did not understand. They were frightened. Kane could not, as a Christian, or a man of decency, hurt these two, no matter how frustrating he found their behavior.

"You know I am here to help," Kane said. "Do you not?"

"So you say," Archer said. His grip on his musket shifted, and Kane saw his knuckles were white.

He is in a rage, Kane realized. *He is barely controlling himself right now.*

This was perhaps not so surprising. Enoch had made no secret that he did not want Kane here. And now, Kane realized, Enoch had become the avatar for the entire village, and its current feelings.

"I say to you again, Enoch Archer: I *have* come to help," Kane said. "I have told no lies since I arrived, and have harmed none." He nodded to them, touching the brim of his hat. "So I shall wish you both a good morrow and promise to see you at the trial today."

He turned and began to walk back to the inn.

"Mind how you spend the hours between now and then,"

Enoch called after him. "Stay away from my wife, Solomon Kane, lest you find yourself sharing a cell with the witch—or worse."

Kane managed to keep his pace, but barely. He also managed not to make a curt reply.

Kane returned to the inn, where he stopped by the stables to check on Holiday. He stroked her mane, whispered soft words of comfort, and fed her from a bucket of oats. She seemed well enough. Whatever else Roger Kidby had been dealing with, he had not neglected his care for Kane's mount.

When Kane went into the inn itself, he found the building empty and dark, a stark contrast to the crowds he had found this morning. Roger seemed to be gone—likely dealing with the necessary business of preparing his mother for burial.

Kane went back to Esther's bedroom. The door stood open. The windows, which had previously been shut against the cold, were now open. The stuffiness and stink were weaker now. The removal of Esther herself had probably helped, as had airing out the room. No doubt the smell would vanish entirely after a good cleaning, and laundering the bedclothes.

Kane looked about. He did not know what, exactly, he was looking for, or if he were looking for anything at all. What did he expect to find here?

The only change he noticed was on the bedside table. Sybil's medicine bottles were gone. No doubt taken by Cheesebrough the physician, for further examination.

Kane knew Cheesebrough visited the village often. The fact had been mentioned to him by several of the people who lived here. But the fact that Cheesebrough was to offer testimony in Sybil's trial—that he claimed to have testified in other witch trials in the past—worried Kane. Men like Cheesebrough made good money, visiting frightened provincial people and making proclamations of guilt or innocence on witchcraft. Kane found such men dubious, their opinions suspect. For a man like Cheesebrough, a guilty verdict was good for business. It grew your reputation and your coin purse far more than proving someone innocent.

But Kane could do nothing about the man's presence now. Cheesebrough was part of the story, the Lord's Providence. All Kane could do was try to understand and work within it.

He returned to his room, and there he prayed, asking God for the wisdom to understand His will. If God was listening, He provided Kane no comfort, or answers.

At the appointed time, Kane hiked back across the village to the meetinghouse, where the trial was to take place. He was unsurprised to see a crowd gathered at the doors, waiting to be admitted. Individuals glanced at him, but none offered greeting. Instead, to a one, they glanced away, as if they had seen something they should not have.

Kane ignored the looks, and shuffled inside with the crowd, through the lobby, and into the large chamber that occupied most of the building. Wooden pews lined most of that space, and an elevated pulpit stood at the head of the room. At the base of the pulpit now stood a single chair, and a small table. To the left of the pulpit, twelve wooden chairs had been arranged in two neat rows. Seating for the jury, Kane assumed.

Kane found a seat in one of the frontmost pews, on the left side of the room. He and the other onlookers were packed in, thigh-to-thigh and shoulder-to-shoulder.

After most of the crowd had been seated, two men entered through a side door: Mayor Bartlett, and Reverend Pelham.

Bartlett mounted the steps to the pulpit, and Kane understood that he would be serving as the judge for Sybil Eastey's trial. Pelham went to the table beside it, setting down a sheaf of papers, as well as quill and ink. He would be serving as the prosecutor then.

Kane stood and approached the pulpit.

"What is happening here?" he demanded.

"Master Kane," Pelham said. "Good morrow."

"There are laws for witchcraft accusations in England," Kane said. "You are required to send for a justice of the peace. I see no justice here."

Pelham stared at him, studying his face. Then, he murmured, "We have not sent for him."

"Then what you are doing here is illegal," Kane said. "I saw the expressions of the village leaders last night. All certain of Sybil Eastey's guilt. How can she receive a fair trial, when everyone's minds are already turned against her?"

"Look around you," Pelham said. "Who are the people in this village?"

"Puritans," Kane said.

"Puritans, hounded and persecuted by the Church and the Crown," Pelham said. "Do you truly think we want to call such attention on ourselves? To offer corrupt officials more chances to hurt us? We are a small village in an impossible situation. Making do with the tools at hand."

"But it does not make things right. If you insist upon circumventing the law, then I shall represent Sybil in this case," Kane said.

Pelham's usually mild countenance broke into a shocked expression, as if Kane had slapped him.

"No," Pelham said.

"You can allow it," Kane said. "Or I can press the issue, and bring the monarchy down upon this village."

"By the time you get their attention, this matter will have long since settled," Pelham said.

"True," Kane said. "But I believe that, once their attention is upon Windsend, it will make life for you and your neighbors quite difficult regardless. It is your choice, Reverend."

Pelham scowled. "Very well," he said. "I will explain it to Mayor Bartlett."

A moment later, the jury shuffled in the side door. It was a mix of men and women, a few of whom Kane recognized from the inn, and from around of the village. He could name none of them. This, at least, the village seemed to have gotten right.

He turned his gaze to the front once more, as Sybil Eastey was brought in by Nehemiah Lockwood and Ezekiel the jailer. She was shackled, her blue dress and coif spotted with dirt. Her blond hair, visible at the coif's hem, appeared greasy, unclean.

Despite her grubby appearance, she seemed in no way downtrodden. She hid not her face from the assembly, but stood up straight, her shoulders erect, her head high. Her carriage was noble—almost royal—and her blue eyes clear and bright as she looked about the room.

Kane gave her a tiny nod as she was seated in the chair near the foot of the pulpit, facing the crowd. Reverend Pelham stood at his table, shuffling his papers, as if refreshing his memory about the matter at hand. Ezekiel the jailer retrieved a third chair, then sat at the table next to Pelham, with quill and paper at the ready. He would be recording the trial, then.

Pelham finished reading his papers and turned to face the crowd. "Good afternoon," he said. "We are gathered here today for the trial of Sybil Eastey, who has been accused of witchcraft. I will be serving as the prosecutor, and Master Kane, our visiting expert on the supernatural, has requested that he be allowed to represent Miss Eastey."

Ezekiel looked up from his papers, surprised by this

proclamation. He then got up, and hurried to find Kane a chair of his own, as Pelham read the charges against Sybil, and called his first witness, Joy Lockwood.

Like her husband, Joy was small, but with dark hair and large dark eyes, which she kept upon her lap as Pelham began his questioning.

"How long have you known Sybil Eastey?" he said.

"For over five years," Joy said. "Since my husband and I came to help found Windsend."

"And how would you describe your relationship with the accused?"

"We were friends for a time," Joy said. "Or rather, I thought of her as a friend during that time."

"An interesting turn of phrase," Pelham said. "You thought of her as a friend, but with the benefit of hindsight, you no longer believe that to be the case?"

"That is correct, Reverend."

"Why?"

"When my husband, Nehemiah, and I moved to Windsend, we were but newly married," Joy said. "We had no children, but assumed that the Lord would bless us soon. That... that did not happen. Although we did as husbands and wives do, I never fell pregnant. After three years without success, I went to visit midwife Eastey. This I did on the recommendation of another woman I once called 'friend.'"

"And who was this woman?" Pelham asked.

"Catherine Archer," Joy said. "Goodwife Archer told me that Sybil Eastey had saved her own youngest son during a difficult childbirth. That Sybil might be able to help a new life quicken in my womb. So I visited Sybil, and asked for her help."

"What happened next?" Pelham said.

"Sybil sat with me for a time, and asked me questions, much as you do now, Reverend. She also examined me, as if she were a physician rather than a midwife. She held my face and looked into my eyes for a long time. And when she let go of me, she turned away, stood up, and walked to the far side of her hut. She would not face me for what she said next."

"What did she say?"

"She told me that she could help me get pregnant. That, under her care, I could conceive and likely carry a child to a successful birth. But she also said that motherhood would be no joy for me. That the experience would only bring me grief, and I should be happier if I went back to my husband and told him she could not help."

"And what did you do?" Pelham asked.

"I scoffed at this advice," Joy said, and here she sat up a little in her chair, looking as haughty as Sybil herself. "I told her that motherhood was my fondest desire, as it is for every good Christian woman. And who was she, to tell me she could help me, and then refuse to give that help? No, I would have her help, whether she thought it wise or not."

Kane glanced at Sybil, sitting chained on the far side of the table from where Joy sat. Sybil's mouth quirked up in the briefest of smiles, and then disappeared. Kane suppressed a sigh. Smiling during one's own trial was a poor choice.

"And did she help you?" Pelham said.

"Yes," Joy said. "She gave me herbs—to be taken by both myself and Nehemiah—and advice about the best times of the month to… perform cohabitation. We did as bid, and within a few months, a new life quickened in my womb." She touched her belly, absently, as she said it, as if she could still feel it now.

"How was the pregnancy?" Pelham said.

Joy actually looked up from her lap. "You already know the tale, Reverend," she said, a plea in her tone.

"I do," Pelham said. "But tell it again, for the record, please."

"It was a difficult pregnancy," Joy said. "Midwife Eastey told me my health was at risk. She directed me to lie in bed for most of that time. This seemed like good advice. I had seen Catherine Archer undergo a similar regimen of bedrest during her own pregnancy. But despite its necessity, it created difficulties in my marriage. My husband was without a partner for several months, and our neighbors often had to come to our home to look after me and attend to my household chores. I could tell he was frustrated, as was I, but we tried to remain positive, because we wanted a child more than anything in the world. And at the end of nine months, I gave birth to a beautiful baby boy. Zachariah. It was the best moment of my life." She smiled as she said this last part, her face radiant, but the smile quickly vanished, and a shadow seemed to pass over her face.

"What happened next?" Pelham gently prompted.

Joy was silent, and the meetinghouse was quiet as well. There was no coughing, no shuffling in seats. Everyone present seemed to be holding their breath.

"Zachariah was… a difficult baby," Joy said. "Frequently sick, and ill-tempered. The exact opposite of what a mother hopes for. I had to take him to Sybil often. Much of my husband's earnings were spent on her salves and remedies, trying to cure this illness or that. But even when there was no physical illness, he often refused to sleep. He seemed full of rage. He screamed and kicked and cried all day and night. He was slow to nurse, yet seemed forever hungry. And I…" She grimaced, and worried at something in her lap.

Pelham placed a hand on Joy's shoulder. "It is alright, Goodwife Lockwood. You are among friends. Please, tell us what happened next."

"A darkness seemed to come over me as well," Joy said. "Almost as soon as I became a mother. It was as though all joy and life had been taken from me. Does that seem right to you? Natural?" She looked up at the reverend with wide, pleading eyes.

"No, indeed," Pelham said. "Motherhood should be the chief cause of joy in a woman's life."

"For four months, I struggled," Joy said, looking back to her lap. "I fed the child, and tended his crying through the night. But I had energy for naught else. If Zachariah did not need me, all I wanted to do was lie in bed and sleep. I had no desire to cook, or clean, or spend time among friends. Nehemiah was... patient with me. He tried to understand, and give me time and space to find my way back to myself. But the weeks went by, and things did not improve. I began to feel... unnatural toward Zachariah."

Pelham's hand remained on her shoulder. "Can you explain?"

She wiped at her cheeks with the backs of her hands. "I mean that I felt he... my innocent babe... was somehow responsible for how I felt. That it was his fault I ailed. I... I cannot explain it any better than that. I began to have dreams where..." She stopped, and licked her lips. "Dreams where bad things befell the boy. Things that would end his life, and set me free of him. I dreamt of strange men coming into the house. Men with hoods, and dark eyes, who would reach into his crib, and suffocate him while he slept. Men who would stab him with sharp knives. Men with glowing red eyes. Servants of Satan himself. And then..." She wiped at her cheeks over and over.

"It is alright," Pelham said. "The Lord knows the content of your heart. He sees your intent, and does not judge you by the phantoms that terrorize you in the night. Be not afraid."

Joy nodded, and sat up a little straighter in the chair, as though the words gave her strength. "And then, just after Zachariah had turned four months old, I woke in the night to find him on the floor outside his crib. He seemed to have fallen and..." She put her hand to her mouth and shook her head a little. "He was cold to the touch. Nor did he breathe. When I tried to lift him, I found his neck broken."

"A terrible tragedy, for certain," Pelham said.

"That was what my husband and I said to one another," she said. "We buried our son. We accepted the condolences of our neighbors, and prayed to understand the Lord's Providence. It was the darkest time of my life."

"I can only imagine," Pelham said, his voice soft.

"It was not until later, when the fog of grief began to lift, that I began to question," Joy said. "After all, Sybil Eastey had warned me not to have this child. She told me that naught but ill would come of it. I wondered, then—did she know something of the future? Did she have powers in addition to her wisdom as a midwife? And if so, from where could these powers originate? Certainly not from the Lord. And then a terrible thought occurred to me: had she a hand in this tragedy? Had she caused the darkness in my heart? Had she used her power to pull my son from his crib, and break his neck upon the floor?" Goodwife Lockwood was in tears now. "I spoke these thoughts to you and my husband, but no one would listen. At least, not then. It was only after the murders began to take place that anyone paid heed to what I said."

Kane tore his gaze away from Joy, and back to Sybil. Sybil watched Joy with an inscrutable expression upon her face.

"Thank you, Goodwife Lockwood," Pelham said. He turned to look at Kane. "Do you wish to question the witness, Master Kane?"

Kane stood, and approached the woman, who continued to dab at her eyes with a handkerchief.

"Goodwife Lockwood," he said. "You say you found the babe next to his crib, with his neck broken?"

"I did," she said.

"It is a manner of death far different from those the town has seen of late, is it not?"

She narrowed her eyes, perhaps intuiting the goal of this line of questioning. "It is," she allowed. "But—"

"Please just answer my questions," Kane said, cutting her off. "Did you, or your husband, ever ask Sybil Eastey if she had a hand in the child's death? Did you seek to understand her whereabouts on the day Zachariah was murdered?"

"No," Joy said. "But as I said, it was months—"

"Once more, I ask you to only answer the questions which I ask," Kane said. "So you admit that the manner of death is different from that of the recent murders, and that, until this moment, you never accused her of any crime?"

"It was not until the recent killings—" Joy said.

"Yes or no will suffice," Kane said.

Her nostrils flared and all hint of weepiness was gone. "Yes," she said. "Yes, I admit to both things."

"Thank you, Goodwife Lockwood," Kane said. He turned to the jury. "What happened to young Zachariah is a crime. It does not seem possible to me that a child so young could pull himself out of his crib. I agree that foul play was at work. But so far I have heard nothing to indicate that supernatural forces caused it. Almost anyone in this room would be physically capable of the act. I would argue that Goodwife Lockwood's tragedy falls outside the scope of this trial, and shows that the prosecution is proceeding based on rumor and feeling, rather than evidence." He looked back over his shoulder at Joy Lockwood. "I have no further questions."

Joy Lockwood stared daggers at Kane, then stood and walked back to the pews. Nehemiah came forward to meet her. He wrapped an arm about her shoulders and guided her back to their seats. There seemed to be genuine concern and love in Lockwood's handling of his wife, and by the way Joy leaned into her husband's embrace as they sat, it seemed that the love went both ways. It was the opposite of Kane's impression of the Archers' marriage.

15

The Testimonies of Roger Kidby and Doctor Calvin Cheesebrough

Next, Reverend Pelham called Roger Kidby to testify. Roger took the same seat Joy Lockwood had occupied a moment before, and listened intently as Pelham questioned him. Roger told the story of both his parents' deaths, as he had understood them. The lad did himself credit, Kane thought. He did not cry, or come close to tears during his testimony, despite having to retell the most harrowing events of his life.

Pelham let Roger tell the story of each death completely before he asked any questions of his own.

"Tell me, Roger," he said. "Who was present at the death of your father?"

Roger listed off the members of the night's watch, himself, a few neighbors who had been drawn from their beds, and Kane.

"And who was present at the death of your mother?" Pelham said.

"No one," Roger said. "She died in her sleep. I found her this morning."

"Who was the last person in contact with your mother, before her death?" Pelham said.

"Master Solomon Kane," Roger said. "But that—"

"Thank you, Master Kidby," Pelham said.

"But—" Roger said.

"Thank you, Master Kidby," Pelham said. His manner had grown sharper since Kane had cross-examined Joy Lockwood. He seemed angry as he said to Kane, "You may question the witness."

Kane stood and approached Roger. "You say that your father was pulled into the air, and murdered before several witnesses?"

"I do," Roger said.

"Would you agree that the manner of his death is similar to that of the other men in town? Murders that happened long before my arrival?"

"I do," Roger said.

"And your mother. Was the manner of her death similar to those of the other men in town?"

"No," Roger said. "Not even close."

"Do you think I had anything to do with either death?" Kane asked.

"Of course not," Roger said.

Kane turned to the jury. "I do not understand why the court is trying to pull in these unrelated deaths, and lay them at the feet of Sybil Eastey. If she committed the murders in question, that ought to be more than enough. Instead, Reverend Pelham attempts to scapegoat the poor woman for every bad thing that has ever happened in this town."

Pelham stood up. "That is *not* true."

Kane looked to Mayor Bartlett, who watched the proceedings like someone both furious and helpless. "Your honor," Kane said. "Is it meet that the prosecutor interrupt me?"

"Do you have further questions for the witness?" Bartlett growled.

"No," Kane said. "I do not."

"Then take your seat, Master Kane, and stop these theatrics."

But Kane did not do as instructed. Not right away, at least. Instead, he turned to Roger. "I am sorry for your losses. And I am sorry that you have to be here, with us, today, when you ought to be at work burying your mother."

Only then did he sit.

Roger nodded silent thanks as he stood and retreated to the pews, rejoining the audience.

Next, the reverend called Calvin Cheesebrough. The little man carried himself with utmost importance as he came to the front of the meetinghouse. As if he were nobility.

Once Cheesebrough had settled into his chair, Pelham asked him for his name and profession.

"I am Doctor Calvin Cheesebrough," Cheesebrough said. "I am a physician who travels the countryside, offering help where I may."

"And what does that help usually look like?" Pelham asked.

Cheesebrough clicked his tongue as he considered. "It takes various forms. Sometimes, it is as simple as prescribing treatment for a sick child. Other times, sorry to say, I am asked to bring my expertise to bear on the matter of witchcraft."

"Indeed," Pelham said. "I am sure I speak for the entire village of Windsend when I express our gratitude to you, Doctor. You are a busy man, and I am sure that witchcraft runs rampant across the countryside in these dark days."

"Across the world, yet," Cheesebrough said. "But it is my pleasure to help do the Lord's good work, wherever I may."

"When did you arrive in town?" Pelham asked.

"Last night," Cheesebrough said.

"Can you tell us what happened upon your arrival?"

"I asked to see the bodies of the deceased," Cheesebrough said. "Unfortunately, all had already been buried—but the latest, a man by the name of Kidby, had only been buried that day. Men were summoned to exhume the body for my examination. I was also able to perform a thorough examination of Goodwife Kidby's corpse this morning, after her son discovered her."

"This was all only a few hours ago," Pelham said. "The town offered to delay this trial, to give you more time to pursue your investigation, did it not?"

"The offer was appreciated, but, happily, not necessary," Cheesebrough said. "The signs of supernatural evil may be subtle, to the average person, but are quickly apparent to the expert. It is the reason you summoned me, is it not?"

"Indeed," Pelham said. "And we ask you to share that expert opinion now: what did you find, when you examined the Kidbys?"

"In the case of George Kidby, it was immediately apparent that the death was unnatural. That, at least, you and your neighbors already knew." He gave a grave a shake of his head. "He was ripped to shreds."

"And you have seen similar deaths, in your travels?" Pelham said.

"This is a far more brutal death than anything I have seen before," Cheesebrough admitted. "And clearly the work of a powerful dark magic user."

"I see," Pelham said. "And what of Esther Kidby? As Master Kane so recently pointed out, she was not torn apart. She had no visible wounds. As everyone in this village knows, she ailed long, and suffered much. And yet, when you arrived this morning, you asked to examine her body as well."

"Indeed," Cheesebrough said.

"Why?" Pelham said.

"You told me yourself that Sybil Eastly—"

"Eastey," Pelham corrected. He said it mildly, but there was a stiffening of his posture. Most probably missed it, but Kane did not.

"Indeed," Cheesebrough said, waving the amendment away. He did seem to like that word. *Indeed.* "The accused. I was told that the accused had been treating Esther Kidby for consumption for the last several years, alternating my own medical treatments with herbal remedies. So I was curious what I might find if I investigated the body."

"And what did you find?" Pelham asked.

"At first glance, all appeared normal. Esther Kidby's body looked like that of any recently deceased woman who had suffered a long ailment. But, given the reason I had been summoned to town, I decided I should investigate further. I went to midwife Eastey's hut, at the edge of the village. It was, as you might expect, full of plants and herbs that might be used in medicines and poultices. I was about to leave the hut, considering the matter closed, but a certain smell caught my attention. It was a smell I recognized but could not immediately place. I went back into the hut and found a hidden compartment in the floor."

"What did you find in this compartment?" Pelham asked.

"A store of herbs that no good, god-fearing, law-abiding woman ought to have in her home," Cheesebrough said. He lifted a bag from his lap, and laid out a series of dried plants upon the table next to him, pointing at each and naming them:

"This is hemlock. This is deadly nightshade. And this last is henbane." Here he paused and smiled. "The henbane was the giveaway. It has a very distinctive, awful smell."

Kane looked to Sybil. Her mask of stoicism had faded. Her eyes were narrowed and her mouth was set. She was working hard to maintain self-control, but it was clear she was angry. Kane shared her frustration. He had examined the hut himself and found no secret compartments. Something dark and dishonest was at work here.

"What do these plants do?" Pelham asked. "I am not familiar with any of them."

"Terrible things, Reverend," Cheesebrough said. "Hemlock is poison. If you know your ancient philosophy, you know that Athens forced Socrates to drink it, when he was sentenced to death. Henbane causes victims to suffer convulsions. In ancient mythology, the dead wore henbane in the afterlife. And deadly nightshade? It causes terrible pains in the stomach, restlessness, blood in the scat, and in some cases? Death."

"Do you have evidence that Sybil Eastey used these poisons on Esther Kidby?" Pelham asked.

"Well… no," Cheesebrough said, his brow furrowing. "Although I had time to make a full autopsy this morning, I could find no signs. However, the marks of poison upon the body of someone already sick are… subtle. And yet, the presence of these herbs in Sybil Eastey's hut—coupled with the fact that she was treating Esther Kidby—is suspicious. And when you add those two facts to the other things of which she is accused? It paints a damning picture."

"And what of Sybil Eastey herself?" Pelham asked. "You were offered the chance to examine her last night."

Cheesebrough nodded. "I did. I had her stripped so I could examine her fully." His round face flushed as he said it, and something ugly turned over in Kane's gut. He had a suspicion that the doctor had quite enjoyed the act of forcing a woman to undress and submit to his gaze, his touch.

Sybil, for her part, kept her stoic façade. If she felt shame, she did not show it. Kane felt a sudden surge of approval for her, refusing to be cowed as men discussed her naked body.

"And did you find the marks of witchcraft upon her?" Pelham asked.

Cheesebrough shook his head. "Physically, she seems pure. A normal woman of middle years, healthy, and having borne no children."

"Did you perform any additional testing upon the subject?"

Pelham asked. "To try to ascertain her guilt or innocence?"

"We performed the scripture test," Cheesebrough said. "Asking the accused to read from the Bible. She read from the Gospel of Luke without issue. But then we moved on to the pricking test, using a needle. When used upon Sybil Eastey, the needle produced no blood. Any ordinary man or woman would have bled when pricked, but not Sybil."

Pelham nodded, as if deep in thought. "Doctor, I am sure I speak for all of Windsend when I offer our thanks and gratitude."

Cheesebrough gave Pelham a sunny smile. "It has been my sincere pleasure, Reverend."

Pelham took his seat, and Kane stood, approaching the doctor. Cheesebrough's blithe cheeriness dimmed as he looked up into Kane's grim face.

"You are a doctor, yes?" Kane asked.

"Yes. I believe that is already in the record."

"Where were you educated?"

"Oxford college."

"And you say that you have offered your expertise in other witchcraft trials?" Kane asked.

"I have."

"And where did you receive your education in this regard?" Kane asked.

"I had no formal education," Cheesebrough said. "I have learned through experience, as a sad side effect of my work as a traveling doctor. My only teachers have been trial and error, refining over time. As I imagine you yourself have done, Master Kane. I doubt you received much education in the supernatural in your family home in Devon, yes?"

Kane frowned, silently admitting the doctor made a fair point.

"You are being paid for your presence here today, are you not?" Kane said.

Cheesebrough frowned. “I do not see what that has to do with anything.”

“It is a simple question. Have the town elders paid you for your presence here today?”

“Yes,” Cheesebrough said. “Have you not been paid?”

“They attempted to pay me,” Kane said. “Last night. But the purse they offered came with strings attached. They did not like what I had to say, and they tried to pay me to leave. But you—you took their coin, did you not?”

Cheesebrough shrugged. “I must make a living, Master Kane. I cannot speak for your circumstances, but I need money in order to live.”

“True,” Kane said. “But tell me honestly: how does one build a reputation as a consulting doctor in witchcraft cases? Does an innocent verdict spread the word? Or does a guilty verdict help you find more business?”

“Are you impugning my morals?” Cheesebrough said.

“I am attempting to understand your character,” Kane said. “When was the last time you found a woman innocent?”

“I cannot recall,” Cheesebrough said. “I am not usually called in unless there is already overwhelming evidence against the accused.”

“If there is overwhelming evidence, what purpose do you serve?”

“Even with all the evidence in the world, it is no small thing to send a woman to her death. As I’ve done here, I investigate further and ensure the evidence has been interpreted correctly.”

“I see,” Kane said. “Have you ever said something your employers did not wish to hear? Have you ever declared a woman innocent?”

“No,” Cheesebrough said. “But I believe that is more a sign of the dark times in which we live.”

“Master Kane,” Bartlett said. “You try my patience.”

"I am glad to hear it," Kane said. "But let us turn to the matter at hand. Doctor Cheesebrough. You contend that Sybil Eastey is a witch. And that, furthermore, she is responsible for at least seven deaths—the six men, and one woman, Esther Kidby."

"I do," Cheesebrough said, sitting up a bit straighter in his chair.

"Do you believe she also murdered the Lockwood child?"

"I was not here," Cheesebrough said. "I cannot say. But the testimony provided by Goodwife Lockwood is damning."

"Damning," Kane said, his tone musing. "It is an interesting word. The six men who were killed—they died horribly. I saw the last of those deaths. I saw a man rent limb from limb, whose blood spilled like a torn wine sack. But you contend that Miss Eastey then turned to poison to kill Esther Kidby? Why would she change her methods?"

Cheesebrough's face puckered as though he had eaten something unexpectedly sour. "Who am I to guess at the motives of a fiend? Perhaps the suspect hated the men enough to cause them great agony, but felt pity in her heart for the widow Kidby? Perhaps, in her sick and twisted mind, poison was a mercy? You would need to ask the witch herself."

Kane's lip twisted. "One final question, doctor: this witch-finder needle you carry. Where is it produced?"

"I cannot say," Cheesebrough said. "I bought it from a clergyman."

"A Puritan clergyman?" Kane asked. "A reverend?"

"There are few Puritan witch hunters," Cheesebrough said. "No, this was a Catholic priest."

"So you admit to bringing papist tools into this village?"

Cheesebrough sighed. "What does that matter, if the tool is effective?"

"Please answer the question," Kane said.

Cheesebrough threw up his hands. "Yes. Yes, it is, by your definition, a papist tool."

"Thank you, Doctor. I have no more questions."

Cheesebrough gave Kane a venomous look as he stood and left the chair.

Pelham rose from his chair. "Mr Mayor, if it please you, I would call a short break, and then continue to interview our witnesses."

"We have already heard from our witnesses, have we not?" Bartlett said, a warning in his voice.

"There is one last witness I would speak with before the jury makes it verdict," Pelham said. "Master Solomon Kane."

16

A Short Recess

Mayor Bartlett scowled down at Reverend Pelham from behind the pulpit. "Do you truly feel this is necessary, Reverend?" he asked.

"I do, mister mayor," Pelham said. His voice was light, but firm. There was some steel in this odd man.

"As you will," Bartlett said, before announcing a recess of ten minutes.

Despite the October chill, the meetinghouse had grown stuffy. Most of the gathered crowd shuffled out into the afternoon for some fresh air. The jury also left through the side door, alongside Pelham and Bartlett. Kane remained in his seat.

Sybil also remained inside, shackled to the table before the podium. Ezekiel the jailor stood and stretched, but stayed close to his charge.

Sybil gave Kane a wan smile that betrayed the kindness and mirth in her heart. Her eyes crinkled, showing her years. This was not the smile of a witch, or a seductress, but perhaps that of a school teacher, or nanny.

"So," she said. "The famous hunter of supernatural evil has taken up my cause. How do you think it is going so far, Master Kane?"

"Cheesebrough is a fool," Kane said.

"On that we agree," Sybil said. "But men tend to listen to fools, when the fools speak loudly and confidently enough. They seem hungry for it."

"On that we agree as well," Kane said.

Ezekiel, the jailer, coughed to make sure his presence was known. He stood a few feet away from Sybil now.

"I am sorry to interrupt, midwife Eastey," he said. "Would you like to go outside for a moment?"

Sybil turned that same sweet, gentle smile on Ezekiel. "It is kind of you to ask, Ezekiel. You have been kind to me throughout this ordeal. I will not forget it."

Ezekiel gave her a nervous, fleeting smile in return, then looked down at the floor. "Thank you. But what about going outside?"

"Not now, thank you," she said. "I prefer the company in here."

"As you say," Ezekiel said. He stood at her side a moment longer, unsure what to do with himself, then retreated to the shadows at the far end of the meeting house, giving her and Kane a bit of privacy.

Once he had gone, Sybil turned back to Kane. "Must you sit so far away?" she said.

"I have been scolded, of late," Kane said, "for appearing too familiar with the women of this village. People think it improper, and have advised that I keep my distance."

"I am on trial for my very life," Sybil said. "My reputation can sink no lower."

"But mine can," Kane said. "And your life may depend on it."

"So why not step outside with the rest of them?" she asked, but there was no weight to the question. She twisted her shoulders from side to side, stretching her back. "No, their distrust is inevitable, I am afraid. The only thing men love more than listening to fools is ignoring true wisdom from a person of intelligence—at least, while listening to that person might make a difference. Look at Christ. Did anyone heed that man while he was alive? No, he had to die to get the world's attention."

"Do not blaspheme," Kane said.

"How do I blaspheme?" Sybil said.

"You compare me to the Lord," Kane said.

"I merely used an example you might understand," she said. "If I mentioned Socrates, as Cheesebrough did, would that have meant anything to you?"

Kane frowned. "Not truly. I know the name, and that he is of repute with scholars, but that is all."

"Socrates was a wise man," Sybil said. "A philosopher. And while he lived, he had loyal followers. But it was not until he was executed, and one of his pupils, Plato, began to tell his story, that anyone paid attention to anything he had to say. And that is my point, Solomon Kane. You are a man of faith, yes, but also seem to be one of reason. That puts you at odds with almost everyone in the world, including the people of this village. Do not base your actions and decisions upon the approval of fools, even if they share your faith. The approval of fools is fickle, and worth very little to begin with. So please, come closer, if you would."

Kane stood up and approached, leaning on his staff. His knee did not hurt, exactly, but it was stiff after such a long sit.

"You have developed a limp since yesterday," she said. "Your knee troubles you?"

Kane scowled at her, meaning to end this avenue of conversation. His expression did nothing to scrub the curiosity and concern from her own.

"Some days, yes," he said, grudgingly.

"Days when you have to do a lot of walking?" Sybil said. "Or when there are extreme swings in the weather? Does it get better or worse, depending upon the length and quality of your sleep?"

Kane struggled to know which question to answer first. Then he remembered that he was under no obligation to answer at all.

"Why do you ask?" he said.

"I am a midwife," she said. "But also a wise woman. It is my job to look after the ailing. Perhaps I can help you."

"And maybe you would poison me, as you poisoned Esther Kidby," Kane said.

"You defend me from my accusers in public, and accuse me yourself in private," she said, annoyed. "Why would I poison Esther?"

"Because you meant to keep her sick," Kane said. "Dependent upon your remedies, and paying handsomely for them. And perhaps you put too much into your last bottle. Or perhaps the widow drank more than she had been prescribed, and ruined your plans."

"Do you believe that, Master Kane" Sybil asked.

"I—" Kane said. "I do not know what to believe, at present."

"And here I hoped that a kind, soft smile might topple your judgement and send you to your testimony singing my praises," she said, her tone making the joke clear. Kane did not smile back.

"Quickly," he said. "Tell me: the creatures I met in the woods. They are nothing to do with you?"

Sybil shook her head. "I do not know what creatures you speak of. Whatever you found out there has nothing to do with me, and everything to do with this unfortunate place."

Kane's gut told him she spoke truth. He wanted to question her further, but was prevented by the sounds of the meeting-house doors opening, returning the crowd to their seats.

"Master Kane? What are you doing?"

The voice came from the side of the room, and Kane turned to see Mayor Bartlett and Reverend Pelham walking toward him. It was Bartlett who had spoken. He sounded vaguely outraged, but Pelham's eyebrows rose as well.

"I am speaking to Mistress Eastey," Kane said. "I am entrusted with her defense, am I not? Would you have my testimony now? Or have I sullied my reputation such that my word will no longer be trusted? If I ever enjoyed your trust, of course."

17

The Testimony of Solomon Kane

Kane took the same chair that had recently been occupied by Joy Lockwood, Roger Kidby, and Dr Cheesebrough. He kept his staff erect in his left hand, and his right hand upon the table.

"Your name, for the record," Pelham said.

"Solomon Kane," Kane said.

"You are the famed adventurer, yes?" Pelham said.

Kane frowned. "I make no claim to any title. Others may say what they will."

"But you have spent your life traveling the world, yes?" Pelham said. "Soldiering? Exploring? Righting wrongs and enacting the Lord's justice upon evildoers?"

Though this seemed an accurate summation, Kane hesitated to own it.

It is a trap, the voice of reason told him. Kane could not quite see the shape of the snare, but he sensed it coming.

"I have done my best to do what seems right, in my understanding of the scriptures, and God's Providence," Kane said. "Like all mortal men, I have failed as often as I have succeeded, but I have tried."

"But you have some experience facing the supernatural," Pelham pressed. "The unholy. You would agree with that, would you not?"

"I would," Kane allowed.

"And what brings you to Windsend now?" Pelham said.

"I came at the request of Goodwife Archer," Kane said. "She considers Sybil Eastey a friend, and trusted me to be able to ascertain the midwife's guilt or innocence."

"Why would Goodwife Archer summon you," Pelham said, "when the village leadership had already decided to consult with Dr. Cheesebrough?"

"I believe she wrote to me before Mistress Eastey was arrested," Kane said. "It took some time for her letter to reach me by courier. As for Goodwife Archer's motives, you would need to ask her."

"Would you indulge me, and speculate?" Pelham asked.

"Goodwife Archer and I have known each other since we were youths. We grew up together and are old friends. She knows about some of the things I have seen in my travels, and trusts my judgement."

"You say you—and likely Goodwife Archer—were not aware of the fact that Dr. Cheesebrough had been summoned, when you decided to come to Windsend. Would it have made a difference in your decision, if you had known?"

"No," Kane said.

"Why not?" Pelham asked. "If the village officials had already made a decision, why would you intervene?"

"The characters and competencies of men are greatly varied," Kane said. "I knew not Cheesebrough, before this morning, and my friend asked for my aid. Perhaps my investigation would be redundant, perhaps not. But this is all speculation. When a friend asks for help, I answer if it is possible to do so. And anyway, does Ecclesiastes not say, 'Two *are* better wages for their labor'? What harm do you see in it?"

Pelham put a hand to his chin and considered. "Harm? Perhaps none, not directly. But that is not the entirety of the story, is it? After your arrival, you met with Goodwife Archer's husband, Enoch Archer, did you not?"

"What has this to do with Sybil Eastey's guilt or innocence?" Kane asked.

"Please, indulge me," Pelham said.

Kane fought down a sigh, conscious of how people watched.

"I did meet with him, yes," Kane said.

"And what did he say?"

"He said he would rather I not be here, but gave me leave to conduct my investigation and bid me leave as soon as possible."

"So you saw his displeasure, and yet you stayed," Pelham said. "Ignoring the husband's clear wish that you go?"

"That is correct," Kane said.

"Did you have any qualms about this?" Pelham said.

Kane's grip on his staff tightened, and he became aware of an ache in his jaw. He'd been grinding his teeth since the trial began, and had not realized it until now.

"I did not," Kane said. "I mean to cause no damage to a marriage, but there is great evil afoot here, and it seemed important that I try to get to the bottom of it. I do not concern myself with appearances, Reverend. I concern myself with right and wrong. Evil and justice."

"Again, I commend you on your noble sentiments," Pelham said, in a condescending tone. Kane had throttled men for less. "You have conducted an investigation of your own, independent of the wishes of this village and its leaders."

Kane sat silent, not rising to the implied question. When Pelham realized he would not draw out an attempt at self-justification from Kane, he sighed. "Can you please summarize your investigation, Master Kane? What did you do? What did you discover?"

Kane obliged, beginning by recounting the night of his arrival. His conversations with the men of the night's watch. His attempt at sleep, interrupted by the bizarre death of George Kidby. He told of his investigation of Sybil's hut and made a point of saying that he had not discovered any hidden compartments, or noticed any smells out of place.

"And would you know the smell of henbane?" Pelham said.

"I would," Kane said. "I have smelled it many times. It is unmistakable. I say to you that there was no henbane in that hut when I searched it. Nor did I find any other signs of devilry or witchcraft. It was, as near as I can tell, an ordinary midwife's dwelling."

"You contend that there was no henbane in that house," Pelham said, "despite Dr Cheesebrough's testimony?"

Kane shrugged. "I did my investigation yesterday. He conducted his this morning. It is possible that someone planted the henbane after my search, and left it for the doctor to discover. There is also the possibility that the doctor brought the henbane with him, and planted it himself."

Angry surprise rippled through the crowd, and Pelham's eyes widened. Kane glanced past the reverend to look at Cheesebrough, seated in the front pew of the meetinghouse. The little man's mouth puckered once more, and he gripped the railing before him with white knuckles.

"That is quite an accusation, sir," Pelham said.

"I make no accusation," Kane said. "I only point out the possibilities as I see them, given the things I know. Are you ready to hear the rest of my testimony?"

Pelham spread his hands, giving Kane leave to speak once more. Kane continued his tale. He told of his interview with Sybil.

"So you interviewed her and physically examined her?" Pelham asked.

"I did," Kane said.

"And, in your estimation, given all that you know of witches and the supernatural, is Sybil Eastey a witch?"

"Sybil Eastey is on trial for murder, is she not? Her status as a witch is not germane," Kane said.

Kane glanced back at Sybil, then into the crowd, scanning the faces there. He finally spotted Catherine and Enoch Archer near the back of the meeting house. Perhaps they had come late? Enoch's face was like granite, carved into a mask of pure hate. Catherine kept her head bowed, and stared at her lap. In the silence, she glanced up at Kane, revealing a bruise around her left eye. Kane could easily guess her assailant.

"You are right, Master Kane," Pelham said. "Sybil Eastey is on trial for the murders of the men of Windsend these last few months. However, it should be stated: even if Mistress Eastey is acquitted of the murders, she may still be found guilty of witchcraft. Per the Witchcraft Act of 1541, witchcraft is a felony, punishable by death and the forfeiture of goods and chattels. So I ask once more: in your estimation, is Sybil Eastey a witch, or not?"

Kane sat back in his chair and licked his lips. He was not a liar. And yet the truth added a deadly wrinkle to these proceedings.

"I found no evidence that Sybil Eastey is a witch," Kane said, schooling his face and his own disgust at himself, for lying in a court of law. *Would a true servant of the Lord lie?* Kane thought himself no better than those he hunted.

No, he told himself, tightening a fist in his lap. *For there are unjust laws, are there not? And is not morality above any man-made laws? I merely circumvent an unjust law now.*

The thought soothed his conscience—but not as much as he might have hoped.

"Indeed?" Pelham said.

"Indeed," Kane said, forcing the word out. He wanted to look at Sybil but kept his eyes on Pelham instead.

"Will you please tell us *how* you determined Sybil Eastey's innocence?" Pelham asked.

"There are methods one can use, but when one has spent as much time as I have in the presence of evildoers, one develops an instinct. The way a midwife might know a woman is pregnant before the woman herself knows. The way a blacksmith knows just where to strike iron, to shape it to his will. A professional knows."

"You avoid the question, sir," Pelham said. "Did you search for a witch's mark? Did you use the needle test? Did you weigh her against a stack of bibles? Did you make a witch's cake?"

Kane scoffed. "Tell me, Reverend: where did you hear of these methods for witch detection?"

Pelham walked over to the stack of books and papers he had brought into the meetinghouse with him, and picked up a fat volume, which he now offered to Kane.

"Surely, Master Kane," he said, "you have heard of the *Malleus Maleficarum*? Is it not the standard manual for witch hunters?"

Kane waved the proffered book away. "Do you know who wrote that book, Reverend?"

Pelham opened the book and paged through it idly, like a man browsing in a shop. "Of course. Heinrich Kramer and Jacob Sprenger."

"Do you know who Heinrich Kramer was?" Kane asked.

"He was an inquisitor," Pelham said.

"An inquisitor for the *Catholic* church," Kane said. "I have read that book. It is rife and stained with popery. I thought Windsend was meant to be a Puritan village, and you a Puritan, Reverend. And yet you wave around the tool of popists as if it were the holy scripture itself."

Pelham's mouth dropped open in a small "o" but recovered quickly, snapping shut. "Kramer is long dead," he said. "He lived in another land, far from here. He would not have had the opportunity to have seen the light of the Puritan movement. Are we to punish him for living in his time and place? And if we are not to use the *Maleficarum* in our investigations, how else are we to proceed?"

"How were Puritans to proceed and thrive, without the guidance of Catholicism?" Kane said. "Somehow, we have managed, through hard thinking and hard work. Yet you—and Dr Cheesebrough—employ the relic of a corrupt perversion of our faith. I tell you, that book cannot be trusted, and I call into question any proceeding that uses the *Maleficarum* as its basis."

Pelham's nostrils flared. His mouth, previously smiling, drew into a small, thin, angry line. Kane had ruined the reverend's fun.

The sight of Pelham's anger caused most of Kane's contained rage to drain away. He felt a flat coolness spreading from the crown of his skull and through his body. He recognized the feeling. This was the centering of his soul that took place before a battle. A gift of calm from God, which Kane used to vanquish enemies. In the past, Kane had experienced this feeling on his feet. It was strange to experience it sitting down now, in an ostensibly civilized place, but he welcomed it, and pressed his advantage.

"Catherine Archer asked me to come here because she trusts my judgement. She knows my heart and aims to be true, and my wisdom hard-won. I am not after profit, like Dr Cheesebrough. I pursue only the truth and the Lord's justice. I came to Windsend to meet the accused without any preconceptions of her guilt or innocence. I spoke to her without prejudice. I listened to what she said. I looked for signs of the evildoer, and found none. Furthermore, she gave me evidence that led me to the actual killers, which I explained to you and the village leaders last night."

"Ah yes," Pelham said. "Please tell the jury about this cave of monsters you found." His smile returned as he said it, but the look was far uglier than it had been before.

Kane reported an edited version of his conversation with Sybil and his trip to and from the cave outside of town. Pelham never interrupted. He merely stood to one side, arms crossed, listening. When Kane stopped speaking, the reverend turned to the crowd, then the jury.

"I heard this story last night, and it still amazes me," he said. "That this stranger comes into our town, and tries to sell us a story, not of witchcraft, documented for years in this country and on the continent, but of little blue monsters, which can, conveniently, become invisible in most lights?"

"My story is easy enough to verify," Kane said. "I offered to lead a party of men back to the cave myself. If you will not follow me, you could at least send a party of your own. It should be easy enough to find."

Pelham's sneer returned. "I suppose you have not yet heard, then? This morning, at first light, Enoch Archer led an expedition into the woods, to attempt to find this cave, and these monsters. They searched all morning, and returned shortly before the trial. Shall I tell you what they found? Nothing. No hole in the forest floor. No cave entrance. No nest of invisible monsters."

Kane shook his head. "That cannot be. The entrance is there. The men are either lying or were misled. Allow me to lead a party myself—"

Enoch Archer shot to his feet near the back of the meetinghouse. "How *dare* you?" he shouted.

Mayor Bartlett slammed his palm upon the pulpit a few times, creating a sharp sound that echoed through the meetinghouse.

"Quiet!" Bartlett said, voice booming. "Or I will have you removed, Enoch Archer."

Enoch was not listening, however, but already making his way up the aisle of the meeting house. His fellows watched, too surprised to move, as he passed the railing into the front of the room, heading straight for Kane.

"I will quiet this liar once and for all!" Enoch growled, rushing the remaining space between himself and Kane.

Kane used the staff to push himself to his feet, made a fist with his free hand, and punched Enoch square in the face. The sound of the impact—a most satisfying *crunch*—gave Kane more joy than it should have.

The blow reversed Enoch's forward momentum, knocking him backward. He stumbled once, twice, and then landed flat on his back. Kane looked down into glazed eyes as blood began to run from Enoch's broken nose.

Enoch had not the presence of mind to wipe at his face. He blinked at the ceiling with eyes that seemed to see nothing.

Kane retook his seat as three men rushed forward from the crowd. They retrieved Enoch, helped him to his feet, and took him outside. No one spoke until the meetinghouse doors clapped shut behind them.

"Master Kane," Mayor Bartlett said.

"I merely defended myself, your honor," Kane said. "What should I have done? Sat here and let him assault me, the same way he assaulted his wife? Believe me, sir. I showed great restraint a moment ago. Had I not, you would be preparing for another funeral today."

A scandalized murmur passed through the crowd. Bartlett continued to glare at Kane, but could apparently find no argument with his logic, and he gestured that Pelham could continue.

"Why not let me lead a group of men into those woods?" Kane said. "I could show them the way, and solve this at once."

Pelham began shaking his head before Kane had finished speaking. "We have spent enough time on your fancies, Master Kane. The longer we wait to act, the more people die. It is my opinion, Master Kane, that your testimony is unreliable. That you are unreliable. You call yourself a Puritan, but you do not live among us. You wander and live a life of dalliance, avoiding the hard labor of being a proper Christian, and then you come to our home and call us incompetent, and worse, liars. You accuse us of being popists. You try to discredit our expert witness. All of this leads me to wonder—and I have to assume that every person in this room is wondering the same thing—just *why* you are so intent on proving Sybil Eastey's innocence."

"Because I seek justice," Kane said. "And what is happening here is not justice."

"Yet my question lingers," Pelham said, his tone becoming mild once more. "That is an interesting staff you carry. From what type of wood is that staff fashioned?" Pelham said.

"I know not," Kane said simply. "No one I have met has been able to tell me."

"And where did you get it?"

"It was given to me by a friend."

"Who was this friend?"

"I doubt you know him, Reverend," Kane said.

"It was told to me that, during your travels, you became friendly with an African sorcerer," Pelham said. "A practitioner of witchcraft. A man you call 'blood brother.' Is that true?"

Kane readied to lie once more. But he could not bring himself to repeat the sin.

Instead he took a deep breath, and said a short, silent prayer for patience. "I understand that you are afraid, Reverend Pelham. I understand that all of you are afraid, and rightfully so. But I tell you, persecuting an innocent woman, and turning your ire upon me, will not end your ordeal."

"Answer the question, Master Kane," Pelham said. "Was the staff given to you by a practitioner of black magic?"

"It was," Kane said.

"And does the staff itself possess supernatural qualities?" Pelham asked.

"Yes," Kane said. "It has saved me on many occasions."

"If that is so," Pelham said, "and, if it is true that you consider yourself a Puritan, you will not argue when I ask this jury to discredit anything you have said, either in the defense of Sybil Eastey, or yourself, and you will not fight when I ask you to stand and surrender all weapons on your person, so that the men of the night's watch may arrest you."

"On what charge?" Kane said.

Pelham gave Kane a quizzical smile. "What else? Witchcraft, Master Kane."

18

Accused

Kane did stand then, so fast and with such force that he knocked over the chair in which he sat. It hit the floor with a *bang*, and Kane found himself reaching for one of his pistols before he was completely aware of what he was doing.

It was only by practicing the greatest restraint of his life that he stopped himself long enough to look around. He looked at Sybil, who watched him with her eyes wide and her eyebrows raised, genuinely surprised by this turn of events. He looked at the men of Windsend, rising from their pews with hard looks in their eyes. They no doubt meant to fight to subdue him, if they had to.

And then he saw Catherine, near the back of the room. Catherine, with her black eye and sad gaze. She must have overheard him telling Isaac about the staff, and N'Longa. The black eye suddenly made more sense. Enoch had beaten intelligence from her.

Catherine shook her head just a little now, silently pleading with Kane not to hurt her neighbors.

The people of Windsend were wrong—murderously so—but they were afraid. And ignorant. And although Kane had no doubt he could fight his way out of this place, he doubted he could do so without killing some of these men.

But you like hurting people, Monsieur Galahad.

The voice was that of Le Loup, who had been in Kane's dream last night.

Do not let your conscience trouble you, mon ami, Le Loup said. *Do what you do best. Show them what fools they are to meddle with you.*

With a scowl, Kane released his staff. It clattered to the ground beside him and he raised his hands in surrender.

He allowed himself to be disarmed by the men of the night's watch, and shackled by Ezekiel the jailer. He allowed himself to be led to the Windsend jail. He wondered if the night's watch might try to beat him, out of the view of their neighbors, but they seemed to think better of it. The worst physical treatment Kane received was a rough shove into the jailhouse's solitary cell. He slammed against the far wooden wall at the back of the building and turned back to see Nehemiah Lockwood and John Howlett smiling back at him, smug expressions upon their faces.

They wanted him to rage. They wanted him to threaten them. But Kane kept control, staring back at them with a mask of stoicism upon his face.

"You are making a mistake," he said.

"I do not believe we are," Nehemiah Lockwood said, but he looked somewhat troubled as he said it. He was not the wall of anger that Enoch Archer had been. There was something deeper and uglier going on behind his eyes, but Kane could not be sure what it was.

Ezekiel locked Kane in the cell, and then he and the other members of the watch left Kane alone in the jailhouse.

He paced the small cell, trying to release some of his rage

through simple movement. Movement only seemed to agitate him further. He had been arrested and thrown into jail by his own countrymen—fellow Puritans—as an accused evildoer. The injustice of it boiled in his chest. He wanted to strike something. To bloody his fists against the bars of this little cell.

Remember why you surrendered, the voice of reason said. *Keep it in your mind.*

He sat on the cell's thin, hard cot, his hands on his knees. He took deep breaths, and reminded himself anew that this was a terrified village. As Christ had said, *Father, forgive them: for they know not what they do.* If Christ could forgive the evildoers who crucified Him, surely Kane could find mercy in his own heart.

But as he worked himself into this frame of mind, something nagged at him. Even if he accepted Windsend's collective fear, their hatred of him seemed extreme, bordering on unnatural. And that look in Nehemiah Lockwood's eyes… what was happening here?

He froze, and let his breaths grow deeper. He closed his eyes and let the world fall away. As he did, he was able to listen to his body, and was only mildly surprised to discover his own exhaustion. He had not had a good night's rest in many weeks.

He laid down on the cot. It was too short for his long body, and his booted feet dangled off the far edge. It mattered little to Kane, who had learned to sleep in almost any condition. He pulled his slouch hat down over his eyes, folded his hands over his chest, and let sleep take him.

Kane looked around. At first, he saw only darkness, but as his eyes adjusted, he saw that he stood in a great stone chamber. In the center of the room, reclining upon a couch lay a young-looking, beautiful Black woman whom Kane recognized at once: Nakari, the vampire queen who had ruled over the ancient city of Negari.

"Welcome, Solomon Kane," she said. "It is a pleasure to see you."

"Nakari," Kane said, shaking his head a little. "I saw you die."

"Did you?" Nakari said. "Are you sure you saw what you think you saw?"

"Do not toy with me, evil woman," Kane said. "I missed my own chance to kill you before, but I would welcome another chance now." He reached for the rapier at his belt, but his hand swiped at empty air. Only then did he realize he wore no weapon belts.

"I once offered you life eternal," Nakari said. "The chance to be my king. And you spat in my face. You were so sure. So self-righteous. It makes me sick to think about it."

"Good," Kane said. "If I had my way, you would feel sick for eternity, drowning in Satan's lake of eternal fire."

Nakari's mocking smile grew larger. "And yet," she said. "You testified on behalf of a witch. You lied to your fellow Puritans to try to save her life."

Kane stepped back, and put a hand to his head. He felt strange. How could Nakari be here? And how did she know about Sybil Eastey, and Windsend?

"You have abandoned your morality," Nakari said. "And for what? The life of a witch? An evildoer?"

"She uses magic," Kane said. "It does not make her evil."

"Let none be found among you that maketh his son or his daughter to go thorough the fire, or that useth witchcraft..."

"Do not quote scripture at me, woman."

"For all that do such things are abomination unto the Lord, and because of these abominations the Lord thy God doth cast them out before thee."

Kane opened his mouth to argue, but the words did not come.

"How do you defend someone your Lord condemns. Are you any better than the men who now try Sybil Eastey? I wonder."

"I wonder too."

The vampire queen's smile broadened to show her sharp, glistening teeth.

"Good," she said. "Then you have taken the first steps on your journey."

Kane's eyes snapped open, and he found himself staring at the ceiling of the cell in the Windsend jail. He had fallen asleep, and had dreamt. He had only woken because of a sound—the jailhouse door being unlocked.

Kane sat up as the door swung open. Sybil Eastey entered first, flanked by Ezekiel the jailer, and then Enoch Archer and the members of the night's watch. Kane watched silently as Ezekiel unlocked the cell door and gently guided Sybil inside, then locked it behind her. The men then turned and left without a word.

Sybil remained by the now-shut door, looking at Kane. A faint smile danced across her face.

"I cannot say I am happy to return to this cell," she said. "But I am happy to have company."

Kane realized what she meant, and looked past her to Ezekiel, who was now sitting at his desk, writing something down.

"You cannot mean to leave us in the same cell all night," Kane said.

"We have but one jailhouse, and one cell, Master Kane," Ezekiel said. "I apologize, but this does seem to be the situation for tonight. It is only for one night, I promise you."

Kane looked from Ezekiel back to Sybil and found her still looking amused.

"I promise I do not bite, Master Kane," she said.

"This is not proper," Kane insisted.

"I will come back with your dinners shortly," Ezekiel said, as he stood to leave.

"Thank you, Ezekiel," Sybil said. She crossed the cell and sat down upon the cot with a sigh, as Kane stood and walked to the bars of the cell. He wrapped his hands around the metal. It was cold to the touch.

"Catherine chose poorly when she chose a husband," Sybil said.

She continued when Kane did not respond.

"I knew Enoch was dense and unkind, and jealous of his wife's attention and affection," Sybil said. "But lately I have seen the true cruelty in that man's heart. I am sure you marked her black eye during the day's proceedings."

"Indeed," Kane said. "It is my fault she bears it."

"Do not speak so," Sybil said. "It is the fault of the man who gave it to her. And you have paid him back for it, regardless."

"No man should lay his hands on the innocent, but those who harm women or children are doubly damned," Kane said.

"Master Kane," Sybil said, a note of mock surprise in her voice. "You are a progressive thinker."

Kane grunted. He was not a man prone to laughter. This sound was the closest he usually came.

"For all the good your punch did," Sybil said. "They let him back into the courthouse after you were taken away. Reverend Pelham asked if anyone else had testimony to offer. Catherine stood and tried to speak. Enoch restrained her. She fought him like the devil, and I swear to you, I thought she might claw his eyes out. But he managed to drag her out of the meetinghouse, with everyone watching. And none did a thing to stop him.

They watched until she was gone, and then turned forward to listen to the mayor direct the jury to their deliberations."

"Are they deliberating still?" And then, for the first time, Kane remembered something Ezekiel had said before he left: *It is only for one night.* What had that meant?

Sybil shook her head. "They were gone only a few moments—so short a time that Mayor Bartlett and Reverend Pelham and Ezekiel did not try to bring me back to my cell. It was as if they already knew that the jury would return within ten minutes. They found me guilty of witchcraft and murder. I have been sentenced to execution."

Kane walked back to the cot. He sat down beside Sybil, leaned back against the wall, and grimaced at the ceiling.

"You are to be executed in the morning?"

"Yes," Sybil said. "There was some discussion about waiting until your trial was over, and you yourself are sentenced, so that the executions could be done in one event. But they are in a hurry to see me dead, it seems."

Kane scowled. "You should not joke about this."

"It is my life, and my death," Sybil said. "I can joke if I want to."

He stood up and walked back to the bars of the cell, grabbing hold of them.

"Are you testing the bars' strength?" Sybil asked. "Looking for a means of escape?"

Kane shook his head. "Nay."

"You mean that you have a different escape method in mind?"

"Nay."

"Why not?" she said.

"The people of this village have arrested me," he said. "They will try me tomorrow, and we shall see what happens then."

"I do not understand," she said. "You could have fought

your way free of that mob earlier. You could be long gone by now. Instead, you let yourself be taken by those stupid men. You let them disarm you and imprison you with me, and now you sit and wait for them to decide to kill you when you know you are innocent. Why?"

"Because most of them are innocent," Kane said. "They are Puritans, like me, trying to understand and execute the will of God. I would prefer not to harm them. But it is more than that. I believe in the Providence of God. He will show me my path. I believe I was meant to be arrested today. That I am meant to be tried tomorrow. And perhaps I am meant to be found guilty and executed, the same as you. After all, have I not strayed, using magic?"

Something struck Kane in the back. The blow was not hard, or painful, but it was surprising, and he whirled to see Sybil sitting on her cot, arms crossed. Only belatedly did he notice that one of her boots was off, leaving her stockinged foot bare. Her missing boot lay on the cell floor behind Kane. She had thrown it at him.

"Why did you do that?" he asked.

"That is the stupidest thing I have ever heard," Sybil said. "Providence. Waiting for God to tell you what to do, how to behave. Do you know what happens when you wait for God? Nothing. Absolutely nothing. Sick people die. Women lose their children or their own lives in childbirth. The innocent suffer, because the evil do not wait for God to show them a path. And yet you, a righter of wrongs, are content to sit here and do nothing?"

Kane picked up her boot, crossed the room and offered it to her.

"You are free with your criticisms, Sybil Eastey, but you sit in this cell as well. Have you no methods to escape this prison? Could you not use your magic to tear down this jail? Or to charm Ezekiel into freeing you? He seems quite susceptible."

"I can hear thee," Ezekiel called, from his seat near the door.

"Do you deny you are enamored of this woman?" Kane called back.

Ezekiel answered only with silence for a moment. Then he sighed and said, "Be not unkind, Master Kane."

Sybil scoffed. "Do you think so little of me, Master Kane? After you have risked your own life for mine? You believe that I would use magic to warp the will of another human being?"

"Why would you not, if your life was on the line?" Kane asked.

She shook her head, disgusted. "Setting aside your low opinion of my character, you do not think through your own reasoning. Why would I not just use this power to charm the whole town and avoid this mess altogether?"

"I doubt it is within your power," Kane said. "Moreover, I risked my life because I knew you were not guilty of the murders. It was the right thing to do. Do not mistake it for a change in my beliefs. I still believe you are damned to Hell."

"And what of you, and that strange staff of yours?" she demanded. "It was given to you by a priest of black magic, was it not?"

Kane nodded, feeling glum. "It may be that I am damned too. We are all on the paths laid for us by God. His Providence determines all that happens, including our salvation or damnation. It is impossible for any one of us to know, for certain."

She shook her head slowly. "Your behavior makes no sense, Solomon Kane. You make no sense. You say you believe in Providence, that the Lord expresses His will and we ought but to listen and follow. But you have spent your life traveling the world. Acting as an instrument for God's wrath. You truly believe that. Is that not so?"

Kane raised his eyebrows. "Who said I believe that?"

"Catherine Archer and I have had many an occasion to speak," Sybil said. "Fret not—we have far more interesting things to talk about than you, most days. But you may have come up once or twice. You called yourself the Hand of God, did you not?"

"I was young," he said. "Not yet in my majority."

"So your feelings about this have changed?" she asked.

"No," he admitted. "I continue to travel and work based upon my teenage revelation."

"You choose to act when you see something wrong," Sybil said. "You chose to come to Windsend. You chose to investigate my claims. You chose to speak up on my behalf, and attempted to save my life. You are a man of action. And yet, as soon as they came to arrest you, you became passive. Why?"

Kane considered this for a while, staring down at his boots. They were crusted with mud and dirt. He wished he could clean them now, while he had nothing to do but wait.

"I am not entirely sure," he said at last. "I am not entirely myself lately. I feel different in a way that is difficult to express. When I last saw my reflection, it startled me. It was as if the face I knew had been replaced by that of an old man."

"I think that happens to all of us," Sybil said. "It is part of being a mortal on this earth. The gradual failure of our bodies is the great tragedy of our lives. I have felt it too. I was once beautiful, you know."

Ezekiel glanced up from his place near the front of the jailhouse, looked ready to speak. It seemed some people *still* found her lovely. But Kane had little interest in the beauty of women, and turned the conversation aside once more.

"Why do you remain?" he asked. "You avoided my question before. I linger because I am not sure the right path forward, or the right thing to do. But if you are averse to manipulating men's minds and hearts, why not use your gifts in some other way, and flee?"

Sybil sighed and leaned back against the wall herself, slouching out of her perfect posture and touching her coif to the dingy wooden wall.

"My 'gifts,' as you call them… are somewhat diminished, of late."

"How is that possible?" Kane asked.

"That," Sybil said, "is a long story."

19

Sybil's Tale

You have heard it again and again, like the chorus of a song, Master Kane: life in Windsend has never been easy.

Five years ago, a group of Puritans came to this valley, with the intention of founding a Puritan settlement. A place they could practice their faith and live their lives free from the eyes and persecution of the Church of England—or as freely as possible, while remaining in England, rather than setting off for the colonies.

I am no Puritan. I had no business coming to Windsend, and I was not among the first group of settlers. But not long after the village's founding, I received a letter from my friend Catherine Archer. None of the founding settlers in this village were midwives or physicians. The nearest doctor was at least a day's ride away. These people needed someone who could look after their health.

I was not enamored of the prospect of living among Puritans. But I was poor, and, as Catherine pointed out, the village would present me with no real competition. Perhaps here, I could make a real living. And I felt that Catherine was something of a kindred spirit. Like me, she had trouble making friends. She is possessed of too much intelligence for a woman in this religious movement—no offense intended, Master Kane. Please take a breath, and let me tell my story.

So I came to Windsend, and with the villagers' help, I built a home in a space just outside the village. It was a small, humble hut, close enough that I could be summoned in an emergency, but far enough that I could live as I chose, without the constant scrutiny of religious zealots.

Once I was established here, I did well. A little too well, to be honest. I had many visitors and callers, almost every day. The people here got sick often, and seemed to stay sick. I did what I could with my herbs and remedies, and yes, magic too, but my work never seemed to end. I had no day of rest. I was constantly in demand, and struggled to find time to explore the forest and replenish my stores. Catherine's youngest son Isaac—he was a difficult birth and a sickly babe, but had seemed to stabilize after a time. Here in Windsend, however, he could not seem to get well. None of my remedies—none of my magic—seemed to solve his breathing problems.

Nor was it only illness that plagued these people. Their livestock were weak. The herds thinned steadily over my first few years here, as cattle and pigs and chicken died in droves. The farmers tried everything—different feed, different pastures. They also asked for my help, although my expertise with animals is minimal. The crops were similarly weak, the harvests meager.

Did people look at me askance back then? Did they begin to grumble about my lack of faith, my refusal to participate in their perfect community? Perhaps. But it was no more than I was already used to. I am a witch, after all. Some mumbling about me is to be expected, especially from religious types. But I saw nothing to be concerned about.

I know how foolish that sounds, in retrospect. But I suppose we all have our blindness, do we not?

My true troubles in this town started with Joy Lockwood. You heard her testimony during the trial today. The first part of her story was true. She and her husband had been trying to conceive a child for some time. She came to me, hoping I could change that.

I did what I normally do. I examined her. I found nothing physically wrong, but I felt something was off when I was in her presence, regardless. It is like you said during your testimony, Master Kane. You do a job long enough and you develop an extra sense for things.

During my interview and examination of Joy, I looked into her future. I did so gently, probing in a way that she would not feel. And I should say, this form of augury is mild. If you think of the future as a meal to be eaten, this is not a tasting of the food, but rather, a sampling of the aromas in the kitchen. A hint of the flavors to come.

When I glanced into Joy's future, I experienced only darkness down the path of motherhood. It was a darkness I had seen before.

This is not a popular thing to say, but some women are better off not becoming mothers. They are not suited for it. They lack the disposition. The prevailing view is that, as soon as a woman knows she will be a mother, a change takes place within her heart. Sometimes that does happen. But sometimes it does not. And when these women—the ones who ought not be mothers—become mothers, they do not warm to the task. In the best cases, they go through the motions, feeding, cleaning, disciplining, rearing. These women raise their children, but they never truly love them.

That is in the best case. In the worst cases… I have seen women go to dark places, after the birth of a child.

I tried to communicate this to Goodwife Lockwood, as gently and with as much compassion as I could. But it is a truth no woman wants to hear. All our lives, it is beaten into us: we are born to be wives and mothers. And when either of those doors is closed to us, what purpose have we?

So she reacted as you might expect. She grew angry. She chastised me. Called me names. I did my best to weather the insults calmly, but, in the end, when she demanded I help despite my warnings, I did as she asked. Because I do not believe in manipulating the will of others, Master Kane.

I knew the right herbs and concoctions for her and her husband to drink. The Lockwoods were open to my help, and conceived quickly. I cared for Joy throughout her pregnancy, looking for any sign of the darkness I had seen before, but for the most part, Joy seemed a perfectly normal young woman, excited for the birth of her first child. She seemed so content that I began to doubt my own augury. Perhaps I had seen it wrong.

The baby, Zachariah, was a swift, easy delivery, especially by Windsend standards. He was fat and healthy, but from the start, an angry child. Some babies are like that. Some emerge into the world aglow, and ready to love. Others are outraged, as if a dirty trick has been played upon them.

Zachariah was one of these latter children. His rage was palpable as soon as he slipped from his mother and into my arms. I felt it, and Joy did as well. As she held the wailing newborn to her breast, she looked at me with grave concern and asked, "Should he be crying like this?"

I did my best to reassure her. I told her that being born is a big shock, and it might take some time for the child to calm. But in truth, I had a feeling about Zachariah, just like I had about Joy. Here was the darkness I had seen. I feel strange, saying that about an innocent newborn. But as you said—the expert learns to trust her feelings and instincts.

Over the next few months, every time I saw Joy Lockwood, she was cradling a screaming child. She brought the boy to me many times, sure the infant must be sick, or suffering some malady. Why else should he bawl and bawl so? But my examinations never revealed an underlying physical ailment. I could find nothing wrong with Zachariah, aside from his temperament. I told Joy this temperament was normal. That the best she could do was endure and wait. Most babies grow out of it.

I remember the look upon Joy's face when I told her this. She was a pale little thing, but looked especially wan that day, her skin like curdled milk, her hair a mess, barely contained by her coif. Dark bags hung beneath her wide brown eyes, and when she met my gaze, I felt she would happily murder me, if she could.

"There is nothing you can do?" she said.

"Babies have their own personalities, and souls. Some are born difficult. Some stay difficult, but most make peace with life in this world. Stay strong, and this will likely get better, in time."

She stared at me. Her mouth kept opening, as if she had a reply, but whatever thoughts occurred to her, she ultimately kept to herself. In the end, she left my hut without another word.

I heard about Zachariah's death like everyone else. Gossip spreads as quickly in Windsend as it does anywhere else. The details struck me as odd. The babe was found outside his crib, with a broken neck. It does happen, but not with babies so young. He would not have had the strength to topple himself yet.

Odder still was Joy's behavior. In the immediate aftermath of the death, she kept her head bowed in mourning and prayer, but I never saw her cry. I know that each person is different, and it is unrealistic to expect all of us to mourn in the same way. If not every woman is meant for motherhood, not every woman will gnash her teeth and rend her garments in grief.

But I noted it all the same. She did not cry at the funeral of the son she and her husband had prayed for. Nehemiah cried. He did so quietly, but his tears gave him away. But not Joy. She stared into the little grave, eyes clear.

Nor did the specter of mourning seem to hang over her for long. She kept her head bowed for about six weeks, speaking more softly than before, seeming like a woman in a dream. But after eight, I heard her laughing. Saw her smiling. She was behaving like her old self—the self I had not seen since before she gave birth.

Nor did she or Nehemiah ever return to me, to ask me to help them conceive again. Most parents who lose a child will try. Once, when Joy came to me for another ailment, I brought it up.

I did not do this because I wanted her to have another child. I stood by my original prognostication, and the evidence of my own eyes. No, I asked because I wanted to see her reaction. I wanted to confirm for myself what I had suspected for some time.

When I asked Joy, she lowered her head, looked into her lap, and then said, "You are kind to offer, Midwife Eastey. But after losing my Zachariah, I cannot bear to imagine losing another. I am not sure my heart could stand it."

Her eyes remained dry as she spoke. Her words sounded rehearsed. Perhaps they were, and for good reason. Friends and neighbors had likely been asking her this question for months. But even taking this into account, something about the way she behaved struck me as false. As I said before—instinct. Not proof.

There followed a silent moment, while she waited for me to offer comfort, the way most people would. When I did not, she eventually looked up at me. I caught curiosity in her gaze, and a hint of frustration. I was not performing my part in the little play into which she had conscripted me.

The nearly hidden frustration turned into alarm. She covered it quickly, looking down once more, but in that moment I knew I had been right: right that Joy should never have become a mother, but also right in my suspicion that she had killed Zachariah herself, and staged it to look like an accident.

Joy left without a word, and neither she nor her husband ever returned for my help again.

After that exchange, the whispers about me in Windsend only grew. Joy Lockwood poisoned the well. Audibly wondering whether a woman could use witchcraft to cause an accident like Zachariah's.

How she had learned, after the fact, that a baby should not have been able to fall out of its crib, so perhaps there was more at work here than some freak accident.

I spent a lot of time worrying what to do with my own knowledge about Joy. Should I try to tell someone what I had guessed? That a filicidist lived amongst us?

But I worried that no one would listen to me, if I voiced suspicions without proof. The only proof I could offer would require me to reveal my powers, which would not help anything.

So instead I kept my head down and did my work.

Life in the village remained difficult, and this last year was the most difficult of all. A thread of disease ran riot through the flesh of our livestock, decimating the animal population. The harvest was pitiful. Most of the crops died early, and what could be reaped was meager. The village was perched on the edge of a brutal winter, and illness was not limited to the animals. It seemed everyone I passed in the street was coughing and sallow, struggling just to accomplish their daily business.

I made medicines for the sick. I delivered babies. I worked hard, and constantly, and there were times I had to turn away paying customers because my stores were empty, my cupboards bare. I think that was part of how all of this snuck up on me. I was too busy to truly feel the shift in the village's sympathies.

There were town meetings to address the prospect of starvation. I attended, because, despite my independence, I was worried about my ability to survive. Eventually, Mayor Doggett announced that he and several men from the village would form a hunting party. They would go into the woods and seek game.

This seemed a sane and rational plan. The part I did not care for was the makeup of the hunting party itself. The chosen men were mostly older, prominent members of the community. I understood the choice, as a political maneuver: he was showing the village that its leaders were looking after the population. But was fat, jolly, loud

George Kidby a good choice for hunting deer? Would not George's young son, Roger, be a better option? But I said nothing. I knew my status here was unstable, but I did not give that knowledge enough concern.

So the men went out. They hunted. They found and killed a few deer. It was more than I expected from them, to be quite honest. The village began to hope.

Then came a day when the men left and did not return at the usual time. They were gone long enough that people began to worry.

There was talk of sending a search party, but the hunting party returned before anyone took action. They came long after sunset, when many people were already abed. They stumbled out of the trees, weary and bedraggled, but alive and intact. A couple of the men were missing their guns.

Something had clearly happened to them, but they claimed they could not remember what. Only that there must have been an accident. Afterwards, they sent younger men out in their stead.

The younger men struggled to bring back food regularly, the same as their elders had. They managed to kill just enough for the village to eke out a survival. We made it, but barely.

The deaths began in the spring. It started with Reynold Mayhew, the tanner. He was found in his tannery, ripped apart, his limbs scattered carelessly about. When they found his head, the eyes were bulging, the mouth open in a silent scream.

The other deaths followed quickly thereafter. One every week or two. At first the people blamed some wild beast. But as the deaths continued, without any mounting evidence of a creature in the woods—no fur, no paw prints, no sightings of strange wolves—the talk turned to speculation. If it was not some horrible creature of the woods committing these killings, who could it be?

It did not take long for suspicion to fall on me. I was questioned multiple times in those early days, but each time, they let me go. It wasn't until the death of Mayor Doggett that they finally locked me up.

And now here I sit, sharing a cell with you, Solomon Kane. And yes, you may well ask, why not use my gifts to escape and leave this village full of ignorant, hateful people?

That is the other part of it, you see. Ever since the night the hunting party returned late—the night the killings began—my gifts have been... unreliable. Sometimes they work, and sometimes they do not. Whatever those men did in those woods—whatever they unleashed upon this village—is affecting me too. Lately, my magic is... erratic. Spells only work about half the time. So yes, I could attempt to magic my way out of this cell, but there is no guarantee I will not be gunned down as soon as I step out of the jailhouse, or grabbed by an angry mob and hanged from the nearest tree, or worse.

I sit here and wait, because, for the time being, I have no choice.

20

Sleeping Arrangements

Sybil had stared into the middle distance while she told her tale, and Kane, sitting beside her at the far end of the cot, had done the same. When she fell silent, he remained silent as well, until Sybil turned to regard him. He looked back at her and saw the question implicit in her gaze. She wanted to know what he thought of her tale.

"So you believe," he said, "that the hunting party went to the woods, found that cave, investigated, and provoked those creatures? That the creatures caught the scents of these men, and targeted them for death?"

"I did not know about the creatures in the cave until you told of them," Sybil said. "I never entered the place myself. I only sought out its location. My senses—my intuition—told me it was a bad place. I retreated as quickly as I could. But after hearing your tale, I agree with your hypothesis. Aside from Esther Kidby and Zachariah, all the deaths in this village have been men who were in that hunting party. From that group, only Jeremiah Bartlett still lives."

"And these creatures are also what is blocking your magical abilities?" Kane asked.

Sybil sighed and rubbed her face with her hands. "I do not completely understand it, but my gifts began to fail at the same time that the hunt returned, confused, and missing guns. The two things are likely linked, although I know not how."

Kane nodded, considering all she had said. "Everything you have told me is true?"

"The only lie I ever told you was my original claim, that I am not a witch," Sybil said. "You sorted that quickly enough. Everything else I've said is true."

Kane leaned forward, resting his elbows on his knees. "When I was fighting those creatures in the corridor beneath the earth, I also used magic to escape. My staff. I called upon my blood brother, N'Longa, for help. He did help me, but… there was something disrupting our ability to communicate."

"An African blood brother? And one who is a practitioner of magic, no less?" Sybil said. "You are doomed, Solomon Kane."

"It is in God's hands now," Kane said.

"Then let us hope that God has a few surprises up His sleeve," Sybil said.

"Count upon it," Kane said. He stood and walked to a spot cater-corner to the cot. He unfastened his cloak and folded it over several times.

"What are you doing?" Sybil said.

"I am preparing a bed for myself," Kane said.

Then he attempted to kneel, but as he did, his knee gave a great twinge of pain. He gasped, surprised by the sensation, and lost his balance. He tumbled sideways into the bars of his cell, and grunted as his head collided with iron.

Kane was absent from the world for a moment, aware of it only in a dim, faraway way. He heard a voice speaking, but it sounded like a conversation overheard down a long corridor.

When he came back to himself, he found Sybil Eastey standing over him, her blue eyes bright with concern.

"What happened?" she said. "Are you hurt?"

"I am fine," Kane said. He sat up and leaned back against the bars of the cell. He took off his slouch hat and gently felt at the bruise forming on his skull.

Sybil bent over and batted his hands away. "Let me see."

Too dazed to argue, Kane let his hands drop to his lap. Sybil's fingers danced across his scalp and through his hair, probing at the sore spot, and Kane was briefly sorry he had not bathed recently. That her fingers had to touch his greasy, unwashed hair.

All of those regrets fled as her fingers pressed the place where he had hurt himself, and he shouted with pain.

"Be not a baby about this, Master Kane," Sybil said. Her voice was sharp, and lacking in whimsy. She sounded as authoritative as any physician. Kane bowed his head and allowed the midwife to continue her examination. When she finished with the top of his head, she took his chin in her hand and turned his face toward her own. She looked into his eyes.

"Your eyes seem fine," she said. "How is your vision? Blurring, or doubling?"

"No," Kane said.

She let go of his face and stood. "You have a fine lump forming atop your skull, but otherwise your head seems fine. What about that knee, though?"

Kane shrugged. "It is nothing. Worry yourself not."

She scoffed. "It is not nothing. The knee seemed to give out under you as you knelt."

She gave Kane a moment to answer and clarify. When he did not, she pressed again: "Does it trouble you often?"

"It comes and goes," Kane said. "Sometimes I can go months without discomfort. But lately, yes, it has been bad."

"It is not uncommon, in a man of your age," she said. "An

ailment in the joints, especially the knees. If I had access to my stores, or if my magic were reliable, I could give you some relief. But I suppose this is the Lord's Providence too? He wants you to suffer?"

"I do not claim to understand His reasoning or wisdom," Kane said. "But I trust him to show me the path." He picked up his folded cloak off the floor, and pushed it up against the wall, near the foot of the cot. He turned his body and lay back, resting his head upon the cloak.

Sybil's face wrenched up as if she meant to argue, but then softened. "We should not argue. Perhaps another time, when we are not both facing execution. But tell me truly: do you mean to sleep on this filthy floor?"

"I do," Kane said.

"You are facing trial, and an almost guaranteed guilty verdict, with execution," Sybil reminded him once more. "Will you not sleep in this cot with me?"

"I have already been chastised for speaking to Catherine Archer without her husband present," Kane said. "Incessantly, since my arrival in this village. I will not give the villagers more fodder for their inane gossip."

"As you will," Sybil said. "Though I know not how you can sleep at a time like this."

"I can always sleep," Kane said. He closed his eyes, only vaguely aware of the sound of Sybil's footsteps, as she returned to her own cot.

21

Skulls in the Stars

The air smelled of the English countryside in the fall, rich and earthy. Kane opened his eyes. He stood in a patch of soft earth, in a clearing just outside a swamp. The sky above was red with evening light as the sun set.

"Death! Death! There are skulls in the stars!"

The voice came from behind Kane and sent a frisson up his arms and across the back of his neck. It had been many years since he'd heard that voice.

He turned and found himself facing an ancient dead oak tree. There was a man tied to the trunk. At his feet lay a skeleton. The man was as gnarled and bent as the tree to which he was tied. His eyes were wide and staring. The eyes of a man from whom sanity has fled.

The man was Ezra the miser, who had lived in the swamp outside Torkertown. The skeleton at Ezra's feet was all that remained of Ezra's cousin, Gideon.

This was another old adventure, from the early days of Kane's life. Kane had been traveling outside of Torkertown when he had been confronted by a terrible apparition, which he had battled to a standstill. When bested, the apparition had told its sad tale to Kane: how it had once been a man named Gideon. How Ezra had murdered Gideon, and hidden the body in the dead tree.

Kane had wasted no time gathering the villagers, whom he had led to Ezra's hut. Together, Kane and his mob had taken Ezra prisoner, and tied him to this tree, in the hopes that Gideon's ghost would kill Ezra and at last find the peace denied him in life.

But how could this be? Kane had already lived this. He had heard Ezra's dying screams, as Gideon avenged himself upon the old miser. And yet here stood Ezra, fastened to the tree, staring at Kane with wide eyes.

As if sensing the direction of Kane's thoughts, Ezra's eyes widened further and his mouth broke into a wide grin. He cackled with glee as his dry lips broke and bled, and his foul breath assaulted Kane's nostrils from several feet away.

"Wonder how you came here, do you?" Ezra said. "Deny it not, Solomon Kane. I can see it in your eyes. You already saw to my death. Years ago, when you were a young man. And yet here you stand. Where you tied me to a tree, and forced me to face the ghost of my cousin Gideon. I begged you to kill me by other means—burning, hanging, shooting. I begged to be flayed alive, rather than face that spirit. You were deaf to my cries. The one mercy you granted was that I be tied 'not too tight.' So that I might wriggle free of my bonds, and face death free and on my feet, as a man should."

"I remember," Kane said. "I regret it not. And yet here I stand before you anew, as if none of that ever happened."

"Fret not, Master Kane," Ezra said. "You but dream. You lie sleeping on the floor of a cell in the jailhouse of Windsend—not too far from where you condemned me, as a matter of fact."

"What are you then?" Kane said.

"A mere dream," Ezra said. "A passing fancy of your sleeping mind. Or perhaps something more." At that, he broke into another round of laughter. Kane merely waited the laughter out.

"I would promise that all your questions will be answered soon," Ezra said. "But that would be a merciful lie, and what mercy do you deserve from me?"

"I did you no wrong, Ezra. I merely led you to your fate."

"Is it so easy for you to deal death to others?"

"Why am I here? What do you want?" Kane demanded.

"Look at the sky," Ezra said. "See how it changes?"

Kane glanced up and saw that, indeed, the firmament had been altered, the red tinge of oncoming sunset replaced with a strange blue glow. A glow that Kane recognized. He had seen it in the corridor below the forest floor outside of Windsend. It was the glow that preceded the arrival of the small, winged beasts that stank of Hell itself.

Kane turned his attention back to Ezra. "I asked you a question, murderer."

"You did," Ezra said, his tone light and lazy. "But what do you mean to do if I do not answer? Kill me again? You would like that, would you not? The chance to hurt someone, and feel justified, doing so?"

Kane lunged forward and grabbed Ezra's filthy shirtfront. "What mean you by that? Speak, damn you!"

In reply, Ezra laughed and laughed and laughed. He laughed until he was overtaken by a fit of coughing. Finally, he inhaled deeply, spat a wad of phlegm onto the front of Kane's tunic. Disgusted and startled, Kane struck the miser across the face.

Ezra favored Kane with his disgusting grin once more. "How does it feel to be on the other side? Locked up in a cell, waiting for a mob to enact their perverse idea of justice—their excuse for committing whatever cruelty strikes their fancy. You are not the only one having strange dreams these days. Facing the darkness in your heart. I came myself because I wanted to tell you that your death will spell the end for life as it has ever been in Windsend. You see that blue glow in the sky? It will soon seep from this dream into the waking world, and when that happens... it will be over for this ignorant, hateful people. They will get exactly what is coming to them. And once Windsend is finished..." He shrugged. "Who is to say what might follow?"

"You lie," Kane growled.

"Do I?" Ezra said. "Tell yourself so, if it comforts you. After all, you have spent your entire life telling yourself comforting lies. About your god, and his Providence. The innate goodness at the heart of creation. Enjoy your lies all the way to your grave, when you shall know no more. Your adventuring days are done, old man. Now wake up."

22

Justice

"Wake up! Wake up, for heaven's sake!"

The voice came in a harsh, ragged whisper, and was accompanied by a rough shake of the shoulder.

Kane opened his eyes to find Sybil crouched over him, her eyes wide with alarm. He was lying flat on his back in the cell in the Windsend jail, his cloak folded under his head for a pillow.

Still more asleep than awake, he grabbed Sybil's forearm to stop the shaking. He blinked a few times, trying to reclaim his hold on reality, the way one does after an especially vivid dream.

"What is wrong?" he asked. "What is happening?"

"The villagers have come," she said. She glanced from Kane's face to her hand on his shoulder, and to his own, which rested upon her arm. When she looked back at his face, he let go of her and sat up.

He became aware of raised voices outside the building. He heard Ezekiel the jailer, speaking in low, reasonable tones, but he could not make out the words. Kane had no difficulty hearing the reply, though. It was Enoch Archer, shouting at the top of his lungs.

"Ezekiel, another man has died!" Lockwood said. "Mayor Bartlett, slaughtered like a hog in his own bed. We cannot wait for the trial tomorrow! We must stop these killings now! Tonight!"

Kane looked away from the doorway and back toward Sybil. For the first time since he'd met her, she seemed genuinely afraid.

"Another death," Kane said.

"And the mob has come at last for its justice," Sybil said.

Kane grabbed the corner of the cot and hauled himself up. He intended to meet whatever happened next upon his feet. He would look it in the eye. He grunted with the effort.

"Your knee?" Sybil asked.

Kane glowered down at her, and almost snapped an ugly reply, but he caught himself. Instead, he gave her a quick nod before he staggered to the front of the cell, facing the front door. He took hold of the bars to support his weight. What he would not give for his staff just now.

The front door of the jail flew open with a bang, and Ezekiel stumbled over the doorstep and landed on his back. Enoch Archer and Nehemiah Lockwood stood framed in the doorway, flanked by a small army of villagers. The two men at the front of the mob had hard, bright eyes—not at all congruous with the grim determination Kane associated with the faces of executioners. Their faces were flush, as Esther Kidby's had been, not long before her death. They seemed delirious.

"Sybil Eastey," Enoch Archer intoned, his voice loud for the benefit of the mob. "You have killed for the last time. Solomon Kane—never again shall you abet an evildoer upon the face of this earth."

"I was under the impression," Kane said, "that my trial did

not begin until the morning. After Mistress Eastey's execution. I thought this village was one of law and order."

"That was before Mayor Bartlett died," Nehemiah Lockwood said. "We will not be mired in the niceties of procedure any longer."

Kane felt Sybil's eyes upon him and turned to see her looking at him with raised eyebrows.

"Are you going to let this happen?" she asked. "Will you call it Providence?"

Lockwood and Archer stepped around Ezekiel, who was climbing to his feet and leaning upon the desk near the door. He had clearly been hurt in the fall.

"I entreat you to see reason," he said. "What harm have I visited upon you? What evidence do you have that Sybil is the architect of these atrocities?"

"You ought to go now, Ezekiel," Archer said. "While we still allow it. Do not think we are blind. That we have not seen the way you look at this witch. You are besotted, and not thinking clearly. I will allow you to walk away if you leave now. If you persist in hindering us, I will not be held responsible for what happens to you."

Ezekiel stood with his back to Kane for a long time, staring at Enoch Archer. It was as though the portly jailer were waiting for Archer to break into a grin, and admit that he had spoken in jest.

"Go," Kane said. "You have done what you can, Ezekiel."

Ezekiel stood a moment longer, and Kane felt a swell of appreciation for this little man. He was not strong, or able. But he had a sense of right and wrong, and courage.

"Go," Kane repeated. "And thank you."

Ezekiel removed the keys from his belt, and handed them to Lockwood. Then he ducked his head and fled. The mob parted to allow him through, then quickly reformed, a wall of men in drab Puritan garb, glaring in at Kane from the night outside.

Kane had faced armies of vampires and demons in the darkest, strangest places on Earth. But never had he guessed that he could feel so great a chill facing a group of his own people.

Have I fallen so far from the path? Kane wondered. *That God would send Puritans to execute me?*

Go ahead, Monsieur Galahad, came the voice of Le Loup in his head. *Hurt them. Go free. You know it is what you want.*

Kane looked back to Sybil. She looked at him, pleading silently for him to do *something*.

"I cannot," Kane said softly, by way of apology. "I do not want to hurt the innocent."

Sybil made a sound of disgust. "If it is a choice between staying alive, and dying a martyr to righteousness, I will choose to live, every time."

And yet she did not resist as Lockwood unlocked their cell. She allowed Archer to shackle her once more. She said nothing, but held her head high, as she had during her trial during the day.

You are brave, Sybil Eastey, he thought. *I was glad to know you, even if our acquaintance is the cause of my death.*

Kane allowed himself to be shackled as well. Enoch Archer did the job, jostling Kane roughly as he performed the task. Kane could feel the blacksmith's anger and desire. It rolled off Enoch in hot waves, like a fever. Something was amiss here, a feeling in the air that seemed to go beyond the borders of ordinary mob bloodlust.

Sybil must have noticed something strange as well.

"Tell me, Master Lockwood," she said. "How do you feel? You look a bit ill."

In answer, Lockwood slapped her.

Kane lunged toward him, his automatic instinct to defend a helpless woman overcoming his desire to remain peaceful during this event. Enoch had a firm grip upon Kane's chains, however, and yanked them taut as Kane lunged. Kane stumbled and fell to his knees, crying out in pain as his right knee barked against the floor. Archer then struck Kane upon the head, in the exact spot where Kane had banged his skull against the cell bars earlier.

Kane hissed and clenched his eyes shut, suddenly awash in agony. It was impossible to think straight for a moment.

He lingered in that painful twilight state as they dragged him out of the jail and into the crisp chill of a late October night. Without his cloak, the air acted like a splash of water to the face. He came back to himself with a sharp intake of breath. His arms were pinioned by Enoch on his right, and, on his left a man Kane recognized but could not name. A few feet behind, Sybil was being similarly manhandled.

"You truly believe that hanging Sybil Eastey and myself will solve your problems," Kane said, trying for patience, "but I promise you that it will not. The killings will continue, and you will know you have spilled innocent blood."

"We shall see," Enoch said.

"And it is not as if we mean to hang you both," the other man said.

At that moment, they led Kane out from between two houses into a wider space at the edge of the village, and Kane understood what the stranger meant. There was, as Kane had suspected, a noose draped over a nearby tree branch. What he had not expected was what he saw in the center of the clearing: a wooden post driven into the earth, surrounded by large piles of firewood.

They meant to burn Sybil at the stake.

Kane had seen such violence before, done by both inquisitors and so-called witchfinders. He had heard the screams of the condemned as the flesh cooked off their bodies. It was a fate worse than death.

"Why, Enoch?" he asked.

"The dreams," grunted the man on Kane's left. "The voice in the dreams has promised us peace if we but burn the witch."

"What voice?" Kane demanded. "What dreams?" He remembered the voices in his own dreams these last several nights. The voices that hinted, threatened, and taunted him whenever he attempted rest. The dreams he had begun to have upon his first night in Windsend. Could it all be connected?

"Quiet, Roger," Enoch said. "He will twist what you say and show you false reason."

"I too have had dreams," Kane said. "I tell you, Enoch, something greater than myself or Sybil Eastey is at work here, and if you do not free us, it will only grow worse."

Enoch let go of Kane and struck him again. Again his blow landed atop the tender spot on Kane's skull, and Kane grunted. In that moment, all thought of Providence and destiny fled, replaced only with white-hot rage. He jerked his left arm free of Roger, and swung at Enoch. Dizzy and disoriented from Enoch's blow, however, his punch went wide, and as he stumbled forward to keep his balance, his right knee gave out once more and spilled him into the mud. His face squelched against soft, wet earth.

Enoch burst into an uncharacteristic gale of laughter. It was loud, brutish, and cruel. Kane lifted his head. Enoch's face was red with glee, but his eyes retained that strange, feverish light.

"I told Catherine not to write to you," Enoch said. "I told her to leave it be. But she did not listen. She never listens. She is a poor wife, and I know not why the Lord tests me so. We have been too free. Too liberal. But there has been a reckoning in this town, and in my home. Things will change now. God speaks to me in dreams, and has showed me the way. We must atone, or die." He looked at Roger. "Help me get him on his feet."

The two men dragged Kane out of the mud and stood him up. He grunted as he put weight upon his knees, and agony shot up his right leg as they dragged him toward the tree with the noose. Somewhere behind him, he heard Sybil shouting. She did not sound afraid, but angry. At least she would meet death well, with rage, rather than fear.

"Why are you smiling?" Enoch demanded. "Look you forward to meeting Satan and answering for your crimes?"

"'Thou sayest it,'" Kane said, quoting Christ.

Kane expected the reference to earn him another punch from Catherine's husband, but Enoch either chose to ignore it, or did not understand it.

"Hold him," Enoch said to Roger. Roger moved behind Kane and put his upper arms in an iron grip. Enoch unshackled Kane, and tied his hands behind his back with thick, bristly rope. The knots were so tight Kane immediately began to lose feeling in his fingers.

He glanced heavenward. Was this it? The end God had planned for him? How could it serve His purpose for Kane and Sybil to die, leaving these people so vulnerable?

His ruminations were interrupted as Enoch lowered the noose about Kane's neck. The rope scratched and dragged at his flesh, and he experienced a fresh discomfort as Enoch tightened the noose.

When Enoch finished, he said to Roger, "You can go, if you wish. I would finish Master Kane myself."

Roger departed without a word, his boots squelching away into the muddy night behind Kane. Enoch stared at Kane the whole time, saying nothing until the sound of the footsteps had faded.

"I warned you," he said, as he walked past Kane. "Did I not? I told you to leave this place. To let us tend our own garden. To let me lead my household, as is my God-given office. But you had to stay. You had to meddle. To stir unspoken longings in my wife's heart."

This last took Kane by complete surprise. "I know not—" he started to say, but his sentence ended with a gurgle as Enoch heaved at the rope. The noose yanked Kane into the air, and conscious thought left him. He became a creature of pure instinct. His hands, tied behind his back, struggled to work free of their binding, for the chance to pull at the noose, and loosen it enough for even a half-gasp of air. His legs kicked uselessly, looking for a purchase that would never come. His body heaved, struggling for air. The bruise on his skull continued to throb painfully.

Enoch continued to heave on the rope, pulling Kane higher and higher. The blacksmith shouted and raved, lecturing Kane as if Kane could hear or understand him. It was only background noise to Kane, as the world began to gray.

In the gray, his body's struggle lessened. No, that was not quite correct. The struggle continued. Kane felt his hands working, his legs kicking, but those things seemed to grow further away. Less a part of Kane's immediate experience. It almost seemed like something happening to someone else.

I am dying. The thought came to him consciously, calmly. This was not at all how he had pictured his own end, but what man could truly say he knew the moment and shape of his passing? God would do as He planned, and men could but wait and see.

I will meet Him soon, Kane thought. *And will learn my soul's fate.*

The peacefulness of the gray ended all at once. There was a lurch in his stomach, a sense of fast motion, and then a burst of pain as he hit something with all his weight. Suddenly he could breathe. The breaths were narrow and rasping, but they were there. The world faded back in. His face was in the mud. He rolled onto his back, and looked up into the tree where he had so recently been hanging.

Enoch, however, was nowhere to be seen. In the blacksmith's place stood Catherine. Kane blinked up at her, experiencing a moment of confusion. What had happened? She stood with hands wrapped around the handle of an axe, and strangely enough, she seemed to be holding the axe backwards, the blade pointed toward her body, and the poll red with blood.

Kane blinked a few more times, and tried to speak. What came out was a horrible fit of coughing. He sat up, and turned to one side to vomit onto the ground next to himself. It was as he turned that he saw the crumpled figure of Enoch Archer on the earth, and understood at last what had happened. Catherine had hit her husband with the blunt end of the axe.

Once Kane had finished vomiting, he looked up at Catherine. She stood above her husband, a shocked expression upon her face.

"Catherine?" Kane said.

She dropped the axe, and walked around behind Kane. He felt her sink to her knees behind him, and a moment later, her fingers were working at the knots Roger had tied about his wrists. Kane stared at Enoch while she worked. He appeared to be breathing. Alive, but unconscious. Catherine was lucky. Hitting a man on the head was tricky business, if you were not trying to kill him.

Behind Kane, Catherine growled with frustration more than once, but managed to make quick work of the knots. Feeling returned to Kane's hands, and he flexed his fingers, wincing at the pins and needles sensation as Catherine loosened and removed the noose from his neck. This hurt, too, but God above, how good it felt to breathe unencumbered.

"You defied your husband," Kane said. The words came sluggishly. His mind remained fuzzy, his thoughts hard to reach.

"I saved your life, and that is all you can think to say to me?" Catherine said. "Now up, on your feet, please—I need you to help save my friend, if there's anything left to save."

She pointed and Kane turned his head to see several men

gathered around a blazing bonfire. He stumbled to his feet, and hurried toward the conflagration. His mind and body still were not quite working in concert, each step was tricky, and any weight on his right knee hurt. He moved as quickly as he could, and Catherine kept pace with him, axe in hand. Whenever Kane glanced sideways at her, he experienced a moment of shock, for she looked not like his old friend, but like some savage warrior woman out of legend: her jaw set, her axe brandished smoothly and surely.

As Kane approached—as his mind cleared and his body returned to a semblance of its normal operation—he became aware of how strange the scene before him was. The men stood before the pyre, unmoving, their hands at their sides, and they did not stir as Catherine and Kane drew closer. It was as if they were in a trance. More worrisome, though, were the lack of cries from Sybil. She ought to be screaming right now. Instead, the night air was filled with susurration rattling the leaves; the licking of the flames; and the strangely heavy breathing of the men nearby. All innocuous sounds in and of themselves, but taken together, sickeningly ominous. Was she already dead? Was it already too late?

"Get water," Kane said to Catherine. "To douse the flames."

"I can but carry two buckets," Catherine said. "Will that be enough?"

"Find aid if you can," Kane said. "Look for Ezekiel, the jailer, and Roger Kidby. But do not tarry. Every second counts now."

He extended his hand toward her. She handed him the axe, and ran back toward the village. Kane turned his attention toward the men gathered around the stake. He braced himself for a fight, but it proved oddly easy to dispatch this small crowd. Moving as quietly as he could, he moved from man to man, striking each upon the head with the butt of the axe. Each crumpled at once, unconscious.

Task complete, Kane looked back to the pyre. He could make out Sybil's figure, a dark shape amid the bright light, but could make out no specific detail. He turned, meaning to head for the well in the center of town, but as he did so, he spotted three figures running in his direction. He recognized Catherine's silhouette. She moved quickly, despite the yoke over her shoulders, buckets balanced on both ends. The other silhouettes Kane had a harder time discerning until they were close enough to make out faces: Ezekiel the jailer and Roger Kidby.

Kane rushed forward to help Catherine with her burden. He pulled both buckets from her yoke, and handed one to her. He had just enough time to see (and feel) how full each bucket was. She had managed not to spill much on the trip.

Together, Kane and Catherine closed the distance to the fire, and tossed the contents of their buckets upon it. Roger and Ezekiel came a moment later, adding their buckets as well. Steam billowed and hissed as the water hit the fire, and Kane pulled Catherine back to save her from suffering burns of her own.

"Was it enough to douse the flames?" Catherine asked. "Should we get more?"

Kane looked into the steamy haze, trying to see if the flames still burned. He could see none, but that was not a sure thing, and embers had a way of re-sparking when least expected.

"I will fetch more water," Roger said. He picked up his yoke and buckets and ran back toward the village. Ezekiel hurried to follow. This left Kane and Catherine alone, waiting for the steam to finish billowing and part.

He put a hand on Catherine's shoulder and attempted to turn her toward him.

"Look away, Catherine," he said. "I would not have you see this."

She huffed impatiently and batted his hand away, keeping her eyes fixed on the pyre.

"Sybil!" she called. "Sybil, can you hear me?"

"Aye," came Sybil's voice, through the steam. "I hear you well, Catherine Archer."

The steam parted, and Kane saw Sybil. The stake to which she had been tied had burned away. So had the rope that had held Sybil to the stake. So had the clothes that had preserved her modesty.

Sybil Eastey stood atop a pile of unburnt wood, ashes, and embers, naked as the day she had been born.

23

Counsel

Kane was no stranger to the human form. In his travels, he had seen many nude men and women, young and old, healthy and unhealthy. Although he was not immune to the sight of a beautiful naked woman, he never dwelt on the image, never let it distract him from his purpose, whatever it might be. He usually averted his gaze, to allow the woman to preserve her modesty.

But he must have looked at Sybil longer than was permissible, because she smiled down at him and asked: "See you something you have not seen before, Master Kane?"

Kane lowered his gaze, his face flushed with a heat that had nothing to do with the remains of the fire before him.

"I am sorry," Kane said. "I was surprised—by your survival." That was true enough. "I have never seen a convicted witch survive a burning."

"Perhaps that is because you never saw an actual witch burned," Sybil said. "You only saw innocent women set ablaze." Kane kept his eyes on the ground, but heard her moving, picking her way among the wood and embers, back to the safety of the damp earth. "Catherine? I am cold. Have you anything I can wear?"

"Of course," Catherine said. She unfastened the cloak about her neck and wrapped it around Sybil. Only when Sybil's modesty was restored did Kane raise his head to look at her. She regarded him with half a smile. Such an odd woman. She had almost died, but looked at him as if they were sharing a private joke.

"How did you survive?" Kane said. "I thought your powers had abandoned you?"

"I never said that," Sybil said. "I said my powers were unreliable. That whatever is happening here is interfering with them." She shrugged. "When they set the flames at my feet, luck was on my side, I suppose. My gifts served me well. They could not save my clothes, but they did save my person, and that is good enough. Perhaps it is that Providence you put so much stock in?"

Kane opened his mouth, to chide her for joking about such things, but before he could formulate his reply, the sound of running footsteps alerted them to the arrival of other people. Kane, Catherine, and Sybil turned to see Roger and Ezekiel hurrying toward them, water buckets balanced across their shoulders. The contents sloshed and splashed with each footfall.

They slowed as they drew near, both men breathing hard. Ezekiel knelt, and Kane went to him, to help take the buckets off the fat man's yoke.

"We came..." Ezekiel gasped, "...as fast as we could."

As Kane unhooked each bucket from the yoke, he glanced inside. Both were less than a quarter full. The rest of the water had sloshed out during the trip.

"You did well," Kane lied. "But all is well. Sybil lives."

Roger frowned at Sybil. "I do not understand. You were set to the flame, and yet you live. How is that possible? Unless...

everything they said about you is true after all?" He started forward, toward Sybil, but Catherine stepped between the two.

"She is innocent," Catherine said. "A witch she may be, but she has committed no murders, young Roger Kidby." She stood her ground, despite the fact Roger was several inches taller than her, and far broader.

Roger looked at Kane. "Is that true, Master Kane?"

"Both things are true, young Kidby," Kane said.

"I thought witches were evil?" Roger said.

"That is what the frightened men who run your churches would have you believe," Sybil said. "There *are* evil witches. Twisted magic users who would harm this world and the people in it. Just as there are evil Christians, who murder and rape in the name of your god. But just as there are good Christians—like yourself, Catherine Archer, and Solomon Kane—there are witches who mean no harm. Who do their best to help their friends and neighbors. You cannot judge a human being by their religion, Roger Kidby. You must judge them by their actions. Their intent. Their character."

Roger nodded slowly as she spoke, as if all of this were getting through to him.

One of the felled men about the bonfire groaned. It would not be long before all of the crowd began stirring.

"We waste time here," Kane said. "We should go somewhere safe. We have decisions we must make."

"My house," Catherine said. "The children are asleep and Enoch will not bother us for some time, I hope."

The unlikely party retreated to the Archer residence. There, all five gathered near the hearth. Catherine warmed up leftover food for Sybil and Kane. Kane ate out of practicality, rather than hunger, but Sybil devoured a bowl of stew as if she had been starving.

"The men in the clearing will wake soon," Sybil said. "With splitting headaches and unsated bloodlust."

"There was something wrong with them," Kane said. "They behaved like men in a trance. Enoch was the only one who sounded like himself, and he seemed peculiar, too. Before they tried to hang me, they spoke of dreams."

Sybil nodded and put a hand in front of her full mouth to speak. "I heard that too," she said. "And I know what they meant. I have been plagued by strange dreams ever since I came to Windsend. At first, the dreams were intermittent—a nightmare once a month, perhaps—but since that hunting party went into the woods, I have been visited almost nightly."

"As have I," Catherine said.

"And I," Roger said.

"And I," Ezekiel said.

"And I," Kane said. "Every night since I arrived here. It is as if there is some power capable of reaching into my mind. This power twists my past. It makes old memories speak my worst thoughts and fears."

"Tonight," Roger said, "before Goodwife Archer came for my help, I slept. In my dreams I saw my mother. She said terrible things to me. She said…" He shook his head. "I will not repeat it here. But it cut me to the soul. I was relieved to be torn away from that dream."

"Something is closing in on this village," Kane said. "Something that guided those men to kill Sybil and myself."

"Why?" Ezekiel said.

"Perhaps because we are the only ones capable of combating it," Sybil said. "It turned the villagers' fear of me into hate, from there… We saw the same thing happen to Master Kane during my trial."

"What will we do?" Roger said.

Kane touched Roger on the shoulder. "You and Ezekiel will go to the jail, and get my weapons. And find me a sword, if there is a decent one in the village." He turned to Catherine. "You and Sybil will go to Sybil's hut. Find her decent clothes to wear, and then pack her a bag. Take only necessities. Money, a change of clothing, some food and herbs essential to your craft. Then head for Sutton Harbor. Find a ship there, one that might take you away from England. Go somewhere new. Someplace no one will know you. Take a new name. Start a new life. Be safe."

Sybil sat back, aghast. "You would have me abandon my home? My entire life and identity? And leave Windsend to its fate?"

"Yes," Kane said.

Sybil waited a moment, expecting some elaboration. None came. None was needed, Kane thought.

"And what do you mean to do, while I flee?" Sybil said.

"I mean to go to that cave and root out this evil, the way a barber surgeon might wrench out a rotten tooth."

She set down her stew bowl with a clatter on the table, much louder than necessary. "You have already tried that, and nearly died in the attempt."

"She brings up a good point," Catherine said.

Kane glowered at Catherine, but she did not quail under the gaze. "I was not properly informed or prepared. This time, knowing what I face—"

Sybil started shaking her head before he finished the sentence. "I have seen how your right knee troubles you. When it gives out, you cannot walk. You will not survive more than a few moments on your own, even armed with all your weapons and experience. Your body will betray you, and you will have died for nothing."

"Do you have a better plan?" Kane asked.

"I can make you a poultice that will alleviate the pain," Sybil said. "But its effects are limited. It will have to be reapplied often."

"Good," Kane said. "You can give me the supplies and show me how to apply it myself. I'll take it with me on the journey."

"You need my help if you mean to go into that cave," Sybil said. "You do not know what you will face. Even if you perfectly memorize the preparation and application of my poultice, there is no guarantee you will have the time, space, or wherewithal to help yourself every time you need it. I am going with you into the darkness."

Kane dropped his head. His face burned with shame. Would he really allow this woman to follow him into danger? As if he were a doddering old man with a nurse who followed him everywhere? Had he been reduced to this?

"Come, Ezekiel. Come, Roger," Catherine said. "Let us be about our errands."

The three exited the house, leaving Kane and Sybil alone in the kitchen. Kane waited until he could no longer hear their footsteps outside before he spoke.

"You said yourself that this evil is interfering with your gifts. It will be incredibly dangerous for you to go. To be closer to the source, you might lose their use entirely. You would be as helpless as anyone else."

"It will be very dangerous," Sybil agreed.

"Then why do you insist upon it?" Kane said. "The people of this village do not deserve your help or mercy."

"Do they deserve yours?" Sybil said. "They just tried to hang you."

"They were driven mad by that evil," Kane said. "It stoked their fears and twisted them against me."

"Is their hatred of me more natural, then?" Sybil said.

"In my experience? Yes," Kane said. "The ignorant fear things that fall outside their narrow, comfortable worldview."

She rolled her eyes. "I would still go with you on this expedition."

"Why?" Kane said. "Why cannot you just leave, as I bid?"

"Mistress Sybil? Master Kane?"

Kane turned, and started to see that he and Sybil were no longer alone in the kitchen. Young Isaac Archer stood in the doorway, rubbing sleep from his eyes.

"Young Master Isaac," Sybil said. "Why are you awake at this hour?" Her voice was soft and gentle, and Kane had his first inkling of what she must have been like as a midwife.

Isaac trudged into the room, coming more awake, and showing not the slightest bit of fear of Sybil. He stopped just short of her, and Sybil reached out to run a hand through the boy's dark hair.

"You ought to be asleep," she said.

"I heard voices," Isaac said. "Where are Mother and Father?"

"They are helping me with important business," Sybil said.

"What sort of business?" Isaac asked.

"Something that cannot wait until morning, I am afraid," Sybil said.

"Oh," Isaac said, turning to Kane. "And you, Master Kane? Are you helping Midwife Eastey as well?"

"Yes," Kane said.

"Can I help?" Isaac said. "I have a sword. Two, in fact. You have seen them, Master Kane."

"The best way you can help," Sybil said, "is to go back to bed, and stay there until either the sun rises, or your mother or father come to get you. Can you do that for me?"

Isaac frowned. This was not the answer he had hoped for.

"Master Kane taught me how to fight with a sword," he said.

"Did he now?" Sybil said. "Well then. I charge you with defending this house against any and all intruders. But to be your bravest, and fight your best, you need to get a good night's rest."

"But you and Master Kane are awake now," the boy said.

"Indeed," Sybil said. "But we are adults. Young boys—even the bravest and most noble—have to sleep. Do you see?"

The boy's frown deepened but he nodded his assent.

"That's a good lad," Sybil said. "Now—back to bed with you."

Isaac turned and left the room, and Sybil turned to look at Kane.

"That is why I will go with you, Solomon Kane," Sybil said. "The people of this village may not deserve my help, but Catherine and her children do. I will not abandon them to this. Do you understand?"

"I do," Kane said. "Better than you might suspect."

Catherine and Roger returned shortly, all bearing what they'd been asked to bring: Kane's weapons, cloak, and staff; and clothes and a traveling bag for Sybil, full of supplies.

"Where is Ezekiel?" Kane asked.

"He has fled the village," Roger said. "He sends his apologies, but he fears he will be killed for helping us."

"You see?" Kane said to Sybil. "At least Ezekiel shows good sense."

"Catherine," Sybil said. "Come help me dress and get me away from this deeply irritating man."

The two women disappeared into the master bedroom, leaving Kane and Roger alone in the kitchen. Kane stood, using the staff to help bear his weight. He donned gun belt, cloak, and hat, and tested the sword that Roger had brought him. It was a rapier, like the one Kane had lost. It was weighted differently but seemed a good enough weapon. Kane swung it through the air a few times before he noticed Roger staring at him.

"What is on your mind, Master Kidby?" Kane said, lowering the sword. He realized now that the young man carried a musket of his own, and a large kitchen knife.

"I would come with you," Roger said. "I would help you defeat this evil."

"No," Kane said simply.

Roger's mouth drew into an ugly line. "No?" he raised his voice almost shouting.

Kane put a finger to his lips. "Children are sleeping."

"These creatures killed my father," Roger said, lowering his voice to a heated whisper. "And his death surely hastened my mother's. I have nothing—no one—left." The truth of his words seemed to hit him as he spoke, and he put a hand to his chest, as though physically struck. "All of my life, I have wanted to be someone like you. To see the world, right wrongs. Help people. Protect the innocent. But the Lord set a different path before me. One of drudgery and toil, caring for an ailing mother, running an ailing business first in one village, and then another. And now that this evil has taken both my parents, you would have me remain behind while you risk injury and death to save my home? You dare refuse me? Who has more right than me to share in this venture?"

"This is not about rights," Kane said. "You are not a warrior. I cannot look out for your safety and my own. It is too dangerous. If you would help, then go prepare."

"Prepare for what?"

"What might happen if Sybil and I fail."

"The midwife can accompany you, but I cannot?"

Kane almost told Roger that he wasn't happy about this arrangement either but held his tongue.

"I do not know what will happen if Sybil and I fail," he said instead. "It may be that the villagers' dreams will lead them to more madness. To self-destruction. Or it may be that the creatures in the woods will come for everyone else. You must be prepared—either to lead an exodus to safety, or to make a last stand. The inn would make a good gathering place for survivors, would it not?"

Roger reluctantly acknowledged this truth.

"Then prepare it," Kane said. "Your neighbors may need you before the end."

24

Return to the Woods

Roger lingered with Kane a few moments longer, though he stopped arguing his case. Instead, the two men sat in silence and waited for the women to return, which happened quickly thereafter. Catherine carried Sybil's bag of supplies, and Sybil was now dressed in proper traveling attire, including a long red cloak wrapped about her shoulders. In a village full of Puritan blacks and whites, it was a shocking burst of color. No wonder the villagers had murmured behind her back.

"Shall we go?" Kane asked.

"Not just yet," Sybil said. "Catherine wants to give us food for the journey, and I need to see to your leg."

"Food?" Roger said. "How long do you expect to be gone?"

"We do not know," Sybil said. "We do not know how deep the corridor goes, and will not return until we can be sure the threat is ended. We may not need the food, but I would rather have it, just in case."

Roger nodded, and stood up from the table. "I can help. I work in the inn kitchen all the time."

"That would be welcome," Catherine said. "Thank you, Roger."

As they moved into the kitchen, Sybil turned her attention to Kane. "To the bedroom, Master Kane. We need to see to your leg."

Kane followed the midwife to Catherine and Enoch's bedroom. It was small and modestly furnished, the bed scarcely larger than the one Kane had at the Falling Star Inn.

Sybil shut the door behind them. "Take your breeches off," she said.

"Excuse me?" Kane said.

"I cannot treat your leg if I cannot see it," Sybil said. "You will have to remove your breeches. Oh, do not look so shocked. It is nothing I have not seen before. But if it helps, here." She turned her back to him. "Once they are off, sit on the bed with your legs fully extended."

Kane took off his boots, belt, socks, and breeches. He sat up on the side of the bed closest to the door, and briefly wondered if this were Enoch or Catherine's traditional sleeping spot. He tried not to think of what else the Archers had done in this bed, over the years. As he settled, he was at a loss for what to do with his hands. He settled for folding them in his lap.

"I am ready," Kane said.

Sybil turned back to face him. She made no remarks about his body, or his undergarments, but instead set her bag on the bed at Kane's feet, and bent over his legs, peering at them.

"The right knee is the trouble," she said. It was not a question.

"Yes," Kane said. His left knee looked much as it always had, but the right was red, and swollen as if there were a bird's egg just under the skin.

She nodded and made a sound. "That is not uncommon. It happens to many of us, as we get older. A pain or inflammation in the joints. Tell me if this hurts." She pressed gently on the bird's egg and Kane grimaced.

"It hurts," he said.

"You are lucky, Master Kane," she said. "Well, as lucky as one may be, when suffering this affliction. Despite your discomfort, the swelling could be worse. You appear to be in the early stages of this condition."

"You mean to say it will worsen?" Kane said.

"Not necessarily," Sybil said. "But there is a chance, yes."

"You cannot cure it?"

She shook her head. "There is no cure for this, but I can treat it with a simple mix of herbs. Wait here."

She disappeared for some time—for so long, in fact, that Kane began to drowse in the bed. His head drooped forward and his chin touched his chest. It was a mark of his exhaustion that he was able to drift this way. Normally, the impropriety of his presence in a married couple's bed would have kept him wide awake.

He was almost asleep by the time Sybil returned, and he snapped back to consciousness with some alarm as the bedroom door opened, and he found himself without a weapon in easy reach.

"Peace," she said, in a soothing voice. "It is only me."

She carried a folded cloth, which she knelt to apply to his knee. "This will feel uncomfortable for a moment. But it will help."

She pressed the cloth to his knee, and he sucked in air through his teeth at the pressure and pain. The sharp intake of breath brought with it a sweet aroma of the poultice.

The pressure lifted almost as soon as it began, and Sybil stood once more.

"Leave it there," she said. "It should only take a quarter hour or so to begin working."

"Every minute we spend here—" Kane started.

"Is a minute well-spent, if it saves us having to stop later," Sybil said.

"Can you not just wrap a bandage about the poultice and let us be on our way?" Kane asked.

"I need to make sure it works," Sybil said.

"You do not know if your own cures work?" Kane said.

"The human body is a strange and fickle thing," she said. "What works for one person may fail another. We must be sure this remedy affects your body the way we hope."

Kane sat back with a sigh. "Very well. I defer to you, Mistress Eastey."

"Very noble of you, Master Kane," she said. "I shall return in a few moments to check on you."

She left, and Kane dozed, startling awake once more upon the midwife's return.

"How do you feel?" she asked.

"Fine," Kane said.

"Let us put that to the test," she said, and without warning, she slapped his right knee. There was some discomfort, but it was mild, compared to what he had felt the last time she applied pressure to the spot.

"I believe it is working," Kane said.

"You are telling me the truth?" Sybil said. "You would not lie to me in order to speed us on our journey, would you? It is far better for us to solve the problem now, than to try to invent a new poultice once we're belowground."

"I tell you the truth," Kane said.

Sybil stared into his eyes a moment longer but seemed satisfied by what she saw. She wrapped a bandage tight about his knee.

"Ordinarily I would insist that you stay off it for at least a day, and then try going about with this wrapped about your knee," she said. "But as you continue to point out, time is not on our side."

Once the bandage was on, she left Kane to dress and arm himself. He stood gingerly, not sure what to expect as he put weight on the leg. It was not comfortable, exactly, but the discomfort was a ghost of the pain he had felt before. Whatever else she might be, Sybil Eastey was an excellent wise woman.

When he returned to the kitchen, he found Sybil, Roger, and Catherine packing dried fruit, bread, and cheese into a bag. He offered his assistance, but they were mostly finished, and quickly the party of four set out for the woods. Kane would have preferred that only he and Sybil go, but Roger insisted on accompanying them to the cave entrance.

"I need to see where you're going," he said. "So that if you do not return, I at least know where the danger originates."

Carrying lanterns, the four took the long way toward the woods, giving a wide berth to the site of their near-execution. Despite the circuitous path, they made good time and quickly found their way into the woods.

They smelled the entrance long before they saw it, a potpourri comprised of the sickly-sweet smell of rotting meat, and the rotten egg stench of brimstone. Kane heard a little squelching sound, and stopped walking to look at Roger.

"Oh," Roger said. He had stopped too, and now stared at the ground.

He had stepped onto the carcass of a bloodhound with long ears and floppy jowls, ripped apart, in a manner similar to the murders in town. Its eyes were open and intact, so the kill must be fresh. Roger's boot was lodged in the dog's middle, which appeared to have been torn open. Maggots writhed around his ankle.

Kane used his staff to hold the body in place so Roger could shake his foot free. He then watched the younger man set about removing the maggots from his boot. Kane was impressed; another man would have shuddered or complained, but Roger set about the task with grim workmanlike efficiency. Perhaps years of taking care of a sick woman had toughened him against physical unpleasantries. Or perhaps his gentleness hid a true strength, one belied by his gentle, boylike manner?

He might have made a fine adventurer or soldier, had he been given the chance, Kane thought.

"I think this is—or was—Max," Roger said, as he turned back to the group. "Jeremiah Bartlett's hunting dog. He got out about a week ago and wandered off. That was unlike him. He was usually so well-behaved. We all expected that he would be home any day…"

"Animals know things," Kane said. "You have seen it yourself, Master Kidby. Before a big storm, how do the horses behave?"

Roger nodded slowly, processing Kane's words. "He looks afraid. Confused. Like he does not understand what happened to him."

Catherine squeezed his arm. "There is nothing we can do for him now. And I would guess he is not to be the last dead animal we see on our path. Are you alright, Roger? You can turn back now, if you need to."

"No," Roger said, standing up straighter. "I will see this through."

They moved on, and Catherine's prediction proved true. The ground before them was soon littered with the corpses of dead animals. Some were well-rotted, and others were fresh.

"You would think animals would know to stay away from this area," Catherine said. "That they would fear it."

"Perhaps these creatures beguile them," Sybil said. "Enchant them so that they're tempted to wander out of safe places."

"Or the evil creatures grow bold," Kane said. "Venturing further out to hunt, and then bringing the kills close to their lair."

"They said that they sent men out to look into your story," Sybil said. "They said they could not find anything."

"They lied," Catherine spat. "They would not take into account any facts that did not fit the story they had already decided to believe."

"Perhaps," Kane said. "It is also possible that they were deceived. When the mob came for us tonight, they had a strange gleam in their eyes. They spoke of dreams. Promises that had been made."

"True," Sybil said. "I think the dreams of this village have been uneasy since its founding. There is more happening here than we know."

Everyone fell silent upon this pronouncement. They walked in silence for several moments more, navigating the increasingly dense and difficult forest, stepping carefully to avoid putting a foot into a dead animal. But even slowed in this fashion, they came to the cave mouth quickly.

It seemed to loom up out of the woods all at once, a gaping darkness that pulled all light, sound, and cheer into itself. The sky above was beginning to lighten with early morning light, but failed to properly penetrate down here.

Kane thought, not for the first time, about the dark places in this world. Places that were *wrong*. Where the Enemy held sway. This was certainly such a place.

As they approached, the hellish stink grew more pronounced. Catherine covered her mouth and nose with one hand, and Sybil gagged, almost losing the contents of her stomach.

"If the creatures down there do not kill us," Sybil said, "then surely this smell will."

The stench had definitely gotten worse since Kane's last visit. "I do not suppose you have an herbal remedy to rob us of our sense of smell for a time?" he said. When her face grew thoughtful, he waved a dismissive hand. "It was only a joke. We shall need all of our senses at their sharpest, even if we do not like what they report to us."

They paused at the cave mouth, and all four of the travelers faced one another.

"This is where we leave you," Kane said.

Catherine sighed. "It feels wrong, not to finish this with you."

"I agree," Roger said. He said it quietly, with his eyes cast down. Like someone who knows he has already lost an argument.

"You will only hinder us," Kane said. "Return and make ready to start the exodus. You may be the last sane people in Windsend. They will need you, if all goes ill."

Roger remained silent, but Catherine nodded. "Then go, old friend. Go do what you do best. Solve the problem. Save us all. And then—please—come back alive."

25

Back into the Dark

Kane and Sybil walked into the cave. Kane could feel Catherine and Roger watching, but he did not look back. It might be mistaken for weakness, a plea for assistance. He knew both were brave, and felt guilt about staying behind, regardless of the tasks Kane had set them.

Both Kane and Sybil carried lanterns, but down here their light seemed weak. As the cave entrance had seemed to swallow light, so did the cave itself. They could scarce see a foot past their lanterns. This slowed their progress considerably, as the brimstone smell grew ever stronger, assaulting their noses and starting a nausea deep in Kane's stomach.

All of this—the drawing of light, of sound, the great stillness all about—put Kane in mind of a living thing, a great beast drawing a breath as strong as a powerful wind, and pulling all things toward it. And if this cave was the beast, and it was inhaling, what happened when it finally exhaled?

Kane spent the first few minutes of the journey on his guard, listening hard for the chittering and clicking sounds that had prefaced the arrival of the monster horde before. But all he could hear for the time being were the sounds of himself and Sybil, making their way deeper into the cave—and those were muted, too.

Sybil made a small noise of surprise, and Kane glanced over at her. She was looking at the floor. Kane looked down as well, and saw that the natural rock of the cave had given way to the rough-hewn stone blocks.

Kane killed his lantern, and indicated that Sybil should do the same. As their fires dimmed and disappeared, the stone floor, ceiling, and walls began to glow, a strange, haunting blue. The witch made a small sound of delight.

"How remarkable," she murmured. She approached one wall, a hand extended to touch it.

"Sybil—" Kane began, but before he could say more, her palm was pressed flat against the rock.

Nothing terrible happened. She did not burst into flame, or melt, or scream. Instead, she ran her fingertips along the stone, studying the intricate carvings, which now glowed an eerie blue.

"It emits no heat," she said. "It feels as cold as any stone in the dark. And yet it gives off light. Have you ever seen anything like it?"

"No," Kane admitted. "Have you?"

"Why would I?" she said.

"You are a witch," Kane said.

She laughed, a bright, happy sound in this joyless place. "I am. But I have no coven. I meet few other practitioners of the craft. I have little opportunity to learn aught but what my own mother taught me. And she knew nothing of glowing stones, Master Kane." She traced her index finger along one of the whirling patterns, leaning forward as it spiraled toward the floor.

"I do not think this effect is natural to the stone," she said. "See how the pattern moves from block to block. It looks as though the stones were laid, and then carved and enchanted thus. All of this—the arrangement, the patterns, the light—speaks of intention. Higher thought and reasoning. It does not match with your previous reports of mindless killing monsters."

Kane nodded slowly. He had been so focused, until now, on proving Sybil's innocence that he had not given the stone corridor, or the question of its provenance, much thought.

"I think you are right," he said. "There is more here than I originally considered."

Sybil looked back at him over one shoulder and smiled. "See there? Are you not already glad you consented to my company?"

They stashed their lanterns in their bags and continued forward, finding their way by the eerie blue glow. The glow provided more light than the lanterns had, cutting the darkness like butter. Kane wondered how this was so.

The brimstone stench grew ever stronger, and soon, Kane and Sybil came upon a gruesome sight: a section of corridor littered with the fallen bodies of the creatures. It was not unlike the sight they had seen so recently on the forest floor, finding the remains of the beasts that had been killed and eaten, except all the creatures were of one kind: small and spindly, with large heads and eyes, and thin, leathery wings like bats. Their hands and feet ended in sharp talons.

Some of the corpses were stabbed and slashed, but others lay partially crushed, as if the very stones had been hauled out of the wall to flatten their victims.

Though the creatures were visible in the blue light, they were difficult to see. They seemed almost to merge into the walls and earth, and trying to get a good look at any of the bodies hurt Kane's eyes. It was as if he were trying to focus on two things at once—something near and something far—and the effort stretched his mind in an uncomfortable way.

This visual difficulty made it hard to keep a count of the

bodies, but Kane would have guessed that there were somewhere between forty and fifty, at least.

"This is your handiwork, I presume?" Sybil said, her words muffled behind the handkerchief held to her mouth.

"Aye," Kane said.

Sybil knelt next to one of the bodies. One hand pressing the handkerchief to her mouth, she used her free hand to examine the creature, touching its skin, running her fingertips along the repulsive wings. She showed no shyness at the task, no apparent disgust. She was as dispassionate as any physician conducting an autopsy.

"So strange," Sybil said. "I have never heard of anything quite like this. If you live in the countryside, and spend time among villagers, you hear all sorts of stories about the ancient little people with whom we supposedly share this land. The fae. And these creatures are certainly smaller than us, but..."

"...But the fae would not interfere with your powers," Kane said.

"That is my assumption as well," Sybil said. "Whatever else the fae may be, I assume they are native to England. That they are as natural as any fox, or deer. I do not believe these creatures are those. I think they are something else entirely." She lifted and then dropped the dead creature's arm, then surveyed the rest of the bodies strewn about.

"You fought bravely," she said. "To stand against so many."

"I was nearly overrun," Kane said. "It was magic that saved my life. My staff."

"I remember you saying something about this earlier," Sybil said. "Have you ever called upon your friend—this N'Longa—this way in the past?"

"No," Kane said. "In the past, I could hold the staff while sleeping, and communicate with him over vast distances. This was my first time attempting to call upon him while awake.

Desperation drove me to such a measure, and given the difficulty of that first attempt, I would not count on being able to repeat the act. We should rely only upon our own strength, for the time being."

"That is a sobering thought," Sybil said. "But not a surprising one."

They pressed on. For a while, the bodies remained thick as carpet upon the corridor floor, but eventually they began to thin, and disappeared altogether, revealing the bare stone.

The corridor seemed to stretch on forever. The only thing that seemed to change were the designs etched into the stone. The etchings, which now glowed bright blue, put Kane in mind of the night sky. Walking down this corridor felt like walking among stars. It was a dark wonder, perhaps, but a wonder all the same.

Through it all, Kane continued to listen for the sounds of approaching enemies. But as before, the only sounds he discerned were the ones he and Sybil made. Their breathing, their footsteps, oddly muted in this eldritch space. They seemed to be alone. Had Kane killed the entire population of these creatures on his previous visit? No, that could not be right. There had been a death in the village last night, while Kane and Sybil shared a cell.

After some time, Sybil stopped and examined the walls, ceiling, and floor again.

"What is it?" Kane said.

"The markings," Sybil said. "They have changed." She pointed to a design. "Can you see it?"

Kane squinted at the spot where she pointed. "They have seemed ever-changing since we first saw them, have they not?"

"Yes and no," Sybil said. "It is almost as if..." She paused and sighed, frowning in thought. "When the corridor began, the designs were more decorative. Random. Things the designers probably found artistically pleasing. But I am beginning to see... patterns. Repeating symbols. Like this." She tapped the spot she was studying. "And this." She tapped another. "It is almost like a primitive glyph. I think there might be some sort of language here."

"Can you read it?" Kane said.

She shook her head. "It looks like nothing I have seen before. But it gives off the... sense of meaning, if that makes sense. It is not unlike overhearing people converse in another room. You cannot necessarily make out individual words, but you pick up on cadence, tone, and the like." She lingered over the glyphs a moment longer, then pulled herself away with obvious effort, shaking her head as if to clear it.

Together, they moved on.

They continued down the corridor for what felt like several hours, if Kane's sense of time might be trusted in this unnatural place. They met no one, and heard nothing. The corridor continued unchanged, unbroken by benches for rest. Whatever had traversed this corridor in the past had done so without relief.

The lack of sounds—of enemies to fight—drove Kane to greater worry and tension. Where were the damnable beasts?

At last, the seemingly-eternal corridor ended at a stone wall with a small doorway cut into its center. Through the doorway, Kane could see a stairway, winding down. This doorway was too narrow for Sybil and Kane to walk through side-by-side.

Kane stepped forward, meaning to go first, but Sybil caught him by the arm and stopped him.

"How fares your knee?" she asked.

"Fine," he said, truthfully. "Your poultice does its job well."

Still she did not let go. "If that staircase goes on as long as this corridor, the poultice will wear off before we reach the bottom. I will change it now."

It was not a question, or a request, but a declaration. Kane could see from her expression that she would brook no argument. He folded his cloak upon the stone floor, and undressed from the waist down, removing his boots, socks, breeches, and weapon belts. He pulled one of the pistols free, so he had a weapon at hand, at least.

He shivered as he sat upon the cloak. The air had grown noticeably colder since they had entered this place.

"I am ready," he said.

Sybil's back remained to him for a moment. He heard her strike flint against steel, and the spark as flame kindled. Abruptly, the blue glow of the corridor vanished, replaced by an almost total darkness, broken only by the feeble orange glow of a lantern.

"Only for a moment," Sybil said, sensing Kane's complaint. She turned and knelt beside him. "So I can get a better look at your knee. The blue light might hide things from me."

She set her bag on the ground beside her, and removed the items she needed for the poultice, laying them out.

Kane looked away as she began to work, focusing on the dark to his left. Although he was used to seeing others in various states of undress, he was not familiar with the sensation of being observed by others. And although Sybil had already seen him unclothed once before, it still felt strange and incorrect now.

She did not taunt or tease, however. She simply went about her work, unwrapping the bandage around Kane's leg and removing the first poultice.

"Oh yes," she said. "That looks much better. Do you see?"

At her prompting, Kane turned his head to look. He leaned forward, taking his back off the corridor wall, to get as close as he could without raising the knee. It remained red, but the swelling had abated considerably, and the pain was gone altogether.

"That is remarkable," Kane said. "Truly. You have worked magic."

"It is—" Sybil said, but she stopped as Kane turned his head up to look her in the eye.

Their faces hung inches apart, their noses almost touching. Her mouth hung slightly open, sentence unfinished, and her blue eyes seemed bright in this pathetic light.

"It is what?" Kane said.

"It..." she blinked slowly, like one in a trance. "It is no magic. Simply medicine."

"Well," he said. "Whatever you are doing, it is working marvelously, Mistress Eastey."

She bent her head to her work. "Thank you, Master Kane. But you must keep in mind that there are limits to what even I may do, without my gifts. The knee may feel normal now, but if you put too much strain upon it, you may trigger discomfort, or pain. You may lose the ability to put weight on it. In fact, we ought to have rested before now, come to think of it."

26

The Descent

Once the new poultice was applied and Kane had dressed once more, Sybil re-packed her supplies and doused the lantern. The blue light shone forth around them once more, and Kane led the way through the narrow doorway and started down the winding stairs on the other side.

The staircase proved to be a long journey. As before, however, they met no one along the way. Nor could Kane hear any signs of life besides their own. It was quiet as a tomb. Once, when Kane glanced back over his shoulder to check on Sybil, he saw that she no longer held the handkerchief to her face. He took a deep breath and realized that he no longer smelled brimstone. Had the smell truly vanished? Or had his nose just grown accustomed to it?

The air around them grew cooler with each step they took. It had been chilly up above, on the surface, but they were passing the threshold into genuine cold now. It bit at Kane's exposed face, ears, and neck, and he drew his cloak tighter about his body.

The stairs went on and on, keeping to their tight, spiral pattern. It had a somewhat hypnotic effect, and Kane fought to keep himself from slipping into a lull. He moved slowly, testing each step before putting his full weight upon it. The last thing he needed was to trigger a trap, or lose his footing and break his neck tumbling down these steps.

Luckily, the stairs did not continue quite so far as the corridor had seemed to, and ended in a small chamber that led out into a wider one. Kane could not quite make out what was in the wider space; only blue surfaces shining in the near distance. He wanted to press on and continue exploring. It was the wanderlust that had set his heart aflame as a boy, drawing him ever further into the depths and darkness, eager to see what he might find.

Instead he paused to look back at Sybil: "We should stop for the night," he said.

"Can you say whether it *is* day or night up above?" Sybil asked. "I cannot."

"No," Kane said. "But regardless, we need rest. This space is defendable."

She lowered her bag to the floor. "I could use some sleep."

Kane picked a narrow space between the last few stairs and the wall of the small chamber. If he slept with his head against the wall here, he would be able to hear anything coming down the stairs from above, and see anything approaching the doorway from without. He sank to the floor, biting back a sigh. He set his hat against the wall, meaning to use it as a pillow. He would have liked to use his cloak, but that would have to serve as his blanket

As if reading Kane's mind, Sybil said, "I am grateful not to have been burnt alive. But I could do with a bit of that fire just now."

Kane frowned. "That is not an appropriate thing to joke about."

"You deal with the darkness of this world your way, Solomon Kane, and I shall do it in mine."

Kane lay down, only the thin fabric of his hat between himself and the stone. The floor was hard and cold, and he shivered within his cloak. He pulled one of his pistols from his belt to hold while he slept, and closed his eyes.

He startled when, a few seconds later, something dropped onto the floor beside him. He opened his eyes. It was Sybil's bag, up against the wall like his hat. She squatted beside it, fluffing it as if it were a pillow.

"What are you doing?" Kane said.

"I am getting ready to sleep," Sybil said. "The same as you."

"We should take it in shifts," Kane said. "And I am already in this spot. It would not be proper for you to be so close."

"I trust us both to wake if the slightest sound occurs," Sybil said. "But am I so repulsive that you would banish me?"

"It is not a matter of repulsion. It is one of propriety."

"There is no one here to see but you and me," Sybil said. "I will not tell if you do not."

"The Lord sees all," Kane said.

She sighed, dropped her head, closed her eyes, and pinched the bridge of her nose between thumb and forefinger.

"I am not attempting to seduce you," she said. "I am trying to survive the night. It is cold. Since we cannot have a fire, we must conserve warmth however we can."

"Very well," he said.

"Thank you," she said, with a hint of dry irony, "for seeing reason."

She lay down beside him, and he turned onto his right side, allowing her to press her body back into his own. He lay at first with his left arm—the one holding the gun—flat against his side. But this felt uncomfortable, so he draped the arm around Sybil, resting the gun against the floor before her. Somehow the presence of the pistol in his hand made all of this feel more proper. He could not actually *touch* Sybil this way.

Still, he could not help but be aware of her body pressed up against his. Her soft, curved frame, exchanging heat with his taller, lankier body. And the smell of her, which had been easy to miss amid the brimstone stink, became clear when this close. She smelled like rose petals. He allowed himself to relax and began to drift. He was almost asleep when Sybil spoke.

"You do not try to take advantage," she said.

"I am a Puritan," Kane said.

"Puritans are still men," she said. "Believe me, I feel the gazes of the men in that village. Before their thoughts turned to murder, they had other things in mind. If any were offered a chance to take your place now, I doubt they would be as chivalrous as you."

Kane came all the way awake. "If you are going to put temptation in my path, you can sleep on the other side of the chamber," he growled.

"I meant no offense," Sybil said. "I only mean that you are strange, as men go. Even Puritan men. Perhaps it is mere Providence. God did not mean for you to want me, and so you do not want me."

She fell silent, but now Kane's mind, fully awake, was working.

"You are a strange woman, Sybil Eastey," he said. "You twist my meanings. You joke. You make me sound less of a man, for my refusal to seduce you. You make my belief in Providence sound silly and childlike. But there is more to my faith than a simple belief that God will save me when I am in peril. I believe that God has a plan, and His hand is at work in the world, and our lives. Just because I cannot understand it—just because it sometimes hurts to live through the machinations of the plan—does not mean it does not exist. Suffering may be the surest proof we have that God is at work in the world. His plan is vast and far beyond man's ability to understand. So if I live? Yes, that is Providence. But if I die? That is Providence too. I trust my God, and while I do my best to survive and help others do the same, I find little use in worrying about whether or not I enjoy my part in this grand scheme. And yes, I am keenly aware that I am a man and you are a woman. But I chose a different path, and no one will make me stray from it, not even—" He stopped himself there, surprised by his own words.

"Not even what?" Sybil asked.

"Not even you," Kane said.

"Why would I be the exception?" Sybil said.

"I do not know," Kane admitted.

He waited a long time for Sybil's retort. When one did not come, he cleared his throat.

"Are you not going to tease me?" he asked.

"I am thinking," Sybil said.

"Thinking what?"

"A woman offers you her body, and you respond with a theological argument," she said, and now he heard the smile in her voice. "There is more to you than I expect. You are not like the Puritans of Windsend. They are plodding, narrow-minded, and cruel. They use their faith as a cudgel. You do not. I believe that good and bad things happen, and most of it means nothing. I believe that people with good intentions often create bad results, and occasionally those with ill will manage to do some good. None of it *means* anything, except what it means to the people living through it. But despite that, I find something beautiful in your faith. It leads you to try to do good in the world. To help, where you may. To fight, when you must. It makes you strong. I do not share it, but I would not change it."

You like to hurt people, yes? Le Loup asked in Kane's mind. *Are you so sure that your faith is so pure, Monsieur Galahad?*

"I am not so sure of myself, or my faith lately," Kane admitted. "I do my best, but I am… shaken."

Sybil reached back and patted one of Kane's cheeks. "Sleep well, Solomon Kane. I hope both our dreams are more pleasant than they have been, of late."

27

Laughter of the Dead

Kane stood in the dark. No, not quite. He was surrounded by an eerie blue glow. It seemed to come from no particular direction, but from all around him at once.

As his eyes adjusted, he realized that he stood in a great stone chamber. That the blue glow seemed to come from the ceiling above, the walls on each side, and the floor below, creating this effect. He also discerned that he was not alone in this space. There were great hulking shapes in the distance—structures of some kind, although he could not quite make out their outlines.

A laughter began, behind Kane, and to the left. He recognized the sound, having heard it so recently, and spun to face its owner. He experienced a moment of confusion, for he had expected to see a man standing before him. Instead, he found himself facing a crumpled figure upon the ground, hard to see in this semi-darkness.

"Good morrow, Master Kane," the figure said.

Kane approached. It was George Kidby, who had, until recently, run the Falling Star Inn. He lay upon the ground in pieces, covered in his own blood and gore, torn apart. And yet, despite his dismemberment, he lay here, looking up at Kane and laughing.

"What dark miracle is this?" Kane said. "You are dead, George Kidby. What message do you come here to impart?"

Kidby seemed tickled by the question, and his laughter increased in volume and intensity. Kane waited, glowering down at the disemboweled and dismembered man. Kidby laughed harder and harder. The laughter took on a hard edge, verging on hysteria. Kane was tempted to slap Kidby, to draw the innkeeper back to his sense, but also did not want to lay hands on this vile abomination. Instead he stood and waited. Let this dark vision speak its piece.

"You can think you make a thing make sense, just because you ask a few silly questions," Kidby said, gasping for breath. "As if the great mysteries are yours for the interrogation."

"What do you want from me?" Kane said. "Why are you here?"

"Why are *you* here?" Kidby asked.

"I ..." Kane closed his eyes. His mind felt strange and foggy. As if his thoughts were not truly his own. "I do not know."

More laughter came from behind. Kane turned once more, and found himself facing a body upon the ground. This one was Enoch Archer, Catherine's husband. Blood ran from his scalp and down his face in thick rivulets.

"Why continue on?" Enoch asked. "Pressing forward, trying to do good. Do you not see it is pointless? We are all bound for the grave. We are all dead here."

"You are not dead," Kane said. "You were yet breathing when I last saw you."

"But you did not minister to my wounds," Enoch said. "I lost too much blood. The blow scrambled my brains. I slipped away while you were eating my wife's stew and lying half-nude with that witch in my own bed."

Enoch's eyes had that same manic glean they had shown earlier, when he had tried to hang Kane. The look of madness.

"Fear not for me, wanderer," Enoch said. "I am dead. But soon, we will all be dead, and down here, beneath the earth in Windsend. When you fail we will be overrun. It is only a matter of time. You only delay the inevitable. Do you not see?"

"I do not believe you," Kane said.

"Believe whatever you like," Enoch said. "Truth cares little for your beliefs."

Kane wondered if the blacksmith were truly dead. It was not impossible, but why should he trust this malevolence?

Behind Kane, laughter began again. Kane spun to see George Kidby. The innkeeper had sat himself up and was attempting to reattach his severed arm, holding it to his bloody stump of a shoulder. His face was scrunched up and tears streamed down his face as he laughed hysterically. The sound hurt Kane's ears, seeming to stretch something in his mind not meant for stretching.

"What are you doing?" Kane asked.

"You... You should have fled," Kidby said, barely squeezing out the words between gales of laughter. "You should have taken the witch and gone. Instead, you have come into our lair. And you will have to face us."

Us? Kane wondered at that. "Who are you?"

"Your days as a knight errant are at an end." This came from Enoch, and when Kane turned, he saw the blacksmith sitting up now, too, grinning. "You made a mistake, coming to this village. Meddling in affairs that did not concern you. And now you will pay, and meet your maker. How will you be judged, I wonder? Interfering in my marriage. Defending a servant of Satan against a village of your fellow God-fearing Puritans. And who knows what else you have done, that I cannot know? Oh, how I wish I could watch you try to justify yourself to your god."

Kane became aware of another sound in the distance. He realized that he had actually been hearing it for some time now. It had begun quietly, while he spoke to Kidby and Archer, but had grown steadily, like a storm blowing in from afar, until it was overhead and so loud one could hear nothing else: a mass of clicking sounds, as of claws scraping on stone, and the soft susurration of thousands upon thousands of wings brushing against one another.

Kane looked past Archer, peering into the semi-dark of the great chamber. A legion of wiry little creatures flowed toward him in a great wave. Kane reached for his rapier and pistol, meaning to at least make a final stand—but where his hands would normally close about his weapons, they grasped only at empty air. He glanced down, dumbfounded, to find himself weaponless.

Enoch Archer's laughter joined that of George Kidby, the sounds barely audible above the approaching horde.

"Enjoy Hell, Solomon Kane!" he shouted.

He barely had time to get the words out before the wave crashed over them all.

28

At the Bottom of the World

Kane opened his eyes in the dark. There was a hand upon his shoulder, and he swung his gun hand toward the owner.

The hand disappeared from his shoulder, and a voice shouted: "Peace! Peace! All is well! You were dreaming, Master Kane!"

Kane looked about, his heard pounding as he tried to see the speaker—to see anything at all. Where was he? He was upon a stone floor, in a dark place. The person speaking to him had been a woman. A woman. Sybil Eastey. They were below Windsend, at the base of the winding stair.

"Will you please stop pointing that gun at me?" Sybil said.

Kane obliged, uncocking the weapon and letting it fall into his lap. He rubbed his face with his free hand, as his eyes adjusted to this dim light, and Sybil took shape before him. She was standing already, holding her bag.

"I dreamt," he said.

"I know," Sybil said.

"The dream was… unnerving."

"As were my own," she said. "As have been all my dreams lately."

Kane nodded slowly. “It is like a coordinated assault by an enemy army,” he said. “It explains why your neighbors have been behaving so poorly.”

Sybil scoffed. “They have always behaved badly.”

“But they have been worse than usual of late, have they not?”

“They have,” she conceded. “It was only recently, for example, that they imprisoned me and attempted to murder me.”

“There is something behind these dreams. Some animating presence, lurking unseen, using my own memories as puppets. Each of these dreams so far has been an attempt to scare me off. To make me leave Windsend. And this latest one was gloating. Threatening me with an ignominious death, and my damnation to Hell.”

“That sounds terrible,” Sybil said.

“What about you?” Kane asked. “What are your dreams like?”

“My dreams used to be pleasant things, you know. In them, I was a cosmic traveler. I swam the space between worlds, looking in here and there, but always on the move. It was as if I lived an entirely different life, one I resumed whenever I slept. Now? It is as if something is clawing at my mind, trying to see inside. When it cannot, it resorts to tantrums, attempting to frighten me with terrible images and sounds. To torture me into compliance. It shows me men from my past, threatening me with torture. Battery. Rape. Gloating about their power over my body.”

“And your latest dream,” Kane said. “It was more vivid than the others?”

“It was,” she said. “We draw near the source of this animating presence, do we not?”

“I think we do,” Kane said. “And I think we have reason to feel encouraged.”

“Oh?” Sybil said. “Why is that?”

“It resorts to threats and bluster,” Kane said. “It fears us.”

"Why would it fear us?" Sybil said. "If it leads the creatures you saw before, then it has an army to easily overwhelm us. What weapon do we have, that it should cower?"

Kane shrugged. "I do not know."

They ate a spare breakfast of bread and cheese, and split a single apple. The bread was tough, and the cheese passable, but the apple was sweet and crunchy, and restored Kane's spirits a little. It was hard to feel melancholy when eating fresh food, grown from God's earth. When they had finished, Sybil put the core into her supply bag. She did not say why, but Kane assumed it might have something to do with her potions and concoctions.

Fed, they gathered their meager belongings, and together they passed through the narrow doorway at the foot of the stairs.

Sybil gasped as they did, and Kane turned to her, hand going toward his sword. She put a hand on his arm to still him.

"I knew we were going into a larger chamber," she said. "But I had no idea it would be like… this."

After the endless hours of low-ceilinged hallways, and the narrow, winding stairs, they found themselves in a space so large that, if not for the blue glow from the stone walls and the ceiling, Kane would not have been able to discern its boundaries. The patterns etched above looked almost like heavenly bodies, constellations of man-made stars. The lights on the walls were like the lights of small villages, seen from a great distance at night.

"This is no natural cavern," Kane said. "It must have been carved from the earth and fortified with stone."

Sybil made a small, thoughtful sound. "I wonder how the builders achieved it. How did they place the stones so high above? It goes beyond any magic I know."

"Perhaps they used mechanical means," Kane said. "Much as men built the cathedrals of Europe. Or the pyramids in Egypt."

"This space is older than any structure on this continent," Sybil said.

"How do you know?"

"I do not have any proof," Sybil said. "It is just a feeling. But a true one, I think."

As they moved forward into the darkness, a great structure seemed to emerge and take shape before them, one commensurate in size with the space around it. It was larger than any castle, fortress, cathedral, or pyramid Kane had ever seen. Aboveground, its size would have blotted out the sun. Kane thought of the Tower of Babel. God had punished the arrogance of mankind for that attempt. Were the builders of this temple similarly struck down? Or had they been under the protection of something darker?

The structure seemed to be built of the same stone as everything else that Kane and Sybil had seen so far—rough-hewn and of a light gray color, glowing blue from the etchings upon it. The shape was more like a towering cathedral than a pyramid or the temples Kane had seen on his journeys.

"This should be impossible," Kane said. "As you said, this place feels ancient. Older than any man-made structure I have seen in any of my travels. The architecture appears far more advanced than any ruins here in England. More advanced than any modern structure I have seen, either."

"And yet here it is," Sybil said.

"Here it is," Kane agreed.

Kane stepped forward, but Sybil, whose hand remained upon his arm, squeezed to hold him back.

"Before we go further," she said. "No matter what we find. I am glad we saw this dark wonder together, Solomon Kane."

"I have been traveling most of my life," Kane said. "But one revelation never grows stale: the world is larger and stranger than I can ever know."

She let go of his arm. "Let us go, and see what we may find, here at the bottom of the world."

Kane's sense of wonder—the rush he felt whenever he saw something no one would believe, were he to share the tale—only lasted a few minutes, at least in its purest form. For those few sweet moments, he and Sybil approached the ancient temple like pilgrims in an alien world.

Then they came upon the first human remains, and the purity was tarnished.

Kane knelt down, wanting a better look. *Body* was too generous a word for this. There was no muscle, flesh, or even frayed and aging fabric to be seen. It was a bare skeleton, lying on its back, arms splayed wide, and staring with sightless eyes at the eerie ceiling above.

Sybil knelt beside him.

"Well, we know at least one human being came down this way before us," Sybil said.

"It is impossible to know how long ago he was here," Kane said.

"She," Sybil said.

Kane raised his eyebrows. "What makes you say so?"

She pointed. "See the pelvis? It's lower and wider in women."

"I wish we could speak with her," Kane said. "I do not suppose you have spells that let you commune with the dead?"

"I am no necromancer," Sybil said. "I try to stay in tune with nature, and necromancy is an inversion of nature's dictates."

Kane thought of N'Longa. Upon their first meeting, Kane had watched N'Longa animate corpses to help them escape execution. He grunted, the sound he made closest to actual laughter.

"What?" Sybil said, with a wary look.

"It is strange to me," he said. "You are a witch. You use magic, and are surely as damned as any necromancer for your use of the dark arts. And yet you make distinctions between the types of magic you will and will not deign to employ. It is all against God; what does the shape matter?"

She stood up, arms crossed. "What an ugly thing to say."

Kane, still crouched before the skeleton, looked up, confused. "I meant no offense."

"And yet I am offended," Sybil said.

Sybil raised her eyebrows, waiting for his next words but Kane was silent.

"We should move on," she said. "The sooner we get to the source of this darkness and root it out, the sooner you may be on your way, and I will no longer be forced to suffer your company."

She stormed off at a brisk pace. Kane lurched to his feet with a grunt, using his staff to hold his weight.

"Sybil," he called after her.

She was almost out of sight, but stopped and looked back at him.

"Do not walk so fast," he said. "It is imperative we stay close to one another."

Her scowl deepened. She was clearly angry, but why? He had spoken true. Was it his fault if she grew angry at the truth? It was not. Though an apology would set this right, something in him rebelled against the idea of delivering one.

He was so preoccupied with trying to extricate himself from this quandary that he did not consciously register the change in the air. The return of the brimstone stench, stronger here than ever it had been above. He perhaps missed another sign too—

the sounds of something moving through the dark, trying not to make itself heard.

Regardless of what he noticed or did not notice, it came to the same, in the end. One moment, Sybil stood before him, fuming and angry; the next, she had been yanked up into the air, into the dark, with a cry.

29

Battle Before the Temple

Kane opened his mouth to shout after Sybil, but the wind was knocked from his lungs as something smashed into him from behind. He stumbled forward, lost his grip on his staff, and hit the ground with a hard grunt.

The world grew far away for a moment. All Kane could think about was air. He was inhaling, but the air did nothing to satiate his body. He rolled onto his back and a weight landed on his chest. It was one of the creatures, lit blue in the eldritch light: spindly and thin, as if starved; tall as a child, its head too big for its body; wide eyes glaring down at him; wide mouth open to reveal sharp, pointed teeth within. Its wings spread as it kneeled upon his chest and screeched in triumph.

Kane smashed his fist into the side of the creature's skull. As it crashed to the ground beside him he regained his feet, switched his staff to his left hand, and drew his rapier with his right. He thrust the tip of the blade into the creature's chest, and yanked it free as he heard the rustling of more wings behind him. He spun to see another creature closing in from above.

Kane swung his staff and the cat-head end struck the monster's head. Blood exploded from the point of contact, and the beast fell to the ground, twitching.

The air around Kane was now full of the clicking, chittering noises he had been listening for since they had entered the cave mouth in the woods. They were here in force now, their sounds so loud they seemed to form a wall in the air. Kane strained to hear beyond it, to know if Sybil was still screaming. If she was, Kane could not hear it.

Kane looked about. He was surrounded on all sides, by a horde that dwarfed the one he had faced before.

Any normal, rational human mind would have quailed at this sight. Any ordinary man would have experienced pure, primordial terror, at being stripped of all the modern illusions of safety and comfort, and faced with a force that wanted nothing more than his death.

Solomon Kane was not an ordinary man. Instead of fear, he felt a surge of rage and confidence boil through him, the mad joy of battle.

"Come, then!" he shouted at the creatures. "Kill me, if you can."

The monsters surged forward on all sides. Kane adjusted his staff so that his hand rested near the bottom. He spun the staff's full length before him, knocking aside his closest opponents. Blood splattered the staff as skulls broke against it. Kane had enough presence of mind to be surprised at how easily the monsters' skulls shattered. Their bones must be more delicate than those of men.

He kept his sword drawn, to thrust at any enemies that made it past the perimeter formed by his staff. He spun and swung with both arms, the creatures screaming as their bones cracked and snapped, as their flesh was rent with steel.

The bodies piled up about him, but the monsters kept

coming. There must be thousands of them. Tens of thousands. Would Kane have to fight them all if he meant to survive?

Each time he swept in a circle, that ancient temple spun past him. Perhaps, if he could make his way there, he could find safety. A place to hide and determine the next step?

Slowly he began to press in that direction. Continuing his circular defense pattern, he began to grow dizzy. It took concentration to maintain defense and move in the correct direction. It left little of his mind to wonder about Sybil, but that small part of him strained to hear any sound or report of how she might be doing. He listened for screams of terror, or the grunts and sighs of a person fighting for her life, but heard nothing.

He resisted the urge to call out for her. Either she lived, or she did not. If she lived, and was safe, it was better that she remain quiet, and not draw attention to herself. And if she was dead she would not be able to call to him now, and would be beyond his ability to help.

The possibility sent a chill through him. The melancholy—the one that had begun upon seeing that first human skeleton—threatened to grow large now, and obscure Kane's battle rage. He gritted his teeth and shook his head, trying to clear it. He could not succumb to darkness now.

He continued to smash and swing, redoubling his fury. Before, his blows merely knocked the creatures aside. Now, each creature struck flew sideways, slamming into its fellows and forcing them to stumble back under the weight of their fallen comrades. The space around Kane seemed to grow. He took his careful steps, over and around fallen monsters, and human skeletons. Those skeletons seemed to grow more frequent as he approached the temple, multiplying by magnitudes with each fourth or fifth step. There were many monsters down here, but it seemed, at one point, that there had been many humans as well. Soon, Kane could no longer step around the skeletons, if he meant to continue toward the temple. He had to step upon them. The bones gave way easily, crumbling to dust beneath his feet. The bone dust soon caked his boots, and the excess kicked up beneath his feet as he shuffled onward. It swirled about him as he spun, filling the air and creating a strange haze. Kane was vaguely disgusted with himself but had no choice but to press on. He could pray for forgiveness later.

He fought on, and fought valiantly. He fought as bravely, and with as much intensity, as a man half his age, and his stamina extended far beyond the capabilities of most younger men. But still, as strong as he was, enraged as he was, *determined* as he was, Solomon Kane was yet a man—and an aging one, at that. He had usually survived in the past by rationing his strength, moving only when necessary. In this way he could outlast an opponent, wait for an opening, a show of weakness, and then strike.

It was long since he had needed to act the part of a berserker, and he found it not as easy as it once had been. The muscles in his arms and shoulders ached, and some part of his red-draped mind noticed that Sybil's poultice was beginning to lose its effectiveness as well. The pain was faint, for the moment, but it was only a matter of time.

He purposely slowed. He continued to swing, to keep a small perimeter about himself, but he let it get smaller, allowed the creatures in closer. This allowed Kane to exercise his sword arm, and create wounds. They did not immediately kill, but did slow the assailants down. Enraged, but wounded, they made mistakes, stumbling into one another, then snapping or hissing at one another in anger. This was also new information: the creatures might basically be human in shape, but they behaved more like beasts. It lined up with everything Kane had seen so far. They did not attack like an army, but like animals.

He was still trying to figure out how he might turn this to his advantage when he stepped backward over a fallen creature, one he thought dead. When he stepped upon its wings, its eyes snapped open, and it screamed in pain. Before Kane could register what he had seen, the creature's head snapped forward, and it sank its teeth into his boot. Its teeth passed easily through the thick, sturdy leather, and into Kane's flesh.

He cried out, and flailed for balance as the creatures surged forward. They yanked upon his staff, pulling it from his hands, and throwing it away. They closed in. Kane used his free foot to stomp upon the creature biting him. He felt its neck snap under the weight of his boot as he used his free hand to pull one of his pistols from his gun belt. He pointed it into the crowd, aiming in the general direction of where he had seen the beasts throw his staff. He cocked the weapon, and fired.

The creature standing before Kane's weapon soared backward as its chest exploded. It coated its fellows in blood and ichor as its arms and wings flew into the air and landed upon others. Lord above, these creatures were fragile.

The act of firing the gun seemed to pause time. The sound was deafening, and in this cavernous space, it rolled over the chamber like thunder, an echo repeating. The creatures paused for a long moment, looking about—first at their dead comrade, then at one another, as if seeking an understanding of what had just happened.

Kane did not waste the moment. He dived forward, tucking the fired pistol back into its holster and grabbing his staff. Planting the butt against the stone floor, he lurched to his feet and spun toward the temple. The creatures continued to stare at him, wide-eyed and confused. Kane sheathed his sword and drew his left pistol, pointing it at the creature directly before him.

The creature, understanding what was about to happen, shrieked and cowered away. So did all the others around it.

Seeing his window of opportunity widen—but also intuiting that it would be limited, that the creatures' bloodlust would eventually overcome their fear—Kane pushed forward toward the temple. The creatures fell away before him, and he quickened his pace to a run. He stomped on skeleton after skeleton, each ribcage, skull, or tibia exploding in a puff of dust beneath his feet. Kane lost count of the bodies. It was sickening—how many men and women and children had these monsters murdered?

He could not afford to lose time mourning and contemplating now. He had to reach the temple, and find refuge before the creatures recovered their senses.

The structure grew larger before him until it took up his entire field of vision. He was close now, only thirty yards or so from the stairs leading up toward the great entrance doors. His way was blocked, however, by a wall of the creatures. Kane holstered the pistol he had already fired, switched his staff to that hand, and drew his remaining pistol. He leveled this at the creatures now, hoping they would quail or fall away at the memory of what he had been able to do before. They did not.

Kane sighed. It had been worth a try. He prepared to fire.

"Hey!"

The voice, high and soft, cut through the quiet of the cavern like a thunderclap. The creatures, and Kane, turned to look at the source of the sound. Sybil Eastey stood upon the temple steps, her dress and cloak torn, her lip bloodied, but intact, and alive. In one hand, she held a lit lantern. Its door was open, revealing the tiny flame inside. The fire dampened the blue light from the stone, and turned the closest creatures translucent, nearly invisible. It made Sybil appear a single figure aloft in darkness, above the heads of Kane and the disappearing creatures alike, reminiscent of a goddess out of primitive myth.

Sybil's free hand moved through a complicated gesture, her fingers contorting in ways that looked painful. The flame in her lantern expanded in size, so large, so fast, that she had to toss the lantern away from herself. It shattered in the air before striking the ground, and the flame grew larger, darkening the world around it, seeming to suck in light.

When it was as tall as two men, and almost as wide, the flame shot from its place on the steps and toward the horde.

Kane dived out of the way and hit the stone floor as the ball of fire hit the monsters. They bellowed and shrieked, their cries digging into Kane's brain like daggers. He looked up. The monsters would have been invisible in the firelight, except that they themselves were aflame. They appeared to him as flame-limned silhouettes, stomping and waving about, screaming their terrible cries as the fire did its terrible work.

Realizing he would get no better opportunity than this, Kane got to his feet and ran for the temple stairs, where Sybil remained. She had snuffed the lantern and stood with a hand extended to Kane now.

He reached for her with his right arm when something whistled past him, disrupting the air. He turned, looking for the source of the sound, but saw nothing—until he looked back toward Sybil. She still held an arm out toward Kane, but now she wore a look of mild surprise, and something protruded from her middle.

It was a rapier sword, buried to the hilt. He would recognize that hilt anywhere. It was his own. The sword he had lost on his previous trip into this place.

Sybil looked at the sword in her gut, then at Kane. Her hands went to her stomach, and came away bloody, a dark stain blooming from the wound. Then she closed her eyes, and toppled to the ground.

30

In the Temple

A coldness spread through Kane's own gut as he hurried up the temple stairs, paused to tuck his staff under one armpit, and kneeled to scoop Sybil into his arms.

Her eyes snapped open and she screamed as Kane lifted her. He grimaced in sympathy, but there was no time for gentleness now. He ran across the wide porch of the temple, and through the blessedly open doors.

He passed through a large antechamber with a domed ceiling, and lined with couches and chairs. Skeletons lounged upon the furniture, as if going about daily business like living people. Others lay upon the ground, limbs splayed. Kane would have loved to stop and investigate further, but could hear the clattering of claws on stone behind him, the chittering calls of his pursuers. Those who had survived Sybil's inferno were in pursuit once more.

The antechamber gave way to a long, wide corridor, much like the one he and Sybil had passed through when they had entered the cave outside Windsend. Unlike that corridor, however, this one was lined with doorways—and most of these doorways had doors in them. The doors appeared to be made of wood. Kane marveled: given how ancient the temple seemed, shouldn't the wood have rotted by now? Particularly given the humidity of the subterranean space?

He shook his head as he sprinted down the corridor. Another mystery that would have to wait for later—assuming there was a later.

Sybil groaned in his arms, and Kane spared her a glance. Her eyes fluttered, and he realized that his own clothes were damp now. She was losing a lot of blood.

"Keep your eyes open, Mistress Eastey," Kane murmured, the words coming between hitched breaths. "Eyes on me now."

"I am so tired," she murmured. "The inferno spell. It… takes much, to make it work. Did you like it?"

"It was both timely and impressive," Kane said. "How did you manage it, so deep? I thought your powers were scarce?"

"I do not know, exactly," Sybil said. "It was as if… they suddenly appeared in full once more. As if the sun had come out from behind clouds. But now I am tired, and would like to sleep."

"I know," Kane said. "But if I am to carry you about thus, I would like to be entertained."

She sighed, as if terribly put upon. "Everyone always wants things of me. No one ever asks what I want."

"What do you want, Sybil Eastey?"

"I want… to be warm, for one thing," Sybil said. "I feel like I have been cold for days. How long do you think we have been down here?"

Kane continued sprinting down the corridor. Heavens, but it was long.

"I do not know," Kane said. "We have only slept once, so I think it cannot be longer than two days."

"It feels like an eternity, when you are in the dark," Sybil said.

"I would like to see the sun. To smile up and feel its warmth on my face. The blessing of the goddess."

Kane scowled at the blasphemy, but this was not the time to argue. The chittering behind him grew louder, but he dared not look back. Would this corridor never end?

"I would like to be among nature, to feel its harmony once more," Sybil said. "Too long have I been in Windsend, where something has been..." She waved a lackadaisical hand through the air, as if searching for the right words. "Off," she finished. "Something is off."

Kane hazarded a look over his shoulder. The horde approached, and his fatigue was no longer just there—it had begun to insist upon itself, and Kane's attention.

At last, the end of the corridor came into view: a wide staircase that led both up and down.

Kane slowed just a little, trying to decide what to do next. He was still attempting to make the decision when the door to his left flew open, and several of the creatures burst forth, slamming into Kane. He reeled across the wide corridor floor, fighting to keep his footing and his hold on Sybil. She screamed in pain, and the sound focused him, allowed him to plant his feet.

He could not fight while holding Sybil. His only option was to continue fleeing. He danced through the creatures, using a lifetime of experience with intricate dueling footwork, and made it to the stairway. He launched himself down, if only because it was easier to descend than to climb, given his current burden.

He rushed down the stairs, his long legs taking them two at a time. When he came to the first landing, Sybil began to speak again.

"I would also like to have a week or two without being disturbed by some new injury or illness. Let the damned villagers stay healthy and happy for two weeks. Let me gather my herbs and prepare them in peace."

"Indeed?" Kane said. "They keep you too busy?"

They came to the bottom of the stairs, and a corridor that split three ways. Kane ran down the one to the right. This corridor was also lined with closed doors, and he swung his head from side to side, looking at each, waiting for another band of attackers to emerge. The hallway stretched on and on and Kane could not see where it ended.

"'My leg hurts,'" Sybil said, in a cruel mockery of a neighbor. "'I cannot stop coughing.' 'My baby is running a fever.' 'Help me to get pregnant.' And then, after I help them? After I make their lives better? Do you know what they do, Master Kane?" She sounded woozy. Drunk.

"What do they do?" Kane said, hardly listening as he looked for their salvation.

"They turn around and speak ill of me behind my back. Poison one another against me. Sully my reputation. Blame me for things they did themselves."

Kane opened his mouth to reply—anything to keep her awake, and talking—but before he could form the words, a door to Kane's right flew open. He danced backwards, already turning to flee, but nothing flew forth. Instead, Kane saw what appeared to be a pale woman peering out. With one hand she held the door open, and with the other, she beckoned him frantically.

Kane had many questions, but none more pressing than the need to survive. He took one glance back up the corridor. The creatures were hot behind but had not yet clambered into view. The stairs and the corridor split must have slowed them. Kane entered the room, and the woman shut the door fast behind him.

31

Surgery

The room was small, and lit, like the corridors and the cavern, by the blue light from the stone. It was decorated with a large wooden desk and two chairs, as well as a few bookcases.

"Set her down here," the woman said, pointing at the desk. "I need your help with the door."

Kane lay Sybil on her side, trying not to jostle the sword buried in her stomach and poking from her back. Then he turned to see the small woman at one side of a tall bookcase beside the door. Kane went to stand on the side opposite the woman. He tested the bookcase's weight, lifting his side. Despite the fact that the case was empty, it was still heavy. He could barely get his corner off the ground. Hopefully the door was made of the same wood. That would offer some protection if the creatures found them.

Together, Kane and the woman braced to begin moving the bookcase but paused as they heard the horde. At least some had entered this corridor and were heading this way. Kane looked to the woman. She made a show of removing her hands from the bookcase, and then put a finger to her lips, gesturing for silence. Kane also let go. He froze, slowing his breath, trying to make as little sound as possible. He kept his eyes on Sybil. She was delirious, probably not aware of what was happening. What was to stop her speaking, or crying out?

But assuming they could maintain perfect silence, how much protection would that give them? These creatures had made their way out of the woods and into Windsend, where they had murdered the hunters who had disturbed their lair. They had probably done so by following the hunters' scents. It stood to reason that the horde would find Kane and Sybil through similar means now. There was also a good chance that Kane and Sybil had left a trail of blood, making themselves easier to follow.

But if Kane and the woman moved the bookcase now, they would surely give themselves away. Silence was their best chance. So he crept across the room to where Sybil lay, and placed a hand over her mouth. Her eyes fluttered open and Kane put a finger to his own lips. Sybil studied Kane a moment, then closed her eyes. He could feel the hot breath from her nostrils on his fingers. At least she yet breathed.

The sounds of the horde slowed as it drew closer. The leathery sound of wings and the chittering grew quieter, and less pronounced, replaced by the sounds of something—a great many somethings—sniffing. The sniffing grew louder, as if a nose were pressed up against the sliver of space between the bottom of the door and the stone floor.

The strange woman moved her hands in a series of gestures, her fingers contorting in a manner that belied the presence of human bone and muscle. A short, sharp, puff of wind sounded from her fingertips, and drifted toward the door.

The sniffing slowed, then stopped. A moment later, the chittering sounds resumed, as the horde moved on. Kane stood beside Sybil, watching her breathe, and listening for the sounds of the horde as they grew fainter, and fainter, and then stopped altogether. The smell of brimstone faded as well, although it never disappeared altogether.

After several moments of silence, the woman said, "Now we may move the bookcase into place."

Kane left Sybil, resumed his place on the other side of the bookcase, and together he and the woman dragged it across the stone. It made a terrible racket, and Kane held his breath through most of the process, terrified that it would draw the creatures' attention once more.

But they managed to get the bookcase into place, squarely blocking the door, and Kane heard no sign of the horde's return.

The woman stepped away from the bookcase. "I think we are safe for the moment. We can relax."

Her voice was strange, light and airy as a breeze through tree leaves on a summer day. She enunciated clearly, and Kane had no trouble understanding her, but her accent was not one he recognized. She looked like a young woman who might live in any small English village—pale and fair-haired, with a long nose and large dark eyes.

Kane pushed past her, and stopped at the desk, looking down at Sybil. The desk was now covered in blood. It had run off the sides and dripped into pools upon the floor. Kane squeezed Sybil's shoulder. She moaned softly, but did not open her eyes. He let his fingers hover near her nostrils. She still breathed, but the breaths were shallow.

"It is a grave injury," the woman said.

"What you did a moment ago," Kane said. "Putting the creatures off our scent. That was magic, yes?"

"It was," the woman said.

"Can you heal this injury?" Kane asked.

The woman shook her head slowly. "I do not think so."

Kane looked about, trying to decide what to do. His eyes

fell upon Sybil's bag, wrapped about her shoulders, now soaked with her blood. He took the bag off her and set it on the desk. He dug through it and removed several items: a bottle of foul-smelling liquid; a few ragged cloths; and a small bag with iron and flint, for striking a fire. These he set upon the desk beside the table.

He looked at the woman. She stood near the door, watching him and Sybil curiously.

"Come and make yourself useful anyway," he said.

The woman approached, stopping beside Kane.

"I have to sew up the wound," Kane said. "It will be messy, and quite painful for her."

"How can I help?" the woman said.

"Hold her down," Kane said. "Cover her mouth when she screams."

The woman raised an eyebrow at this but moved around the desk to grab Sybil's shoulders.

Kane took a deep breath. It had been a long time since he had needed to dress a wound in the field. Usually there were men at hand better suited to this task. But in this moment, he was Sybil's only hope.

Moving as quickly as he could, he opened the foul-smelling bottle on the desk, and its aroma filled the air of the little room. Vinegar had a nasty stink, but it was a bit better than the brimstone stench of the creatures, he supposed.

He leaned forward. "Sybil," he said.

She moaned faintly but did not open her eyes.

"I am going to remove the weapon now," he said. "It will probably hurt worse than any agony you have ever known."

She made no response. Kane stood up and nodded to the woman. "Cover her mouth."

The woman cupped one palm over Sybil's mouth, just beneath her nose.

Kane held Sybil's right shoulder with one hand, and grabbed the rapier handle with the other. He took a moment to find his focus and calm. Then, in one swift, sure motion, he yanked the sword from Sybil's body.

Her eyes flew open and she screamed.

The woman kept her hold over Sybil's mouth, muffling the sound, which wrenched Kane's heart. He had heard men cry like this during surgery, but never a woman.

He handed two cloths to the woman. "Press these to the wounds. One to the front and one to the back. Press as hard as you can."

"I will not be able to muffle her shouts," the woman warned.

Kane bent down and put his head level with Sybil's. He looked into her wide, wild eyes.

"We have to staunch the bleeding," he said. "This will hurt, too. You must be quiet, Sybil, or you will give us away to the monsters."

Her breath came in ragged gasps. She licked her lips, and tears streamed down her cheeks. She nodded her understanding, and Kane in turn nodded to the woman, who pressed the cloths to the wounds.

Sybil reached up and muffled her own screams this time.

Kane turned his attention to the rapier, which he held in his left hand. With his right, he took a cloth from Sybil's bag, and used it to wipe blood from the blade. He tossed the bloody cloth aside, and picked up a fresh one. He set the sword down on the desk, picked up the open bottle of vinegar, and poured a small portion onto the cloth. This he used to wipe the clean blade, disinfecting it. Then he set the cloth down and used the flint and iron to spark a flame. He held the tip of the blade over the fire until it glowed orange, superheated.

"This too is going to hurt," he murmured to Sybil. "I am sorry."

Ah, but you like to hurt people, Monsieur Galahad, Le Loup said in his head.

Kane gestured for the woman to step away. She moved to the head of the desk and grabbed Sybil's shoulders once more.

He took another deep breath, then pressed the sword tip to the wound in Sybil's stomach. Her screams this time put Kane in mind of what he had seen and heard of the Inquisitors and Witchfinders. Men who took great pleasure in hurting others—particularly women.

He didn't relish this, but his nerve never failed, either. He worked quickly, applying the metal to the wound in quick bursts, first to her stomach, and then to her back, until the bleeding had stopped and the skin had closed.

He quickly doused a final cloth with vinegar, and this he wrapped around Sybil's abdomen, with the woman's help. Sybil whimpered through it all, tears flowing freely.

"I am sorry," Kane repeated. "But I cannot let you bleed to death. I need you, Sybil Eastey."

She did not answer with words, but reached out and took his hand. Her touch was light, but he thought he felt her trying to squeeze. He squeezed back.

"Rest now," he said.

She dropped his hand. He unfastened his cloak and draped it over her like a blanket. He looked up to find the woman watching him.

"Who are you?" she asked.

"My name is Solomon Kane," Kane said. "My companion is Sybil Eastey. We have come from the village of Windsend, to root out the evil in this place."

The woman smiled faintly. "I came on a similar purpose. I descended to this place with the intention of wiping out a darkness that had invaded my home and destroyed my people."

Kane frowned. He had heard of no women in Windsend who

had gone missing. Nor was this woman, in her green gown, dressed like a Puritan.

“Where is your home?” he asked.

“The woods above,” the woman said. “The valley.”

Kane glanced back at Sybil, wishing she were awake. She might be able to clarify now.

“I am sorry,” Kane said, shaking his head. “I do not understand. I have been several days in Windsend, and have heard tell of no woman who lived in these woods.”

The woman’s smile grew a bit. “I have never heard of this Windsend you mention, but that is no great mystery. My guess is that my time in those woods ended many years before your Windsend was founded. Many years before you were born. My name is Rhiannon. And men once called me the goddess of this place.”

32

Rhiannon's Tale

1

I cannot tell you how old I am, for I believe I was born before men began measuring time in years. In truth, I believe I was born before men ever walked the Earth. I do not know for certain. I do not know for certain that I was born. I have no memory of the event. In this way, I suppose I am no different from most mortals—for what living, thinking being can remember the moment its life began?

In my earliest memories I just... am. Wandering my woods. Tending to the trees, and the beasts that lived among them. I think this went on for a very long time. I watched my trees grow from saplings into a mighty forest. I watched the beasts make their homes. Some of them foraged. Others hunted. I looked after them all, as best I could. I did not choose favorites. Instead, I kept the balance. I... Somehow, I understood this was my task. Why I was put in this place.

I followed the dictates of my function. I kept all things—the beasts and the plants—in harmony. I summoned rain, and wind, and snow, and, when necessary, flames. I made sure the laws of birth, life, and death were obeyed, until my charges learned what you now call "instinct," and could almost look after themselves.

For a time, things were good. There was pain, and strife, but those are natural parts of life, and I grew accustomed to them. All was as it should be, in my valley, and my woods.

I do not know how long this went on. Time is a strange concept to an immortal. But I think I must have tended my charges for many hundreds of years, if not thousands, before the first men came.

The first men were a startling sight—tall, hairless beasts that stood upright, with dark skin and pronounced brows. Creatures with incredibly dexterous hands, and long fingers. Creatures who communicated through gesture and vocalizations more complex than anything I had ever seen or heard. They wore the furs of other beasts, and carried long shafts of wood, tipped with sharpened bits of rock or bone.

They came from outside the valley and wandered among the trees, and I watched them for a time, not revealing myself.

As I watched, they moved slowly, carefully. They spread out among the trees and hunkered close to the earth, moving almost silently. I understood their purpose. I had seen beasts behave this way. They were hunting. They had no claws of their own, and their teeth were not sharp like other predators, but, working together, they managed to fell two large creatures.

They dragged the bodies away, leaving trails of blood in their wake, and left the valley thereafter. I was not offended by the killing or the death. I understood the central contradiction of mortal life: life must feed upon life in order to sustain itself. It was neither moral nor immoral in my view, but simply a fact.

The tall, hairless apes returned only a few days after their first appearance. They knew my forest was rich with game, and they came to hunt often. In the early days, I let them take as much as they liked. After all, the other creatures I tended only took what they needed to survive. Why would these new beasts be any different?

And yet, they were different. They took, and took, and took. And I quickly realized that, if allowed, these new beasts—these men—would deplete my woods of all the creatures that lived within.

So I took a step I had never felt compelled to take before. The next time the men came, I showed myself to them, and made clear my displeasure.

That was my first time taking a physical form. Before, I had existed only as a presence, unembodied. Now, I took the shape of a great beast, a thing of teeth and fur and claws, with dark holes where eyes ought to be. A thing that appeared to be both living and dead.

The men screamed, and wailed, and fled.

I thought that was the end of the matter. That I would be able to return to my task, much as I had before.

I am probably not the first immortal to have underestimated the tenacity of men.

I still remember my shock, on the day they returned to my valley. They came in force, in greater numbers than before, moving with both fear and determination. I felt a grudging respect for these creatures, who were clearly afraid, but who also refused to retreat.

I waited until they were close to my woods and took the same shape I had used before. I came roaring toward this host of men. Several of them quailed and fled, but the rest, to my surprise, stayed in place. A few turned the tips of their weapons—spears—toward me, in postures of defense. But the majority froze. I could sense their fear, their absolute terror, and yet they remained and faced me down. My admiration grew.

One among them—an older man, dressed in more ornate clothing than the rest, came to the front of the group. He raised his arms and lowered his head and made a series of vocalizations. When he finished, two of the men brought forward a beast which walked on four legs, had long, shaggy fur, and a pair of horns curled out on either side of its head. It was a goat, although I had no name for it at the time. They led the goat forward, a rope wrapped about its neck, and stopped it just a few feet away from me.

The old man in the ornate furs shouted and raised his arms. The men leading the goat set a stone bowl on the ground, then produced a sharp stone. One of the men held the goat fast while the other placed the sharp stone beneath the goat's chin.

I realized what they meant to do. They would cut the goat's throat, and spill its blood into the bowl below. I was not sure why, but I suspected it had something to do with me.

I am not squeamish. You cannot live among wild nature if you have a weak stomach. It is beautiful, yes, but also terrible, in its way. You will see much pain, much bloodshed. But most of it serves a purpose. As I said, life must consume life. But this—the killing of the goat—did not seem to be about eating. It was about something else. Something I could not understand.

I changed forms. I became smaller, closer in shape to the men before me, although I imagine it was clumsy, since I was not familiar with their forms yet. I rushed forward and put my body between the man with the sharp stone and the goat.

Both of the goat handlers startled. They dropped the weapon, and the rope. The goat bleated in anger or terror and disappeared into the woods.

The gathered men stared after the goat before turning to me. Then, the man in the ornate furs knelt and bowed his head. After a moment, the other men all did the same. Again, because I knew little of men, I did not understand what was happening, but I intuited this was a solemn moment. That these men were offering me something sacred.

I walked among the kneeling men, my small, human-shaped paws making soft sounds on the grass. I approached the leader—the man in the ornate fur—and took his hand. He looked up at me as I pulled him to his feet, and I sensed fear, yes, but also wonder. He was in awe of me.

He spoke a single word to me, then: "Rhiannon."

One by one, the other men stood, all repeating the word: "Rhiannon. Rhiannon. Rhiannon."

2

That day, I led the men into my woods. I removed myself from my physical form, and guided them using sound and light and wind. I helped them find good plants to eat, but kept them from killing any of the beasts. I was not opposed to the eating of meat, but they had taken too much too soon. The population needed time to replenish itself. The balance needed to be restored.

The men seemed grateful for the food. They gathered it, and took it away with them. I watched them go, but this time, I assumed they would return, and soon.

In this assumption, I was correct. They returned quickly, and this time, they brought no small hunting party, no single sacrifice. They came with others—women, and children, and animals of their own. It was overwhelming to see so many of them at once, making such a racket.

I hid in my woods to watch as they raised great round structures of stone and wood and straw. I watched as they built pens to house chickens, goats, sheep, and cattle. I watched as they cleared the fields of rocks and debris, and turned the soil, and sowed seeds in it.

These other types of men—women, and children, I mean—were fascinating to me. The children were like the men, but much smaller. And they took so long to grow to maturity. The creatures of my woods rarely needed more than a season or so. Children of men were small and weak, and needed constant looking after.

And the women were interesting, too. They were, for the most part, smaller than the men, and shaped differently, beneath their furs. Men were often blocky and broad, and woman tended to be softer of shape, more contoured. They seemed more of a piece with the nature I was used to. I fell in love with their form, and decided that, in the future, I would take the shape of a woman.

The humans of my valley spent most of their time trying to eke out survival. But one night out of every seven, the men and women in ornate furs would lead a procession to the edge of my woods. There they would kneel, and start a fire, and they would chant, and sing, and dance. Still they chanted that word: "Rhiannon."

I eventually came to understand that this was their name for me. I was Rhiannon. And these ceremonies were for me. An appreciation, yes, but also an invitation. And so I began to appear to them on the fire nights. I took the shape of a young woman, and I danced among them.

The dancing was great fun. I had never experienced the exhilaration and joy of movement like this before. I had never—to be honest—experienced the exhilaration and joy of existence like this before.

Life among these people—these men and women—was good. And it remained good. As with life in my woods, there was pain, and heartbreak. People got hurt. People died. People hurt one another, with words and actions. But that is not so different from the way animals live, is it? Perhaps it is sadder when people do it, because people ought to know better. But when you think of humans as just another animal, the sting goes out of the thought.

Measuring life as I did in the woods—in births, strife, life, and death—things were good for a very long time. I took care of my people as best I could. I advised them on what to hunt, and when. I helped them plant and harvest. They paid me homage with their worship and dances. They called me Rhiannon, goddess of the valley and woods. I can see the look upon your face, Solomon Kane. You must understand that I make no claim to divinity myself. This is what they called me. The name and title to which I answered.

It is funny, to reflect upon it now. I am not prone to reflection. But when I force myself to do so, I realize that, before the coming of humans, I was content. But once they arrived? I knew happiness. I knew joy. I knew pain and sorrow, too, but they seemed a fair trade for the company of humanity.

If you look for any proof that I am not, indeed, divine, you need look no further than my own folly, Solomon Kane. My happiness with the people of my valley went on for so long that I grew comfortable. Complacent. I stopped guarding against darkness from within or without. It did not seem possible. Not in my woods. Not in my valley.

3

The darkness started in dreams. I do not dream—indeed, I do not sleep—but people began to come to me and tell me of their own dark dreams. This was not so new. Men and women have always dreamt, and pondered the meanings of these nighttime visitations. I have no special gift for interpreting the workings of the human mind in its unconscious state.

I listened, however, when petitioners wanted to tell me of dreams. Although most made no sense to me—sounded, in fact, like the confused ramblings of a drunken fool—I did my best to offer counsel.

I thought it no different when my petitioners began to tell me of the new dreams. The first two or three souls told a similar tale: a dream of a voice that spoke to them in darkness, seeming to come from everywhere and nowhere at once. This voice proclaimed itself a true god but said it needed help to emerge from the darkness. The voice promised wealth, and unnaturally long life, if the dreamer but helped the god make its way out of the darkness and into the light. And then—before the dreamer could respond to the voice's offer—the dreamer was overwhelmed by a flood of screeching, a sound like thousands of leathery wings beating about them, and the sensation of claws and teeth ripping at their flesh.

The dreams all ended here, with the pain and agony of being torn apart.

To the first petitioner who related the dream, I recommended more exercise and time in nature. He was getting older, and his physical health was beginning to fail. I hoped some changes to his habits would cure his mind's cries.

But then a second petitioner told me the same dream. Then came a third. And a fourth. And before that day was done, I had met with over a dozen men and women who had experienced the same dream.

To each petitioner after the third, I asked for time to think about a response. The petitioners seemed perturbed by this request. In the past, they had received immediate answers and counsel. To be denied instant relief after such an upsetting dream set off alarms in their hearts. I could not blame them for this.

The following day, I took leave of my physical form, and went to the woods. I did this sometimes, absenting myself from the humans, moving among the beasts and plants, existing as I had before I met men. As much as I enjoyed life among the humans, I also treasured time alone in the woods. Free of expectation, or demand.

I had barely begun my exploration when I felt something wrong. There was a darkness in the woods. I felt a pull like gravity. Tell me, Solomon Kane—have men discovered gravity yet? Do you know what it is? No? Then do not worry about it.

I followed the pull, and it did not take me long to find the source: a hole, in the forest floor, that looked like the entrance of a cave. I had never seen it before. Perhaps it had always been there, and I had not noticed? But I doubt it. I think this was new. I knew that something about this place was wrong. It was—I do not know exactly how to say it. I know that the earth shifts and changes and transforms. That is a natural part of its life. But this place was unnatural. This hole had not opened on its own. Nor had it been fashioned by men. Men's work has a feel to it, too, a flavor that is difficult to explain but easy to experience, for one like me. No. This felt like neither.

As I drifted near the cave mouth, I felt the same sensations my petitioners had previously described to me. A darkness that went beyond the mere lack of light. I felt a desolation of spirit.

For the first time in my long existence, I experienced fear. Fear of what that hole in the ground might mean for me and the people, beasts, and plants in my charge. Fear of what might emerge from that hole.

I returned to the temple my people had made for me. I took my human shape, and summoned all the people. I told them of what I had seen. I told them a darkness had impinged upon our home, and I charged several of the men—the bravest warriors and hunters—to go into the woods and fill this hole, and block the opening however they might. I told them not to enter the cave—that to do so would be to court death, and I would not be able to help them.

The men I charged with this duty had my complete trust. They had been brave and loyal all their lives. And I admit I had misgivings when another man, not originally tasked, asked to join the expedition.

This man—Berach—was also a brave and able hunter. Under normal circumstances, I would have asked him to lead the expedition. But Berach had been one of the petitioners, the ones who had experienced the nightmares. I had specifically sought to spare him this duty.

Berach was a broad man, thick of limb, with small eyes, reddish hair, and a thick beard. He spoke and moved slowly, and gave the impression of an unintelligent, lumbering giant, but his slowness belied his cunning. He was capable of deep thinking and incredible speed, when necessary, and often bested his fellows when sparring or wrestling.

He wore a perpetual frown, as if thinking through some deep and difficult problem. He also usually stared at the ground, preferring this to looking other people in the eye. He was no different when he approached me that day and asked to join the party. Large as a bear, but shy as a young man courting a girl for the first time.

"Are you sure you want to do this?" I asked him.

"Yes, my lady," he said. "I feel that I must."

"I will not deny you, then," I said. But as I said it, I felt discomfited. The words rang false. I realized that what I actually wanted was to stop him, by any means necessary.

I did not know why I felt this way, and could see no logical reason to stop him. So I said nothing. Instead of trusting these feelings, I trusted logic. I let him go.

Looking back, I wish I had asked him why he felt he needed to go. That would likely have made much else clear, and perhaps saved me some heartbreak.

I am also ashamed that I asked these men to go into the woods and perform this task for me. I ought to have done it myself. I was their goddess. Their protector. I served them, did I not? But years of worship had blinded me. I forgot the pact I made with these people. In my mind, they served me, and not vice versa.

So many things I would have done differently. But the correct path is often clear in hindsight, is it not?

4

The men of the hunt ventured into my woods. They traveled light, carrying only the supplies they would take on a day's hunt. I followed them, invisible, unseen and unheard. I do not believe they sensed my presence.

The men followed my directions, and came shortly to the cave mouth. They gathered about it, and peered inside, wearing expressions of worry, doubt, and fear. One man put a hand to his middle, turned away, and spilled his stomach upon the earth. The vomit steamed in the cold morning air.

The others broke their circle and went in search of things to fill the hole. As I had directed, they searched for large stones and fallen trees, although I had given them permission to chop down trees, if the job required it.

All the men did this except Berach. He remained in place, standing over the hole in the earth, staring into it, wearing his habitually perturbed expression. Then he stepped over the edge and dropped into the hole. It happened so quickly. There was a slight thumping sound as he hit the ground below, and his grunt drifted up out of the dark, muffled.

I took form then and embodied myself on the lip of the cave mouth to shout after him. When he did not answer, I went in search of the other men. I found them, told them what had happened, and ordered them to rescue Berach. The men were alarmed to see me so far from my temple, but rushed to obey.

They tied a rope about the waist of one man, and lowered him into the hole. This man, Patraic, ventured forth some way, almost to the end of the rope, before he found Berach.

"How is he?" I called.

"You will not believe this," Patraic said, his voice oddly muffled, "but he is asleep."

Patraic was not able to wake Berach himself. The men had to lower a second fellow into the cave, and together, Patraic and the second man carried their fellow hunter to the entrance. They tied a rope about Berach and pulled him back into the light.

Once all were safely above ground, they set about trying to wake Berach. None of the usual methods—calling his name, shaking his shoulder, or making loud noises—drew him back to the waking world. He slept so long and so soundly that the men began to discuss making camp right there. I warned them that this would invite disaster, so, although reluctant to do so, they carried Berach back to the village, and, at my direction, brought him to my shrine. Exhausted, they went to bed, and left him in my care.

As night fell, the hole in the woods remained open, and my problem unsolved.

I watched Berach as he slept. He lay unmoving, but his face

showed signs of life. His eyes moved beneath closed lids. He frowned, his heavy eyebrows drawing together. He murmured, although he spoke no words I understood. I took all of these as good signs. Perhaps he would recover after all.

In the morning—scarcely after the sky had turned gray with predawn light—petitioners were at my temple, calling for my help. I left Berach and emerged to greet them. Most of the adults in the village were outside my door, in their nightclothes, looking fearful.

They had dreamed of the dark. Of a terrible stench, and a voice that seemed to come from nowhere and everywhere, all at once. A voice that enticed with promises of riches in one breath, and threatened suffering and death with the next.

All had had this dream. When they heard one another's stories, and realized this, they grew more afraid. They begged for my counsel and intervention.

I urged them not to panic, and promised them all would be well.

"But how?" one woman demanded.

That gave me pause. I did not know yet. My only plan was to block the cave entrance. But what would that accomplish? Could a stopped-up hole prevent a force capable of invading dreams?

The villagers saw my hesitation. They murmured among themselves. I could feel their fear growing. I needed to soothe them. I needed to think of a way to help.

I was still thinking when a voice spoke up behind me:

"My friends! Do not fear!"

I was startled to turn and find Berach in the temple doorway, wide-awake, and, at first glance, perfectly well. But a closer look, as he approached, showed me that there was a strangeness in his eyes—a manic glean that reminded me of the look in the eyes of very sick people, who are unable to tell the difference between dreams and waking life.

"Berach," I said. "You should be resting."

He did not look at me. Instead, he marched down the temple

stairs and stopped there. He kept his back to me, facing the crowd as he spread his arms.

"My friends," he said. "I know that you have shared the dream. You have heard the voice in the darkness. You have heard its promises of wealth and security, but also its threats of suffering and pain. I know that you are afraid, because I too was afraid when I had this dream."

I was completely taken aback. Berach had rarely ever said more than a few words at a time, and when he spoke, he usually mumbled. He had never been one for public speaking. But here he stood, like a leader.

"Yesterday," he went on, "I accompanied several other men into the woods, to investigate a hole that has opened in the earth. We were sent by Rhiannon, and told to fill the hole in. But when I grew close, the hole called to me, so I entered it, and there, I was struck by a magical spell, and put to sleep. In my dreams, I heard the voice in the darkness, but louder and clearer than before. It told me truths. Truths that I do not think Rhiannon wants us to know."

Finally he spared me a glance over one shoulder. It was a look full of scorn, and it stung.

"What truths?" called someone in the crowd.

"The voice I heard," Berach said, "the voice we all heard, belongs to the Deep God. He is a true god."

"So is Rhiannon," called Patraic.

"Is she?" Berach asked. "Or is she merely a woodland spirit that has allowed us to worship her? Tell me—has she truly made a difference in our lives? Or do we continue to struggle and toil each day, as if we had no god at all? We still fall ill. We still suffer. We still die. But we go on paying homage to Rhiannon, and following her dictates as if she offered true help, instead of pretty words."

A wave of murmurs passed through the crowd. I could feel the doubt as it took hold.

"The Deep God, though," Berach said. "He has the power to

shape our lives. He can protect us. He can end the pain and the darkness, or multiply it tenfold, if he so chooses. I tell you, He is a true god. And He has appeared in our dreams because He wishes to make us an offer."

"What offer is that?" Patraic asked. He stood with his arms crossed, skeptical. His expression gave me hope.

"Long ago, a trickster trapped the Deep God beneath the earth and put a sleeping spell upon him," Berach said. "He needs our help to break the spell and emerge into the light. To take His rightful place as the ruler of this valley."

"If this Deep God is so powerful," Patraic said, "why does he need our help?"

"Did you not hear me?" Berach snapped. "He is trapped under an enchantment."

"Why was a trickster able to trap him?" Patraic said.

I silently cheered Patraic on. He was asking the questions I would have liked to ask myself.

"Perhaps He will tell you, if you go to Him in supplication and ask," Berach said. "That is your choice to make." He turned to the crowd and raised his voice. "Indeed, we all have a choice to make now. The Deep God has struggled for untold years, and at last, has opened a tiny hole in the Earth. He has offered His blessings, if we clear the way for His return. Today, I will leave our village, and make my dwelling in the woods. I will begin the work of widening and deepening that hole. I will clear the path. Any who care to join me will be offered the same love and protection."

"And what of those of us who stay behind with Rhiannon?" Patraic asked.

Berach shrugged. "You have been warned about the Deep God's strength. His ability to help, and to hurt. Would you tempt such a power to anger, Patraic?" He turned back to the crowd. "You have heard the offer of the Deep God. I will pack what I can carry and leave for the woods at midday. All who wish to join me are welcome."

He lowered his arms then and walked away, toward the roundhouse where he had lived all his life. He did not stop to speak or look back at either me or his neighbors, and none tried to stop him.

When he had disappeared from view, the gathered crowd turned to look at me, waiting for my response.

"I have long lived in these woods," I said. "Longer than men have walked the Earth, I think. I have cared for the woods—and then for all of you—as best I can, or know how. Never have I spared any effort or chance to keep you safe and looked after. But it has never been given to me to defy the dictates of life itself. Pain is part of life. So is suffering. These are natural parts of existence. I cannot offer you what is not natural.

"I do not know what this Deep God is," I continued. "And I cannot tell you whether or not he is capable of honoring the promises that Berach has made. Perhaps this Deep God is capable of miracles. But I tell you that what he had promised is not natural. It is not of this earth. It is not..." And here I struggled for words. "It is not right. I cannot say it any better than that. Something about this hole in the ground. This voice in your dreams. It feels sinister. Wrong. All of you, and your parents, and their parents before them. All of you have known me all your lives. You know I am not a miracle worker. You also know that I am not violent. I will not hurt you. If you choose to leave and follow Berach into the woods, I will not try to stop you. But I also warn you: I truly believe this path will lead to ruin for any who follow it."

I left them then, and returned to my temple. I spent the day in solitude, and did not emerge until sunset. I drifted above the village, disembodied, and took stock. By my own count, half the population had gone to join Berach in the woods. Half. So many, gone.

Those who remained eventually gathered outside my temple. They looked lost, and confused. I knew the look. It was the one humans wear in the aftermath of a devastating loss. I took form and walked among them. I held those who needed holding, and murmured comforts to those who needed to hear them. I wiped away many tears.

There was a fire that night, but no dancing, and no celebration. Our community had been split in two. There were now two peoples in my valley—my followers, and the followers of the Deep God.

5

Those who had remained with me went on with their lives as best they could. The others—the ones we came to call "the Departed"—set about the task that had been set for them by the Deep God.

I kept busy. In the old days, I had come and gone from my temple as I wished. Petitioners never knew if they would find me present to hear them or not. I was also arbitrary about doling out help. Humans, as I had learned, would take and take if allowed. They would deplete the world if left unchecked. So I was careful when granting their requests.

But after the departure, I stayed in my temple. I saw each and every person who came to ask for aid. And if I could help them, I did. I shortened illnesses that ought to have run their course. I helped grow crops that ought to have failed. I gave them permission to hunt the woods and take more than ever before.

Those who remained with me were as needy as children that year, but so was I. I needed their need for me. Whenever I was alone with my thoughts and feelings, I found myself melancholy in a way I had never known before. This was my first experience with sorrow. I had seen it in others but never felt it myself. I did not want to admit it, but the departure of Berach and his followers had wounded me. I had loved and cared for these people, and they had walked away, into the arms of something that worried me deeply.

I stayed embodied and in my temple for a season. Eventually, my followers, sated and healthy, stopped lining up outside my door, and I was left to my dark ruminations.

The Deep God. Where had he come from? What was he? For countless years, my forest had been immaculate. And then one day, there was a hole in the earth, and a voice speaking to my people in their dreams.

I have never had access to the dreams of men or beasts. How could this Deep God visit dreams? He must be powerful. That worried me. As did the message that came through those dreams, the promises and threats.

And why had he never reached out to me? Tried to touch my mind?

Finally, one night, my curiosity outweighed my fears. I took to the skies, a mere whisper on the wind, and entered the woods. I wasted no time, but went straight to the opening.

The Departed had only been gone for three cycles of the moon. And yet, when I visited the Deep God's opening, I was shocked at the change. A small community had sprung up in the woods. Trees had been felled. Houses had been built. There were pens for livestock, fields for crops. There was a well. And, in the center of all of this, the hole that had started all this trouble. It had been made larger, and a pathway had been built, a ramp leading down into the dark. The entry was now wide enough that several broad men, standing shoulder-to-shoulder, could easily have entered.

Two men stood at the entrance to the opening. Both held torches in one hand, and spears in the other. Were they… guarding the hole?

Unable to stem my curiosity, I took form before the guards. I recognized both, men named Eithne and Rian. Both had been farmers before. They startled at my appearance, and Eithne cried out.

"Peace," I said. "I mean you no harm. What are you doing?"

"Standing guard," Eithne said.

"What are you guarding against?" I asked.

"They stand guard against you and your followers," came a voice from behind me. I turned to see Berach stalking out of the darkness. He still had the ruddy, broad features of a laborer, but now he wore dark robes, like a priest.

"Berach," I said. "How did you know I was here?"

"The Deep God warned me," Berach said. "He said you were on the winds tonight, and out to interfere."

"I have not come to interfere," I said. "I have come to see how it goes with you."

"Fine, as I am sure you can see," Berach said. "You can leave now."

"You used to speak to me with respect," I said.

"I used to think you a goddess," he said. "Now I know you for a pretender. Now, will you leave, or will you make trouble for us?"

"Why are your men guarding the entrance?" I said. "My followers and I are no threat to you."

"We do as He commands," Berach said. "We are fashioning a mighty road. Someday, it will be a path walked by the pilgrims of the world. But for now it is little more than a cave opening. While it is small, it needs to be guarded from outside forces, who would hinder its progression and growth."

"If this Deep God is so powerful," I said, "could he not guard it himself?"

Berach crossed his arms and did not answer, but cocked his head. It was clear he was finished with this conversation.

"I do not mean to make trouble," I said. "I meant it when I let you go. You are not beholden to me. But what I see here is worrisome. Please, Berach. Be careful."

"Do not threaten me, witch," Berach hissed, and the venom in his voice shocked me.

"I will go," I said. "I wish you well. I hope you find paradise." I left my form and took to the skies again.

I should have known it would not end at that. There was too much rage in him. The Deep God had poisoned him too thoroughly. But I had not yet had enough experience of the hearts and minds of men. I had many more surprises ahead of me.

6

Berach's men had guarded the Deep God's road. I should have set my loyalists to guard their village. I should have learned from Berach and the Deep God. Started thinking suspiciously. Is innocence any excuse? I think not.

The Departed returned to my village less than a moon-cycle later. They came on a foggy night when visibility was low. The people of my village were all asleep in their beds. They had no warning. I had no reason to expect such treachery. I had let the Departed go in peace. Why would I expect anything less of them in return?

I was away, on that night, in a distant part of the woods, tending the final hours of a doe with a broken leg. Perhaps it was bad luck, or perhaps Berach's men had hurt her and left her there to draw me away. I suspect the latter, but I do not know for certain, even now.

Whatever the truth, a band of the Departed arrived in my village in the dead of night. They moved quickly and efficiently. They had grown up here, and had to make no guesses about how and when to strike.

They set fire to the roundhouses. Some of my people, deep in dreams, inhaled the smoke, and they drifted away on the tides of their dreams.

These were the lucky ones.

The unlucky ones—the ones who woke and stumbled from their homes into the night air, gasping and coughing—met the Departed in the fog. These poor souls had to look their former friends and neighbors in the eye as they were murdered, their lives cut short by spear and axe.

I was sitting next to the doe, coaxing her to peace, when I heard the screams. I took to the air and flew to the village as fast as I could, but I returned only to find a scene of slaughter. My people—every single man, woman, and child—were dead. Most had died of smoke inhalation. The others lay in their bloodied bedclothes. They had been left where they had fallen.

I walked among the bodies, too shocked to weep. And then I came to Patraic's body. He had managed to flee across the village, and had fought his way to my temple before he died. He lay upon the steps, on his back, his eyes wide, his throat slashed, his clothes caked with already congealing blood.

This was the sight that brought me back to my senses. I did not feel grief. I felt rage. My tears burned hot on my cheeks as I balled my hands into fists and sprang into the sky.

I caught up with the murderers in the woods. They had not yet reached their settlement. I acted as only the most vicious predator can, tearing and rending the flesh in the ways I knew hurt the most. I moved among them too quickly for them to strike back. All they could do was scream, shout, and flail uselessly until they were, to a man, dead.

I lifted the bodies—a dozen in total—and dumped them in the center of the Departed settlement, at the feet of the night watchmen.

"Where is Berach?" I demanded.

"I am here, witch," Berach said. He emerged from the dark, as he had during our last encounter, wearing the dark vestments of his priesthood. He stopped just short of the entrance to the Deep God's Road, and looked at the broken and mangled bodies piled there, between his two guards. Both men stayed at their posts but looked deeply discomfited to be so close to the corpses.

Berach regarded the bodies dispassionately, before looking back at me.

"I see you have finally revealed your true nature," he said.

"You know why I have done what I have done," I said. I was shocked to feel tears upon my face once more. I was full of rage, and yet I wept.

"Why?" I demanded. "Why have you done this? The people you killed—you have known them all your life. They were peaceful. They did not interfere with your work. They were no threat."

"We do the Deep God's will, and we do not question," Berach said.

"Why would the Deep God want this?" I said.

"We do not question," Berach said, his smile as placid as a pond on a still night. "But if I were to speculate? You came here uninvited. You made veiled threats. The Deep God needed us to send you a message."

"Threats?" I said, disbelieving. "I never threatened. I came. I visited. I asked questions."

"The Deep God does not tolerate dissent," Berach said.

"Are questions considered dissent?" I asked.

"We do the Deep God's will, and we do not question," Berach said. "But, seeing what you have done to my men—" here he gestured to the pile of corpses, "—I think the Deep God was right to stand up to you."

I was too baffled to make a proper response. This was delusion, willful delusion made into a system of belief. I already knew that men were capable of great things when they believed in something beyond themselves. I had not known that they could be capable of such darkness, too.

"I took rightful vengeance on a band of murderers," I said at last. "They slaughtered innocents."

"They did the Deep God's will, and paid a heavy price," Berach said. "But know this, witch—they are now in a paradise beyond this world, where you can no longer harm them."

"And what of the souls they slaughtered?" I asked.

Berach shrugged. "The Deep God offered them his protection, and they rejected it. I do not know what has become of them in death. It is not my problem."

He was so flippant about the murders he had facilitated. I could not stand it. I lunged toward him, meaning to carry him into the sky, and break his body slowly. I wanted him to suffer, to feel the terror of the innocents he had killed. The guards were behind me. There was nothing between us.

I was inches away from him, my arms already extended—perhaps I would break his arm first, to clarify his thinking with a sharp bit of agony—when something hit me from behind and knocked me to the ground. There was a chittering sound in my ear, and a sudden stink filled my nostrils. It smelled like rotten eggs. Brimstone. I felt a weight upon my back, and looked over my shoulder, but saw nothing.

I tried to climb to my feet and wrestle the weight off me. A great pain exploded in my shoulder, and my neck, and back. I cried out. I screamed as the pain struck me. Something—several somethings—seemed to be biting me, all at once. Like a pack of hungry, angry wolves. And yet, when I looked about me, I saw nothing. Whatever was attacking me was invisible to the eye, and it stank.

I struggled, but could not free myself. The weights upon me increased, as did the pain. I fought, but I was overwhelmed and confused. I looked up at Berach, who stood with his arms spread. Behind him, I saw a crowed emerging from the trees—members of the Departed, come to watch.

I had been lured into a trap.

"See!" Berach said. "The Deep God makes his vengeance known! This witch posed as a goddess, and now she pays the ultimate price!"

I screamed. I struggled. But my invisible attackers were too great. There were too many of them.

The world went dark around me, as Berach and the congregation of the Deep God began to sing.

7

I was... gone, for a time. Unaware. I wish I had better words to explain how it felt. Perhaps it is not unlike what it is like to be asleep, when one is not dreaming. I drifted in darkness. Not myself. Not anything.

Was this death? I am not sure. I have been with many creatures as they breathed their last, but have never been able to travel with them, to see what experience, if any, lies beyond that moment.

All I know is that I was gone.

Gradually, however, I came back to myself. It happened slowly, in tiny bits and pieces. Much like a ball of snow, gathering mass as it is rolled along the ground. Little bits of mind, consciousness, and perception returned to me. I do not know how long this process took, only that one day, I was fully myself again, bodiless and drifting over my woods and valley on a sunny summer day.

At first, I experienced pure peace and bliss—to be myself, to be whole once more, on such a beautiful day, in such a beautiful place. Then, more recent memories returned, and I remembered Berach's ambush, the invisible attackers, and my dissolution.

In a panic, I returned to the place in the woods where I had been attacked. The settlement of the Departed.

I found a strange sight. Although it was only midday, there were no people about. No children playing. No men and women hard about the day's work. There were no sounds. Not even birdsong, or the tiny sounds of creatures moving through the woods.

And then there was the Deep God's Road. It had widened since I had last seen it; they had finished their work.

Wary of attackers, I remained disembodied, but drifted down into this entrance.

My tale is already long. I will not try your patience by describing what I saw, for you must have seen it yourself. Long corridors of blowing blue stone. The remains of the Departed. Some looked as if they had died peacefully. Others were posed as if they had been struck down while trying to flee.

The remains were old. The clothing long decomposed, along with the meat and sinew of the bodies. Only skeletons remained.

How long had I been gone?

I drifted along, exploring the massive cavern, and the temple built at its back. I explored the temple, too, finding more remains. I explored its highest floors, and then its lowest. At the bottom of its lowest dungeon, I found a doorway, which led to another staircase, and at the bottom of this staircase, I found yet another doorway. This one opened out to a long, narrow bridge of stone. The bridge traversed a great empty space below it—a pit that seemed to have no bottom.

At the other side of the bridge, across from the temple stood two unfinished stone pillars. About these pillars swarmed dozens—hundreds? —of small creatures, whose like I had never seen before. They were human in shape, but only the size of large children, on the cusp of adolescence. Their heads were large, as were their eyes. Their mouths were full of sharp teeth, and each had a pair of leathery wings folded at their back. These creatures were hard at work on the pillars. On either side of the pillars were dozens of small doorways—doorways which a man would have to stoop to enter.

My mind had fully recovered at this point, and I made some assumptions about what had happened. The Deep God had used the Departed. Had encouraged them to open the road, and to build him a great temple in the Earth. How many years had this taken? It was truly a great work.

Then the Departed had built those smaller doorways, and let in the little creatures—the ones I saw working before me now—and the Deep God had had no more use for his human servants. He had killed the humans, then.

I wondered if he had promised them paradise as he murdered them.

It mattered little now, they were all dead, and these winged creatures seemed to be completing the work. I thought I understood what the creatures were doing, then. They were not building pillars, but rather, had started upon a doorway. A gate for the Deep God. It made little sense at first, because beyond the pillars stood a wall of stone. This doorway would open onto nothing. But perhaps the Deep

God—or these creatures—knew of some enchantment that could turn an empty doorway into a portal? One through which he could travel, from his imprisonment, into freedom?

I did not know what the Deep God was. I still do not know. But I had seen what this being did to people. It had killed every single person under my care. Who knew what it might accomplish, if let free into the natural world?

I made a choice then. I would protect my valley, no matter what. There in the darkness, I gathered all my strength to myself, and released it in a great sunburst of energy. This sunburst was meant to kill the monsters working below, and to seal the cave entrance up above in my woods. It was meant to be my final act, my sacrifice to save the natural world.

It was successful, at least in the short term, I believe. The creatures—the Deep God's True Servants—were not killed but put into a deep slumber, their work stopped. The cave entrance was sealed. I saw all of this before I was consumed by darkness once more.

8

I came back to myself only recently. I am not sure why it happened now. Perhaps my enchantment worked upon me, too? And that I have slept here, in the dark, beneath my woods, for untold years. I think I woke when the cave re-opened itself.

I awoke confused, sure that I had been dead. And then I realized that time had passed once more. Humans had returned to the valley. They were in the woods. And the Deep God had somehow, over the course of years, re-opened the entrance to his road. I do not think he was fully awake yet. His Servants attacked the men, hunted them like animals. But I think he is waking now, and his door is close to being complete.

The Deep God approaches, Solomon Kane.

33

A Goddess's Request

Rhiannon's final words hung in the air. The spell she had woven with her tale was so complete that it took Kane a moment to realize she had stopped speaking.

He shook his head to clear it, to return to the present moment.

"Will you tell me your own story?" Rhiannon asked. "I would hear it."

Kane obliged, going over his journey to Windsend, his nightmares, the murder he had witnessed, the trial, his and Sybil's retreat to the woods, and their journey here.

When he had finished, she sighed and said, "Then I am right. The Deep God is awake, and completing his work."

"I do not understand," Kane said. "If these creatures—the True Servants, as you call them—are doing the Deep God's work, why would he be bothering with the humans above?"

"Perhaps he wants their help to widen the road for him once more," Rhiannon said. "Or he has realized he will need human servants in our world. I cannot say for certain."

Kane studied Rhiannon's face. She was beautiful, and

otherworldly. For the first time since meeting her, he realized that she glowed faintly green. Somehow, the color did not make her look like a sickly sailor, but rather full of life and health, though her expression was sad and pensive.

It was an incredible tale, but Kane had seen too much in his life to cling to any pedestrian beliefs regarding the supernatural. He believed her. It was the option that seemed most logical, and explained the most, and there was something about Rhiannon that felt inherently trustworthy.

So now he had answers: the Deep God was the source of his nightmares. The little creatures were its minions. This Deep God was preying upon the hearts and minds of Windsend. Turning the darker parts of their souls against one another. Creating chaos, and trying to remove obstacles to its return. It had worked to remove Kane and Sybil. Kane had been correct: the Deep God saw them as threats. This was good news.

"You have stopped the Deep God before," Kane said to Rhiannon. "Could you not just do so now? Use all of your power to put him and his Servants back to sleep?"

"I could try," Rhiannon said. "But the spell would work upon you and your friend here, as well."

"That seems a fair price," Kane said, "for the lives of those above."

"A noble sentiment," Rhiannon said. "But I worry that the spell might also extend to the people above, in the village you describe. I would not be killing them, but I would be robbing them—and you—of life. You would sleep away the years until your hearts stopped."

Kane frowned. He could agree to sacrifice himself. But all those people? Some of whom were mere children? Could he sacrifice Isaac and Catherine?

"I cannot make that decision," he said. "There must be another solution."

"The creatures," Rhiannon said. "True Servants. They have already completed their work on the doorway. One of these minions appears to be working upon an enchantment of his own. I believe that they are almost ready to open the doorway for the Deep God. Once that doorway is open, the Deep God will come through, and I do not know what will happen next. I do not suspect it will be anything good."

"How do you know that the doorway is complete?" Kane asked.

"I have seen it," Rhiannon said. "It was the first thing I went to see when I awoke from my slumber."

"Our task is simple, then," Kane said. "We have to go to the bottom of the temple, out onto the bridge, and kill the Servant enchanting the doorway—or at least interrupt him in his work long enough to destroy the doorway itself."

Rhiannon sighed. "That is but another temporary solution. You have heard my tale. You know what the Deep God does. If we destroy the doorway, he will still have access to the thoughts and dreams of any people who wander near. He can plague them, even if we manage to bring down the temple and this entire subterranean labyrinth. How long until he finds another Berach, to follow his orders and begin the work anew?"

"What do you suggest, then?" Kane said.

"We must kill the Deep God, once and for all," Rhiannon said.

Another man might have laughed at the audacity of this statement. Kill a god? Why not ask Kane to drain the ocean with a ladle, or build a wooden bridge between Europe and Africa?

But Kane was not a man given to mirth. He only glowered at Rhiannon.

"If everything you have told me is true, then the Deep God is powerful," he said. "I am only a man. And my companion—" he gestured back at Sybil, lying on the table behind him "—has some powers, but they have been disrupted by this Deep God. Even if they had not been, she is injured. You yourself, once worshipped as a goddess in these lands, have not been able to stop him so far. What is different now?"

"The doorway is complete," Rhiannon said. "The Servants prepare to open the way. Until now, I have only battled the Deep God's influence. His followers. But if the door is open, and he comes through… perhaps he will be vulnerable to an attack. Perhaps he will be susceptible to bodily harm, and death."

"Or perhaps he is like you, and will merely reform, in time."

"I do not know what he is," Rhiannon said. "He may be something different from me entirely. But if you are right, and in time, his essence reforms, my solution is the only one that offers life to the people you want to save. The only solution that does not end with you and your—" she stopped speaking then, and it seemed to Kane that her glow softened a bit, as her mouth turned down in a small frown.

"Oh," she said.

"What is wrong?" Kane said.

Rhiannon pointed behind him. Kane spun about to look at Sybil. He gently shook her shoulder, and spoke her name. Her head lolled to one side, and she did not respond. Her shoulder was cold to the touch.

Trying not to panic, he put a hand beneath Sybil's nostrils, checking for breath. None came.

34

A Bargain

Kane touched Sybil's cheek, and recoiled at the coolness there. Dead? How could this be? She had survived being burned at the stake. She had saved Kane from the horde. And now she was just… dead?

He turned back to Rhiannon. "How long has she been dead?" he demanded.

"What does that matter?" Rhiannon said.

"Did she die while I listened to you prattle on? Did you feel her go? How is her flesh already so cold? Were you so concerned with the sound of your own voice that you, who claim to be one with nature and life itself, could not feel her departure?"

"I did not feel her go," Rhiannon said. "It does not always work that way."

He seethed, teeth gritted, and planted his fists upon the desk, attempting to master himself. He wanted to throttle Rhiannon.

You must get control, he told himself. *You have seen many die in your life, and have never lost control like this before. She was an ally, yes, but you have seen scores of allies die in the past. Why is this different?*

Rhiannon put a hand upon his shoulder. "This one meant much to you?"

Why bother with control? Le Loup spoke up in his head. *All is lost. Let yourself free, mon ami. Have at her. She let your poor witch die. Make her pay.*

Kane turned his head to glower at the one-time goddess. He towered over her.

"Bring her back," he said.

"That is not how life and death work," Rhiannon said.

"Why not?" Kane said. "You have died at least twice, in the story you just told."

"I am not mortal. She was. A mortal is born, lives her life, and dies. And after death, she returns to the earth from which she came. It is the cycle."

"I do not need an education in the basics of life and death," Kane said. "I am not some primitive for you to educate. I have not come to cut a beast's throat, to beg your favor. I am Solomon Kane, instrument of God, and I am *demanding* that you return this woman to life."

"I am of nature," Rhiannon said. "I cannot go against what I am."

"You say you want to kill the Deep God," Kane said. "You say you need help to do it. Well, I need *her* help."

Rhiannon regarded him for a long time. Her eyes grew glassy, and she reached out as if to touch Kane's cheek. Kane turned his face from her touch.

"I am sorry," she said. "But I cannot. It is not a matter of choice. It is a matter of ability."

"If you will not grant me what I ask," Kane said, "then I will not help you with what you ask."

"You would do this?" she asked. "You would put all the

people at risk, for this woman's life?"

He hung his head. "She is an innocent. She tried to care for others, even when they did not care for her. She is only here because I could not make the trip alone."

Rhiannon waited for him to finish his sentence. When it became clear he would not, she sighed. "I say to you again that to bring her back would not be natural, and is outside the scope of my power. I am sorry for your pain, Solomon Kane, but believe me, it is as natural and common as the air we breathe."

Kane left his head hanging. Sybil was gone, then. A coldness, more terrible than the great chill of this labyrinth, washed over him.

"But perhaps..." Rhiannon sighed. "Perhaps there is another way."

Kane said nothing. He would not dare to hope.

"I have lived long," Rhiannon said. "And across the many long days and nights of my existence, the true constant—the thing that lingers with me—is regret. I have made a mess of my time in this world. Perhaps it is time to give another a chance. Perhaps your friend—this innocent you speak of, the woman who cared for her neighbors, even as they hated and distrusted her—can do better?"

Kane frowned, trying to follow the path of her reasoning. "You mean to transfer your power to her?"

"Yes," Rhiannon said. "In the past, I could speed the healing or passing of a wounded creature or person by sending a little of my essence into its body. What I propose to do now is to gift my entire essence to your friend, draining myself."

"You would sacrifice yourself?" Kane said.

"I do not know if it *can* be done. But if it can, she will be restored to life, and will find herself in possession of all my gifts and responsibilities. It means she will never grow older. She will never die, unless she makes a choice like the one I am making now. But it also means she will never be able to leave the valley. She will be tied to it, and its health, forever."

Kane at last understood. There were strings tied to this gift. Sybil would live, yes, but she would never leave Windsend.

"Do you feel comfortable making this decision for her?" Rhiannon said.

Most people Kane had met rarely traveled far from the village, town, or city where they were born. Travelers like himself were quite rare. So in a way, Sybil would be no different. And yet, this would mean that she could never accompany him on an adventure. She could never leave the place that had tried to kill her. She would be trapped close to the inhabitants of Windsend—and their descendants—forever. She might well come to hate Kane, for damning her to such a fate.

And yet he could not let her go. He needed to see her breathing and well once more.

He placed a hand on Sybil's cold cheek. "Forgive me," he murmured. Then he looked into Rhiannon's eyes. "She will have your powers? She will be able to do what you do? Her own gifts are… interrupted by the presence of these unnatural creatures."

"Mine are muffled as well," Rhiannon said. "But I *can* access them. It should be the same for her."

"Do it. If you can."

Rhiannon placed one hand upon Sybil's middle, and another upon her upper chest, just below her throat.

"May you have all the joy that I did," Rhiannon said to her. "But may you have the cunning to safeguard that joy. May darkness never take you by surprise. May you do better than I did."

It was as good a benediction as Kane had ever heard.

Rhiannon's body glowed brighter as she gathered her power to her. The glow rippled down her arms, through her hands, and spread over Sybil's body, enveloping her. It came in waves that pulsed like a silent heartbeat. It was one of the strangest, most beautiful things Kane had ever seen.

Rhiannon gasped and squeezed her eyes shut. "I think it is working," she said.

"Does it hurt?" Kane said.

"It is not entirely pleasant," she said, with a small smile. "But it is… oh, is this what it truly feels like, to be mortal? To face death?"

Kane stepped around the desk, meaning to put a comforting hand on her shoulder.

"Do not touch me," she warned. "It could interfere with the transfer." She turned her head to look at Kane, and a tear rolled down her cheek, glistening like a tiny star. "I can feel her. All of her memories. Her thoughts. Her pain. Her feelings." And now the tears flowed freely. She closed her eyes.

"Rhiannon?" Kane said.

"I had no idea," Rhiannon said. "The intensity of mortal life. Everything you experience. It all means *so much*, because it is so fleeting, and ends so quickly. I am glad to experience it now. To see all of my own experiences, given shape by the arc of a birth, a life, and now, a death. I am glad I experienced Sybil's as well. I hope these memories and experiences will sustain her, over the many years to come."

She closed her eyes and leaned forward, laying her head upon Sybil's breast. The pulsing lights stopped, and became a shimmering glow. Then this, too, faded, leaving Kane in the dim blue light from the stone.

He touched Rhiannon's shoulder, and startled as her flesh gave way beneath his fingertips. Her body lost its shape all at once, dissolving into small, individual pieces. Some of the remains drifted onto the desk, and the rest softly landed upon the floor. Kane picked up a flake. It felt papery, and crunched between his fingers, and his senses at last reported what he held.

It was a fallen leaf. Rhiannon had dissolved into hundreds of fallen tree leaves.

It was a fitting end for the goddess of the woods.

Sybil began to glow, softly at first, but the light quickly intensified. Kane had to drop the leaf to shield his eyes.

He saw, rather than heard her first intake of breath. Then she began to scream.

35

The Final Descent

Still keeping one hand over his eyes, Kane scrambled forward, groping for Sybil's mouth.

"Sybil," he hissed, as if his quiet could help them now. "Sybil, it's alright!"

She continued to scream, stopping for breath between cries.

He found her shoulder, her neck, and then her face, and wrapped a hand about her mouth, muffling the shouts.

"Peace!" Kane urged her. "Peace, Sybil Eastey. All is well."

Her eyes, which had been darting about the dark room, unseeing, locked upon his. Kane put a finger to his lips. She nodded once, and he let go of her. They both remained silent. Kane closed his eyes, listening for sounds from outside the room. They came quickly: the clicking of long nails on stone, the chittering voices of the Deep God's Servants as they came to investigate the racket. It did not sound like many. Certainly not the horde they had fled from before. Half a dozen or less.

Sybil looked from Kane's face to the bookcase pressed up against the door, then back to Kane's face. Sanity seemed to return to her. He removed his hand from her mouth. She remained still as the sounds outside grew closer, moving up the corridor outside.

A great bang sounded nearby. Sybil startled, but remained quiet. That had been the sound of a door being opened. It was followed a moment later by another bang, this one closer. They were working their way down the corridor, checking each room. What would happen when they reached this room? Kane and Rhiannon had blocked the door with the bookcase. That would prevent the Servants from entering but would also alert them that something was afoot.

"Can you move?" Kane whispered to Sybil. "Do you have your strength?"

She looked down at her body—at her blood-soaked clothes, at the drying pool of blood on the desk. She touched the place in her stomach where she had been wounded. There was a tear in the front of her dress, but the exposed skin beneath was smooth and unblemished. Although her raiment and the room bore the marks of her injury, her body did not. Not even the scars from Kane's cauterization.

She looked back to Kane, her confusion plain. "I do not understand."

"I will explain, if we survive the next few moments," Kane said. "Can you stand? Can you help me lift that bookcase without making a sound?"

Another bang sounded, this one closer than the last. They did not have much time.

"Why would you want to move it?" Sybil asked. "It is the only thing standing between them and us."

"You must trust me," Kane said.

Sybil licked her lips, then hopped off the desk. She landed on the floor without a sound, as lightly as a bird on a tree branch. She stood on one side of the bookcase, and Kane went to the other. He nodded to her, and, as one, they lifted it. It came up so easily that Kane almost lost his grip and dropped his side. Sybil held her end as if it weighed nothing at all.

But he did manage to keep his grip, and together, they moved it aside, clearing the doorway. That done, Kane gestured to Sybil to stand in one of the corners of the room, on the same side as the door, where she would not be immediately visible to any intruders. He pressed himself upon the wall next to the door, his staff gripped in both hands.

He slowed his breathing, and tightened his grip on the staff. The red fog descended over his mind, enveloping him in his battle calm. All worries, cares, aches, and pains fled before it.

The door to the room flew open, and slammed against the wall, kicked in by one of the Servants. The creature marched inside. Kane held still, waiting. A few seconds later, two more creatures entered. Kane counted two heartbeats, then moved.

It was nice to have the advantage on these creatures at last. He stepped forward quietly, gracefully, grabbing one from behind and easily snapping its neck. He lowered the body to the floor soundlessly, then stepped forward, crouched, and swung his staff in a wide arc. He knocked the legs out from under the other two creatures. They crashed to the stone floor upon their backs, and before either could make a sound of reaction, Kane stepped forward, sword drawn in his right hand. With his left arm, he slammed the staff down to crush one Servant's skull, and with his right arm, he drove the tip of his sword into the throat of the other. It tried to cry out, but only thick gurgles emerged from its bloody, sharp-toothed maw.

The execution of these creatures took only a few seconds. As Kane lifted his bloodied weapons from the bodies, he felt an immense satisfaction. He truly felt like himself, for the first time in some while.

Then he heard the click behind him, and spun to see the

fourth creature standing in the corridor. It was hard to read expressions on these creatures' faces: their eyes did not communicate emotion like a human's. But Kane suspected he saw surprise and dismay in the rigidity of the creature's posture, the way its head was drawn back.

Kane's sword arm tensed as his battle-mind offered him options. Perhaps he could hit the creature with a thrown weapon, and at least slow it down? Give himself enough time to close the distance and finish the job, before it could make a sound and alert its fellows?

All of this blazed through his mind in the space of a breath—and yet, he was still thinking when the green light flashed across his field of vision, and the creature crumpled to the floor. Its eyes remained open, but there was no mistaking what had happened. It was dead.

He turned to see Sybil standing beside him, her arms raised, a green glow about her body. She slowly lowered her hands, and looked at them.

Kane poked his head into the corridor. He saw no other Servants. He and Sybil appeared to be safe, for the moment.

When he re-entered the room, Sybil was staring at her hands.

"What has happened to me?" she said. "I..." She put a hand to her head. "I can feel... goddess... it is..." She put her hands to her head, and sank to her knees.

Kane knelt beside her, and put a hand on her shoulder. It was so much warmer than it had been a few moments ago. He felt a rush of gratitude for Rhiannon, diluted only by his concern for Sybil, who cradled her head in her hands and softly groaned, like a woman in great pain.

"What is it?" Kane asked.

"It is everything," Sybil said. "I feel *everything*. Eternity itself. It is so much... too much..." She gasped, as if in pain. "What has been done to me?"

Kane opened his mouth to answer, but she put up a hand to preemptively silence him. She closed her eyes and frowned, hand in the air. She seemed to be listening to something Kane could not hear.

"I can feel her," she said. "Inside me. Her memories. Her life. Her pain and regrets. I see it all. I see… Oh." Her eyes snapped open and she looked at Kane. Her expression contained some of that playful shrewdness he had come to recognize during their short acquaintance. For the first time since she had drawn breath a moment ago, she looked like herself.

Kane waited for the next questions. Why had he done this? Why had he bargained with Rhiannon for Sybil's life? Why had he chained Sybil to this mortal plane, to this valley, for all time? Kane thought he could *feel* those questions in Sybil's expression, lurking just behind curled lips.

But she did not ask questions. Instead, she said, "I have been joined to Rhiannon. Given a task to help you complete."

"Yes," Kane said. "We must kill the Deep God."

Kane dragged the body of the fourth Servant out of the corridor and into the office. He stashed the bodies of all four creatures in the darkest corner of the room, and shut the door. While he did this, Sybil went up the corridor and closed all the other doors that had been opened during the Servants' search a few moments before.

It would not fool another search party, if the party was thorough, but it would slow them down. Kane and Sybil would be long gone by then.

Sybil led the way, navigating from Rhiannon's memories. They moved down the corridor, down another set of stairs, which ended in another corridor, almost identical to the one above. This new corridor ended in a heavy wooden door with an ancient padlock upon it. Sybil flicked her fingers and the lock crumbled.

Beyond the door stood another staircase, this one grand and wide, like something in a great city, or a palace, and ended in a grand archway.

When Kane and Sybil reached the archway, they found themselves outside the temple. They'd emerged at the far end. Behind them, the temple wall rose to the cavern ceiling. This was a change from the front of the temple, where the cavern ceiling had stretched far above the temple roof. The temple must bridge the space between two separate caverns, he guessed—its entrance in one, its exit in the other.

The archway that Kane and Sybil had passed through opened out to a narrow, winding stair that seemed to have been carved out of the rock itself. The stairway descended in a series of switchbacks, without railing or protection against fall. Far below, the stairway ended at a small landing, which opened onto a narrow stone bridge across a great chasm. The chasm was so deep that Kane could not see its bottom from his current vantage point.

A single Servant stood about three-quarters of the way across the bridge. This Servant wore a strange raiment on his person, a robe of furs. He carried a staff as well, which he held in one hand. With his free hand, he made small, sharp gestures in the air. Blue light burst from his fingertips with each gesture, and then moved through the air like living smoke. It all drifted toward a great empty doorway at the far end of the bridge. Kane recognized the doorway. Rhiannon had described it for him.

"The Deep God's portal," Kane breathed. "It is bigger than I imagined. What creature could need such a door?"

"Either one of great stature, or great ego," Sybil said.

"I do not understand," Kane said. "If it is so large, what was the purpose of this temple? The creature could never fit through any of its corridors or doorways. And what about the Deep God's True Servants? How are they here? Did they come through a different doorway? Why can the Deep God not arrive how they arrived?"

Sybil shook her head. "I do not know. I do not think Rhiannon considered these questions. Perhaps the temple and labyrinth were only ever meant for the Deep God's human servants. Places for them to live and worship while they went about the work of preparing for his arrival. Once the Deep God comes, perhaps he will be able to change his size or shape. Or perhaps he means to destroy all of this, and just batter his way to the surface? And as for the True Servants, I only know that they *are* here, and have been for a very long time. Speculation seems pointless, with time so short."

Kane scratched his chin, his face rough with stubble, as he surveyed the scene and considered his next moves. The great doorway was growing opaque. Although Kane could still see a blank stone wall behind it, it was difficult. A glowing blue film was taking shape and filling the empty archway. It looked almost like the surface of a pool of water reflecting a midday sky. There was also a small legion of the Deep God's True Servants arrayed before the doorway. They stood in neat rows, like a battalion of soldiers.

Once more Kane found himself tempted to change the plan. To disrupt the ritual below, and delay the Deep God's arrival. To allow such a being into this world seemed an unacceptable risk.

As if sensing his doubts, Sybil squeezed Kane's arm.

"Courage," she murmured. "Rhiannon's plan is the only path that does not end in ruin for Windsend. It is a small hope, but the only one we have."

Kane's doubts remained. How was he supposed to defeat a legion of these True Servants, their wizard, *and* a thing powerful enough to call itself a god? He supposed he would find out shortly.

36

The Deep God

The Deep God's wizard stood upon the bridge, approximately three-quarters of the way across from the stairs at the bottom of the temple. Its eyes were affixed to the portal, and its free hand moved in increasingly frantic and severe gestures, its fingers twisting about unnaturally. Blue light burst from its fingertips and flew through the air to join the gathered mass in the portal.

The mass filled the entirety of the portal, the way water spreads to fill and take the shape of a container. With each gesture from the wizard, the mass glowed brighter and brighter. When Kane and Sybil had first seen it moments before, it had appeared almost translucent. They had been able to see the stone wall beyond. Now it was solid, and shone like a great bonfire, casting all the darkness about it in an eldritch blue as bright and vivid as the midday sky.

A small army of the True Servants were lined up on either side of the portal, standing at attention like human soldiers awaiting an inspecting general.

At last, the wizard finished its chant, and, gesturing with a final flourish, a final blue burst flew from its hand and coalesced in the doorway. The glow increased once more, and became almost blinding for an instant, before softening into something less intense.

The wizard lowered its free hand to its side and stood up straight, eyes forward. The army of Servants turned their heads to look as well. They all waited, in perfect stillness, for what would come next.

A deep growl sounded from the portal, and the air itself seemed to vibrate like a plucked harp string. The stone shook, and loose pebbles and rocks fell from the walls and into the chasm below. If they made a sound, it was lost in the echo of that growl.

The sheet of light in the portal was pierced as something pressed up against it from the other side: a single balled fist, the size of a grown man's torso. The fist pushed forward out of the solid mass, seeming to gather the blue light about itself, the way a body emerged, soaking wet, from a lake. The fist unfurled, three great digits and a thumb flexing, experimenting with the sensations of the cavern air. Apparently satisfied, it withdrew slightly, and then punched forward, revealing a length of thin, jagged arm, and shoulder. A huge face followed, flat and skull-like, with nose. It seemed too large in proportion to the arm that preceded it.

The rest of the body followed, emerging all at once, as if now, having tested the air of the cavern, it was eager to finish the transition. Its head and torso were shaped like that of a man, although the arms were too long, the head too large for the spindly neck and shoulders. Below the waist, it had a ridged abdomen like an insect, with two thin legs on either side. Each leg was lined with spiky protrusions. The abdomen ended in a giant stinger.

Kane was surprised to see that the Deep God was not just a larger version of its Servants. It was some more advanced and terrible form.

The Deep God stood outside its portal, freed at last, after countless centuries of planning and work. It opened its eyes upon the cavern. They glowed white, like tiny suns. It opened its great mouth, tilted its head back and made a sound of triumph, like the chittering of its Servants multiplied a thousand-fold. The stone trembled at its cry, and the Servants near the portal struggled to keep their balance. The wizard upon the bridge planted his staff and clung to it, as if the bridge were trying to buck him off and into the chasm below.

The Deep God's True Servants chittered and waved their arms about in triumph and adulation. Their long labors had been a success. Their leader—their god—was here.

Now, in the monster's moment of triumph, a single figure strode out of the darkness and onto the bridge. It made no attempt to hide itself. It had no need of secrecy. The Deep God and its Servants were too busy celebrating to notice the figure, and so it was able to approach the wizard from behind, and did not make itself known until the wizard cried out in pain, its note of distress discordant among its fellows' exultation. The other Servants paused and looked. The Deep God turned its head in time to see the sword tip emerge from the wizard's chest, coated in dark blood.

The wizard screamed and flailed, trying to get at its attacker. But Solomon Kane held his blade at arm's length, and remained safely out of its reach. He—and the army of monsters before him—watched the wizard's struggles lessen. Together, he and his opponents listened to the wizard's cries soften, then stop. And when at last the little hierophant had ceased moving, Kane tilted his arm down, and allowed the body to slide off his sword and fall onto the bridge like a bundle of sticks.

Kane kicked the wizard's body aside as he stepped forward. It tumbled off the side of the bridge and into the chasm below.

"I have not slept well of late," Kane said. "I believe I may lay that blame at your feet."

The Deep God opened its mouth in a snarl. It made no vocalizations, but Kane heard its voice in his head as clearly as if it were speaking in his ear.

Are you not dead yet, old man? Must I kill you myself?

"You are welcome to try," Kane said.

The Deep God skittered forward on its many legs, as the red fog of battle dropped over Kane's mind.

It is in your hands now, Sybil, he thought.

In his right arm he continued to brandish the rapier, and with his left, he drew a knife. He had left his staff behind with Sybil, assuming it would be of little use in the Deep God's place of power.

The Deep God scuttled onto the bridge. It wielded no weapon other than its huge fist, at the ends of long arms. It would have the reach and strength to swat Kane into the abyss, if it got close enough.

Kane took a few steps back the way he had come. The Deep God scuttled forward. Kane watched it approach, and forced himself not to glance back and up toward Sybil's hiding place.

The plan was simple: Get the creature out onto the bridge; then destroy the bridge. The Deep God would plummet, and hopefully break every bone in his body at the bottom of the chasm.

"You are strangely silent, Deep God," Kane said. "For days, you have ceaselessly prattled in my dreams, threatening and cajoling. Now that you face me, you have no words?"

The Deep God glared down at Kane with those too-bright eyes. Kane could see no pupils within. If Kane met a man or woman whose eyes looked thus, he would know the person was blinded by cataracts. Could the Deep God actually see Kane? Or was it blind as well?

You do not fool me, little fanatic. The Deep God's voice did not come from its mouth, but rang in Kane's head. It hit him like a blow, and he had to stop moving to keep his balance, and this gave the Deep God a chance to close some of the distance between them.

I smell your weakness, it spoke in Kane's mind. *I can feel your exhaustion.*

The voice was like a physical force pressing down upon Kane. It pushed him down to one knee, and pressed against his skull, forcing him to lower his head. He now knelt before this dark abomination.

You have fought long and hard, but you are no match for a god.

"There is but one God," Kane said. With great effort and gritted teeth, he lifted his head to look up into the Deep God's unknowable face. "And I did not come alone."

As soon as he spoke, a great *crack* split the air. The bridge shook beneath Kane, and the whole world turned bright green. The Deep God whipped its head about, looking for the source of the light and sound. Its attention—its grip—on Kane loosened, and he stumbled backwards and to his feet, putting a few steps between himself and the great beast.

Sybil's bolt had struck true. Cracks had appeared all along the stone bridge, starting at the place where the Deep God stood, and stretching all the way back toward the portal. These cracks spread and splintered quickly, reminding Kane what it was like to step on thin ice seconds before it shattered.

Kane had enough time to take a single step backward before half of the bridge broke into hundreds of small pieces, and fell into the darkness below. The Deep God fell with them. It made no sound as it plummeted. Perhaps it was too surprised.

Kane did not hear its cries in his mind as it disappeared into the depths.

The creatures arrayed near the portal roared and chittered. Some of them took to the air on their wings. Kane turned and ran as fast as he could, heading toward the stairs at the base of the temple. It would be a long journey back, and his back would be exposed the entire way, but perhaps Sybil could cover his retreat—

Pain exploded in his right knee. There had been no warning this time, no slow build of discomfort. One moment, it felt fine, and the next, it refused to hold him upright. Kane collapsed for the second time in as many moments, and shouted with pain as his knee struck stone. The intense agony replaced all thought with bright white light.

He was in the midst of this light when something hit him from behind and knocked him prone, on his stomach, upon the bridge. His sword bounced out of his hand and over the side, into the darkness. Kane fought through the agony and managed to keep hold of his knife, but barely.

He tried to roll onto his back, to shake loose whatever had landed upon him. The weight was too great, however, and his struggles proved fruitless. He was pinned so thoroughly he could scarcely draw breath. All he could do was turn his head, to try and see who had bested him.

The Deep God loomed above Kane, one of its arms pressing Kane into the ground. Kane tried to think through the fog of pain. How was this possible? He had seen the creature fall into the chasm.

Then he became aware of the sound of some great object slicing through the air, creating wind with each movement, blowing stone dust into his face. Wings. The Deep God had wings, like its Servants. Kane had not lured the monster to its death. He had merely annoyed it.

In the air behind the Deep God, its servants soared toward Sybil's hiding place at the top of the temple steps. Great flashes of green light burst from her location, cutting the smell of brimstone with one of trees. Sybil was occupied. She could not help Kane now.

Godspeed, Sybil Eastey, he thought, before straining his neck to look up into the Deep God's face.

"Go on then, foul beast," he said. "Get it over with."

The Deep God's mouth parted in what might have been a smile, exposing a mouth with several rows of razor-sharp teeth. It raised its free arm, and spread the digits of its hand. The flesh of its palm parted, and something emerged. It looked like a cross between a tooth and an insect's proboscis.

The Deep God held the proboscis at eye level for Kane for a long moment, making sure he had plenty of time to look at it.

Are you afraid? it asked.

"Of death?" Kane said. "No. God sees me, and will judge me."

Who said anything about death?

The monster's hand shot forward. The proboscis plunged into the base of Kane's spine, and the world disappeared in a wave of blue light.

The Blue

For a time, Kane knew only pain, and blue light. There was nothing else. But, gradually, the initial burst of discomfort quieted to a low hum. The ache remained, but he could think now.

As they did, he realized that he was no longer being pressed into the stone bridge. There was no hand upon his back, no stone beneath his stomach. He was still prone, but there was no great cavern all around him, no temple steps before him. There were no creatures flying through the air above, battling flashes of green.

Kane pushed up onto his knees and looked about. He seemed to be in an immense, empty darkness, tinged with a dim blue light. And although he knew he was in pain, the pain was relegated to his spine, where the Deep God had stabbed him. His knee bothered him not at all.

Welcome home, little fanatic. The Deep God's voice killed Kane's mind and reverberated in his skull. Kane winced at the sheer force of it, and clamped his hands to either side of his head. It felt as though fingers were rifling through the contents of his mind, examining his every thought and feeling. He saw images flash past, of Rhiannon and her tale. The Deep God was learning of Kane's journey through the labyrinth.

You have been with the little green witch, the Deep God said. *I thought she had killed herself when she last attacked me. But it seems she survived, and enlisted your aid? So she must be with you now. Only… oh.*

In that simple syllable, Kane heard the Deep God's profound surprise.

She willingly surrendered her life essence to a mortal? A chuckle bounced through Kane's head, rocking him to and fro. *What a foolish waste of power. What goddess would willingly give up her existence?*

His tone was full of scorn, but Kane heard something else beneath. Unease? Confusion? It was hard to think straight with this foreign presence in his head.

"Where am I?" Kane demanded. "What is this place?"

You are with me, little fanatic, the Deep God said. *I have never named this place, but my first human priest, Berach, called it* The Blue.

"Berach had been here?"

Indeed, the Deep God said. *He was the first human to visit this place. When he first came to my cave, I put him to sleep and brought him here. I bring all my priests here.*

"Your priests?" Kane said.

Yes, the Deep God said. *You are strong, little fanatic. You have resisted me long, and confounded my efforts to remove you and your influence. And yet, your body fails you. I see much potential, but you must shift your focus, if you are to continue to thrive. With the right... education... I believe you will serve me well.*

"I will never serve you!" Kane growled. With all his will, he pushed against the presence in his head, trying to remove the invader. The Deep God's laughter filled Kane's head.

So said Berach, once upon a time. You have heard Rhiannon's tale. You saw how his resistance worked out for him. In the end, he served me all his life, and was happy to do so. Your life will play out no differently. You will resist me. You will fail. You will become a tool, not for some fictional god of another land, but for me, a true god. You will be my right arm. You will bring the valley under my control. And in the end, you will thank me for it.

"My God is as real as the sun and wind and rain," Kane said. "And He will—"

Shall we begin? the Deep God said, interrupting as though he could not hear Kane. *Yes. I think we shall.*

And before Kane could protest, the presence in his mind expanded, driving out all other thought. It was not painful, but rather like a great ocean wave crashing against his consciousness. It drowned all other thought. Kane was not himself anymore. All was blue.

38

The Trial of Solomon Kane

When Kane came back to himself, he was no longer in the blank, blue-tinged darkness. Instead, he seemed to be in the Windsend meeting house, arranged as it had been for Sybil Eastey's trial. Kane sat in the same chair where Sybil had sat while her neighbors and so-called experts bore false witness against her. Reverend Gideon Pelham stood before Kane now. Behind Pelham, the meeting house seemed to be full of spectators.

"What is this?" Kane said.

Pelham studied Kane for a moment, then walked to a table nearby, where he rifled through a stack of papers.

"Solomon Kane," he said. "Born in the year 1554. You grew up in Devon but were forced to flee at the age of fifteen, after killing a man with important friends. You have spent your life traveling the world?"

"Yes," Kane said.

"And in those travels, you came to see yourself as the wrath of the Christian God?"

"I make no such claim for myself."

"Perhaps not aloud," Pelham said. "Perhaps not so that anyone else can hear. For humility is prized in the Christian faith. But you feel it in your heart, do you not? That you were chosen by God for this purpose."

Kane did not answer, but he also could not meet Pelham's eye.

"Your silence speaks louder than any words," Pelham said. "So you spent your life as God's sword. You tried to protect the innocent, but took far more pleasure in punishing the guilty. Is that not so?"

Kane glared at Pelham, but remained silent.

"There is a rage in you," Pelham said. "There has been, for as long as you can remember. You love to save an innocent maiden here and there, because it allows you tell yourself you are an angel of mercy. But in truth, you harbor a darkness that only violence can quench. It felt good when you killed those men at the age of fifteen, did it not?"

Kane flushed with shame. It was as though Pelham had access to Kane's deepest thoughts and feelings—the parts of himself that he hoped never to show any man or woman. How could Pelham know this?

Because this is not Pelham, he realized. *This is the Deep God.*

"What do you want, monster?" Kane said.

The thing wearing Pelham's face smiled and raised its eyebrows in mild surprise. "That was fast. It took the others much longer to understand."

"Why put on this farce?" Kane asked.

"To help you acclimate to the truth of yourself, little fanatic," the Pelham-thing said. "You wear the garb of a Puritan. You were raised to pray to the Christian god. But your soul has been at war with itself all your life. You have always wanted to hurt. To injure. To kill. You only ever preserve life to preserve your own illusions. Helping others does not satisfy you the way hurting does. Is that not so?"

"It is not so," Kane said, but he lowered his head as he said it, and the words tasted like dirt in his mouth. It was the way he felt when he lied.

"You cannot even lie to yourself convincingly," Pelham said. "I am offering you a chance to embrace your true nature. As my priest, the darkness in your soul would be allowed free rein. Violence would be your art. You could hurt and punish to your heart's content. You might not be able to travel or fight as freely as in the past, with that knee of yours, but in my temple, subjects would be brought before you for judgement. You would be free to carry out my justice as you saw fit. You could spread great fear across my kingdom."

Kane kept his head lowered as his mind flooded with images. He saw himself, garbed in purple robes, sitting upon a throne of judgement in a great hall. Swinging the axe to behead rapists, murderers, and thieves. All cowering before his holy justice. The fire in his heart could burn freely.

"Do you say that my god is a false one?" Kane growled.

Pelham did not answer right away, and Kane lifted his head to see the reverend looking back with a tilted head and confusion plain upon his face.

"Why ask me this?" Pelham said. "I know of no god like the Christian god. I have never met him. He may be real, or he may be a story. What does that matter?"

"It matters..." Kane said, but trailed off as he glanced past the Pelham-thing and into the crowd. On the front row, the eager spectators were Kane's old enemies: Le Loup; Nakari; Sir George Banway; Jonas Hardraker, the Fishhawk; Ezra the miser; and many, many others who had met their ends at Kane's hands. These villains sneered at Kane.

"We do not judge you, Monsieur Galahad," Le Loup said.

"You need to hurt others, just as we did. Only we had the courage to look our desires in the eye. We hid behind no false pretenses of morality. We pursued our appetites. Do you have the decency to do the same now?"

Kane sat back in his chair, his back pressed to the hard, uncomfortable wood. He could feel the rogues' eagerness from across the room. They leaned forward as he leaned back.

Then something else caught his eye. A young woman—a girl, really—sitting toward the back of the room. She stood up, and Kane thought she looked familiar, but could not quite place her face.

Pelham spun about as the girl began to speak, his surprise evident in his posture, the way he held his narrow shoulders.

"You found me among the trees, miles from home. I was already hurt. Stabbed by Le Loup. But you held me as I died. You gave me comfort at the end. And you avenged my death, putting Le Loup to the sword."

"Be gone!" Pelham said. "We will have no more interruptions."

Two other figures stood, a blue-eyed young man and a lovely young woman, holding hands.

"My name is Jack Hollinster," the man said.

"I am Mary Garvin," the woman said.

"You saved Mary and myself from the clutches of George Banway and the Fishhawk," Hollinster said. "I would have been killed, and Mary would have..." He trailed off, his face flush with rage.

Mary stroked his arm and spoke softly. "I would have suffered worse than death," she finished. "But you saved us both."

"Quiet, all of you!" Pelham said. His voice rose an octave. It did not sound particularly commanding, but then, Pelham did not have that kind of voice. His was a light and nasal tone, more suited to the bookish scholar than a preacher meant to lead a flock.

Another figure rose, near the back. Catherine Archer. When last Kane had seen her, her face bore the marks of her husband's fists. This version of Catherine was clear-eyed and untouched.

"You were kind to me when we were young," Catherine said. "I wanted you for myself. You loved Bess better, but you were kind to me. And when I asked for your help in Windsend, you came. Although we had not seen each other in many years. Although you have many demands upon your time and attention. You came home to England, to help me ferret out the truth, and save my friend."

Another figure rose. Sybil Eastey. Like Catherine, she did not bear the marks of her recent hardship, but instead wore a light blue dress, her golden hair straight and free down her back.

"You treated me honestly," she said. "Though I am a witch, and worship forces you consider blasphemous. Despite your discomfort with my faith, you listened to me. You treated me fairly. You investigated honestly, and did your best to prove my innocence. When you realized my trial would be a sham, you lied for me. You compromised your morals in pursuit of a higher truth and justice. Because you thought you could save my life."

A final figure rose at the back of the room, a Black man with a playful smile upon his face, his dark skin a sharp contrast to the small ocean of pale European faces throughout the room. Kane recognized N'Longa at once.

"You allied yourself with me," N'Longa said. "You accepted the gift of the Staff of Solomon. You call me blood brother, despite the fact you believe me damned to Hell."

"How did you get in here?" the Pelham-thing demanded. "I demand that you leave at once!"

Instead of leaving, N'Longa walked toward Kane. The Pelham-thing cut him off, and with a gesture, slammed the priest to the floor. N'Longa did not cry out. Instead, he looked at Kane from his new vantage on the floor as Pelham straddled his chest.

"Some of what the Deep God says is true," N'Longa said. "You have a darkness in you, a barely contained fury, and that darkness is part of your strength."

Pelham interrupted N'Longa's speech with a fist to the face. N'Longa's head rocked back and blood flew from his mouth. Still the priest looked at Kane, and continued to speak, his teeth streaked red.

"But the Deep God is wrong about you in another important way," N'Longa said.

Pelham hit him again. And again. "Shut up! Cease your prattling!"

"You have used your darkness in the pursuit of the light," N'Longa said. His words remained clear despite the battering he was receiving from Pelham. "You fear the darkness within, but you put it in service of the highest good you know. You want to hurt, yes, but more than that, you want to *help*, blood brother. And that—"

Pelham lifted N'Longa's head and slammed it hard against the wooden meetinghouse floor. Kane heard a loud *crack* as something in the priest's skull gave way.

"Are you done?" Pelham screamed into N'Longa's face. "Is it over?"

N'Longa stared up for so long that Kane was worried Pelham had indeed killed him—or at least successfully banished him from this strange dreamscape. But then the priest blinked a few times, and looked back at Kane.

"That..." he murmured, "...is the difference." He let out a last, strangled breath, and then fell still.

Kane looked about the meeting house. All the other figures were gone—both the rogues and Kane's friends and allies. He was alone in the meeting house with the Pelham-thing once more.

The Pelham-thing remained upon his knees, kneeling over the place where N'Longa had been only seconds before. He whirled about as Kane stood, and Kane read something new in the reverend's eyes: panic. The Deep God was worried.

"I have never seen anything like this before," the Pelham-thing said. "I do not understand."

"I think I do," Kane said. "You invaded my mind, meaning to break it and rebuild it in your own image, as you did to Berach. But you have miscalculated, demon. My body is aging. It does not serve me as well now as it did twenty years ago. But my heart and mind are as sharp and strong as ever. They come forth to defend me, in the shapes of my friends, wearing the faces of those I have saved. My faith in my god—the one true God—makes me strong. I am as He made me. I put my light and darkness into His hands, to carry out His will, and act my part in His plan. I believe in His Providence. If He has deemed it meet that I die at your hands, that is how I shall die. But I do not think that is what He has in mind for me."

He jumped to his feet and closed the distance between himself and the Pelham-thing. With a shove, he knocked the Deep God's avatar to the floor. It struggled as Kane straddled its chest, pinned its arms with his knees, grabbed its skull, and pounded it twice against the floor, much as it had done to N'Longa only a moment before. The Pelham-thing's eyes glazed as Kane fastened his hands about the avatar's throat and squeezed.

Kane was not entirely sure this gambit would work. After all, he was in the Deep God's place. Could the Deep God simply escape, or change the rules of engagement to give himself the advantage? Or was he bound to the form he had chosen for this encounter? Kane desperately hoped it was the latter.

The Pelham-thing writhed and bucked, trying to dismount Kane. Its legs kicked wildly, slamming against the floor, the knees digging into Kane's back. None of it made a dent in Kane's steady strangulation of the avatar.

The intensity of the avatar's struggles lessened. The kicks became taps. The writhing became slow spasms.

As the light disappeared from the Pelham-thing's eyes, the light in the meetinghouse dimmed as well. Kane's view of his opponent dissolved, and the sensations—of the throat in his hands, and the body beneath his own—faded too.

Kane was alone in darkness.

And then, suddenly, he was not.

39

Collapse

Kane felt pain.

His whole body ached, the way it sometimes did the day after a hard battle. But his knee and his back hurt worst of all.

He groaned, and opened his eyes. There was still a great weight pressing down upon him.

He turned his head to see the Deep God hovering above. It hung perfectly still in the air. Its wings had stopped moving. Its eyes, once bright white, had gone dark.

It hung, motionless, for a long moment. Then, silently, it fell. The weight upon Kane's back let up, and the sharp pain in his back spiked once more as the god's proboscis withdrew from his flesh.

The Deep God fell past Kane, one moment visible in the blue glow, and in the next, swallowed by darkness and gone.

Kane pushed up onto his hands and knees and took a deep breath. He coughed out stone dust, and then sneezed. He watched the darkness, waiting for his adversary to rise. When it did not, he clambered back to his feet. His knee held him, but barely, and he had to duck immediately, as one of the Deep God's True Servants swooped down out of the air, swinging a spear. Kane sidestepped the thrust and grabbed the shaft of the weapon. He used it as leverage to flip the creature onto its back. He yanked the spear free and slapped the base into the creature's face. Its head burst like an overripe tomato.

He leaned on the spear and looked about. The air was full of these flying creatures. So many of them! Dozens, no, hundreds flying through the air, enraged at the death of their god, and heading for Kane.

He sheathed his knife and took up the spear in both hands. It was small for him. It would have fit more easily into Isaac Archer's hands as a toy than in his own, but it was the weapon at hand. He looked back toward the temple. Green light continued to flash and sizzle up there. Sybil was still alive and defending herself against the onslaught. That was something.

Kane limped toward the end of the bridge that remained intact, the side that ended at the base of the steps leading back toward the temple. God above, but there were a lot of stairs. So many. He had no idea how he would traverse them, with his knee in such awful shape, but he could address that problem when he got there. First, he had to survive this bridge.

He had only taken three steps when he felt the first tremor. The entire cave shook around him, and he planted the spear in the stone to preserve his balance. The blue lights—the ones that shone from within the stone itself—flickered, like a candle flame which has been disturbed. A wave of darkness passed through the cavern. The lights reappeared briefly, flickered twice more. Kane had just enough time to see the first chunks of the ceiling fall. Then the lights went out altogether, plunging the entire cavern into darkness. The tremors increased into a full, steady rumble.

Kane thought he understood. The Deep God had died, and now, its magic was failing. The labyrinth was collapsing. Kane felt a burst of savage happiness bloom in his chest. The Deep God was truly dead. Not just incapacitated. Not just dissolved, as Rhiannon had dissolved herself all those centuries before. But well and truly dead. The labyrinth was collapsing. It would crush all of the True Servants. The people of Windsend were safe.

He sighed, and stopped moving upon the bridge. He and Sybil were days from the surface, they had no hope of escaping in time.

"Greater love than this hath no man, when any man bestoweth his life for his friends," Kane said. If this was the Lord's Providence, then so be it. He looked up toward the top of the stairs, where Sybil's light continued to flash.

"It is enough," he murmured, barely hearing his own voice. "Enough."

Suddenly the darkness around him disappeared, and he was blinded. Kane raised his free hand to cover his eyes as he felt his feet leave the stone bridge. He opened his eyes, squinting against the brightness. He was enveloped in a bubble of green light and hurtling through the air.

The bubble soared up, up, and up, to the temple entrance, where Sybil Eastey stood, arms raised. With one hand she fired blasts of green light, and with the other, she controlled the bubble holding Kane. She directed the bubble to the ground beside her. It then grew outward until she herself was inside it.

She knelt to pick up Kane's staff, tossed it to him, then whipped her fingers through the air in another quick, sharp gesture. The bubble around Kane and Sybil rose to hover a few feet off the ground, then lurched forward at great speed through the dark, fast as wind, trying to outrace the collapse.

Great chunks of stone fell about them and bounced off, harmlessly, with a strange, hollow *thunk* sound. With each *bonk*, Sybil grimaced and her shoulders hunched a little more, as if she felt each blow.

"What can I do?" Kane asked, shouting to make himself heard.

"Just shut up for a moment," she said, through gritted teeth. "This is much more difficult than it appears."

The stone fell and fell. The bubble continued to rise, but its progress slowed. Kane looked down at his staff. He'd attempted to enlist N'Longa's help before, but had barely been able to get a message across the world. That had been while the Deep God was still alive, and disrupting all other forms of magic, though. Perhaps now…

Kane tightened his grip on the staff and closed his eyes.

N'Longa, if you can hear me, he thought, *I need your help once more.*

The staff warmed in his hands, and began to vibrate. Kane raised his head and opened his eyes to see the cat's head release a stream of white light. It joined to the green bubble about himself and Sybil, the white and green blending together.

The sounds of falling stones grew softer and more distant. Sybil stood up a bit straighter. She still looked as though she carried a great burden, but that burden appeared more manageable now.

They rose and rose. The sounds of destruction outside the bubble grew more frantic and intense, even though Kane's ability to hear them had lessened. Kane wondered what would happen to the earth above. So much had been hollowed out and enchanted for the Deep God. Without that enchantment, would the woods collapse? They would find out, provided they did not die down here.

After several more moments of ascent, the bubble outpaced the wave of destruction. Through the semi-opaque barrier, Kane saw the insides of the temple. They now rose through one of its endless, winding stairs, spiraling up and up as the carved stone walls rumbled on either side.

"I am not sure," Sybil grunted, "how much longer I can hold this together."

At the top of the winding stair, they emerged into a great hallway with a low ceiling. Kane's heart leapt. He thought this was the corridor that led to the surface.

"We are nearly there," Kane said. "Hold on another moment."

Sybil bared her teeth and let out a long, low cry. It sounded almost like the shout of a woman in labor.

Kane reached out with his free hand and squeezed Sybil's shoulder.

She growled and the bubble put on another burst of speed, hurtling down the tunnel. Hope bloomed in Kane's chest.

The corridor shook and rumbled as the destruction caught up with them once more. Chunks of ceiling began to fall, ricocheting off the bubble's membrane. They sounded louder once more.

Kane opened his mouth to encourage Sybil, but as he did, the bubble flickered about them, then disappeared entirely. Kane's stomach lurched as he fell out of the air and hit the ground. His right knee flashed with pain and he leaned upon the staff to stay upright.

Sybil landed beside him, down on one knee, hands over her head once more. She managed to throw a dome up over Kane and herself, and the white light from Kane's staff joined it. Kane watched Sybil's face. It was drenched with sweat, and drawn with effort. Her breath came in short, sharp gasps. She pushed her arms higher, as if trying to extend the dome's reach. The barrier expanded briefly, then collapsed inward once more, becoming smaller than before. Kane had to duck his head.

"I cannot… go… any further," Sybil said. "I am sorry."

Kane kept his head down, staring at the floor. "You have nothing to be sorry for, Sybil Eastey. You have performed well.

The Deep God is dead. The people of Windsend are safe. The woods and valley are safe. And you are likely safe now as well."

"Am I?" she said. "Because I do not feel safe."

"Rhiannon died twice before she transferred her essence to you," Kane said. "You will return from this."

"But you will not," she said.

"It is not so bad," Kane said. He had felt death haunting his footsteps for some time now. His only wish had been to die doing something of which he could be proud. This would serve.

The world grew dark around Kane and Sybil. The dome remained in place but was now completely boxed in by fallen stone. Only the slight green glow of Sybil's magic allowed Kane to see at all.

"You never answered my question," Sybil said. "Why did you ask Rhiannon to transfer her essence to me? To bring me back to life, when she could have accompanied you the rest of the way through this adventure."

"I did not want Rhiannon's company," Kane said. "I wanted yours."

Sybil was silent for so long that Kane twisted his neck, trying to see Sybil's face. Despite the clear exertion and exhaustion in her expression, she managed to look wryly amused.

"Is that all you mean to say on the subject?" she asked.

"It is all there is to say," Kane growled.

"Very well then," she said.

"What will happen now?" Kane said.

"The stones will continue to fall," Sybil said. "More and more weight will press down upon us. The dome will continue to shrink, as my strength fades. Eventually, the dome will be crushed, and so will we. If we are lucky, we will run out of air before that happens."

Kane nodded. He would have preferred to die on his feet, weapons in hand, rather than crouched in the dark. But no man was given the right to choose the moment of his own end. Kane would have to be content here, with Sybil.

"I am glad—" he said, but before he could finish the sentence, the whole world shook around him. Sybil grunted in surprise, and then there was a sharp pain in the back of his skull, and all went dark.

40

Providence

Kane felt pain. His entire body ached from head to toe.

It means you are alive, old man, he thought. But in truth, he was sick and tired of waking up in pain. Was this all he had to look forward to in his old age?

Something soft and wet was pressed to his forehead. His eyes snapped open and his hands rose by instinct. He could see nothing at first—the light above him was too bright—and his fingers closed about something narrow and soft. A woman's arm.

"Peace, Solomon Kane. You are safe." It was Sybil Eastey's voice. It must be her arm in his grip. She had pressed a wet cloth to his face.

He let go of her, and put a hand over his face to shield his eyes. He squinted as he looked around. He appeared to be lying in a small clearing on a forest floor. The air was cold, but sweet and fresh. The sun shone down through the leaves.

"We're alive," he said, his voice hoarse. "And aboveground."

"Indeed," Sybil said.

"How?" Kane said. He sat up and looked about, taking in

more details. They were not just aboveground in the forest, but there was a small campfire burning nearby, and Kane lay upon a pallet. "We were trapped beneath the rubble. Did you find some new reserve of power to draw upon?"

"It was not me," Sybil said. "But perhaps your beloved Providence."

Kane frowned at her, not understanding. She pointed over Kane's shoulder, and Kane turned to see Roger Kidby step through the trees, carrying a freshly caught rabbit over one shoulder.

Roger smiled, his ruddy face bright with cheer.

"Good morrow, Master Kane," Roger said. "It is good to see you awake."

Kane sat all the way up and turned back to Sybil. "Roger rescued us?"

"We were trapped beneath the stones," Sybil said. "I was at the end of my power. But he found us. He heard my call for help, and dug us out. He helped me carry you the rest of the way to the surface, and has looked after us through the night and into the morning."

"She makes it sound more impressive than it was," Roger said, as he set the rabbit down and settled before the fire. He put his hands toward it, for warmth. "The two of you had nearly made your way out on your own. I traveled scarcely a few hundred feet past the cave entrance before I came to the rubble and heard Mistress Eastey calling."

"How did you know to come for us?" Kane said.

Roger shrugged. "I did not know. I had no great vision or premonition. But you had been gone for days, and I began to worry, so I took it upon myself to search for you. I know you told me to stay behind, but I am not sorry I disobeyed."

"Nor should you be," Kane said. "Mistress Eastey and I owe you our lives."

Roger shook his head. "Mistress Eastey told me what happened below. You have avenged my father. You have saved me, and my neighbors from something worse than death. You owe me nothing."

Kane nodded, then looked back at Sybil. "I take it the village does not know we are back yet."

"No," Sybil said. "We thought it best to decide on a plan after you woke."

"We will face them together," Kane said.

"Are you sure?" Sybil said. "It might be easier if we snuck you out of the village before anyone knows. I doubt we will receive a hero's welcome."

"I will not cower, Mistress Eastey. My horse is in Roger's stable, and I owe Catherine a proper farewell," Kane said. He looked from Sybil to Roger. "How fares the village, since our escape?"

Roger's good cheer vanished. "Things have remained in an uproar since your departure. Nehemiah Lockwood has been arrested. The day after your escape, he... killed Goodwife Lockwood."

"Joy?" Sybil said. "Joy is dead?"

"She is," Roger said. "Nehemiah said that God came to him in a dream and told him that Joy had killed their son, Zachariah. That she had smothered him, and then staged it to look like an accident. That Sybil Eastey had had nothing to do with the crime at all. He also admitted to planting the poisons in Sybil's hut, at Joy's insistence."

"The Deep God's work?" Kane asked Sybil.

"Perhaps," Sybil said.

"Nehemiah is in the town jail now," Roger said. "Along with Catherine Archer, they share a cell and await trial. There were too many witnesses who saw her aid your escape."

Kane looked about and found his staff nearby, upon the

ground. He grabbed it and used it to haul himself to his feet with a loud groan.

"We have no time to waste, then," he said.

Sybil rose as well, putting a hand upon his shoulder. "I have just brought you back from the brink of death," she said. "My powers can only do so much to speed nature's course. You need time to rest and heal."

"I cannot rest while Catherine Archer sits in jail," Kane said. "You insisted upon coming below with me. Will you deny me your help now?"

"I suppose not," Sybil said. She looked to Roger, who still warmed himself before the fire. "Pack up the camp and follow as soon as you can, young Providence. Master Kane and I have one last bit of urgent business."

41

Return

Less than an hour later, Kane and Sybil marched out of the woods and into Windsend. It was mid-morning and many of the villagers were about their daily business. Although the harvest was past, the farmers found much to occupy their time, tending to their livestock, cleaning their instruments, and preparing their crops for market, as women set laundry out to dry in the cold air.

All looked up as Kane and Sybil passed. Some looked away at once, their faces reddening with shame. Something in their consciences nagged at them, now that they were free of the Deep God's influence. This was a good sign. Others gawked in open curiosity, and left off their chores to follow Kane and Sybil through the village, and straight up to the jailhouse itself. Sybil stopped Kane there with a gesture, and mounted the steps herself. In the open sunlight, her green glow was obscured, but still there, for those who knew what to look for. She rapped upon the door three times. Kane wondered why she did not barge in, but held his tongue. Let her make her move.

Behind them, the crowd had grown. No one had said anything yet, but Kane felt their curiosity, a welcome change from the previous hostility. They reminded him of children woken from a deep sleep, who have wandered into the kitchen at night, confused and still half-dreaming.

The jail door opened, and Ezekiel the jailer peered out. His mouth opened in a little "o" of surprise.

"Mistress Eastey! You are back!"

"I am," she said. "I see you are back as well. Roger told us you fled, the night of the attempted executions."

"I fled that night, the same as you and Master Kane," Ezekiel said. "But something in my conscience rebelled. I could not abandon the people here."

"Good man," Kane said. He found himself liking the fat little jailer more and more.

"Is Catherine Archer locked up within?" Sybil asked.

Ezekiel nodded. "She is here, awaiting trial."

"You will release her at once, Ezekiel," Sybil said.

"I beg your pardon?" Ezekiel said.

"You will release Catherine Archer at once," Sybil said. "She is under my protection."

"Mistress Eastey," Ezekiel said. "It is not up to me."

"You followed your conscience when you helped douse the flames meant to kill me," Sybil said. "Did Catherine do any different? Do you feel it is right to hold her?"

Ezekiel silently wrestled with the right and wrong of it, but in the end, he stepped out of Sybil's way and held the door for her.

Sybil and Kane hurried up the steps, Kane wincing as his knee complained. Sybil walked past Ezekiel and approached the holding cell where she had so recently been prisoner. Catherine Archer and Nehemiah Lockwood sat on either sides of the cell's single cot. Lockwood had dark circles beneath his eyes and wore a haunted expression. Catherine's face was bruised purple and black, and one of her eyes was swollen shut. Kane felt rage bubbling up within. Enoch Archer had been disciplining his wife again.

At Kane and Sybil's appearance, she sat up straighter on the cot.

"Catherine," Sybil said. "Can you walk?"

"Well enough," Catherine said.

Sybil gestured at the door of the cell. "Come with me, then, friend. You have tarried long enough in this place."

Catherine stood, and grimaced at some other, less visible injury. Kane added it to the tally of what he now owed Enoch Archer, as Catherine limped forward and took Sybil's proffered hand.

Sybil put a hand to Catherine's cheek. As Kane watched, the bruises upon her face faded. They did not disappear entirely, and some discoloration remained, but the swelling receded, and both her eyes became visible once more. Catherine blinked, and stood up a bit, straightening her shoulders.

Sybil then turned her gaze toward Nehemiah. He remained in the cell, staring into the empty space before him. He seemed not to have noticed anything that had happened in the last few seconds. Sybil turned away from the carpenter, saw Kane's questioning glance, and shook her head.

"There is nothing I can do for him," she said. "He is beyond my touch, and will have to find his own way back. Or not."

Kane looked at the man, who continued to stare into space. Lockwood had killed his own wife. But his wife had killed their infant son. At least one of those murders had been committed under the Deep God's influence. Kane wondered if Joy had been under the sway of something evil herself. He felt no rage for the Lockwoods, only a hollow sadness. It was an ugly, messy business. Sybil left the cell door open as she retreated, but Lockwood did not move.

As they approached the jailhouse door, the three met Ezekiel once more. He held his hat in both hands, looking unhappy.

"Mistress Eastey," he said. "I will lose my job over this."

Sybil paused in the doorway, and touched his shoulder. "You are a good, and gentle soul, Ezekiel, and too good for this job. Come find me later, and together we will find you proper employment."

Kane, Sybil, and Catherine exited the jailhouse, finding a larger crowd than the one they had left behind. It seemed the entire village was now gathered outside, packed shoulder to shoulder. At the head of the crowd stood Enoch Archer, and the council of elders, led by Reverend Gideon Pelham.

"Solomon Kane and Sybil Eastey," Pelham cried, voice raised to be heard by all. "You are both wanted for witchcraft and murder. You will surrender and return to the jail at once, or—"

Green light flashed from Sybil's fingertips and hit Pelham square in the face. Where his mouth had been a moment before, there was now only a patch of skin. His hands flew to the space, and his eyes widened in panic.

"Sybil," Kane said.

"I will restore him in a moment," she said. "After I have had my say." She turned to face the wider crowd.

"People of Windsend! A great change is upon you. You came to this place to live in peace and worship in the way you wish. And yet you have been plagued by bad fortune and dark dreams since the founding of this village. I tell you that those days are at an end. There was an ancient evil in the woods here—one stirred up and awoken by your council of elders. It was this evil that committed the murders. It was this evil that poisoned your hearts against one another. Against me, and Master Kane. Master Kane and I have done you a great service, by venturing into the woods, and destroying this evil once and for all. You are now free to live and worship as you wish. But there *will* be changes.

"This valley is now under *my* protection. That includes both the creatures and plants of the woods, but also you. I will do my best to see that you live happy, healthy lives, in harmony with the land. I will not interfere with your beliefs, as long as you live in peace, although I will give my help whenever it is asked of me. Your lives are your own, to spend as you see fit. However, my non-intervention only extends as far as your goodwill and kindness toward one another. Should you raise a hand against your neighbor, or family, you will pay for it."

"Shut your mouth, witch." It was Enoch Archer. Kane noticed for the first time that Archer carried a hammer from his smithy. It hung loosely in his right hand, but the implied threat was clear.

"You expect to live as some pagan priestess in a community of Christians?" Enoch said. "You expect us to live by your dictates, and obey you, in blasphemy against God?"

"You are free to leave, if you do not like it here, Enoch Archer. But before you do, I think you will help me make a point."

"The devil may have stopped you facing justice before," Enoch spat, "but I shall set things right now." He swung his hammer up and gripped it in both hands. He stepped forward and Kane did likewise, but Sybil put a hand upon Kane's chest and pushed him back.

She took a step toward Archer. With the same hand she had used to push Kane away, she made a gesture in the air. Enoch's forward progress stopped. He hung suspended between steps, knees bent, hammer at the ready. He grunted, and cords appeared on his neck as he tried to force his way forward.

Sybil gestured, and Enoch dropped the hammer. It smashed against his right foot, and he cried out. Then his arms spread to either side, and he rose into the air, until he was high above the crowd. He hung, almost crucified on the air itself, toes dangling.

"Put me down, you vile bitch!" Archer cried.

Green light flew from Sybil's fingertips. Enoch's body went rigid, and the blacksmith screamed. Kane had heard cries like this before, in the dungeons of the Inquisition.

"Sybil," he murmured.

"Enoch Archer," Sybil said. "You are a vile, small, petty, jealous, close-minded slug wearing the guise of a man, and hiding your ugliness beneath a mask of religious righteousness. You pretend to love God when in fact you simply hate. You hate your life, your station and women—your wife, in particular. She is too good for you. You know this. You know she settled when she married you, but rather than being grateful for your good fortune, you allowed resentment to fester in your heart. Resentment eventually turned into hate, and now you do not blink an eye before laying your hands upon her. You are among the worst and lowest of men, Enoch Archer, and I will make an example of you now. I will show you true hatred, Enoch. I will show you real power."

Enoch was beyond speech. He could only wail in reply. Kane noticed that trickles of blood were now running from both the blacksmith's nostrils and ears.

Did Sybil mean to kill Enoch? Surely, if a man deserved punishment for his actions, it was Enoch Archer. And who was Kane to tell Sybil not to kill an evildoer? Still, it seemed an ill omen, for Sybil to start her guardianship with such brutality.

"Sybil." It was Catherine. She put a hand on Sybil's shoulder. "Do not kill him. Please."

Sybil glared at Enoch, then sighed. With a flick of her wrist, she drew Archer through the air until his face was inches from her own. He whimpered with fear, and Kane could smell something foul about the man. He had soiled himself.

Sybil leaned in so that the tip of her nose nearly pressed to Enoch's. "You will live the rest of your life in my valley. You will never lay hands on Catherine in an unkind manner again. If you do, I will know. No man or god will be able to save you if you draw my ire. Do you understand?"

Enoch whimpered in reply, and Sybil's frown deepened.

"Do... you... understand?" she demanded. The green light about Enoch's body flashed, and he screamed.

"I... I understand," he said.

"You will thank Catherine now," she said. "For convincing me to spare your miserable life."

"Thank you," Enoch said, staring at the ground. "Thank you, Catherine."

Catherine said nothing, but instead turned to Sybil. "Enough."

Sybil let Enoch fall to the ground. Catherine stared down at her husband, then sighed, and walked down the steps. She helped him to his feet, and led him, limping, away, back toward their house.

Sybil turned back to the crowd. "Let this be a warning to you all. I am the power in this valley. You cannot harm me. You cannot stop me. Even if you left and returned with an army. This is my place of power, and I shall never leave. You live here at my mercy. If you do not like it, you may leave. If you stay, I will look after you and your families. Now go. Disperse. And for pity's sake, try to behave like *Christians*."

42

Departure

The following days were among the most peaceful and restful Solomon Kane had ever experienced. He returned to the Falling Star Inn, and slept the better part of two days. His sleep was deep, and dreamless, and when he woke at last, he felt like a man reborn, his aches and pains gone, his mind clear. While he had slept, Roger Kidby had found him fresh clothes to wear, and when Kane at last stepped from his room, ready to face the world, he did so in clean black Puritan garb.

He came downstairs to find an empty common room at the inn. All of the benches were upon the tables, and Roger was sweeping the floor.

"Are you not open, Master Kidby?" Kane asked.

"No," Roger said. "Not today. But I can fix you some breakfast, if you're hungry."

"Starved," Kane said.

Roger disappeared into the kitchen, and Kane wandered about the first floor. Everything was clean, and put away. Esther

Kidby's room had been cleaned out. A faint stink in the air was the only hint of its former occupant.

When Roger returned with Kane's breakfast, Kane sat at the bar to eat while Roger caught him up on the events in town.

Life had more or less settled back into a rhythm of normality while Kane had rested. Sybil had returned to her hut just outside of town, and was accepting callers. No one had yet tried her patience or her threats of retribution.

"It is as if the whole town has made a silent agreement not to speak about the change," Roger said, keeping his voice low.

Kane smiled wryly. It was remarkable how people could contort themselves to avoid looking the truth directly in the face. The way Nehemiah Lockwood had so long avoided looking at his wife as the murderer of their child. The way the town lived with Sybil before the accusations, praying to the Christian god but seeking pagan remedies for their illnesses.

The way I use magic in tandem with my own beliefs, Kane thought. *As Sybil pointed out upon our very first meeting. We all blind ourselves, so that we can stand to live.*

"And what of the change I see here?" Kane said. "Normally the inn would be bustling with customers at this hour."

"Yes, well," Roger said. "I think I have had enough of Windsend. I never liked it here. When my parents made the move, I was too young to stay behind, but when I reached my majority, Mother was sick and Father needed the extra help. He could not afford to hire anyone else. So, because I loved them, I stayed. But they're both gone now, and nothing remains to tie me to this place. I think it is time I was gone myself."

"Where will you go?" Kane asked.

"Mistress Eastey has offered me a job," Roger said. "Because of her recent… change… she can no longer leave this valley. She is not content with this state of affairs, and wants to consult with other magic users. Ezekiel and I will serve as her messengers and couriers. We set out for Paris tomorrow."

"What of the inn? Will you sell it?"

"Mistress Eastey has agreed to broker a sale for me. I do not want to think on it. I want to be away."

"The adventuring life is not an easy one," Kane said.

"My life has been nothing but hardship," Roger said. "That being so, I would rather have hardships doing what I want to do, rather than seeing to inherited responsibilities."

Kane, hearing true wisdom in the young man's words, made no further warning or argument.

After breakfast, Kane set about preparations for departure. There was little to do. He had few enough belongings. Once his bag was packed, he went to the stables to check on Holiday. She seemed content in the safety and warmth and plenty there, untouched by the conflict and strife of the previous days.

"Are you ready to do some work, after days of lazing about?" Kane asked her, as she ate an apple form his hand. "I hope so."

"Planning to sneak away, Master Kane?"

Kane turned, startled, to see Catherine Archer in the stable doorway. She had approached without him noticing. Her face already looked much better. The bruises had faded almost altogether.

"My work here is finished," he said.

She shook her head and sighed. "At least come to my house for lunch, before you go. Noon sharp," Catherine said. "We will expect you."

She left before Kane could argue, or ask the more pressing question: who was *we*?

Solomon Kane returned to the Archer house at midday. The air was crisp and chilly, but the sun was shining this afternoon, and it felt good to be out of doors. Catherine, apparently in agreement, had set up a table on the back porch, where she directed Kane upon his arrival.

As he stepped through the kitchen door and onto the back porch, he was only half-surprised to find Sybil Eastey already seated at the table, in hushed conversation with Catherine's daughters, Mercy, Faith, and Grace. They were all giggling about something. Out in the yard, Isaac was dueling some great invisible opponent. He threw himself about with abandon, rolling in the grass.

When the girls noticed Kane, they covered their mouths to stifle the laughter. Sybil only smiled and cocked an eyebrow.

"Master Kane," she said. "I admit I am surprised to see you. I thought you would be long gone by now."

"Soon," Kane said and sat down in the chair opposite Sybil.

Catherine saved him from the awkwardness of further conversation, arriving with a loaf of bread and bowls of pottage for everyone. She called Isaac in from the yard, and for a time, the party sat in silence, happily eating.

Enoch did not join them for the meal. Kane could hear his hammer, clanging away in the smithy adjoining the house. Was it the same one he had brought with him to the jailhouse, meaning to bash Sybil's head in? What dark thoughts haunted the blacksmith's mind now? Hopefully his fear of Sybil would keep him in line, but Kane had his doubts. He heard danger in every *clang* of that hammer next door. Perhaps Sybil should have killed Enoch. Perhaps Kane should have done it himself.

After the meal, the girls cleared the table and washed the dishes, while Sybil joined Isaac in the yard to play some game to which only he seemed to know the rules. Kane and Catherine sat in silence for a time, watching them play.

"Thank you for coming," Catherine said. "I do not know what would have happened, without your intervention."

"It was Providence that brought me here, and guided my hand," Kane said. "I am glad that you and your children are safe, and that all is well in this valley at last."

"She suits you, you know," Catherine said, nodding to Sybil. "In a way I never could have. She is your equal. She could be a true partner."

"She is damned to the fires of Hell," Kane said.

"No. You saved her from that fate," Catherine said. "She told me of the deal you made with Rhiannon. You have granted Sybil eternal life. So long as this world persists, she will never die. She will never suffer Hell."

"Eventually this world will end," Kane said. "And God will deal with all manner of sinners, mortal and immortal alike."

"I am not so sure she is damned," Catherine said. "She has the purest heart of any woman I have ever met. I suspect God knows it, regardless of how she worships."

Kane kept silent, tightening his hand into a fist upon the table. Catherine had been through much. Let her speak as she would. It changed nothing.

"Why did you make the deal with Rhiannon?" Catherine asked. "Why not let Sybil die?"

"It would have been a poor thing, to have come so far, to have worked so hard to prove Sybil's innocence, only to see her die in the bowels of that evil place," Kane said. "She is your best friend. I would not leave you bereft of that comfort."

"How selfless of you," she said, her tone dry. "Are you sure there is not more to it?"

"It was not a matter of the heart," Kane said. "At least, not in the way you imply, or hope. No. It is difficult to explain, even to myself. But I suppose that, in this town of God-fearing

Puritans, I feel like an outsider. In Sybil, I see a kindred spirit. She sees the darkness, and tries to help. And I could not let that go without a fight."

To that, Catherine had no reply. Together she and Kane enjoyed watching Sybil and Isaac play in the yard.

Although Kane would have liked to set off from Windsend right after lunch, he stayed one more night in Roger Kidby's closed inn. He needed guidance before he left. So that night, as he lay in bed, he wrapped his arms about his cat-headed staff, and when he slept, he found himself sitting next to a campfire deep in the African jungles. N'Longa sat across from him, eating something out of a bowl.

"It is good to see you, Solomon," N'Longa said. "Alive and well."

"I am ready to resume the hunt," Kane said.

"Good," N'Longa said. "While you tarried, the undead have continued to kill their way across Europe. They were subtle at first, stopping in small, out-of-the-way places. Picking off drunkards and the elderly. Small children who could be tempted out of their bedrooms. Now they grow less shy. They have emptied entire villages in France and Germany."

"How?" Kane asked.

"How indeed?" N'Longa said. "I am not sure. That is why I need you, my friend. I see the death, but not the details."

"I will set out first thing in the morning," Kane said.

"Good," N'Longa said. He stood, as if to conclude their meeting, but Kane remained seated by the fire. "You had more to say?"

"I wanted to thank you," Kane said. "Two times I called for your help. And both times, you saved my life."

"What are blood brothers for?" N'Longa asked. "If not an occasional bit of life-saving?"

"Yes, well," Kane said. "Thank you, N'Longa. You are a good friend."

N'Longa smiled, but he did not say it back.

Kane woke with his knee paining him once more. It was too bad. He had not experienced much discomfort since waking in the woods, but he supposed this would be his life now. So he limped down the stairs of the inn and across the yard to the stables. He limped as he led Holiday out onto the road, and found his way blocked by Sybil Eastey.

She wore her red cloak, and held a small parcel in her hands. In the predawn darkness, her glow was particularly pronounced. She looked to Kane like the power of life itself.

"Sybil," he said.

"I wanted to say goodbye," Sybil said. "And I have something to give you. A parting gift." She approached him and placed a hand upon his arm. His knee stopped its complaints at once. All the little aches and pains through his body disappeared as well.

"Is it better?" she asked.

"It is," Kane said, standing up a bit straighter. "Thank you."

"It is no panacea," Sybil said. "Merely a temporary alleviation of the pain. And since I cannot be with you at all times, you will need this as well." She offered him the parcel in her other hand, a small bag tied with a leather strap. Kane opened it, and the smell of herbs drifted up toward him.

"Poultice ingredients, for your knee," Sybil said. "And a list of the ingredients you will need, when these run out. You will have to apply the poultice yourself, since I will not be near to do it for you. Indeed, I cannot follow you from this valley."

Kane tied the bag closed once more, and put it in Holiday's saddlebag. He did not look at Sybil as he said what came next: "I am sorry if I chose poorly when I made my bargain with Rhiannon."

"I am eternally in your debt, Solomon Kane. You have saved my life twice over."

"I do not tarry with debts, Mistress Eastey. We have more than repaid each other."

"You are bad at receiving praise, Solomon Kane. But you are a good friend. To Catherine, and myself, and all the people of this valley." Her hand slid from his arm up his shoulder and neck, until it cupped his face. She smiled at him, glassy-eyed, then stepped out of his way and gestured down the road.

"Go forth and do good," she said. "Serve your god well. And perhaps return some day, if you can. I feel your gloomy countenance will always gladden my heart."

Kane did not know what to say to this, so instead of speaking, he mounted his horse, and set her at a canter down the road which would lead him up out of the valley and back into the world, where he would meet the adventures God had set before him.

He looked back, once, but Sybil was already gone.

THE END

ACKNOWLEDGMENTS

The first Robert E. Howard story I ever read was a Solomon Kane tale, so it feels almost like Kane's beloved Providence that, nearly twenty years later, I was allowed to write the first novel starring the character. It has been a great honor and terrific fun. I hope I have captured a bit of Howard's magic and managed to add a few threads to the grand tapestry, but of course I didn't do this alone, and there are individuals who must be thanked:

My editor Daquan Cadogan, who thought of me for this job, and who helped refine an initial pitch ("What if Solomon Kane had to defend a witch against a village of puritans?") into a full-bodied work of fiction. Working with Daquan has been great fun, and I hope we'll get more opportunities to collaborate in the future.

My agent Kent D. Wolf, who handles the business end of things so I get paid to tell stories. I only have a career because he whipped my first novel into shape. I remain in his debt, always.

Chris Butera at Heroic Signatures, one of the guardians of Howard's oeuvre, who kept me from straying too far from the essence of Howard's characters and world. (Chris is also a terrific novelist. Do yourself a favor and pick up his book *The Darkest Deep*, posthaste.)

My history buff father, Rick Hamill, who made himself available to answer my random questions about England in the early 1600s, and hopefully saved me from embarrassing myself on the page.

My girlfriend, Sara Montañez. Sara and I started dating shortly after I began writing this book, and at least half of it was written, re-written, and revised at her kitchen table, between the hours of 4 and 6 AM. Sara happily made space for me to write in her home, and never complained about the half-asleep man crashing around her kitchen in the wee hours and chugging through her coffee stores.

And finally, Sara's cat, Ash. Ash is an early riser like me, and proved good company in those predawn hours, settling on my laptop bag to receive pets and distribute occasional bites while I worked. Ash, if you're reading this: first of all, good job learning to read, that's amazing, but secondly, I couldn't have done it without you, buddy. You have a good heart, and very sharp teeth.

ABOUT THE AUTHOR

Shaun Hamill received his bachelor's from the University of Texas at Arlington and his MFA from the Iowa Writers' Workshop. He is the author of *A Cosmology of Monsters* and *The Dissonance* as well as *Alien: Perfect Organisms*. He is the host of *The 616 Files* podcast and also a frequent cohost of *The Dungeons & Dragons Lorecast*. He lives, works, and games in north Texas.

A NEW ERA OF BRAVERY AND HEROISM!

COMICS AND COLLECTIONS

CONAN THE BARBARIAN VOLUME 1

CONAN THE BARBARIAN VOLUME 2

CONAN THE BARBARIAN VOLUME 3

CONAN THE BARBARIAN VOLUME 4

CONAN THE BARBARIAN VOLUME 5

CONAN: BATTLE OF THE BLACK STONE

THE SAVAGE SWORD OF CONAN VOLUME 1

THE SAVAGE SWORD OF CONAN VOLUME 2

THE SAVAGE SWORD OF CONAN VOLUME 3

SOLOMON KANE: THE SERPENT RING

REMASTERED. OVERSIZED. OMNIBUS EDITIONS

CONAN THE BARBARIAN ORIGINAL COMICS OMNIBUS VOLUME 2

CONAN THE BARBARIAN ORIGINAL COMICS OMNIBUS VOLUME 3

CONAN THE BARBARIAN ORIGINAL COMICS OMNIBUS VOLUME 4

CONAN THE BARBARIAN ORIGINAL COMICS OMNIBUS VOLUME 5

THE SAVAGE SWORD OF CONAN ORIGINAL COMICS OMNIBUS VOLUME 2

THE SAVAGE SWORD OF CONAN ORIGINAL COMICS OMNIBUS VOLUME 3

THE SAVAGE SWORD OF CONAN ORIGINAL COMICS OMNIBUS VOLUME 4

THE SAVAGE SWORD OF CONAN ORIGINAL COMICS OMNIBUS VOLUME 9

KING CONAN ORIGINAL COMICS OMNIBUS VOLUME 1

KING CONAN ORIGINAL COMICS OMNIBUS VOLUME 1

EXPLORE THE FULL RANGE ONLINE!

TITAN-COMICS.COM

TITAN COMICS

CONAN: SPAWN OF THE SERPENT GOD

Tim Waggoner

A new chapter of the Titan Comics & Heroic Signatures massive narrative event: Scourge of the Serpent.

"What do you know of the Cult of Set?"

In Zamora, the city of thieves, Conan meets Valja, a thrill-seeking thief. She entices him to join her on a heist, where they steal a golden statuette of Ishtar, said to contain the goddess herself. After killing a dozen guards and failing to escape, the pair are saved by priestesses of Mitra. But Conan knows that nothing is free.

The priestesses have need of their skills. They have waged war against Set, god of chaos and serpents, who demands constant sacrifice from his subjects and massacred thousands of his followers. Yet they are no match for Uzzeran, a powerful sorcerer, who has been performing unspeakable experiments on humans in the name of Set. To defeat Uzzeran, they will need a legendary warrior on their side. They need Conan the Barbarian.

CONAN: CULT OF THE OBSIDIAN MOON

James Lovegrove

A new chapter of the Titan Comics & Heroic Signatures massive narrative event: The Battle of the Black Stone.

Still mourning Bêlit, Conan attempts to drink away his sorrows. In his tavern-hopping journey he meets and befriends married couple Hunwulf and Gudrun and their son, Bjørn. A decade ago, Hunwulf eloped with Gudrun after killing her betrothed, they live on the run from her tribe, who are desperate for revenge.

Bjørn has the makings of a shaman, while Hunwulf is prone to having strange fits which bring him visions of past and future lives. When a descendant warns Hunwulf of imminent danger, he and his wife ride out to ambush the tribe, leaving Bjørn with Conan, who vows to protect the boy with his life.

Unfortunately, Conan is betrayed by a former accomplice, and Bjørn is kidnapped by the tribe. Conan and Bjørn's vengeful parents search for the lad. They catch up to the tribe, only to find Bjørn has been taken by murderous bat-winged figures, who fought with talon and sword. The boy, and other "gifted" children have been taken to the Rotlands, a place plagued by a contaminating supernatural force that warps all who go there. To save Bjørn, the trio must go to the heart of the Rotlands, where strange, horrifying fates await at every turn.